D1558777

Dedication

**This book is dedicated to my family,
Gini, Johnny and Nat**

"... all sorrows can be borne if you put them into a story or tell a story about them."

Isak Dinesen, author of "Out of Africa," in a 1957 interview.

"You could say a happy man has no biography—who'd want to read it?"

Walter Houk, friend of Ernest Hemingway. From the book "Hemingway's Boat."

Front Cover Photograph: The 50-foot-tall sculpture called Stargazer by Linda Scott, part of her Stargazer project, sits on the eastern side of County Road 111 in Manorville, NY just before the Sunrise Highway juncture and marks the beginning of the Hamptons in Long Island's Suffolk County.

Back Cover Photograph: By Annick Couillard taken on the Île Saint-Honorat off the coast of the French Riviera.

Book Cover Artwork: By Paul Rocheny of Rocheny
Photography & Framing Studio, Bayonne, NJ.

Table of Contents

Prologue

I still was not sure. Escape? Would I go tonight? If they caught me, I knew they would move me up the hill to the Acute Care Unit. So, if I went, I had to be careful.

I lay there, keeping track of the nurses' rounds. At night, they checked on me every fifteen minutes. I stared at the window. Outside, the tall light pole lit both the building and the bushes two floors below.

Should I go? Should I?

I didn't know.

Betty, the short nurse, gently pushed open my door and peeked in.

"He's still sleeping, Alice," I heard her whisper.

Nurses. They can't help me. No one can help me.

The large outdoor lamp snapped off. 4 a.m. Now there was nothing in my room but darkness and the sound of the two nurses walking the halls.

I hate this claustrophobic box. I'm trapped inside it. I clenched the sheet and gritted my teeth. *I've got to get out. I've got to get back to my family. I have to get back to New York and find a new job.*

Quietly, I slipped out of my pajamas, rolled them in to a ball and put them under the covers. I'd made up my mind; I would go tonight! I found my underpants in the top dresser drawer; hid my sneakers under the bed. I got back under the covers and waited for the next bed check. Then I put on my socks and shirt and pulled on my chinos. I took the vial of Zoloft from the night table, stuffed it in my pocket, then took it out again.

Fuck it! Doesn't work anyway, and threw it across the room.

After the nurse closed my door, I walked to the window and struggled to work the screen free. It came loose with a jar, and I hid it on the floor behind the old, stuffed armchair. 4:50.

When will I go? Will I go? I have to!

I kept watching the sky to see if the summer night was starting to lighten.

You're going to let them keep you here? Are you? Or are you going to do something about it? It's now or never, asshole. Have you got the guts?

I practiced in the dark going back and forth from the bed to the window, measuring my 5' 7" frame against the size of the opening that led to the ground two floors below . . . to the ground and to freedom. Back and forth, back and forth, from the bed to the window. But each time I went to the window, fear forced me back. The magnetic pull of the room held me, froze me, just like two months ago when I stood alone on the subway platform beneath the World Trade Center.

Stay by the mouth of the tunnel, I thought that afternoon. *Then he won't have time to stop the train.*

I remembered picking up my new attaché case and walking to the end of the station platform where the subway would come in to wait for the next train, hiding next to the tunnel wall. I straightened my suit coat and fixed my tie.

What will people think? I wondered.

Successful, young insurance executive, dressed in felt-collared overcoat, gray pin-striped Paul Stuart suit, Hermès tie and well shined Gucci loafers, carrying a Gurkha attaché case, killed today in the World Trade Center on the tracks of the R train. It is not known if his death was an accident or a suicide. There was no note.

My thoughts were the same now.

Do you have the guts?

Now, like then, I could not make my body move.

It's only two floors. What's the big deal? What's the big deal!

I studied the darkness outside.

You've got to go before it gets light. You've already lost an hour. It'll be light soon.

Again and again, I tried to force myself through the open window, but my body would not go.

That's right, just stay here! You never had the courage to kill yourself. So why should this be any different?

Then, in an instant, it happened. As though watching from across the room, I saw my body move in slow motion towards the open window. Something grabbed me, pulled me, pushed me. As if in a trance, one moment I was in the room, the next, outside, sliding down the white siding of the Main House to the bushes below.

Crash!

Chapter 1

As the old yellow bus slowly rattled to my stop, I watched Buttons through the smudged windowpane. He streaked across our huge front lawn and sailed over the small boxwood hedge at the end of the yard onto the pebbled sidewalk. His black spots blurred as he dashed beneath the tall maple trees, down the dirt path, to meet me at the corner.

With my eighth grade book bag swinging, I bounded down the worn, black rubber steps and landed on the grass beside him. I bent to one knee and scratched him hard behind his ears. I knew Buttons loved this. And I loved him. He was my best friend and we would never part.

"Hi, Boy. Ya miss me? Come on. I'll race you home!"

Off we went, splashing together through the muddy puddles and racing past the black mailboxes, before turning up the long winding driveway towards our large white house.

Above the porch, in the middle of the railing, was the big new 'W' that my father had recently added. 'W' for Walker, high above the street, for all to see from the road. I remembered Mother arguing with him last week after the carpenters left.

"You never ask me anymore!" she yelled. "You never ask me anything anymore. Why didn't you tell me you wanted to put *your* initial in the middle of the railing? How could you? Why don't you just put your statue up there, too? It's like buying that damn car—red and white. What were you thinking? You've got your goddamn firedog, don't you? Did you need a fire engine too? And a Packard of all things. If you really want everybody to know you're in the insurance business, don't be so subtle. Put up a flashing sign for God's sake. *Cheap Insurance.*"

We sprinted around the side porch, away from the 'W', to the front of the house. Mother had told me that years ago our home had been a large dairy barn. Cows had come in from the east, so the structure was turned that way with the entrance facing away from the road. Ours was one of the biggest houses in Garden Village with two tall white columns on either side of the red front door and a heavy brown-shingled roof high above.

Haskell was sweeping leaves off the front steps where a black metal jockey in red vest and white jodhpurs stood holding out a welcoming ring for my father's imaginary horses.

"Hi, Haskell."

Haskell smiled his deep warm smile, took off his straw hat and knelt down so Buttons could lick his wrinkled face.

"Good day at school, Master Jay?"

"Fine, Haskell, except for that old Mrs. Applebee. She's a witch."

Haskell laughed his deep Southern laugh and scratched his short grey hair. "I suppose you just have to let things be, Master Jay. Just concentrate on those three Rs: readin', writin' and 'rithmatic."

"Gotcha. Is Mom home?"

"I do believe she is."

I walked up the steps and tried the brass knob, but the door was locked. Buttons stood tall on his hind legs, scratching excitedly at the red door while I rang the bell. No answer.

"Mom? Mom! I'm home," I called.

I rang the bell again. Finally, Mother slowly unlocked the door and pulled it open. Buttons pushed his way past her and scampered down the long waxed hallway with his legs flying every which way over the Persian throw rugs and parquet floor.

"Oh, hi, Honey. Sorry, I was in the back," she said holding her glass. "I had some laundry to do."

Her face was lined and haggard, her hair stiff from too many bleachings. No longer did she look like the pretty young woman in the Red Cross uniform smiling out from the silver picture frame on the living room table. Now, her body, once firm from sports, was undernourished and thin. The blue shine in her eyes had gone pale. She put her arm around me and hugged me tightly. As we kissed, I smelled her breath reeking of alcohol.

"Jay, why don't you run upstairs and put on some clean clothes?" she said. "Your friends will be here any minute."

Buttons came galloping around the corner from the kitchen and scampered after me up the first flight of stairs that led to the spacious master bedroom. As I passed my brother Harry's room, I thought how Mother would punish me when I did something wrong. She would have me lie on Harry's bed and whip me with one of his belts. Sometimes, by mistake I guessed, she used the wrong end, and the belt buckle would hit me hard on my side. I brushed the memories aside, and bounded up the next flight, taking the stairs two at a time, to my bedroom on the third floor.

I sat on the lower bunk next to my crystal radio set and peeled off my school clothes. Across the room, as Buttons whipped his tail against my battered desk, my father's ceramic Princeton tiger teeter-tottered back and forth on its remaining three legs. I rifled through my drawer, found a fresh T-shirt, then pulled on a pair of old blue jeans, and tied my Keds. I found my beaded Indian belt mixed in with my LPs of Elvis and Frankie Lymon.

"Hurry up, Honey!" Mother called from downstairs. "Billy's here."

I pushed aside the blue and pink riding ribbons that hung from my mirror's wooden frame and checked my hair. Decals of my baseball heroes—Pee Wee Reese, Duke Snider, Whitey Ford—fought for space on the glass with the multi-colored chiffon scarves doused in sweet perfume that were given to me as souvenirs by my new girlfriend Judy. With one more pass of the brush, I called for Buttons and we ran down the stairs together.

Bill Schumacher was waiting in the main hallway. He was a couple of inches taller than me, about 5' 9", and thinner, with a thick, black flat top.

"Hi, Bill."

"Hey, Jay. Hi Buttons. Good dog."

Buttons rolled over thrashing his tail back and forth while Bill scratched his spotted belly.

The front door pushed open and Jack O'Neil clambered into the vestibule. Jack was covered with freckles and had a thick chunk of bright red hair sticking out from under his checkered hunting hat. Right behind him came Andy Barret, a gangly kid of over 6'. Andy was wearing a blue-and-white Yankee's jacket that matched his baseball cap. And his blue-and-white t-shirt proudly proclaimed New York as the winner of this year's '56 World Series.

"Hey, Andy. So, what's with all this baseball stuff?" I asked. "I bet you're wearing Yankee u-trou too, right?"

"Come on, Jay! Lay off. It may have taken seven games, but we finally beat those Brooklyn bums."

"Hi boys," Mother said as she came into the foyer carrying her drink. "Well, it looks like we have the 'Happy Hackers Club' duly assembled. Here's your wet washcloth. Now remember, stay away from the crystal. Last time you broke the candlestick. It's 3:15, so you can play tag 'til four. I've put the record player down in the basement. After your snack, you can listen to the Edgar Allen Poe tale. Jay, why don't you start?"

"OK."

I took the washcloth and covered my eyes.

"One, two, three . . ."

My friends scattered. We chased each other around the house throwing couch pillows about the living room, messing the rugs in the side hallway and sneaking under the majestic table in the foreboding dining room. I ducked into my favorite hiding place—deep in the back of the hall closet—way in the back where no one could see me. My father's heavy Polo coats and tweed Chesterfields swallowed me up as I pressed into the far corner. From the shelves overhead, the rich, clean scent of Vitalis cascaded down from the sweatbands of his many hats from Brooks mixed in with the smell of mothballs. Smothered by his heavy winter overcoats, I wondered, *Why can't we spend more time together? He's always too busy with his work to concern himself with me. Why is he always working?*

"It's four o'clock," Mother called. "Come on boys. Snacks in the kitchen."

Mom sat and joked with us as she sipped her drink and we ate our cookies and finished our milk.

"Now are you sure you eighth graders are old enough to listen to this record player by yourselves?" she asked. "Edgar Allen Poe can be pretty scary."

We looked at each other nervously, hesitated, then all nodded our heads tentatively. The doorbell rang and we jumped.

"I'll get it, Mom."

I ran into the main hall and tugged at the heavy front door. Mrs. Phillips, our neighbor from across the street, stood on the step outside with my brother Harry.

"Hi, Mrs. Phillips. Hi, Har'."

"Hi, Jay. How's your mom? Hope she's feeling better. Well, I have to run. Tell her I said 'Hi'."

Harry, almost five years younger than me, had just celebrated his eighth birthday. Like mine, his hair was platinum blond and his eyes were dark blue. But he was thinner than me and a head shorter.

"Jay, take your brother with you downstairs."

"Ah, Mom, not Harry."

"Yes, Jay!"

"Do I have to?"

"Yes!"

"O.K. Come on Harry. Jack, Bill and Andy are here. We're going down to the basement. Hurry up. We're going to listen to *The Cask of Amontillado*."

I led my friends down the shaky steps from the pantry to a rickety metal card table and record player in the dank basement. We huddled together on five small folding chairs under a dim lightbulb that hung from the low cellar ceiling. When the record began, Mother handed me the flashlight, turned out the light, went up the steps and closed the pantry door. Quietly, we sat together and listened as the phonograph needle scratch out Poe's penetrating words in the dark:

"...I replied to the yells of him who clamored. I re-echoed, I aided, I surpassed them in volume and in strength. I did this, and the clamorer grew still. It was now midnight, and my task was drawing to a close. I had completed the eighth, the ninth and the tenth tier. I had finished a portion of the last and the eleventh; there remained but a single stone to be fitted and plastered in. I struggled with its weight; I placed it partially in its destined position. But now there came from out the niche a low laugh that erected the hairs upon my head..."

Harry looked at me wide eyed and grabbed my arm. It

was only then that I heard it. From above, there was a low
groaning sound and the rattling of chains. The noise grew
louder. Heavy footsteps were coming down the stairwell. In
unison, we jumped from the table and fled for safety. Up the
storm door steps we ran, forcing ourselves against the double
doors, pushing, pushing, until they flew open. We erupted out
onto the back lawn into the safety of daylight. Timidly, we
peered back down the stairs into the dark cellar well. A rau-
cous laughter came from the kitchen. Standing in the back
doorway, Mother was doubled over in hysterics. In one hand
she held the snow chains from the garage and in the other her
glass. We looked at one another, nervously at first, and then
we began to laugh, harder and harder.

"Some Mom you've got there," Andy giggled.

"Sure had me scared," Bill smirked.

"Me too," Harry added, still shaking.

I smiled. "That's my mom," I said, and pushed Harry
and Andy back towards the kitchen.

The gang picked up their jackets and hats in the large
main hallway and got ready to leave.

"Hey, Jay. Want to ride our bikes over to Judy's tomorrow?" Andy asked. "I mean if you don't crash into any more
parked cars."

I could still feel the black and blue marks around my
groin from last week's accident.

"Lay off will ya? Us Happy Hackers have to stick together. I wasn't looking where I was going. OK?"

"Maybe she'll give me more scarves." Andy said. "I've
got more than you, you know."

"Are you kidding? No way! I've got seven. And I'm
crazy for her. We're all crazy for her. Right? I wish more girls
would move here from California."

"Maybe we can have her over," Andy whispered with a
smile. "You know, get her upstairs, and play doctor."

"Are you nuts? It might have worked with Suzy. She's

only eight. But Judy'll never fall for that. She's thirteen." I shook my head. "She's stacked, not stupid."

"Yeah, I guess you're right," Andy said.

"What about that Rock 'n Roll show in Brooklyn on Saturday?" Bill asked. "Alan Freed's at the Paramount. Why don't we take her to Brooklyn to see the Flamingos? They're so great. Right?"

"Or we could take her to the Saturday matinee to see *African Jungle*?" Jack offered. "It's playing in Pleasantville in 3-D. We could sit in the back, and, you know, make out. See this? Got it last week."

"What's that?" I asked, looking at the purplish red mark on Jack's neck.

"Don't you know anything? It's a hickey."

"A hickey? What's a hickey?"

"It's from kissing, stupid. Judy gave it to me last week back by the lockers."

"Does it hurt?"

"Nah. It's my love bite."

"Hmmm." I looked at the others and shrugged my shoulders. "Anyway, if we go to the movies, we can't go with Mom," I said. "Last week the two of us went to see Gary Cooper in *High Noon*. We couldn't agree on where to sit and got in to a huge fight. So, Mom ended up sitting in the row behind me for the whole show. She said it was my fault. It's been bugging me ever since. Anyway, let's talk about it tomorrow."

"Yeah. We'll put on our Flapjacks and go on over there," Bill said.

"We gotta go, Jay." Jack pulled on his windbreaker. "Come on, Andy. Hurry up, Bill."

"Hey, Jay, did you ever find that retainer I dropped on your front lawn last week?" Bill asked. "My dad's really pissed."

"No, but I'll keep looking for it."

Andy grabbed me by the arm as he walked to the door. "Jay, you wanna go over to Lamstons tomorrow after school?" he whispered in my ear. "We can swipe some more of those plastic soldiers?"

I looked around to see if the others were listening, then whispered, "I don't know, Andy. Maybe we should lay low for a couple of weeks. We'll be screwed if we get caught. Let's talk about it tomorrow. OK? See you later alligator."

Andy winked. "OK then. After a while crocodile."

When my friends left, Mom helped Harry and me start our homework at the kitchen table. She freshened her white wine and finished up cooking our dinners.

"OK. It's ready," she said. "Go sit in the dining room. I'll bring it in before it gets cold."

I sat at one end of the glistening mahogany table with Harry at the other.
Mom pushed through the swinging door with our dinners, but as the door swung back, the two plates she carried crashed to the floor.

"Oh, don't worry," she smiled, cleaning up the mess. "I have extras in the kitchen."

Mother took the broken plates back into the kitchen, and then quickly reappeared.

"Here you are," she said. "Now, I want to see you two clean those plates."

As I looked down at my food, I saw that both the hamburger and the peas were covered with lint from the carpet. I shook my head.

Why does she have to drink so much? I wondered.

After television, on my way up to bed, I watched Mother from the first landing. She was pushing the heavy hall table in front of the stairs leading up to the seven bedrooms. Then she brought pots and pans from the kitchen to put on top of the hall chairs to block the steps.

"Mom," I called. "What are you doing? How's Dad going to get up the stairs tonight when he comes home?"

"Don't worry about your father. Just go to bed, Hon'. Good night, Jay."

She pushed two more chairs in to place, completely barricading the way to the bedrooms, and wiped her brow.

"Good night, Mom."

Upstairs in my bed, I heard her crying at the foot of the stairs and mumbling to herself.

"Nineteen years of marriage this Sunday. Nineteen! I can't take it anymore. I'm so sick and tired of him coming home drunk and smelling of perfume. And he's still fucking me . . . even when I'm having my period. Even then he wants to fuck me. I'll show him. If he comes home tonight, he'll have to stumble over this mess to get to bed. Bastard! And if he makes it up the stairs, then there'll be hell to pay . . . I'm going to divorce the bastard! Where's my drink?"

I pulled the pillow over my head and thought about my family. I didn't understand why my mother drank so much and why some nights my father never came home. I always looked forward to meeting him on his way from the station. Tired and disheveled in his rumpled suit, he carried his briefcase in one hand, his torn newspaper in the other. I would watch him walk slowly down the gravel sidewalk with his rep club tie pulled down from his sweaty custom collar. When I ran to meet him, I would hug him tightly around his portly waist. He would bend down next to me under the trellis at the neighbor's house and give me the package of Spearmint gum that he always brought from the station. Tonight, instead of hugging him tight, I hugged my pillow and tried to make the unhappy thoughts in my head go away.

"Please God, let me have a happy family," I prayed before falling asleep.

Saturday was the day mother always took my friends, Harry and me to Coney Island to go on the amusement park rides. It was our weekend ritual. We waited eagerly in the car for Mom to finish up in the kitchen. The day was bright and warm. When she climbed in, she put the top down on the red and white Packard. We always stopped at Byron's for ice cream cones. And, as Mother zoomed along the expressway towards Brooklyn, the wind painted sweet multi-color drippings along the side of the car. It wasn't long before we could see the tower of the tall Parachute Jump. Its iron skeleton rose high above the Steeplechase and the Cyclone.

Mother paid the parking lot attendant as Bill, Andy, Jack, Harry and I scampered off towards our favorite rides.

"Hey! Wait!" Mom called. "Come back here. Here's five dollars each for the arcade and the rides. Now be sure to be back here by four."

From the top of the roller coaster we could look out over the Atlantic before diving straight down on the tracks, catching our stomachs in our throats. We did four trips on the Cyclone, then walked over to the steeplechase. Harry liked the white horse and I liked the black one. When the bell rang, the five of us dashed off on our steeds around the outside of the building. We darted up to the second floor on our rails, then inside the building to the finish line. Each time, Bill's dapple-gray horse beat us by a nose. After the rides, we played the pinball machines and went through the Fun House, posing with funny faces in front of the curved mirrors. Mother finally rounded us up between the rows of concession stands as we ate our sugary clouds of pink cotton candy. It was time to go home. We walked together towards the exit, our stomachs aching from Nathan's hot dogs, candy and Cokes—tired but happy.

On our way to the car, we came to a crowd of men, women and children circled around two boys who were fighting. A small black boy was defending himself with a broken fishing pole from a taller white boy. Cautiously, they stalked each other from opposite sides of the circle's edge. Never did they take their eyes off one another fearing an attack while their guard was down. The crowd stood and watched.

"What's going on?" Mother asked one man.

"The white kid tried to steal the little colored boy's fishing rod."

"Well why isn't anybody stopping it?"

"Lady, what are you—nuts? The white kid's got a knife."

Mother pushed her way through the crowd and stepped between the two boys.

"Give me that," she said to the white boy.

"Get out of here lady," the big boy shouted.

"Mother, be careful, he's got a knife," I yelled.

"Give me that knife," she said to the boy, "or I'll take it from you."

She stared directly into the boy's eyes. The boy began to cower.

"Well, he has to give up the rod too," he said.

"Alright then." She turned to the smaller boy. "Hand them both over right now," she demanded.

The frightened little boy gave Mother his splintered fishing rod and the bigger boy gave her his knife.

"What happened?" she asked the black boy.

"I was just sitting on the pier fishing when this guy tried to take my new pole." The little boy wiped the tears from his eyes. "He took out this big knife. We started fighting and he broke my pole. Now all I have is my broken rod."

Mother put her arm around the little boy.

"Here. Take this and get a new pole."

She put a twenty-dollar bill in the boy's small, callused hand. The little black boy looked up in amazement. Then he picked up his tackle box. Mother watched him as he walked away before turning to the other boy.

"As for you, go home!" she said. "And in the future, if you want to bully someone, bully someone your own size. Come on children, let's go."

The stunned crowd watched as Mother turned and headed for the parking lot. As we walked to the car, I listened to my friends whisper amongst themselves.

"I can't believe she did it," Andy said to no one in particular.

"Did you see that?" Jack replied.

"Wow! You've got some Mom," Bill said slapping me on the back. "She sure is brave."

My chest swelled and my step was lighter. I felt taller. I was so proud of my mother.

That night at dinner, Mother said, "Now hurry up, boys, and finish up. We have to go into New York City tonight."

"Oh Mom, not again?" I complained. "We went into town just last week."

"I know, but I want to see if I can find your father tonight. I think he's in
Greenwich Village again. Hurry up. And Jay, when we get back, I'm going to need another one of your back rubs with the ointment. My back's killing me." Mother smiled. "I love the way you do my shoulders with the rubbing alcohol. And when you use the Heat, the ointment always feels so good."

As she drained her glass, I felt my heart sink.

Harry and I reluctantly finished our meals, put on our coats and got in the car.

The drive to the city went quickly. Before long, we were cruising up and down the dark tree-lined streets of Greenwich Village that had now become so familiar to us.

"Look for a white '55 Thunderbird with a red convertible top. It's his girlfriend's."

"Mom, we know," Harry sighed.

After spending an hour peering at parked cars under city street lamps,
I said, "Mom, it's ten o'clock. I'm tired. Can't we go home?"

"Mom, I've got to go to the bathroom," Harry whined. "Why do we always have to come to Greenwich Village anyway?"

"OK. OK. One more block and then we'll stop," Mother said. "We can go to The Bonsoir."

"Oh, Mom, not again," Harry whined. "I want to go home."

"Just for a little bit. You can have your Shirley Temples, and I'll give you quarters for the jukebox. Maybe we'll see your father there. And there might be a floor show tonight."

Minutes later we squeezed inside the tiny nightclub on 8th Street, and sat in mother's corner booth. Harry and I had become used to spending time at the Bonsoir sipping our drinks and munching our cherries. Mother would usually stop

here for an hour or two at the end of her futile nocturnal esca-
pades in search of our father before heading back to Garden
Village. Tonight she listened to the torch singer in the red
dress, and swayed back and forth on the banquette humming
along while drinking her drinks.

"*Come down, come down from your ivory tower,*"
mother sang as she downed her Rusty Nail.

"Jay, tomorrow night, if your father comes home . . .
Jay, are you listening to me?"

"Yes, Mom."

"Tomorrow night, if your father comes home, as you're
going up to bed, I want you to say to him Bonsoir."

"What?"

"Bonsoir. It means good night in French. Understand?
Say it."

"Bonsoarr."

"No. No. Like this. Bonsoir."

I pursed my lips. "Bonsoir."

"That's it. Perfect. Now Jay, don't forget. OK?"

"Yes, Mom. I won't."

The young waiter walked over to our table.

"Ma'am, we're closing now. Here's your bill."

Mother blinked at the tab, then looked up and smiled.

"I thought I already paid." Her eyelids had grown heavy.
"You know, some of the other waiters give me my cocktails on
the house."

She paid the tab and left a ten-dollar tip. Walking to the
exit, she stopped and looked over her shoulder and smiled
again at the waiter.

"I'm a good customer, you know. We'll see you next
Saturday."

Uncomfortable and embarrassed, I thought, *Why is she
doing this?*

I looked at mother, then Harry.

"Come on, Mom. Let's go home," I said. "I'm tired."

Harry and I slept on the back seat as mother slowly
navigated the Packard back to our enormous empty house on

Long Island.

    The next morning, I was combing my hair in the down-stairs bathroom when Mother called me from the kitchen.

    "Jay, there's something I have to tell you. It's important."

    "What, Mom?"

    "You know, you'll never be able to drink alcohol."

    "What do you mean?"

    "I mean in our family, you just can't drink alcohol."

    "No?" I pushed up my pompadour. "Well then I'll just drink beer or wine."

    "No . . . no, I mean you can't drink any alcohol at all—ever."

    "Why not? You and Dad . . ."

    "Jay, please. You just can't drink alcohol! All right? Never forget that, Jay. Remember what I just told you. Do you understand?"

    "Sure." But I didn't. *What does she mean? I can't drink any alcohol ever. Why is she telling me this now?*

    "There go the church bells," she said. "It's twelve noon. Jay, why don't you take your brother outside and play. I have something I have to do."

    "OK. Harry? Harry!" I yelled. "Come on, Harry. Let's go out front and hit some pop-ups. Go get your glove."

    We pushed open the terrace door and ran across the pebbled driveway to the massive front yard. I put Harry down by the hedge next to the street. Then I trudged back up through the thick green grass to the top of the lawn with my bat. When I turned, I laughed. Way at the other end, Harry looked like a miniscule Charlie Brown with his big head, my old Rawlings mitt and Yankees cap and his tiny body.

    We had been playing ball for a while when Mrs. Thomas drove up in her station wagon, waved and stopped.

    "Hi boys. I'm here to pick your Mom up for golf. Nice cap, Harry. Go Yanks!"

    She pulled around the side of the house to the front door and parked her car behind the high hedge. Not long afterwards, while I was hitting fly balls to Harry, an ambulance came racing up the drive followed closely by a squad car with its red lights flashing and siren blaring.

I watched as the two policemen ran in the front door.

"Com'on, Jay! What are you looking at?" Harry yelled. "Let's go. Hit me some more pop ups!"

I turned away from the house and picked up the ball and hit a line drive over Harry's head.

Minutes later, Harry and I watched as the two vehicles sped back down the driveway into the street.

We started for the house when Mrs. Thomas came out the side door and walked quickly across the lawn. As I looked at her, I could tell by her eyes that she had been crying.

"Jay, promise me you'll wait right here. I'll be right back. I have to take Harry over to the Phillips'. They can watch Harry. I'll be right back to get you. OK, Jay. Are you OK?"

"Sure, Mrs. Thomas. I'm fine," I said. "Don't worry about me. I'll wait right here."

"Harry. Come on. Harry! Hurry up. Get in the car. We have to go to the Phillips' right away."

After Mrs. Thomas left, I tossed the ball in the air, took some practice swings, bounced the ball on the bat. The sun was hot and I was thinking about the ambulance. And why was Mrs. Thomas crying? I wanted to get my soccer ball in the laundry room, so I wandered up the drive and walked inside the front door. As I entered the front hall, I noticed the smell of gas and followed its scent towards the kitchen. I tried to push open the kitchen door. It would not budge. I pushed again, harder. Finally, with difficulty, I jarred the door open. Inside, wet towels were placed on the floor along the openings of all the doors and along the windowsills. I gagged from the strong odor of gas. Buttons lay still under the kitchen table by his dog bowl. The door to the stove was open. Next to the bowl of fruit on the counter top was a handwritten note. I covered my nose and mouth with a washcloth and picked up the piece of paper.

My hand shook as I read the message. Mother had written the words from her favorite song . . . the song from the movie we saw last week, *High Noon*.

Do not forsake me, oh my darling,

On this, our wedding day,

Do not forsake me, oh my darling,

Wait, wait along.

"What has she done?" I looked around the kitchen frightened. "What do I do?" I sobbed. "What do I do?"

I gagged as the tears ran down my face. I held myself, my body shaking with despair. The back door opened and a massive black silhouette stood blocking the sunlight.

"Where's my mother?" I gasped.

A tall policeman walked into the kitchen and put his hand on my shoulder.

"Come on, son. You can't stay in here. You've got to get outside and get some air."

Confused, I stared at him.

"But, where's my mother gone?" I stammered.

"Don't cry, son. I think she'll be OK."

"But, Buttons . . .. What about Buttons?"

"Let's go outside, son."

Chapter 2

Sandpiper Beach

I walked quietly into Mother's small bedroom. Her plastic neck brace hung over the white wicker chair in the corner. At the edge of the night table, her glass of vodka sweated, half- finished. *Watchtower* magazines held open the red leather Bible from Billy Graham's wife. The passage *If God be for us, who can be against us*? was underlined. A pale afternoon sun lit the clock on the dresser.

3:05. She had asked me to wake her at 2:00.

The muffled sound of the Atlantic's breaking waves blew up from the beach below through the sheer white window curtains.

"Mom? Mom. It's time to get up."

She lay sleeping on the bed in her nightgown with a sheet pulled across her body. Her dyed blonde hair, tangled and wet, stuck to her brow. I reached out and touched her, but she did not stir. I shook her shoulder. Slowly, she began to rouse.

While I sat on the edge of the bed, she reached up without opening her eyes and pulled me down to her. Her lips touched mine, and I felt her tongue in my mouth playing with mine. She lay back with a smile, her eyes still closed, still only half-conscious.

"Where were you, Bob?" she mumbled.

I quickly pulled away and left her bedroom, ashamed and bewildered.

What the hell was that? I wiped the kiss away with my sleeve and headed for the kitchen. *I'm not Uncle Bob, or any of those other 'uncles'. Jesus!*

Mother's kiss brought me back to that summer night two years ago on Nantucket before her divorce—a memory that still haunted me.

I was upstairs reading in my bed across from the room where Harry was sleeping.

Mother called me. "Jay? Jay, come down here."

I put down the Hardy Boys, climbed out of bed and went downstairs to her bedroom. She was covered with her bedspread and propped up by several pillows, her vodka next to the lamp.

"Jay, do you know about the birds and the bees yet?" she asked.

"K-kinda," I stammered.

"Well, you're almost twelve now. It's time you learned. Come here, I want to show you something."

She drew back the sheet. Her white panty girdle held her wrinkled stomach cinched beneath her bare, tired breasts.

"Now, when you make love to a woman . . . you get on top, like this."

She pulled me on to her.

"You put your hands on her breasts like this. And then you put your penis inside her, down here."

"Mom . . .." I pulled away, frightened and confused. "I'm really sleepy. I have to go."

I fled her room, raced upstairs, closed my door and

quickly turned on my radio.

"Jay. Jay!" Mother shouted. "Come back down here."

As I lay dazed on my bed, I turned the radio louder and louder until Dinah Shore's "Love and Marriage" drowned out her calls. I curled up into a tight ball beneath my covers and held myself until I finally rocked to sleep.

I shook myself from my daydream and came back to the bright Florida sunlight.

"Where've you been?" Harry asked. He had been waiting for me in the kitchen.

"What?" I looked at Harry. "Oh . . . nowhere . . .. I was just thinking about something."

"You OK?" Harry asked.

"Yeah, I'm OK," I snapped. "Are *you* OK?"

"Yeah, I'm OK. Well, come on. You said three o'clock. It's 3:15. Let's go. We're late. It's time to play Skeet Booze."

I laughed. My brother had dragged the two large garbage pails out of the kitchen onto the small second floor landing that overlooked the vacant lot next door.

"I go first," he said.

Harry rummaged in his garbage pail for an empty liquor bottle and then found one for me.

"Ready?"

He winged his bottle far above the thick palmetto brambles that covered the empty lot. As it sailed up through the air, I reared back and flung mine as hard as I could.

Bang!

Our two bottles exploded into a thousand shards of glistening glass before tinkling down like tired fireworks onto the sand in the dense underbrush.

We took turns rifling bottles high into the air—green Scotch bottles, clear vodka bottles, yellow wine bottles, brown beer bottles.

Bash! Boom! Smash!

A car pulled into the driveway below. It was Uncle Bob. He sat behind the wheel of another new used car. This time it was a blue and gray 1950 Chevrolet. He fought to get his door open, then stepped out into the sun, unsteady, and pushed back his oily white hair. His faded blue eyes, opaque with sadness, glanced up at us.

"Hi, Bob." We waved. "Nice car."

"Fourth one in ten weeks. I almost couldn't get the insurance this time. Your mother's hit almost every light pole on A1A. It's amazing she made it all the way down from Long Island with you two last month."

Bob's flabby arms struggled to pull the packages from the liquor store off the rear seat. He waddled, huffing and puffing like a giant penguin, up the path to the stairs, careful not to be pricked by the treacherous sandspurs; he always wore thick white socks with his sandals for this very purpose. Bob stopped to catch his breath at the bottom of the stairs, and then began trudging up the flight of steps like a proper English butler—formal, pudgy, fairly short and balding. He was in his mid-50s but looked older with his ruddy complexion from years of drinking. Bob usually smelled like mothballs or whiskey, or often both. He hardly ever spoke.

Bob stopped at the landing and wiped his forehead with his handkerchief "Can you give me a hand?" he sighed. "Where's Jean?"

"In the bedroom," I said. "I think she's expecting you."

"This Chevy better last longer than the others. If she smacks it up, it could be her last one."

Mother pushed open the kitchen door wearing her white nightgown and neck brace.

"Oh, Bob, she's a beauty. Really. Much bigger than that tiny Hillman. From now on Jay'll drive us home from The 19th Hole. I promise. Now that he's fourteen, as long as I sit next to him, he's allowed to drive at night in Florida. No more light poles for me. I've had it with all those hospitals." She gave Bob a long kiss. "Boys, why don't you run down to the beach for a swim? Uncle Bob and I have to freshen up." She smiled at Bob. "We'll go to the Kon-Tiki for dinner tonight. I love that organ music. And those Mai Tais with the little red parasols are delicious."

After we got our swimsuits and flip-flops on, Harry went out to the back porch. When he slammed the screen door shut, chameleons skittered every which way across the wooden planks, disappearing through the cracks to safety. He shoved aside the small red trailer by the Ping-Pong table and found his pail and shovel hidden back in the corner.

"Happy Hour's from 5:00 to 7:00," Mother called as she led Bob into the bedroom. "So, be sure to be back by 4:30."

I took two towels from the worn clothesline in the back-yard and helped Harry drag our rafts down the wobbly steps to the path that led through the marsh grass to the beach.

Across the large expanse of white sand, I spotted Sam, my sometimes girlfriend since the beginning of August. She was folding up the large striped cabanas at her father's stand and wearing the same small yellow bikini she had worn all summer long. It made her mahogany skin shine. Her jet-black hair was wet and pulled back into a long ponytail as always. As I approached, Sam squinted into the sunlight and scrunched up her nose.

"Hi, Jay. I missed you last weekend. You said you were coming down. What happened?"

"Yeah. Sorry. I had to bag groceries at Winn-Dixie. Mom wants me to pitch in for the motorcycle, so I had to get a job. Some job. I help women carry their packages out to the parking lot for tips. You know, sometimes, after I've put the bags in their cars, they start touching me . . . holding my arm. They tell me, 'Young man, I'd like to give you something more than just a tip.' It's kind of embarrassing."

"They're probably just lonely like your mom." With her dark tan, Sam's white teeth sparkled when she smiled. "They all come down here to Florida to get their quick six-month di-vorce, just like your mom's doing from your dad. There're a lot of women like that here, especially at the beach."

"Maybe it's these stripped clam diggers. What do you think? They're kind of tight. Right? Do you like the rope belt? Maybe it's my T-shirt. You know what? Some of them, after they give me a dollar tip, they ask me to go home with them when I'm finished with work. They scare the hell out of me."

"Not doing so bad for a fourteen-year-old, eh? Just tell them, 'That's OK, I'm only allowed to accept tips, nothin' else,' then grab the money and hightail it back to the store." Sam laughed. "I guess some of those old broads are super horny. And what's this about a motorcycle?" She cocked her head and looked at me. "Didn't you just get a Cushman scooter for your birthday?"

"Well, yeah. Right after I passed the driver's test and got my license. But now I want a motorcycle. All the guys at Sandpiper Beach laugh at me when I show up for classes on that red piece of tin. They all ride cycles. I feel like a jerk. Besides, I'm joining Freddy's motorcycle club, *The Dominoes*. I have to have a bike, not a lawn mower. Everybody else has one. I want to fit in … be part of the gang. Mom says when she gets her next check from my father, we should have enough money by October."

"What about that Dick Chester? Does he have a bike?"

"No. But he's different. Sam, I tell you, he'll never fit in. And he doesn't want to—he doesn't care. The guy's crazy. I mean *really* crazy. I guess that's why he's in the gang. And Freddy has a Vespa. He's our President. But I want to get a cycle — a Harley."

"Well, I don't know about that."

"Yeah, and it's gonna have straight pipes.

"Straight pipes? But aren't they illegal?"

"Yeah, but I don't care, all the other guys have them."

"O.K. Come on, Jay, give me a hand with these before it starts to rain."

As the clouds darkened, I started to help Sam fold up the last of the green cabanas while Harry played by the water's edge. He darted back and forth, trying to catch the sand crabs with his pail and shovel as they scampered across the sand to escape the ocean's froth.

"Hey, Harry! Get up here and help us put the umbrellas and chairs away before it starts raining," I called. "Then you can go up and watch your cartoons."

Harry grabbed his bucket and joined us for the last of the work. Then he waved good-bye and headed back up the creaky wooden steps to spend the rest of the afternoon sitting in front of the TV, escaping from his life by joining his cartoon friends in their fantasy world.

Sam opened the flap of the main cabana, and we went inside to watch the storm. Most of the sunbathers had left by now, and only a few cars rolled slowly by on the hard-packed sand. I looked at Sam. Salt water still dripped from her hair and clung to her long eyelashes. Her deep brown irises were framed by the whites of her eyes. They hid beneath her thick, black eyebrows that nearly met above her brown, chiseled nose. Many summers of working for her dad on the beach had darkened her skin to a glistening ebony.

We lay side-by-side on the large blue air mattresses and looked out from underneath the flap as the rain walked down the white sand in sheets. Sam's body was lean and firm, covered with the clean smell of Coppertone. She rolled over onto her back and closed her eyes. Her high hip bones stretched the elastic band on her yellow bikini bottoms taut above her flat stomach that rose and sank like a wave. As I stroked her cheek and neck, Sam let her head fall back onto the inflated pillow. The scent of honeysuckle from the nearby dunes swirled throughout the cabana. Gradually, I let my hand slide down her arm. At her waist, I brushed the golden hairs on her belly and drew small circles with my fingers around her bellybutton. Her eyes stayed closed. Cautiously, I rubbed my hand back and forth along the drawstring of her swimsuit from one hipbone to the other. Then, slowly, I slid my fingers under the elastic of her bikini panties down to her crotch. I felt her pubic hair and stroked it as I tried to work my fingers between her lips. Suddenly, she stirred and pushed me away.

"Next time you say you're going to meet me—meet me, goddamnit!" I saw the fire in her eyes. "A date's a date, Jay. Maybe I'm not rich, but I'm not just some beach rat, you know. I thought you liked me. I thought we were friends."

"I do," I gulped. "We are."

"Come on! The rain's stopped. Help me get this place cleaned up. I have to get home."

I sulked after her, disappointed and frustrated, as we organized the remaining cabanas.

"Will I see you next weekend?" she asked.

"Of course."

"Are you sure? Don't say it if you're not sure."

"Yes. I'm sure. I want to see you."

"Good. I hope so."

Sam dusted the sand off her hands, wriggled her faded blue jeans up over her hips and pulled on her Sandpiper letter sweater.

"Hope I'll see you next weekend," she said. 'Bye."

"Me too. I hope I'll see you next weekend. 'Bye."

She walked barefoot to her old red Dodge convertible and drove away down the beach. I watched her tire marks in the wet sand until they disappeared under the pier.

By the time I got home, Mother had slipped into a floral sundress and put on her make-up and neck brace.

"Hurry up, Jay. We're going to miss Happy Hour," she said. "Here're the car keys. You know how to drive a stick shift, don't you? After dinner we'll go to the boardwalk and play putt-putt if you want. You boys love that."

Mother, Harry and I all piled into our new used car. Bob had already taken the bus into town to meet his drinking buddies at The 19th Hole, and then go with them to the dog races.

We drove through the twilight of a wonderful, warm Florida night up A1A in the Chevy. At The Bellaire Plaza, I pulled in and parked in front of the Kon-Tiki with its pointed thatched roof and palm trees. Two 20-foot carved Polynesian statues stood guard on either side of the front door.

Mother found her booth by the dance floor where she could flirt with the organist. His name was Geno. Tonight, he wore a light blue shirt with black ruffled sleeves. As was his custom, he left the shirt open to his navel. His black, slicked-back hair was held in place with pomade and dyed to match the thin moustache that crept across his upper lip.

"Play that one I like so much, Geno . . . Geno, play 'Stormy Weather,'" Mother asked. "I love the way you flick the lights. You make it just like a storm."

She put a five-dollar bill in the glass on the top of the organ and walked back to her drink at our table. As she sang along with the song, Mother played with the tiny paper parasols in front of her empty plate. She took a long drag on her Picayune, drained her Mai Tai and ordered another while Harry and I ate our hamburgers. Sitting between us, looking tired and alone, she clutched her stem glass with an iron fist, lost in thought. Finally, she reached across the table and took my hand.

"Come on, Jay. Let's dance."

She led me onto the small wooden floor and held me tight against her bosom.

"Since my man and I ain't together," she mumbled, "keeps rainin' all the time."

Mother forced her knee between my legs. I felt uncomfortable and moved stiffly as she steered me slowly around the dance floor. Geno flickered the lights so that it looked like thunder.

"Don't you just love this song, Jay?" She mumbled. "It's 'Stormy Weather. And you're a better dancer than your father.'"

I had heard the song so many times before that I knew every word as well as the inevitable consequences of dinners at the Kon-Tiki.

Finally, the music stopped. Mother put her arm around my neck for support and wobbled back to our banquette. She slouched against the shiny red vinyl seat and tipped back her drink.

"Ahh." She banged the glass down on the table and smacked her lips. "OK, boys. Let's go. It's time to go. Up! Up! Up!"

She fumbled in her purse and put a $50 bill on the table. Hoisting herself out of her seat, she lost her balance and knocked the line of tiny paper umbrellas off the edge of the table onto the floor. We followed as she zigzagged to the exit and then out between the two tall totem poles into the dim light of the parking lot.

"Jay? Jay? Look. You have to do it like this," she slurred. "See? Put the gun in your mouth just like this. See?" She put her index finger to the roof of her mouth, cocked her thumb, then quickly pulled her middle finger like a trigger.

"Bang!"

She laughed, spun her head around and looked at us through glazed eyes. "Let's go to the dog track, boys. I'm feelin' lucky. Here, catch, Jay. You can drive."

She tried to throw the keys across the car's hood, but they fell on the pavement beneath the car.

"Let's go to the track," she muttered and stumbled into the car.

No longer did she remember the miniature golf game she had promised us; she never did. I found the keys by the muffler and got behind the wheel. Mother's door was open; her head tilted back against the front seat with her neck brace unsnapped. She slept, snoring. I shook my head.

"Close her door, Harry. When we get home, you can watch TV."

That night, as I drifted off to sleep, I thought to myself, *Tonight was just like all the others—I have no mother to talk to . . ..*

Gently, I pushed open the door to my mother's bed-room. She lay passed out on her bed. I sat next to her and slowly pulled the covers off her and raised her nightgown. She did not stir. Her matted hair was wet with perspiration, and her head rested heavily on the pillow. I reached out and gently put my hand on her thigh, then gradually slid it higher up her leg. My heart was racing. I watched her heavy breath move her wrinkled stomach up and down. As I reached up to touch her . . ..

I awoke with a jolt from this fantasy in my bedroom to the morning's strong sunshine. My pajamas were stuck to my leg, and there was a stiff spot on the bed sheet.

Jesus, I thought. *Couldn't have been my dream about Mom. No way! Maybe it was Sam . . . or maybe the Playboy magazine. Goddamn! My first wet dream. How 'bout that? I'm finally a man! Damn. At last, I'm finally a man!*

I jumped and went to find my brother in the bathroom.

"Harry, guess what?" I smirked. "I came."

"You came where?" His nine-year-old eyes looked at me in a curious way. "What are you talking about? You came?"

"Don't you get it? I had a wet dream . . .. Oh, never mind. Forget it. I'll explain it to you later. I have to go tell Tommy."

I brushed my teeth quickly, ran the Remington across my peach fuzz, hopped in and out of the shower, spritzed on some Vitalis, combed my hair back into a perfect D.A., sprayed my pits and splashed on some Canoe that my father had given me for my fourteenth birthday. On my way back to my room, I took my towel and snapped Harry's ass. I found my pegged pants under the bed by the *Playboy,* yanked on my T-shirt and rolled up the sleeves.

"Belt? Belt? Where the hell did I . . .? Ah, there it is."

I threaded the two thin silver buckles through the loops and arranged them so they hung low on the right side of my waist over my hip. I found two white socks in my drawer, slipped them on, then poked my feet into my blood red Thom McAnn Flapjacks. With a snap, I pulled the tongues shut.

On my way to the kitchen, I noticed Mother's bedroom door was cracked open. Mom and Bob were still asleep nude on the bed. Bob looked like a white whale, Mother more like a skinny eel. A half-finished bottle of Smirnoff lay on its side on the carpet.

I gobbled down two raspberry Pop-Tarts and chugged a glass of milk. In the carport, I grabbed my black leather jacket from the peg, took the scooter's starter cord in my hand and gave the rope a hard, excited yank.

"Owwwwww!"

The rubber handle slipped through my fingers,

smashing my first two knuckles against the metal side of my Cushman.

"Piece of shit!"

I sucked the blood and kicked the rear wheel. I pulled the cord again, and the engine caught. Off I rode through the cold morning air to school, the throttle fully open, pushing the governor's 40 mph top end to the max to look for Tommy.

Three greasers in motorcycle jackets and black jeans were huddled against the radiator in the boys' room, warming their hands from their early morning rides. The hoods wore their collars up and had thick taps on their heavy black boots. One was busy fixing his skinny white belt, sliding its two tiny buckles back and forth along the waist of his tight pants. The other two were crooning in harmony like the Del-Vikings and snapping their fingers while bogarting their Camels.

Tommy was posing in front of the mirror like a gun-slinger, his white jeans riding low on his hips, his feet spread apart, his knees bent. Carefully, he watched as he coaxed the sides of his peroxided blond flat top back into a D.A.

"Yeah. There. That's it," he muttered, stepping back to study his hair again. "No. Damn it. That's not it." He started over, pushing his wings back and parting them down the middle in the back with the end of his comb.

"Tommy. Guess what?" I whispered. "I'm finally a man."

"Wait, wait. Can't you see? I'm busy. OK? Ah, that's it. OK. What?"

"Tommy, I'm a man! Finally, I'm a man!"

"It took you long enough." He smiled. "You get laid?"

"Shhh . . .. Not so loud. I don't want the other guys to hear. Tommy, I came."

"Well, it's about time. Tell you what. Seems like you're ready to meet my step-sis. Scotty's eighteen. Dig? Maybe Friday after she gets off work at the White Castle we can go to the drive-in. Better yet, there's a beer party on Sandpiper Beach Friday night. We can watch the submarine races." Tommy winked. "See if you can't get the car from your mom. There might be some drag racing too. Wait 'til you see Scotty

in her new sack dress. Man, she's hot. She's kinda weird —
she loves to read the Bible, but she also loves to have fun, if
you know what I mean."

My eyes lit up. "Great. But Tommy, don't tell her I'm
fourteen. You know, chicks like older guys. Hey, Tommy. You
know, we *Dominoes* have to stick together, right?"

Tommy smiled. "Don't worry, she likes to break in
young guys like you —believe me, you'll see."

"So, Tommy, do you think she'll go all the way?'

"Like I said, Jay, you'll see."

Friday afternoon, I pulled into the Calhouns' driveway in
Mother's Chevrolet. A new pink and white '57 DeSoto Firedome sparkled beneath the shower from Tommy's hose. Its
silver Lake Pipes slid beneath the long rear fender skirts, hugging the raked bottom. Purple pinstripes swirled around the
door handles and flamed back towards the fins. When I
honked, Tommy looked up and waved as he finished spraying
down the shining chrome spinners that glittered inside the
whitewalls.

"Right on time." Tommy wiped the louvered hood dry
and threw the towel in a bucket. "I'll take Scotty's car. She'll go
with you. Hey, Sis?" he shouted. "Let's go, Sis! Jay's here.
Come on. Hurry up."

"Wait a minute, will ya?"

Scotty ran out the front door, her backless red high
heels clip-clopping on the flagstones.

"Can't you see I'm still putting on my make up?" she
pouted, tucking her lipstick into a small red purse.

I could not believe my eyes.

Tommy's stepsister was petite with short, black hair.
She wore her new red sack dress tied around her alabaster
neck and again just below her knees.   Blazing from behind
her, the strong Florida sun inked the black hourglass silhouette of her breasts and hips hidden beneath the soft summer
cloth of her crimson package.

"Hi, Jay. Tommy's told me a lot about you." She put her
hands on her waist and cocked her hips. "I heard you joined

The Dominoes." Her wet lips glistened.

"Yeah, I'm part of the gang now," I boasted.

"Scotty, you ride with Jay," Tommy said. "Come on, hurry up, we're gonna be late." He slid onto the white leather bucket seat of the Firedome and fired up the glass-packs. "Jay, you follow me. We'll take the Silver Beach Bridge. Got the beer?"

"I took some Scotch. Mom's got so much, she'll never know it's gone."

"Come on then. Let's go. And don't you two get stuck in the sand." Tommy winked.

Tommy peeled out of the driveway, laying rubber down the block, and I cruised after him through the salt-scented breeze towards the ocean. Our cars traveled together in a close caravan through the warmth of this perfect day. We sped through a tunnel of palm trees that took us to the bridge. I locked on to the Firedome's rear bumper and watched the silver plaque jingle jangle beneath the shining Continental kit and dual exhausts. It said, *Lil' Fox.* The deep rumble of Tommy's sedan ricocheted off the cement causeway walls and snarled at the saffron sky. Scotty moved closer. When she reached to search the radio for rock 'n' roll, her soft skin brushed my arm.

"Listen, Jay."

Each time she smiled, her green-brown eyes sparkled in the city lights.

"It's WAPE!" Scotty giggled. "That's my favorite station."

When she rolled her window down and let the wind blow through her hair, the car filled with her jasmine perfume.

"Listen, Jay. It's 'All Shook Up'!" She swayed side to side excitedly in her seat. "Isn't Elvis sooooo great? I'm crazy about Elvis," and she gave me a kiss on the cheek.

We passed the bars on Main Street, the recreation center, the YMCA, then turned down the sandy tunnel ramp under the aged Halifax Hotel onto the beach where we found our friends gathered next to the lifeguard station.

Couples were dancing the Lindy in the sand as *Blue*

Suede Shoes spilled from a transistor radio. Others lay about on checkered blankets warming themselves in front of a small bonfire, drinking beer and necking. Sparks jumped from the driftwood's flames and carried on the evening's breeze out over the white crashing waves. Above, hungry gulls hung in the night's purple sky hoping for scraps of hot dogs or fries. Their shrill cries mixed with the screams from the arcade's bumper car rides and the Ferris wheel. Not far away, beneath the strings of twinkling honky-tonk lights, couples strolled arm in arm along the boardwalk, sipping Cokes and eating cotton candy. Tommy pulled up next to Bobby's yellow, chopped and channeled '53 Studebaker coupe. He revved the mufflers, then cut the engine.

"Hey, you guys, we made it!" he shouted.

"Where's the action?" Scotty yelled.

Peggy and Bobby waved. "Over here."

"Come on, Jay." Scotty took me by the hand and pulled me towards the fire. "Let's get something to eat."

We huddled together with our burgers on an old drift-wood log and listened to Buddy Knox chirp out the words to *Party Doll.* The strong scent of azaleas blew down from the dunes and across the beach on the evening wind. Waves swelled and crushed the shore before their froth slid back into the black Atlantic. Scotty squeezed my arm.

"Can I have a drink, Jay?"

"Sure."

I twisted the red cap off the bottle of Dewar's and poured two Scotches.
We clinked our plastic cups, and I choked down the first warm swallow with a grimace.

"Look, silly. It's not that bad." She took a long swig. "See?"

"Sure is strong." I winced. "It kind of burns."

"You'll get used to it. Wine's fine, but liquor's quicker," she giggled.

At first, I hesitated. But then I wrapped my arm around her thin waist.

She moved closer, put her hand on my leg and whispered, "When we finish our drinks, why don't we go back to my place? My folks left for Orlando this morning. They won't be back 'til Sunday."

"S-sure," I stammered. I emptied my glass. "I'm done. Let's go."

"OK. Oh, Jay! Don't forget the bottle. We can have some more in the car."

"Oh, yeah. Right. OK. Let's go."

"Howdyyyyyyy everybody! It's the Wooooooolf-mannnnn here," the car radio howled. "Friday night on Florida's number one radio station. And this one's going out to all you hepcats."

Scotty moved closer to me, took my hand off the gearshift and wrapped it around her shoulder. She turned the music up and sang along.

"Wake up little Susie, wake up . . .."

When we pulled into her driveway, only the outside porch light was on.

"Come on in, but don't turn on the lights," she said. "I like it dark. Go in the living room. There's an LP by the Platters on the Victrola. Why don't you play it? I'll get some ice."

I switched the record player on and watched the 33⅓ drop down the spindle onto the whirling turntable. When the arm swung over and gently placed the needle in the first groove, *One In A Million* jumped from the Mercury label and filled the room with soft music.

Scotty pushed open the kitchen door and came out carrying a tray with a bowl of ice and two glasses that she put on the coffee table. She took a match and lit the candles on either side of the couch and then poured our drinks. When she moved closer to me, I could tell she had freshened her perfume. The fragrance was heavy, rich and sweet.

"Jay, let's get drunk. Whaddya say? Do you want to?"

"Sure."

"Let's have some fun," she purred.

She clinked my glass, and we gulped the Scotch.

"I think I'm starting to like this stuff." I smiled. "It feels good going down now. I think . . . I think I'm getting bombed. I like it. Yeah, let's have some fun."

I poured two new drinks. Scotty took my glass and put it on the table, then took me by the shoulders and pulled me to her. We sank down on to the large throw pillows, and I began to kiss her cheeks and neck. My hands found her breasts, and I began to rub them firmly up and down. She reached down under me and started to massage my groin. My cock stiffened.

"The Bible sayeth, 'Do not lust after her beauty in your heart'," she whispered in my ear.

I wrapped my fingers in her hair and pulled her to me. I kissed her hard on the mouth. Our lips pushed apart, her tongue played with mine. I fumbled with the drawstring at the top of her dress.

"No, silly, it's a sack dress. Remember?" She giggled. "Here. Let me show you."

She reached behind her neck, undid the bow and lowered the front of her dress, then unhooked her bra. I could see the tan lines that circled her nipples in the candlelight. She loosened the bottom string of her dress and murmured, "I have perfumed my bed with myrrh, aloes, and cinnamon. Come, let us take our fill of loving until the morning."

I forced her dress up to her waist and rushed to pull her panties down over her ankles. Madly, I began to go up and down on top of her.

"No! No! Wait!" she gasped. "Not like that. Let me show you. Sllllooowly, Jay. Sllllooowly."

She unzipped my pants and reached inside my underpants to pull out my hard-on.

"There," she said. "Now you're free. Like this." She guided me into her, receiving me easily.

"The Lord said, 'Giving themselves over to fornication, and going after strange flesh'," she groaned.

We began furiously rocking up and down on the soft couch, my hips banging down hard upon her again and again. White light flashed through my body. Instantly, I exploded up into her, feeling the waves of cum drain my energy. I shuddered and collapsed on top of her. I rested my head against her moist neck. Her wet hair smelled of jasmine. I could feel her holding me underneath my underpants.

"Thou didst trust in thine own beauty, and playedest the harlot because of thy renown," she hissed, "and pouredest out thy fornication on every one that passed by. Amen."

We lay on the couch in the dark, breathing heavily, until headlights swept
across the living room.

"Jay! Get up! Get up! Quick! Put your clothes on."

I quickly pulled up my pants and did my belt buckle as the front door swung open. Tommy bounced into the hall with his beach towel whistling *All Shook Up*.

"Hi, guys. Mighty dark in here. What's up?"

Scotty and I sat next to each other on the couch sipping our Scotches.

"N-not much," I stammered. I looked at Scotty.

"How was the party?" she asked.

"Not bad. I almost got a blow job from Susie." He smiled and yawned. "I'm beat, Sis. Off to bed."

He started up the stairs, then turned.

"Oh, Scotty dear. Aren't those your panties under the coffee table?" He smiled and left us sitting in the dark.

Late the next day, I rode my brand new red and white 165 Harley over to Freddy King's house. The black motorcycle jacket I wore was one of the five we had stolen from Sears and Roebuck the week before. On the front, above my heart, it said, *Jay*. The back was covered with a large black and white number five domino indicating my rank in our club. *The Dominoes* stretched across the back from shoulder to shoulder.

When I pulled in the driveway, Freddy's spastic seventeen-year-old brother Carl was sprawled out on the cement floor of the carport. He kneeled with his double-jointed legs splayed out behind him like spaghetti. Six or seven empty glass Coke bottles lay scattered about him. Against the wall was a large white refrigerator. Its door was open, displaying his stash of stacks and stacks of Coca-Cola. As I revved my engine, Carl jerked his head around, throwing the drool from his mouth. When he smiled, the rotted spaces between his yellow teeth showed the damage done by a ten-year diet of sweet soft drinks. In his crooked hand, Carl held a dirty rag that he was using to clean his brother's midnight blue Triumph motorcycle.

"Hi, Jway. How you doin'?" he slobbered.

"Good. Playing with Freddy's bike again, huh?"

Carl dropped his eyes, embarrassed. He stared at the concrete floor.

"Is your brother home?"

Carl snapped his head around towards the kitchen door.

"Fweddy," he slurred. "Fweddy. Jway's here."

Freddy banged open the screen door. He was slightly shorter than me, about 5' 5", with greasy hair and long side-burns. His ruddy face was covered with acne. Freddy had just been made President of The Dominoes.

"Carl! I told you to stay away from my bike," he grumbled. "You're dribbling all over it. Wipe the spit off your mouth and get inside. You can watch TV 'til Mom gets back."

"I was just twyin to shine it for ya. 'Bye, Jway." Carl dragged himself across the cement carport floor and up the steps through the kitchen door.

"God. That imbecile never listens. I've told him a hundred times not to touch my bike. You'd never know he was my *older* brother."

"So, Pres, you ready for some rock 'n' roll tonight?" I asked. "The sock hop should be hot. Can you believe that Jerry Lee Lewis will be there?" I hunched my jacket up on my shoulders and pretended to run my thumb along an ivory keyboard. "*You shake my nerves and you rattle my brain*," I shouted. "Man, it should be sooooo cool."

"You bet!" Freddy dropped to one knee like Jerry Lee and reached up to pound an imaginary keyboard. He shimmied and howled, "*You broke my will . . . oh what a thrill . . .*

Goodness gracious great balls of . . . Hang on. Hang on. I've got to fix my 'do." He stared in to the rearview mirror on his Triumph. "The damn thing won't stay no matter how much grease I put on it."

"Freddy, your mop looks fine. You're just going to get more zits from all that stuff anyway. Let's go. We're going to miss the dance and Jerry Lee if we don't hustle."

He pulled a comb from the back pocket of his tight jeans, propped up his sagging pompadour, then pushed the oily sides back into wings. Freddy studied himself in the mirror before sliding the point of his comb down the middle in back to make his D.A. perfect.

"That's it!" he chuckled with a wolfish snarl.

"You know, Pres, we've got to be careful tonight. The damn cops are looking for us again. That crazy bastard Chester really pissed them off last week spinning those doughnuts in front of the station house. They've been laying for us ever since. And swiping these jackets from doesn't help any. If they catch us, we're screwed. They know we're not allowed on the roads after dark."

"I told Tommy and Dick to go ahead. We'll meet 'em at the gym. If we traveled in a pack tonight, our goddamn mufflers would wake up the whole precinct," Freddy warned. "We have to be quiet if we're going to drive at night."

We kick started our engines, turned on our headlights, and headed down the back street. As we rode together, Freddy signaled to slow down.

"Damn it! Jay, I forgot to get gas. I'm just about out."

"OK. Let's go to Ted's on US 1. He likes us."

We swung around, dropped down to the Highway and headed north for the gas station. As we pulled up to the pumps, headlights flashed on from behind the service bays at the far end of the repair shop.

"Shit! Freddy! It's the cops. Quick! We've got to get out of here. I'll try to get them to follow me. Get going and get some gas. I'll meet you at the dance."

I gunned my cycle and raced past the cop to draw the

cruiser away from Freddy. I hit the curb, bounced up onto US 1, and sped up the right lane. The police car swung out after me, its red lights swirling and siren howling. Shifting down from third to second, I threw open the throttle and hugged the gas tank with my chest. When I slammed it back in to third, the speedometer hit 70. My front wheel began to shimmy on the pavement, and my studded leather saddlebags clattered against my rear fender in the wind.

Ahead, at the intersection, the light was slowly turning from yellow to red. I sped through the crossing, just as a green convertible jumped the light and came barreling at me from the right. I hit my brakes, skidded sideways—missed the sedan's rear fender by a foot. I glanced over my shoulder. The cruiser had run the red light and was right behind me with its headlights flashing.

Fuck. Don't those guys have anything better to do on a Saturday night?

I turned back to look up the road. Five feet in front of me, at a dead stop, I suddenly saw the letters **F O R D** on the tailgate of a shiny red pick-up. I slammed on both brakes and lay the cycle down, waiting for the collision. My front chrome roll bar caught the road and spun the bike up wildly. I bounced off the truck's rear quarter panel, wrenched the handlebar back to center, and flew down the right side of the long line of traffic. All at once, a massive beige and white Mercury pulled out into the breakdown lane, forcing me up over the curb onto the grassy shoulder. My jacket's shoulder ripped as I clipped the car's long tailfin.

"Get out of the way!" I shouted.

The thirtyish driver gave me the finger.

I skidded across the grass, past a palm tree and his two-tone Merc. Behind me, the squad car was charging in the left lane, its siren blaring. I looked up. Just ten feet ahead, there loomed the solid brick wall of a bridge abutment. Squeezing between the line of cars and the thick concrete blocks, I screeched back onto the street, then turned hard right. As I sped around the sandy corner, my roll bar caught

the road and fishtailed my rear wheel throwing me off my cycle. I ducked as I slid across the sand slamming hard into the
curb. I shook my head and saw my bike was lying next to me
on its side spinning circles on the pavement. I wiped the blood
form my mouth and grabbed the handlebars. When I cranked
open the throttle, my rear wheel snapped back underneath
me, spraying a rooster tail of gravel as I raced up the road.
Flying over the crest of the next hill, I saw the sign ahead:
DEAD END. I screeched to a halt.

A momentary quiet fell across the evening's twilight.
The heaving from my idling engine sounded like the heavy
snorting of exhausted racehorses gasping for air. With each
piston stroke from beneath the red and white gas tank, my cycle shivered. I looked back down the road through the cloud of
dust, then up ahead. The only thing further on was a driveway
leading to a large white house. I stared at the house, then
back down the road again. Suddenly, the cop car came charging around the corner—racing up the hill. The flashing red
lights were getting bigger and bigger.

"Shit!"

I revved the engine and popped the clutch. Spinning
the bike around, I raced up the road, straight down the driveway, onto the side yard. I skidded under a clothesline, tore
across a flowerbed and punched through a small opening in a
thick hedge. Quickly, I cut my engine and peeked back at the
road from behind a large palmetto bush. My heart was pounding.

Two massive police officers with black sunglasses and
guns stood alongside their cruiser at the edge of the lawn.
They rocked back and forth in their tall boots for a moment
with their arms crossed, then climbed back in their car,
slammed the doors hard, turned around and drove away.

"Thank God," I muttered. "No Juvenile Court tonight."

I kick-started my Harley, turned it around and began my
ride up Sandpiper Boulevard. Just before the school, I saw the
gang joking amongst themselves in front of a grove of palm
trees that hid their motorcycles. All of them were wearing their

black leather jackets from Sears. As I pulled up, they all waved—all except Dick Chester. He was busy combing his thick red hair back into a ducktail.

"Close call, I see," Tommy said. He popped his gum. "You've got blood on your lip and your jacket's ripped. Guess we're going to have to make another trip to Sears."

Freddy smiled weakly. "Jay, thanks for getting those guys off my tail."

"Look, Freddy, if you're going to be our leader, the leader of The Dominoes, you gotta have enough brains to keep your gas tank full at night."

"OK. OK. You're right, Jay. I'm sorry."

"Let's get going," Tommy urged. "We're gonna miss Jerry Lee."

Dick Chester looked up from the silver ID bracelet he had gotten from Joanie Funichello. It glistened as it hung down from his freckled wrist. His washed-out green, beady eyes darted about above his slack jaw. Like Elvis, he curled his lip and threw his leather collar up in the back.

"Yeah. And get some ass," he drawled with his maniacal grin.

His lazy tongue moved the dangling toothpick from one the side of his narrow mouth to the other.

"You dig it?"

Chester pulled a pint of Jack Daniels from the hip pocket of his pegged jeans, twisted off the black cap, and took a long pull. As he downed half the bottle, I watched his Adam's Apple jump with each gulp. He re-capped the bottle and put it back in his jeans. He wiped his mouth with the back of the sleeve of his black leather jacket, then gave his lips a smack. He pulled a comb from his pocket and raked his thick, red hair back on the sides into a perfect D.A.

Suddenly a blast of music came from the gym, shaking the night.

"Come along my baby, whole lotta shakin' goin' on . . . Yes, I said come along my baby, baby you can't go wrong . . ."

Jerry Lee was pounding on the ivories.

We all joined in, screaming loudly, *"Come along my baby . . . you drive me crazy . . . Goodness, gracious, great balls of fire!"*

Chester looked across at us with his green, wolfish eyes, and said with a snarl, "Come on, you pussies, we're gonna miss the dance."

He threw one leg over the handlebars of his scooter and spat. The studded belt he wore rode low on his narrow hips. With a swagger, Chester walked off into the night towards the gym.

On Sunday night, Mother left Uncle Bob to watch Harry and went off with her friends for drinks at The Nineteenth Hole. I wanted to get out of the house and go to the movies to see *I Was a Teenage Werewolf*, but I had to have someone eighteen years or older sitting next to me when I drove Mom's car. I called Scotty, but she was just going out the door on her way to work at the White Castle. So I decided, *Screw it. I'll take the Chevy anyway and drive into town to see this week's current horror film by myself.*

It was past midnight when I left the dank, dilapidated movie theater. I stood under the faded marquee that touted the scariest movie of the year and stared out at the pouring rain. On the billboard above, six or seven of the twinkling lights that heralded the Boone Theatre were out. The *W* in *Werewolf* was hanging upside down by a nail, swinging back and forth in the blustery wind, and the *O* in wolf was missing.

On the other side of the dark street, Mom's Bel Air was being buffeted by sheets of rain. I tossed up the collar of my jean jacket, ran through the puddles in my motorcycle boots and jumped shivering onto the worn upholstery. I slammed the door hard as the rain pelted the windshield. Strong gusts rocked the Chevy from side to side. When I turned the ignition key, only the dashboard instrument panel glowed a faint red. I tried again . . . then again. Finally, the engine turned over. I switched on the windshield wipers, but they did not budge.

"Great car, Mom. How do I get home?" I said to no one. "I can't see a thing."

I rolled down the window to get my bearings. Barely did the eerie, blue city lights illuminate the slick, black, glistening streets. As I drove slowly through the empty town up Route A1A past rows and rows of darkened motels, I prayed no banshees, zombies or lycanthropes would attack me.

It was 1am when I finally arrived home. Three cars were parked in the driveway. I killed the headlights and shut off the engine. Voices of men arguing loudly came through the slats of the jalousie windows. It sounded like they were in the living room.

"Get out of the way, old man, and you won't get hurt," someone said.

"If you don't leave right now, I'm going to *make* you leave." It sounded like Uncle Bob.

Another voice said, "Put down the bat, old boy. Put it down now!"

I peeked in through the carport door and saw a young man in a white Orioles T-shirt and baseball cap lunge for Bob. Another grabbed my baseball bat that Bob was holding and twisted it away from him.

"Give me that, you old geezer. We're the baseball players. Not you."

The one in the T-shirt wrestled Uncle Bob to the living room floor, pinning him down with one knee. Mother was in the corner leaning against a tall man in a Yankees jersey. They all looked drunk.

"Get off of me, you bastard!" Bob shouted. "Get out of our house!"

"*Our* house?" The man holding Mother laughed. "I thought this was Jean's house."

"I'm sick and tired of you bush league ball players always following her home," Bob said. "Don't you know any young women?"

"Look, Pops, we're leaving now. I'm going to let you up. But when we come back, you better not be here. Let's go guys. It's almost curfew. We gotta get back to the stadium. 'Bye, Jean." Mother looked up wearily.

The three men walked out the front door and up the driveway, laughing.

Uncle Bob shouted after them, "Don't come back again! If you do, I'll call the police."

They turned and gave him the finger as they got in their cars and drove off.

I came into the house through the side door. Bob brushed back his oily, white hair and smoothed his soiled shirt and trousers. He turned and smiled at Mother. She was slumped in a chair at the kitchen table.

"It's time for bed, Jean. Let me help you," he said gently. "You have to stop flirting with these baseball players at the bars."

He ducked his head under her arm and took her wrist in his hand. With his other arm around her waist, he collected Mother against his hip. His face was flushed.

"Good night, Jay." He carried her unsteadily towards her room. "We'll see you in the morning."

"Sleepy . . . so sleep . . .," Mother slurred.

I looked around at the sparsely decorated living room—the flimsy folding TV tables, the cheap armchairs. I pulled the Scotch from the liquor cabinet and took a long swallow before putting it back with all the other bottles. I walked to my bedroom, closed the door and sat down on my bed.

Why does it have to be this way? She's always drunk, and my father never calls. I lay my head on the pillow. As I stared at the ceiling, a tear ran down the side of my face.

Monday night, Mother, Harry and I sat huddled together in silence eating our TV dinners off aluminum trays and watching the end of *The Ed Sullivan Show*.

Finally, Mother turned to me and said, "Jay, your father called this morning while you were at the beach. He wants to know if you want to stay on at Sandpiper High next year or go away to boarding school in Connecticut. He said he can get you into Dunbarton. That's where he went to school. You'd have to repeat your freshman grade. But that's OK. You're only fourteen, so you won't be the oldest one in your class.

And you'll probably be repeating some of your classwork, so your first year should be easy and you'll get good grades. He said you can stay with him and his new wife over the holidays if you want. He just bought a big new house on Long Island. Or you can fly down here and visit Harry and me." Mother finished her beer. "What do you think?" she said with hesitation. "Do you want to go, Jay? You don't have to if you don't want to."

I thought hard, surprised by this opportunity to escape. I did not want to leave Harry behind. He would have to go through this hell all by himself. And I would miss the Dominoes. I would even miss Mother. But I thought how mixed up this past year had been—going to Florida with Mother for her quick divorce—all of the drinking and the chaos. I did not want to be with my father. But I did not want to be with my mother either. This was my chance—my chance to break free—my chance to get away. I stared at the floor, and then looked at Mother.

"Mom, I love you . . .."

She smiled a weak smile.

"But, yes, I do want to go."

She turned away, as if struck by a blow. She seemed smaller in the flickering pale light of the TV screen.

"Mom . . .? Mom . . .? Mom, can I have a beer?"

Chapter 3

Eric Tempelton III

"A-a-all right gentlemen, quiet down!" Mr. Furgeson bellowed. He cast a stern eye over his new students. "According to the Dean of Boys, it seems as though some of you have already forgotten the schedule at Dunbarton. So, let me remind you again. We rise p-p-promptly at 6:00. Breakfast at 7:00. Classes 'til 3:00. Then a-a-athletics, chapel and dinner. After dinner, study hall is from 7:30 to 9:00. A-a-and lights out is at 9:30 sharp. You should all know this by now. And above all, remember that

Dunbarton is a school for gentlemen. That's particularly true for you Third Formers. Do not ever forget this. I hope I'm making myself clear . . . c-c-crystal clear!"

Mr. Furgeson was one of the two dorm masters in Larson House, a timeworn white frame building nestled in the dogwoods on one corner of the school's campus. With his stutter, baldhead, potbelly and short stature, his nickname was Porky Pig.

"Are there a-a-any questions?" He scanned our young, bewildered faces. "A-a-alright then. Dismissed."

My roommate, Jim, and I walked back upstairs with two of my new friends from down the hall, Paul and Chris. It amused me that my roommate, Jim, and Chris both had the same last name, Chapman, if not the same build or mental agility. Although they were both heavy, Chris was over six feet, talked all the time and was not very bright; Jim, on the other hand, was slightly taller than me, said very little, and was an A student. Chris's roommate Paul was my size: 5' 7", 145. He wore a flat top and used pomade to push it up from his widow's peak. His thick hair gel certainly did not help the acne that he covered with Clearasil. Like Jim, he was one of the brightest students in the Third Form. But, unlike me, Paul was clumsy at sports.

Jim's father was a banker in Providence, and Paul's a well-known surgeon in Hartford. Chris' dad owned a large finance company in New York. All three seemed to have happy families. None came from broken homes. I grasped at my new friends and held them tightly.

During the first few weeks of school, I had learned to compensate for my poor academic skills with my athletic ability. Paul and I complemented each other this way in the school curriculum. Paul helped me with my studies, and I was the jock who was his best friend. We were proud of each other.

"You wanna get together after lights tonight?" Paul asked. "I can help you with your Math, and then you can show me how to do those clapping pushups."

"Sure. I've got a test tomorrow. I don't want to be stuck in the fifth quintile forever."

"OK. We'll be over when the masters finish their rounds." Paul laughed. "And I've got a funny idea for French tomorrow. I'll tell you about it later after lights out."

I sat at my desk across from Jim, staring at my Math

book and thinking about being at Dunbarton. Mother was wrong. Despite dropping back a year to get into this top-ranked prep school, my grades were a disaster. But, regardless of my dismal academic showing, this was still a time of great excitement for me. Everything here was different from the high school life I had left behind in Florida. Being on my own, meeting new teachers, exploring the classrooms in the different buildings, finding my way around campus—all of this filled me with a feeling of exhilaration that I had never known before. I loved the independence. Being away from my parents and on my own was the best part of it all. This new, unknown place in Connecticut thrilled me. Never before had I been amongst the elite—those who dressed and carried themselves in ways other boys didn't. These boys were special, and certainly not part of any Dominoes motorcycle gang. Being a part of Dunbarton filled me with pride. It challenged me daily to fight to improve my academic standing as well as my limited wardrobe. I would not give up easily this place to which I had been allowed to escape—a place where, for the most part, I finally felt secure.

Contrary to my Floridian life that only offered nights of lonely TV dinners with my brother Harry, this privileged boarding school gave me a newfound camaraderie in the dining hall. Instead of beers with Mother at the drive-in, or—if she drank too much—late night motorcycle rides on the beach with Scotty, now my weekends were filled with the excitement of football games.

My father's large house on Long Island, four times the size of my Mother's home, was no better for me. It lay in Old Westerly, on Long Island, covered by a cold cloud of constipated wealth. Father's icy demeanor matched it's chill. Never did he allow time for us to be together to talk. Instead, he lived his life only to restore the fortune his parents had lost in the Great Depression. His focus remained fixed on rebuilding the prestige of the Walker family that vanished in 1929. There was not a minute to waste on being a father. Rather, it was either hard work at the office regaining his family's lost power, or, on weekends, concentrating on the manicured putting greens at one of his five famous golf clubs with business associates.

His new wife, Florence, my daffy stepmother, ignored me as much as my father did. If it was not her bowling leagues, where, oddly enough, my mother had introduced her to my father, or her beauty salons, then her afternoons were spent with her oddball son Ronald. Evenings were reserved for her drinking and maudlin memories of a career in ballet that was never realized.

Only Fritz, her German shepherd, and my old friends in Garden Village, two towns over from Old Westerly, gave me the happiness that I so desperately sought.

The door creaked opened. Paul and Chris squeezed into my room from the darkened hallway with their flashlights.

"Hey, check this out," Chris said with a smile. "What do you think?"

I looked at Chris. His face was streaked with orange lines.

"Chris, what did you do?" I said.

"What do you mean?" Chris asked. "It's my new tan. I used that Man Tan stuff. Cool, huh?"

"You look ridiculous. I told you not to use that stuff. You look like an orange. Put some iodine in baby oil and sit in the sun if you want a tan."

"Hey, guys," Paul said with excitement, "Let's have some fun in French tomorrow. What do you say?"

"Shh . . . the masters are going to hear you," Jim whispered.

"OK. OK." Paul lowered his voice. "So, here's my plan . . ."

"What?" I asked.

"You know how Professor Gallard always comes to class looking like he doesn't have a dime?"

Chris nudged me and smiled. "Listen to this," he giggled.

"Well, tomorrow, when we're in French class, let's give him one of our old clean dress shirts as a joke." Paul laughed.

"We can even stuff some fake money into it."

"What? Give him a shirt?" I looked around embarrassed. "I've only got four shirts—not to mention only one
sports coat and three ties. I can't give him a shirt. The only
reason I've got four shirts is because of those forged notes
you write for Chris and me so we can go down to the laundry
and tell them we lost our shirts. I need my shirts — even if
they do belong to somebody else."

"Don't worry, Jay." Paul gave me a friendly pat on the
shoulder. "I've got an old tux shirt we can use."

"You know, Gallard always wears the same shirt," Chris
laughed. "I bet his shirt could follow him to class by itself."

"You should talk," Paul said with a smile. "You've been
wearing the same pair of corduroys since school began. Look
at them—they're worn clear through at the crotch."

"Well, yeah . . . but whaddya expect? They're corduroys, for God's sake. I told ya. I'm going to wear them all year
long. Why not? There aren't any girls here. Right? Why not?
And, look . . . .. See? The safety pins hold them together just
fine. They're just fine. So, lay off."

Jim dug into his bottom drawer. "Here's some Monopoly money. We can stuff it in the shirt since he's always broke.
The poor guy probably doesn't have a dime to his name."

"OK. I'll bring it to class," I offered. "Hey. You guys better push off. I'll get my ass in a sling if I get caught with you
guys in my room after lights out."

"But what about the Math?" Paul asked. "You have to
study."

"Study?" I gave him a hard stare. "Look, Paul, when I'm
not reading Playboy, I'm up all night guzzling coffee and pop-
ping NoDoz like M&Ms in that goddamn closet. I've been studying in there with my flashlight 'til 3 a.m. almost every night for
the past three weeks. But, don't you get it? It doesn't help at
all. How can I learn anything when my fucking family's falling
apart? Paul, without you . . . without your help, Paul . . . if you
weren't writing my English papers for me, I'd have flunked out
of here by now. It took you four weeks to finally make me

understand that the fifth quintile isn't the best place to be academically. Last week, I cheated on one of Casey's Chem quizzes, and I still only got a 63. Screw Math tonight. I'll never get it anyway. I'm probably the dumbest kid who ever went to Dunbarton!"

"You're sure, Jay? You're sue you don't want me to help you?"

"Paul, you know I've been busting my butt studying. I study all the time. But no matter how much time I spend studying, I just don't get it. It just won't sink in. I think the Headmaster's Weimaraner's got better grades than me. Last quarter I was 128 out of 134 for God's sake. And with my luck, those six other Neanderthals will probably go right by me this semester, so I'll fall even further behind. At this rate, I'll never get my class ring. But, thanks, Paul . . . thanks anyway. I really appreciate your help."

"O.K. See you in French class. Oh, and Jay, don't beat yourself up . . . you're going to get it. Just hang in there."

After Paul and Chris crept back down the dark hall to their room, Jim and I turned out our lights.

"Gnite, Jay."

"'Nite, Jim."

Before falling asleep, I lay in bed staring at the ceiling and thinking about my classes. They were so hard for me. This was the first time I had ever really had to study. And with the constant chaotic distractions of my shattered family life always rolling around in the back of my head, my concentration was nil. I was just barely getting by.

Still, I looked forward to French. I had never taken a foreign language before, and the lifestyle and culture of France intrigued me. Plus, Gallard's funny accent made me laugh. I cherished his tales of bohemian nightlife in Paris.

"Jay. Telephone. Jay! Wake up. It's the telephone." Mr. Barsten shook my shoulder. "Telephone, Jay. You have a call from your mother up at The Cottage."

I stared up at the old master with his wire-rimmed glasses and thinning white hair.

"What?"

"Phone call."

"Oh. OK. OK. I'll get dressed."

I rubbed the sleep from my eyes and pulled on my shirt and khakis. As I walked up the hill to Stengel Cottage, I thought, *Why does she have to keep calling?* The clock atop Sweeny Hall glowed 11:25. *Can't she just leave me alone?*

In the basement, a phone dangled from its cord in one of the old wooden booths.

"Hello?" I mumbled.

"Jay? Jay, Honey, it's your mother. You're gonna haveta come home," she slurred. "I'm sorry, Honey. I just can't afford to keep you there anymore. Your father . . . your father isn't sending me enough money."

"Mom. It's OK. Go to bed," I pleaded. "Dad takes care of the tuition. I asked you before, please stop calling me here at night."

"But, you don't understan . . .," she muttered.

"Mom, I love you. I'm going to hang up now. Good night."

As I walked back across the deserted campus, I thought of all the nights she came home drunk after spending time at the local taverns with her entourage of young lovers— the brawls, the shouting. I drew my hand across my forehead, trying to wipe the thoughts from my mind.

"God, please help her," I said with gritted teeth.

Thursday afternoon, I waited outside French class in the dark hallway of Dryden Hall. Under my arm, with my books, I held the small package for Gallard and listened at the door.

"*Watteau. Répétez.*"

"*Watteau,*" said the class.

I pushed the door open a crack. Professor Gallard had his back to me and was pointing to a nude in a French painting on the board. I slid into my seat and hid the bundle under my small desk.

"*Non! Non! Non! Comme ceci. Vvvvwattoe.*"

"*Vvvvvvvwattoe,*" the class yelled.

Gallard, a man in his forties, stood lean and straight holding a large book of French art. As he turned, his oily, thinning hair gleamed in the afternoon sunlight shining in from the window. His clothes as usual were soiled and rumpled. His shirt was the same one he had worn yesterday. Obviously, he did not care how he looked, or he had very little money, or both.

"Boys, see how Fragonard painted his women?" He pointed to *The Bathers* on the board. "Fragonard. *Répétez.*"

"Fragonard," the class repeated.

"*Non! Non! Non!* Frrragonarrrrr."

"Frrrrragonarrrrrrrrr!" We all laughed.

"Now, boys, pay attention. As you get older, you will learn to appreciate Fragonard's plump ladies. Women, you know, do not all have to be blonde with blue eyes and long legs. Beauty is more than that."

We all stared in quiet disbelief.

"You should look for brains, not breasts...as you get older, you will learn this. In Paris, my affairs were with French women who were bright but not necessarily beautiful. Fragonard saw this. He was '*le fils*' of eighteenth century French Rococo painting. Gentlemen, who knows what '*le fils*' means?"

Mr. Gallard surveyed his students through his smoked reading glasses. I scrunched down in my seat.

"Ah! Monsieur Walker."

"*Le fils*?" I stammered. "Let me think. Ah. *Le fils.* That means the office. Le fils. The office. Like l'office, right?"

"*Non.* Fragonard was not the office of the eighteenth century."

The class burst out laughing.

As I floundered and squirmed, a tall slender boy with blond, wavy hair raised his hand. His name was Eric Templeton. He sat in the front row and seemed to always make things look easy. Eric carried a nonchalant air about himself. He struck me as both pretentious and aloof. Having no wardrobe of my own, I was envious of how well he dressed—tweed sports coats, belted polo coat, tasseled loafers. It seemed that even his notebooks were monogrammed.

For me, every morning I had to carefully plan what I would wear from my meager wardrobe. My only jacket was the blue blazer my father bought me the day before I left for school. After we had finished our Bloody Marys and steak sandwiches at 21, Dad took me to J. Press. Still tipsy from the vodka, he stood behind me grinning into the three mirrors as the tailor worked at the jacket's cuffs. Later that night at home in the kitchen after dinner and too many after-dinner drinks, he tried to open the buttonhole of my new blazer with a carving knife. By the time he finally sent me off to bed, the lapel was ruined.

"*Oui*, Monsieur Tempelton?"

"*Le fils veut dire l'enfant mâle de ses parents*," he answered with a casual air. "*Le fils* means 'the son.'"

"*Trés bien*, Monsieur Tempelton. Correct!"

Eric turned in his seat and smirked at me.

"Pompous ass," I whispered to Paul.

"Relax," he said under his breath. "If his father wasn't in the goddamn Ambassador in Paris, he wouldn't be so goddamn good in French."

"Jay Walker," Mr. Gallard said, "you have to study harder."

"I have been, Sir. But I've been a little busy. You see, some of us boys have been putting together a small present for you."

"*Vraiment? Un petit cadeau?* And what would that be?"

"I guess we've noticed that most of the masters wear Ivy League clothes, but you seem to wear the same shirt all the time."

"Young man, in France, body odor is considered to be an aphrodisiac." Gallard winked at the class, and the students erupted in laughter.

"Monsieur, we'd like to give you a gift." I handed him the package. "I hope it fits."

He tore open the brown wrapping paper and held the

shirt across his chest, then raised his eyebrows with mock astonishment as he ogled the Monopoly money.

"*Merci*, Monsieur Walker. But still, you must try harder."

"I will, Sir. I promise," I muttered.

As soon as the class bell rang, I left for Harmon Hall to pick up my socks, jock and T-shirt for football practice. Today's scrimmage would determine the starting positions for Saturday's game against Old Standish.

So much for hitting the books, as my father always says. Now it's time to hit heads.

Winding amongst the tall fir trees, a red brick path took me down the hill through the clean smell of fresh-cut grass to the playing fields. There, the white yard lines pointed across the gridiron to the other side of the valley. On the distant hillside, the red September sun was brushing a kaleidoscope of fall's mottled golds across the soft heather peaks. Fall's palette of changing patterns had started to blanket the campus.

In the locker room, downstairs at the gym, the chalk talk by Coach Davis was brief and firm.

"So that's it, boys. Got it?" His piercing brown eyes bore through each one of us. "Good. Let's get to it then. And remember . . . no mistakes!"

Wooden benches screeched across the cement floor as we pushed them aside to make our way through the fetid stench that fouled the locker room. The thirty-two of us gushed up the concrete cellar stairs in our new game uniforms while the clatter of our low-cut cleats ricocheted off the brick walls of the old building. We ran across the road beneath the freshly painted goal post onto the white striped turf. Above the froth of dark blue jerseys and bulging shoulder pads, our shining Riddell helmets floated like gold bubbles splattered with decals of wild boars for exceptional performances. The large blue Ds on the helmets' sides shouted 'Dunbarton!' Spikes churned the emerald sod; gold game pants glistened in the autumn light like yellow sparks jumping across a murky sea. With faces covered by cages, we charged across the hallowed pitch—a throng of fierce gladiators. Both the energy and the strength of our youth crashed down upon the playing field like a tsunami.

I thrived on this competition. It excited me. The adhesive tape that bound my wrists and ankles, the hip guards and thigh pads that slapped against my body as I ran, the sweet smell of foam rubber and sweat from inside my helmet, the number 22 that stretched across my chest—all of this made me feel alive.

Coach Davis stood before us with his muscular legs spread wide apart and a tight, white Dunbarton T-shirt stretched across his powerful chest. His black hair was cropped short and his nose flattened from his playing days at Yale. He gave a sharp blast on his whistle and tugged his cap down over his eyes.

"Calisthenics!" he shouted.

The team droned out the cadence for jumping jacks in unison: "One, two, three, four. One, two . . ."

Offensive and defensive plays followed the blocking and tackling drills. Then he broke the team into two groups. I was one of the first picked as running back for the Red Team, but so was Eric Tempelton.

By the end of the scrimmage, the Red Team trailed 10—7. With two minutes left in the last quarter. Our QB, Jenkins, brought us into the huddle.

"Listen up. 22. 22 dog left on 3. Walker! Got it? 22 dog left on 3. Let's do this!"

My number was called.

At the snap, I ran out eight yards, faked right, then brushed past the linebacker for the end zone. As I crossed the goal line and went up for the catch, the bright sunlight blinded me from the ball, and it bounced off my shoulder pad on to the turf.

Coach Davis flung his cap to the ground and kicked it.

"Get out of there, Walker!" he bellowed. "Eric, take his place. And remember . . . no mistakes!"

Tempelton pushed his long blond hair back and pulled on his helmet. "Nice catch, Walker," he said sarcastically as he trotted on to the field.

"OK. Tempelton. Fade in, then cut sharp for the corner," I heard Jenkins say as he tightened his chinstrap. "Guys— same play. 22 dog left on 3. Let's make it work this time. It's there."

The team broke the huddle with a loud clap.

"Readyyyyyy . . .. Hut! Hut!" Jenkins barked.

He took the snap, dropped back five yards and lofted a perfect spiral. Alone in the corner of the end zone, Tempelton reached up for the ball with one hand and pulled it in.

"Touchdown!" the Red Team yelled, as the final horn blew.

Eric walked off the field surrounded by his teammates, hugging the football. As he jogged past me, he snickered, "Hey, Walker, try holding on to this," and he tossed me the ball. "Whenever you want a lesson, just let me know."

I showered without speaking to anyone and sulked back to my room. Jim ducked as I flung my books against the Dunbarton blanket that hung on the wall.

"How the hell did that Tempelton bastard make .... Turn that thing off!" I snarled.

"Come on, Jay," Jim pleaded. "It's *Kookie, Kookie, Lend Me Your Comb.*"

"I don't care if it's *God Bless America*—turn that shit off!"

"I'll turn it down," Jim grumbled.

"How the hell did Tempelton make that catch? Son of a bitch!" I yelled. "I would've had it if the sun hadn't been in my eyes."

Paul looked up from my *Playboy*. "Jay, you're 5' 7". He's six inches taller. No wonder he made the catch. Next time put some of that black greasepaint he uses under your eyes—it'll cut the glare."

"First the bastard makes me look like a clown in French class . . . I studied that stuff just last night! Why can't I get it? And now, just when my sprained ankle's healed, he's won the goddamn starting position for Saturday's game."

"Easy, Jay. It's just a stupid game," Paul said. "The guy

lives in France, for chrissakes. His father works at the Embassy. No wonder he speaks the language."

Sunday evening, after Chapel, I found an empty phone booth in the basement of Stengel Cottage and pulled the glass door shut. I dreaded the collect calls I had to make to my father each week. He wanted me to call him every Sunday night at 7:00. Exactly 7:00. Finally, the minute hand nudged the 12.

"Hi, Dad, it's me."

"How are the grades, Jackson?"

I shuddered at the nickname. I hated it.

"Well, Sir, I'm not flunking French anymore."

"You know, Son, when I was at Dunbarton, I hit the books. I hit them hard. Good grades just came rolling in. Then off I went to Princeton. I don't know why you're having so much trouble. I don't understand it. Just hit the books, Jackson."

"Yes, Sir. I will."

"I never had a problem with good marks when I was at Dunbarton."

"I'll study harder, Sir. I promise. I'll call you next Sunday at 7:00. Good night."

I hung up the phone and kicked the glass door open.

Hit the books. That's all you ever say. I am hitting the goddamn books. How did you get into Dunbarton and Princeton anyway? It couldn't have been your parents' money, could it? Hit the books. Shit. I study hard. Why can't I get good grades?

Monday morning, I got up at 6:00 to drag myself over to Dryden Hall for my work detail. Chef Leonard ran the kitchen like a tyrant. He was 6' 3" and had a ferocious temper. Even at 63, he was feared by most of the student body. And everyone knew about the metal plate he had in his head from the war.

Don't even think about being late, I told myself as I scrambled into my corduroys and loafers.

I brushed my teeth, combed my hair, jumped down the front steps pulling on my blazer, and ran up Chapel Street with my tie in hand.

"You're late," Leonard snapped as I whirled around the corner into the kitchen. "Try that again, and I'll send you to the Dean of Boys."

Late. How could I be late? I wondered.

"I'm done here, Leonard. What's next?"

I looked across the kitchen counter and could not believe who I saw standing in front of the dumbwaiter—that bastard, Eric Tempelton. He gave me a sarcastic smirk as he put away the last tray of glasses.

I clenched my fists and glared at him.

He even looks good in a goddamn apron, I thought. *He's got everything—money, looks, smarts.*

I fumbled around behind the counter with the silverware while Eric strutted about the kitchen putting the plates in order. Each time he looked over, my stomach churned.

After breakfast, back in my room, I found my roommate lying on his bed reading about the new Rambler in *Hot Rod Magazine*.

"Jim, I can't take this Tempelton guy anymore. He's driving me nuts. He's so goddamn perfect. Did you know he's Eric Tempelton the third for chrissakes? And he's got four fuckin' names — Eric N. E. Tempelton. What the hell do N E stand for?"

"Figures. Well, we'll do something, Jay. Don't worry. There's got to be something we can do."

Paul opened the door and came bouncing into the room.

"The way he dresses . . . it's like he's right out of the Brooks catalog," I said. "I can barely scrape together a tie and a sports coat."

"Talking about Tempelton again?" Paul asked.

"I just can't stop thinking about him, Paul. He's driving me nuts."

"Me too," Jim said. "He's always got that . . . that . . .. What was that word Mr. James taught us today in Etymology?"

"You mean insouciance?" Paul said.

"Yeah, that's it. That's what he's got. My father wants me to have it too. Dad calls it sprezzatura," Jim said. "He wants me to have that easy manner of studied carelessness. I guess he hasn't noticed I'm 5' 9" and 185, and no James Dean. It's kind of hard for a tank to be nonchalant."

"Wait a minute! I've got an idea." Paul's eyes were opened wide. "His clothes are out of the Brooks catalog, eh? Well, you know what?"

"What?" Jim and I both asked.

"At the bottom of Harmon Hall, the wombats drop off the laundry on Tuesday afternoon—right?"

"Yeah," Jim said.

"Well, why don't we help Eric cut down on his wardrobe?"

"What do you mean?" I asked.

"Tomorrow after class, we can watch from the bathroom window to see when they drop off the baskets. And when they leave, we'll help ourselves to Tempelton's finest dress shirts."

"Holy shit! That's brilliant! But what if you two get caught?" Jim cautioned.

"Us? We won't get caught," Paul said with a smile.

"OK, Paul, I'm in. I'm definitely in," I said. "Paul, you're a fuckin' genius. And I get his pink shirts."

On Tuesday afternoon, crowded together in a stall in the basement Boys Room, Paul and I stood on the toilet seat and peeked out the dusty window. Finally we heard the *clang, clang, clang* of the large canvass baskets full of clean clothes being pushed down the wooden steps from the laundry. We watched through the dirty pane as the workers lined the bins against the far wall, then shuffled off towards the library. We sneaked out the bathroom door, and checked the empty halls. Each of the five baskets was marked by a dorm house name.

"Larson House, Middle Hall, Chapel House," Paul muttered. "Aha! Here it is! Harts Lodge."

We dove in, windmilling through the brown paper

packages. Tempelton's two bulging bundles were at the very bottom of the white canvas tub.

Carefully, I undid the white string and opened the first package.

"Paul, look at these! Oxford shirts. My God! Pink! Blue! Green striped! And they're all from Brooks. Look at this! French cuffs. And they're all my size! He's got tab collars, club collars, button-downs."

"Be careful, Jay. Don't take anything with his initials on them. Check the chest and the cuffs."

As I quickly flipped through the clean stack of shirts, the stairwell door swung open behind us.

"Boys! You boys there," Dean Kravitch shouted as he stepped forward from a group of underclassmen. "What are you two doing there?"

"Nothing, Sir." I quickly dropped the opened bundle behind my back on top of the pile of brown paper packages in the large white tub.

"That's my laundry!" Eric Tempelton shouted. "What are you doing with my clothes?"

I felt the iron grasp of Dean Kravitch's fingers around the back of my neck. He kicked open the basement door and dragged Paul and me up the stairs to his dark sanctum.

As we stood shaking on the red Persian rug, Dean Kravitch sat down behind his large mahogany desk. He peered at us over his half frame glasses with a scowl across his face.

"Do you know what the punishment for stealing is at Dunbarton?" he shouted.

His face shook scarlet with anger.

"But, Sir, we were just looking for . . ."

The dean lunged at me.

"Don't lie to me, Walker!" he roared. "You're getting forty hours of yard work. Both of you." He wiped the spit from his lips. "You're lucky I'm not throwing you both out of school." He flashed his silver letter opener towards the door. "Now get out of my chambers."

We slunk back to Larson House and climbed the stairs to Paul's room.

"What? Forty hours! Goddamn that Eric Tempelton," Paul moaned. "We've got to get that son of a bitch."

"I'll find a way," I mumbled.

The fourteenth was Fall Festivities weekend at Dunbarton. Paul had invited his girlfriend Sue from Darien to come up to Waterville for the dance. She was bringing her friend Barbara as a date for me. So, during the week, Paul and I did little else but dream about seeing the girls and try to deepen our tans with an illegal sun lamp.

At last Saturday came. When Fifth Period was finally over, I walked down Hill Street with Paul towards the old train station. My chinos were freshly pressed, heinie-buckle well cinched and oxblood Weejuns brightly polished. I had fixed my tab collar firmly so that the refreshing mid-autumn breeze swept my rep tie over my shoulder. Brylcreem held my blond, slicked back hair in place, and the musky scent of English Leather swirled about my head. The blue and gold crest on my blazer's breast pocket made my chest swell with pride. My step had a jaunty spring to it. Paul opened his sports coat, put his hands deep in his pockets and began to whistle. We quickened our pace.

Strung out along the rickety station platform, a line of students from school prowled back and forth alongside the rails like a pack of hungry wolves. One took a clean linen handkerchief and wiped the perspiration from his brow. Another nervously checked his hair in one of the dirty station windows and patted down his cowlick. Then, from far down the track, came the faint sound of a locomotive.

Paul elbowed me and winked. "Get ready for the slaughter."

The train crept in to the station with a screech of brakes and explosion of steam. Porters rushed to put down small metal step stools with loud clanking sounds and helped passengers to the landing. Most of the girls got off waving to their boyfriends for help with their bags. A few were more timid.

They peered out the train windows hoping that their dates would be there. Paul spotted Sue waiting by the last car.

"There she is."

Sue was about 5' with short, blonde hair and bright blue eyes. Next to her was a taller brunette in a forest green suit.

"Barbara? That's Barbara!" I blinked.

"Come on, Jay. Let's go help them with their things."

We took off in a jog towards the rear of the train.

"Hi, Sue. How are you?" He gave her a kiss. "How was the trip?"

"Well, it would have been just *awful* if those two cute guys from Yale hadn't sat down next to us on their way up from Grand Central," she teased. "Too bad they had to get off at New Haven." Sue smiled at me. "So, Jay? You must be Jay—right? Jay, I want you to meet my friend, Barbara . . . Barbara Lockland. She lives in New York City."

I stared into Barbara's eyes. They were the most beautiful greenish-brown eyes I had ever seen.

"Hello, Jay." She offered me her hand.

"Come on, Jay. Let's get going," Paul said. "The dance starts at 7:00."

I pulled my eyes away from Barbara's and groped about for her luggage. Together, we walked back up Hill Street towards campus. It was the first time in a long while that I had felt so happy. At last, it felt as though I truly fit in.

Before long, we were in front of Janson Lodge, an old clapboard house covered in tangled ivy where the girls would stay for the weekend.

"We'll see you about 6:30," Paul said.

"Yes. S-s-see you soon, Barbara," I stammered.

As I turned to follow Paul, Barbara called after me. "Oh, Jay. May I have my bags?"

I looked down, then blushed. "Oh, sure. Sorry. Here you are. See you later."

Paul and I hustled back to Larson House to get ready for the evening's big
event—a black tie dinner-dance with candlelight, and music by

Lester Lanin's Society Band.

I shaved off what little peach fuzz I had with my Remington Electric, doused myself with more English Leather
and struggled with my cufflinks and studs for my pleated shirt.
I found my silk, over the calf stockings in my sock draw and
pulled them on—I liked their sheer look. I hooked my suspenders to my trousers with the silk stripe running down the side of
the pant legs. Their grosgrain band circled my waist just perfectly and closed with a round button covered in black silk
cloth. My black, patent leather dancing pumps still lay
wrapped in tissue paper inside the Brooks Brothers shoebox. I
admired their flat bows that matched my lapels, suspenders
and cummerbund. I slipped them on over my silk socks,
clicked my cummerbund closed and spun its clasp around my
waist to the back. Before attacking my bow tie, I checked the
folds of my cummerbund. Were they facing up? This was one
of the few things my father had ever taught me—the folds
have to be facing up to catch the crumbs that fall during dinner, he said. I grabbed my toothbrush and used its plastic end
to help tie the knot of my butterfly tie—a trick learned from one
of the Sixth Formers.

When I went to the mirror to tighten the bow and check
my hair for a second time, it was hard for me to recognize the
happy face that was smiling back at me. I snapped my suspenders, slipped on my dinner jacket and straightened my
handkerchief.

"Hey, Jay. Close the door," Paul whispered. "Come
over here. Check this out."

He rummaged through the back of his closet and
yanked out one of his old cowboy boots.

"Check this out."

Paul reached in and pulled a fifth of J&B.

"Holy shit!" I gasped. "Where in the hell did you get
that?"

"Dad's not very good at hiding the key for the liquor
cabinet." He twisted open the red cap with a crack. "I've been
saving it for a special occasion. And now we have one. Here,

have a swig."

I pulled hard on the bottle's dark green neck. The warm, raw Scotch burned as it went down.

"N-n-not bad," I choked, and wiped my mouth with the back of my hand.

Paul lifted the bottle and took a long swallow.

"Ahhh. To Festivities!"

He wiped his lips with his sleeve and handed the bottle back to me.

"Have another. Say? How'd you do on that book report?"

Paul reached for the bottle again.

"The book report? I flunked it. Sukany said I missed the point completely. He said the whole point was that Holden Caulfield was surrounded by a world of phonies. Then he stopped and looked at me and said, 'Just like you.' Can you believe it? Just like me. And then he just sat there and stared at me. I hate the guy. He's the one who's a phony if anyone is!"

I took another gulp.

"Nice guy, your English teacher."

"Yeah. Really nice guy! So, then I looked up 'phonies.' It means a fake or a fraud . . .. Paul, do you think I'm a phony?"

"No way, Jay! Absolutely not. If anyone's a phony, it's that guy Tempelton."

"You know, I'll probably end up just like poor old Holden if I keep flunking my classes. Maybe I should get a goddamn red hunting hat. What d'ya think? Of course Tempelton got a goddamn A+ on his book report."

Paul spritzed his mouth with Binaca.

"Here. Use some of this."

Once we freshened our breaths, Paul put the bottle back in his closet, and we pinned on each other's boutonnieres.

"OK! Let's go, Pal." He winked. "Let's have some fun tonight!"

When we got to the lobby of Janson Lodge, I saw Barbara standing tall next to Sue in a long pink taffeta dress. Her white gloves reached above her elbows. Pearls were sparkling from her earlobes and from around her long neck. There were pink ribbons that dangled from her white corsage. My eyes brightened.

We walked as couples across the quadrangle, arm in arm, beneath the large elm trees. In the distance, the dining room candles flickered through the evening's twilight. Swing music washed out over the white trim of the large open windows and spilled down from the second floor on to the bricks in the courtyard.

"Let's hurry," Paul urged. "They've already started."

At the top of the stairs, smartly dressed couples in evening wear pushed about at a large glass punch bowl laughing and jostling for drinks. Others mingled around the fifty circular tables adorned with white linen tablecloths, shining silverware and fresh-cut flowers. A large oil painting of the headmaster and his wife hung above the flames that crackled in the huge two-sided fireplace in the middle of the hall. At the far end of the room, propped up on a makeshift stage, Lester Lanin swiveled his hips to the orchestra's fast tempo. He tossed his monogrammed souvenir hats high above the packed crowd that was franticly dancing the Twist in front of his bandstand. The swing band's drums clashed loudly against the electricity that filled the room and drove the dancers to a faster rhythm.

Paul led us beneath the somber gallery of oil portraits of past headmasters that decorated the mahogany walls to a table halfway between the fireplace and the orchestra.

As we sat by the window, I watched the wind carry Barbara's auburn hair back from her high cheekbones and full red lips. The gentle smell of her light perfume intoxicated me. It stoked the fiery courage already set ablaze by the Scotch.

"Barbara, let's dance."

I followed her to the dance floor and took her in my arms. She was just my height. Our bodies fit together perfectly. The waltz began—"It Had To Be You"—and I pulled her to me. As we danced, I could not believe how light she was. I felt the warmth of her glove and the softness of her cheek. Her arm cradled my shoulder; her hips swayed with the music; her satin gown rubbed against my tux trousers. I could feel her fingers brushing the back of my neck. All of it excited me.

Here I am holding this woman, dancing in black tie at Dunbarton, I marveled. *I must be dreaming. Am I in a fantasy world, or is this really real?*

The song ended and, as we returned to our table, the dinner chime rang.

Headmaster Rockwell, a lean man in his sixties, stood straight and tall looking out over the gathering from the main table. Wearing an immaculate double-breasted dinner jacket from the '30s, he hooked his thumbs into the pockets of his trim white waistcoat. His black, thinning hair was combed back and his brown eyes sparkled.

Just as he stepped to the microphone to welcome the gathering, Mrs.
Richardson came clip-clopping across the polished hardwood floor in front of him in her pigeon-toed way. All eyes focused on her low-cut, red satin ball gown and the rhinestones that glittered from the bows on her black patent mules. She glided across the room with an air of nonchalance, timing her arrival, as always, just *after* all in the dining hall were seated.

"Who's that?" Barbara asked.

"Mrs. R," I whispered. "One of the masters' wives."

As she approached her husband's table, her blue eyes twinkled beneath her thick, black lashes. And casually, as she went to sit, she let her left hand brush across Shawn Ketchum's broad shoulders.

"Looks like she's sleeping with Shawn this week."

"What!" Barbara's eyes widened.

"Two years ago, her husband had a heart attack. So, he's out of commission. Ever since, she's been looking to the

Sixth Formers to keep herself happy."

Shawn stood up eagerly and pulled out her chair. She settled down beside him, slowly crossing her legs, while smiling across the table of ten at her husband like an ingénue.

Rockwell pulled heavily on his waistcoat, swallowed hard, and began again.

"Welcome. Welcome all, to our Fall Dance. I hope our lovely guests will have a wonderful weekend with us here at Dunbarton." His chest swelled as he went up and down on his toes with his hands clasped behind him. "Don't worry," he smiled. "I won't take up any of your time. And dinner will be served shortly. Please enjoy yourselves. Have fun!" He gave a little wave and rejoined his wife.

I leaned over to Barbara. "Archer's a funny old goat, but he means well."   She smiled.

"So, tell me," I asked. "What do you do in New York?"

"I'm studying fashion." She cocked her head and looked up at me. "My father found me a job last summer at one of Manhattan's top design houses," she said in a nonchalant way. "I love fashion. So, I'm going to study at an art and design school in New York after high school. What about you, Jay? What are you taking?"

I stared into her eyes. I could not get over her beauty. "Jay? What about you?"

"What? Oh, me? Math. French. Nothing special."

"I've always wanted to be a designer. That's my dream," she said. "I made my dress. Do you like it?"

"Do I like it? Barbara, you look great. I mean really great."

She smiled.

"You know, I've got dreams too," I said. "I'm going to work for my ol' man in New York after college. One day, I'll take over Walker & Company. And then when I get old, I'll leave it to my kids. And then they'll leave it to their kids. That way, the company will go on and on, and on and on . . . .."

"Your father owns a company?"

"An insurance brokerage firm. I'll wait to get married.

You know, take my time. Make sure to find the right one." I tried to sound older. "I don't want to get divorced like my parents. No way. Get married maybe at twenty-eight or thirty-two. I don't know. Then have a couple of kids. Boys . . . and maybe a girl. And a nice house with a white picket fence. You know, like the Nelsons—Ozzie and Harriet. I want to live happily ever after in Connecticut. Has to be Connecticut."

"Connecticut? Why Connecticut?"

"Blue license plate."

"Blue license plate?"

"Yeah. I want a blue license plate for the station wagon. You know, a station wagon for the kids and the dog . . . a Dalmatian."

"A Dalmatian? How come a Dalmatian?" Barbara asked.

"I had one once in Garden Village. His name was Buttons. He was my best friend."

"Buttons. What a great name."

"We'll be a happy family. That's my dream—to have a happy family. You see? I'm a star gazer."

"A what?"

"A star gazer. You know. I try to imagine things the way I hope they'll be one day. I always want to be looking up . . . looking up at my dreams—gazing at the stars."

"That's a funny way to put it, star gazer. I kind of like it—star gazer. I'm going to remember that."

The band began playing "Puttin' On The Ritz."

I smiled. "Well what do you say, Barbara? Do you . . . "

"Barbara, I can't believe you're here."

Eric Tempelton stepped between our two chairs.

"I haven't seen you since the Beach Club last summer. What a great gown. Did you make it? Come. Let's have a dance."

Before I could react, they were on the floor dancing cheek to cheek. I watched as Eric guided her gracefully around the room with a confident air. Finally, the song ended. But instead of leading Barbara back to our table, he took her to his table next to the fireplace. He sat close beside her and introduced her to his coterie of friends while sliding his arm across the back of her chair. I watched Barbara's eyes sparkle while they chatted and laughed.

"Paul, look!" I hissed. "He's got his hands all over her."

Feverishly, I thought of how to get her back. I racked my brain. When I looked at Eric, I saw his left arm fall around Barbara's pale shoulders. Suddenly, I exploded. In a fit of sudden rage, I jumped to my feet, knocking over my chair. I rushed across the room, pushing dancers out of my way. I grabbed Tempelton by the lapels and tore him violently from his chair. I flung him onto the parquet floor and pounced on top of him. He was strong but stunned. We wrestled back and forth on the brickwork next to the flames in the fireplace. He tried to throw me off, but I pinned his shoulders.

"She's mine, not yours," I spat through clenched teeth, our faces inches apart. "Keep your hands off her." And then I hit him.

The crowd grabbed me and pulled me off him. They dragged me out of the dining room into the hallway where Dean Kravitch was waiting, shaking with fury.

"That does it, young man," he snarled with a crimson face. "You're finished with the dance. Finished. Do you hear me?"

"Y-y-yes, sir," I stammered.

"Now, for God's sake, Jay, tuck in your shirt and fix your tie, and get out of
here at once. I expect to see you in my office tomorrow morning at eight o'clock sharp. Do you understand?"

"Yes, sir."

I walked alone away from the dining room down the path through the night to Larson House. At the top of the stairs, I turned and went to Paul's room, took the Scotch from his closet and wolfed down the soothing blend. The liquor sloshed from my mouth as I gulped my ambrosia that mixed with the tears running down my face. I flung the empty bottle back into Paul's closet, and banged my way down the hall to my room. I threw my rented tux on the floor and climbed in bed.

How can I get even? How?

The room began to turn, slowly at first, then faster and faster. I struggled to get up and held onto the wall to stop the spinning. I wobbled to the open window, doubled over, gasped, then puked all of the Scotch and dinner onto the porch roof below.

Sunday morning at eight, I pushed myself into Dean Kravitch's dark inner sanctum. He was sitting behind a large heavy desk dressed in a tweed sports jacket, white shirt and repp bow tie. A small reading light glowed beneath its green hood in front of him. Through the dark, he looked like an angry bloodhound with his dangling jowls and wrinkled face. He peered over the gold rims of his lunettes with fierce blue eyes. I stood trembling.

"Sit down, Mr. Walker!"

I found one of the tall red leather chairs in front of his desk. As I eased myself down onto its thick cushion, the pain of my hangover rocked forward and hit hard against my forehead.

"Mr. Walker. You know your admission to Dunbarton was due to your father who went here many years ago. You, young man, are what we call a legacy; your application received preferential treatment. Without it, you never would have been admitted to Dunbarton with the grades that you had at Sandpiper Beach High School."

My mouth was dry as cotton. I swallowed hard as the Dean's stern face grew larger.

"As you are well aware, in the short time that you have been here at Dunbarton, you have been able to distinguish yourself not once, but twice, with inappropriate behavior—first stealing and now fighting. This is not the caliber we expect from Dunbarton men. Therefore, Jay, you give me no choice. I am suspending you from Dunbarton for a period of three weeks."

His image blurred as my eyes filled with tears.

"You will pack your bags after classes on Tuesday and be on the 4:25 train to New York."

I looked about the room, staring at the heavy velvet curtains and the patterns on the Oriental rug. I was lost.

What will my father say? I wondered with trepidation.

"Jay, is that clear? Do you understand?" he asked.

"Yes, sir. I understand," I offered in a meek voice.

"Fine. That will be all. You may go."

As I walked to the door I heard him say, "And Jay, for God's sake, fix your tie."

I pushed out the front door of Harmon Hall and wandered down the steps of the red-bricked building shaken. At the oval drive, I stopped and stared across the campus. I looked beyond the road, past the Cottage. Above the distant hills and the cotton clouds, geese were flying south in front of a turquoise ski. Through my tears, I saw the football fields . . . the football fields that I loved so much . . . the football fields that I was now leaving behind . . . all of this, I was leaving behind. I was losing all of this . . . this school that had become my family. Never would I find in Garden Village or Sandpiper Beach an echelon of boys like these here at Dunbarton. I had flossed, brushed and gargled before kissing their asses—but now, they had become my family, and I had lost them.

I've been given this opportunity, and what do I do? I throw it away. Why?   My body was empty. I was hollow inside. Loneliness engulfed me.

I'm losing this. I'm losing all of this. I ran my hands through my hair. *What will my father say?* Suddenly, I decided. *I won't tell anyone anything.*

Back at Larson House, I found Paul in my room thumbing through the Maidenform Bra ads in the *Sunday Times' Magazine* section and listening to *Tom Dooley* on my Kingston Trio album.

"That was some meeting with Kravitch. He really busted my balls," I said.

"Oh yeah? Well guess what. There's something else. You're not going to believe this. Tempelton and Barbara have rekindled their old friendship. He's going to put her on the train to New York this afternoon."

My eyes narrowed. "What?"

"And that's not all. It's worse. She's coming back up next Saturday to watch him play in the game against Saint Dominic's. Jay, I'm really sorry. I didn't even know they knew each other."

I grabbed my study lamp, smashed it against the closet door, bounded down the stairs and slammed out the front door. In the shadows behind Larson House, I hid my face against the shingled siding and tried to smother my sobs in the ivy.

Monday afternoons were for 'Extracurriculars' at Dunbarton. At three o'clock each week, the Gun Club assembled in the basement of Memorial House. Tucked away in a cement crawl space was a small shooting gallery with string pulleys hooked to tiny paper targets. The team had six rifles that we used for practice.

Shooting was easy for me. I felt comfortable with the stock against my shoulder. As part of my instruction, I had learned to take my rifle apart—first the bolt, then the barrel, clean and oil the mechanism, and then re-assemble it. I was one of the best shots on the team. And, as one of the co-captains, I was given the responsibility of cleaning up the gallery as well as locking the door at the end of the day. This afternoon, after the last marksman left, I broke my rifle down and put it in my gym bag with several rounds of ammunition before locking the door.

After dinner, Jim greeted me as I walked into our room.

"Hey, Jay. How's it going?"

I slid my gym bag under my bed.

I looked at him. "You'll never guess who I have kitchen detail with tomorrow morning."

"I give up, who?"

"That prick Eric Tempelton's working with me again."

"No shit. After Festivities?" Jim shook his head. "You just can't catch a break, can you?"

"Yeah. Well, I've got to get up early tomorrow. Leonard will tear my balls off if I'm late again."

"Tell me about it."

That night, I set my alarm for five instead of six and lay in bed excited by the thought of the bag beneath my bed.

Now I'll finally be rid of him!

At midnight, I fell asleep.

Tuesday morning was crisp and clear. The strong rich fragrance of fall swirled through the chilled air. Tiptoeing down the front steps of Larson House, I felt the bolt of the rifle in my gym bag bounce hard against my back. I checked my watch.

Forty-five minutes and he'll be coming up the path from the Lodge.

The autumn leaves crackled beneath my loafers as I pushed up the hill past Dryden Hall and then down the path. There in the distant shadows, the chapel's bell tower rose tall before the pink clouds of sunrise. At its top, the school flag flew proudly for all to see.

Standing alone in the morning mist, I shivered, and cast an eye over the empty campus. Not a sound. I tugged on the front chapel doors. Tugged again. Both were locked. The small side door was locked too.

"Shit!"

But when I pulled on the back door, it opened with a low groan. I squeezed inside the dark chapel, stopped beneath the stained glass windows and listened to my heartbeat. I gathered myself, then crept up the center aisle towards the front chapel doors. I quietly climbed the narrow stairs in the back that took me to the choir loft on the second floor. Behind the organ, I found the tiny door leading to the ladder that led to the balcony high up on the roof. I struggled to drag my gym bag behind me as I mounted the last steep steps to the belfry.

I stood tall on the steeple platform, looking out across the cold clear campus, and inhaled the pungent smell of fallen leaves that blew across Fall's canvas. From high above, my view of the path that Eric would take on his way to the kitchen was perfect.

The cold, fresh morning air called me back to my task. With care, I assembled the rifle, and adjusted the scope to 400 feet. I took the shoulder strap and wrapped it tightly around my arm. Despite my shaking hands, I managed to get the bullet into the chamber and close the bolt. With a silent sigh, I rested the rifle barrel on the tower rail and waited.

Soon, through the quiet haze, the sound of footsteps came from the other side of the sprawling lawn.

I squinted through the scope. *There he is.*

Eric Tempelton walked up the asphalt path between the pines with his hands deep in the pockets of his Loden coat. The elk horn buttons gathered the soft green cloth about both his slim body and his yellow cashmere scarf. I watched as his breath circled his hood in the clear morning light.

Slowly . . . slowly now . . .. Wait . . . wait for him to get between the crosshairs. Slowly . . . slowly . . .. Now squeeze back on the trigger. Now squeeze back on the trigger. Squeeze the fucking trigger!

Tears blurred my eyes as I watched Eric walk by. I let the gun slip from my hands. The butt of the rifle hit the belfry floor with a crash, and the sound echoed across the empty campus. Eric stopped. I crouched down behind the narrow wooden slats and held my breath. He looked up at the steeple, then continued on nonchalantly to the kitchen.

I picked up the rifle, climbed back down the ladder and left the church through the back door for the dining room. Next to the rear door of the kitchen, I hid my bag behind a dumpster and smoothed my hair in place. At the top of the stairs, I found my apron hanging by the sink. Eric was at work cutting the cinnamon buns for the morning meal.

"Morning," I said to Leonard.

He huffed.

After breakfast, I replaced the rifle, and packed my clothes. Looking up from my suitcase, I saw my black leather jacket and motorcycle boots staring out at me from their hiding place in the back of my closet. Across the chest of the jacket, *'Jay'* was written proudly in small white script. The silver buckles of my boots glistened from their twisted straps.

Come . . ., they whispered, *Come home, Jay. You don't fit in here. Come back to where you belong.*

With a shudder, I closed the closet door and left the campus for the train station.

As I walked to town, I thought of Eric Tempelton, and felt my remorse.

What could have I been thinking? Kill him? Kill him? How could I? For Christ's sake! What was I thinking? How could I think of doing such a thing?

I stopped in front of the old post office on Main Street and read my letter one more time before dropping it in the mailbox.

Dear Barbara,

I'm so sorry for the way I behaved Saturday night at the dance.

I guess it was because for the first time ever, I felt something that I had never felt before for someone. You made me feel so happy. And I did not want to lose you.

I hope you will forgive me.

Please see me again in New York.

With love,

Jay

Chapter 4

Homeward Bound

Shortly before noon, I boarded the *Rapide* for Paris at the Gare du Nord. Passengers stood packed together in the narrow corridor talking and smoking, some shouting parting comments to friends on the platform below. I pushed my way through the crowd and leaned out one of the

dirty train windows to tell my French family goodbye. I did not want to leave the city of Lyon, nor my French family, but my Junior Year was over now, and it was time for me to quit La Belle France and return home. I was leaving my family behind.

"Merci! Merci beaucoup! Thank you. Thank you again," I shouted to Madame Mollière. "Thank you for all your kindness. I'll never forget you— all of you. Thank you Jerôme, Pierre! Au revoir, Monsieur Mollière!"

The stationmaster blew a short blast on his silver whistle; stragglers scurried into the wagons pulling their worn luggage behind them. The conductors gathered up the tiny step stools, doors banged shut, and the train gave a sudden jerk.

I watched Madame Mollière use the handkerchief I had given her to wipe away her tears. Her husband Maurice waved his felt hat with an unhappy expression across his face.

Why do they look so sad? I wondered.

Their son Jerôme, 18, stood between them puffing as usual on his clay pipe. He smiled warmly and shook its long stem in my direction. His older brother Pierre, 20, looked up at me indifferently. He was smug and aloof, almost bored in the typical French snob fashion. As was his custom, Pierre kept his hands pushed deep down into the pockets of his smartly tailored double-breasted blue blazer. He was probably happy to see me go. I had been a diversion of his parents' attention towards him.

"Say hello to Marie-Claire and Phillip for us when you get to Paris," I heard Madame Mollière call as this family that I had grown to love became smaller and smaller. Huddled to-gether on the platform, they seemed draped in a heavy cloak of melancholy. Slowly, their speck dissolved. I turned, dried my eyes, and went to find a seat.

Halfway along the corridor was a small compartment partially empty. I pulled the doors apart, tossed my bags up onto the overhead rack and took the empty seat by the win-dow.

On the wicker bench across from me sat an old man wrapped in a black wool overcoat, much too heavy for the summer heat. His threadbare left lapel was lined with small frayed ribbons of past military campaigns. He had not shaved, and gray bristles covered the wiry blue veins crawling across his flushed red cheeks. Next to him, his white-haired wife sat draped in a thick, black crocheted shawl. She untied a small package of crumpled brown paper and began to fix their lunch on her lap. Her strong hands were rough and callused, her fin-gers gnarled with arthritis. She tore their *flûte* in half with a tug and spread pâté from one end of the sandwich to the other.

Her yellow teeth twisted the newspaper stopper from its green wine bottle. Like her husband, black gaps crossed her mouth.

These are the hardworking French, I thought, *not like my aristocratic Lyonnais family that I have already begun to miss.*

The train swerved north through the *banlieue* of Lyon, along the riverbank of the Rhône, through the vineyards of the Beaujolais country. The day was clear; the sapphire sky lit with a radiant sun. Its warmth shone on my face through the windowpane. The rolling fields and farmlands brought me back to my voyage to Corsica last month. Exhausted from last night's party that had lasted till dawn, I laid my head back against the wicker seat and gradually drifted off . . .

Carol and I walked out of L'Hôtel de Marseilles into the cool night's air leaving Sybille and Betsy at the restaurant inside. How happy I was to at last be alone with her. We sat at a small table by the sidewalk and I waved to the young waiter leaning against the hotel's large front window. He tightened the white apron strings around his thin waste, smoothed back his oily black hair and strutted over to our table.

"Something to drink?" he asked through pursed lips.

"Perrier," Carol said.

"I'll have a Scotch on the rocks."

His blue eyes stared at me from under his long black lashes. "One Perrier, one Scotch." He spun on his heel and left for the bar.

I turned to Carol. Her long brown hair, dark skin and deep hazel eyes all shimmered in the evening's light.

"Do you like those two?" I asked.

"Who? Sybille and Betsy? Sybille's not bad. She's been a lot of help to me with my French this year. Betsy's been a pain in the neck ever since the beginning of the semester. She's always complaining about how she doesn't like this, or doesn't like that. I don't know why she came to France. They're OK to travel with, but I don't mind leaving them behind tonight."

"I'm not looking forward to leaving all this behind," I said looking out over the harbor. "Did I tell you I got a letter from my father yesterday? Typewritten of course on his company's letterhead stationary. I'm surprised he doesn't have his secretary sign them for him as well after he dictates them. He said that my brother told him he was gay. How does someone dictate that kind of stuff to his secretary?" I shook my head. "No wonder Harry's gay. My father's such a tough son of a bitch. Dad says he's sure it's just a phase . . . that Harry'll get over it. Kind of like a cold, I guess. Harry probably goes to other men to get the love he can't get from our father." Then he told me that my mother's back in the hospital again for some reason. He asked me if I thought she should be institutionalized. I wrote back and told him that I thought it was the only way to keep her safe."

"Your father's really something . . .." Carol paused. "Do you suppose he'll ever change?"

"I don't know. But that's the kind of stuff I had to get away from. I didn't want to leave my brother behind, but I couldn't stay around my parents anymore. I had to get out. I remember so well that night when the plane's wheels lifted off the tarmac at Kennedy—the feeling of freedom that washed over me. I shouted inside me, 'Go! Go! Take me away!' There was an incredible feeling of relief that I had never felt before. I had no idea what I'd find in France, but I knew what I was leaving behind in the U.S."

"I'm glad you came, Jay . . .. You know, my family's different. We moved so often, from one Army base to another; we were always packing or unpacking. We never had time to just sit and be with one another, or even ignore one another."

I looked at her and squeezed her hand.

"You know, Carol, I've grown up with my Dad's penthouse apartments, expensive cars, private clubs, polo ponies and summer homes. And I've tried to understand why these things are so important to him. There seem to be a constant need for him to prove his importance; to prove he is just as good as those who are the *elite*—that he is one of them . . . whoever they are. He seems to have this need inside him for others to see the *things* that he has—his wives, his clubs, his clothes, his cars. But, these are only *material* things. It seems to me that he has this constant need to project an image of himself that will make others look at him and feel envious and small—less than him. I think that's how he validates himself. He creates this image to prove he's on an equal footing with society's 'best.' I don't think I can ever remember seeing him care for others; he only seems to care about himself. I just can't stomach this kind of stuff, I just can't—it's too toxic."

There was a long silence.

Then I said, "When I look at his life, except for his work, it seems empty. When he gets something, no matter what it is, it's not long afterwards that, whatever it is, it's no longer good enough for him. He not only upgrades his cars, his clubs, and his homes for bigger and better, but he also upgrades his wives for richer and prettier."

"Why do you suppose he's that way?"

"I've tried to figure it out. I often wonder if he's just driven to win back the money his parents lost in '29. And there was also the humiliation of having to drop out of Princeton before graduating because of The Crash—losing his parents' large Park Avenue apartment for a cold-water flat. All of that must have been hard."

"But the same thing happened to my grandparents," Carol said. "Wall Street took all their money too. I know things like that change people, Jay. And it can make them hard. But, still, people go on . . . they find a way to keep on living."

"I think you're right. It must have made him hard . . .. I've always wished I could have his approval . . . have his love . . .. Is it wrong for me to want this? And, if this is too much to ask for, then, perhaps just a small sign of affection or even recognition."

"Jay," Carol looked at me with her warm eyes. "Do you think having his approval, having his love, is really worth it . . . all the torment . . . all the angst?"

"What . . .? 'Really worth it.' I don't know, Carol. I've never thought of it that way. Maybe you're right. Maybe it's not worth it. Maybe it's just not possible. He always seems to hide behind a facade of compassion. But it seems to me that the only thing that's important for him is prestige."

"Certainly there's more to life than prestige." Carol smiled. "Sometimes my dad was very warm towards me. But I'm sure, being an army man, it was hard for him to have a daughter."

"I'm sorry to say I've never seen any warmth or feelings from my father. Isn't there more to life than a successful business?"

"Much more." She looked at me. "But some people just can't see it, Jay. For some reason, they're not born that way."

"You know, Carol, in twenty-one years, there's only one thing he's ever really taught me."

"What's that?"

"How to make the *perfect* Bloody Mary. You know what his secret ingredient is?"

"Lea and Perrins?"

"Close. It's ketchup."

Carol laughed. "Come on. He must have given you some kind of advice or guidance as you were growing up."

"Well, there were several nuggets that he always reminded me of. One, never chew gum. Two, walk with your toes pointing straight ahead. And three, when you shake hands with someone, always use a firm grip and look them in the eye. You see? These were all external things. Nothing from the inside. When our family went out for dinner, my father would always reminded me to order from 'right to left' on the menu. In other words, look at the price first. He wanted to make sure that I understood that it was he who was paying for the meal, and that I should start out by looking at the prices and not order anything that was too expensive."

"Well, cheer up, Jay!" Carol squeezed my hand. "Remember, it's Spring Break. And we're off to Corsica tomorrow. Be thankful for that."

"Here we are." The waiter took the drinks from his small zinc tray and put them on the table in front of us. He looked at me. "Is that all, Madame?"

I looked up with a scowl. "Monsieur, not Madame! Yes, for now."

He turned with his hand on his hip and walked away laughing.

"Let it go, Jay. He probably thinks you're cute."

We clinked our glasses, laughed and sat back with our drinks to watch the night sky turn from purple to black over the Mediterranean.

"I'll miss you, Carol," I said.

She looked at me. "I'll miss you too, Jay."

I drained my drink and tapped the empty glass at the waiter. "Garçon, un autre."

"Vous désirez, Madame?" he asked with a smile.

"God damn it! It's not Madame; it's Monsieur. Bring me a Scotch."

"Oui, Madame. Tout de suite," he said with a smile and a small bow before disappearing into the hotel.

"What's wrong with that guy, anyway? He's screwing up a perfect night."

As Carol sipped her Perrier, I noticed how pretty she looked in her rose-colored tank top and short khaki skirt. Her high cheekbones and long tanned legs were accentuated by the florescent lights overhead. I thought again of sharing the room with her tonight. How lucky I was. After a year of studying with her in Lyon, finally, tonight we would be together. It was all I could think of—the chance to be alone with her for one night.

The waiter returned carrying my drink and put it between us. I looked up and frowned. He cocked his head, winked and walked away.

"Are you looking forward to going home?" Carol asked.

"Not really. My father . . . you know, I've never once heard him say 'I love you' to me. I guess he only has love for things . . . not people. Or maybe he can't love. I don't know. And, I'm sorry to say my mom's a drunk. But I told you that already. My father sends her an alimony check the first of every month, but still, she's always broke. I almost couldn't go on this trip because I didn't have any money. Mom always forgets, or maybe she doesn't have the money to send me my monthly allowance. Sometimes, I go for a week or two flat broke. It seems like she spends every nickel on booze, emergency rooms or used cars. She's always in and out of hospitals. Once, when I was thirteen, she tried to kill herself. I've tried to help her, but half the time she's not even there."

I looked at Carol and saw the tears in her eyes.

"What's wrong?"

"You made me think of my dad. Before . . . before he killed himself, he would tell me 'I love you' all the time."

"Oh, Carol, I'm sorry . . . .. I didn't know."

"It's OK. I've learned to accept it . . . .. He waited until I left. Maybe he thought it would be easier for me that way."

"I've only thought of suicide once—last year at a football game. There must have been 50,000 people there. Everyone was yelling and cheering, but I felt totally alone. At halftime, I walked up to the top row in the stadium and stared down at the pavement outside. I remember watching a leaf drift quietly down onto the concrete sidewalk thirty feet below and thinking, 'That could be me'."

"Why didn't you do it?"

"I guess I believed that you never know what's coming around the next corner. That if you can just stick it out, there could be something great coming, so why not try and wait and see? I know that's easier for some than for others. I'm glad I waited."

"I wish my father had waited. We were so close; we talked all the time. But he never told me he had a problem."

"My dad's just the opposite. For him, there is no problem. He's got plenty of money. And he stays busy all the time by substituting things for love. He doesn't have time for anything else, including me. It seems that he always needs more . . . more cars . . . more homes . . . more wives . . . but never more love."

"Aren't most people like that?" she asked.

"I don't know. It seems to me that when your life comes to an end, all the wealth, all the prestige, all the status . . . it will all be irrelevant. I think that's true for everyone. In the end, for me, I think that, during your lifetime, what matters isn't what you got, but what you gave. You know, I'm sorry to say it, but when my father's gone, I don't even know if I'll miss him."

Carol looked up at me and said, "But, Jay, don't you have any good memories of you dad? There must be some good memories."

"I don't think it's a *good* memory, but one of the things I remember was when I was eleven. It was the summer night in '56 when Elvis was on *The Ed Sullivan Show* for the first time. We were all having dinner at a place called McGuiness's. I pointed up at the TV in the corner and said to my father, 'You know, Dad, he makes more money than you do.' He went nuts!"

"My dad wasn't like that. He was a military man. He just did what he was told to do. And my Mom was the Army wife. So, she was the same way . . . always in the kitchen with her apron on doing the dishes or cooking. I miss not being with her. Do you miss your mother?"

"Sure, but it's much too hard to be around her. And I miss Lui . . . and I also miss The Hall."

"Lui? Who's he?"

"Not *he*, she," I laughed.

"Oh, Lui's a she?" Carol looked upset.

"Yeah. Lui Daniel. She was great! I met her one night at college when I was in town at the Rathskeller. Kind of a hippie. Long brown hair in Indian braids straight down to her waist. You might say she was a flower girl. Lui always wore these rainbow shades and white wrinkled muslin shirts with big puffy sleeves. She had those sandals from India—you know, the leather ones with the ring for your big toe. I don't think if she ever wore anything else, even in the winter. She had such a nice, soft smile, and the best brown eyes. She kept to herself pretty much—I guess she was kinda shy. But, boy, was she smart. She loved books. On Saturday nights, I'd meet her in the reading room of the main library at nine and pretend to study until she finally finished her work at midnight."

Carol squirmed a bit in her chair. "The library?"

"Yeah, she loved libraries. At twelve, we'd pack up our books and find a couple of bikes outside to 'borrow' and ride into town. We always went to this place called The Mole Hole for pitchers of beer—sit in the back and talk. We'd talk about philosophy mostly. She called it the 3 Ks—Kafka, Kant and Kierkegaard.

"How 'bout K for kissing?" Carol said with a smile.

"No. We never kissed and we never talked about sex . . . just philosophy. Sometimes, after a few pitchers, we'd sing my anthem, '*I am a rock, I am an island*' with the jukebox. You know that one, right?"

"No."

"Come on, Carol.

She blushed. "'*I am a rock*'? Tell me. What's that, '*I am a rock*'?"

"It's from Simon and Garfunkel. I love 'em. 'I've built walls, A fortress deep and mighty, That none may penetrate, I have no need of friendship, friendship causes pain, It's laughter and it's loving I disdain, I am a rock, I am an island.' That was my anthem back then. 'I am a rock'. . .pretty upbeat, huh? I felt completely cut off then. . . cut off from everyone—everyone except for Lui. I guess now it's '*Homeward Bound*'. You know that one, right?"

"No. I'm not very good at music. You know me. I usually just keep my nose stuck in books. Like you said, I spend most of my time in libraries. Have you ever noticed?" She laughed. "They don't allow jukeboxes in libraries."

"It's another by Simon and Garfunkel. '*All my words come back to me in shades of mediocrity, like emptiness in harmony, I need someone to comfort me.*' That's something I've been looking for—someone to comfort me. I just wish I could shake this damn sadness that gets me so often We had so much fun. And I felt like she was the only one who really understood me then . . . the only one who really cared about me . . .. You know what?"

"What?"

"I think I just realized . . . I don't think I ever knew it before. . . I think I must have been in love with her."

Carol frowned.

"Before I left for France, we agreed we wouldn't write. But, even so . . . even now, I still feel very close to her. And she's got grit. She's going to apply to the Peace Corps for a post in South America after graduation. You know, Carol, in many ways, you're just like Lui. I don't feel cut off when I'm with you."

"Thanks." Carol smiled. "How 'bout the Hall? What's that?"

"The Hall? The Hall's a frat. I kind of just fell into it when I got to college. They wanted preppies. Saint Barnabas Hall. It's kind of a snobby group of northern prep school guys who couldn't get into Harvard, Yale, or Dartmouth. We try to be radical, bohemian, avant-garde. It really shakes up the southerners on campus. But for the most part, we're just a bunch of preppies from rich families who like to drink and have a good time. Some of the guys say they're writers and painters. I think they really just want to be, or pretend to be. We have some jocks too. Any more questions?"

Carol looked sad. She used her finger to twirl her drink, then took a sip. She looked up at me with her lovely brown eyes.

"Just one more, Jay. Jay . . . what about after graduation? What are you going to do then?"

"I've already taken care of that. I have another plan to get away . . . as far away as I can this time. I can't stay in America with my parents. It's impossible. So, I'm going to do the same thing as Lui. I'm going to go into the Peace Corps. Only I'm going to go to Africa."

"Africa?"

"Yes. Last March, during break, I went up to Le Mans. There's a US Army base up there. I took the Peace Corps tests, and passed. So I'm supposed to start training next June in Ohio right after graduation. Before I left France and went back to the States, I had to know that I was going to get away again. Carol, I can't be around my family. It hurts too much. For now, the only one I can count on is me."

Carol looked hurt. She finally said, "But why the Peace Corps, Jay?"

"Being a guy, once I graduate, it's either teaching in the Ivory Coast or getting shot in Vietnam. Since I have a choice, I'll go to Africa."

"But Africa, Jay. Why Africa? Aren't there other places you can go? Safer places?"

"It's because of Hemingway. I've always been a huge fan of his. That's why I came to France. I want to follow in his footsteps. I guess it's hard to understand. And maybe a little foolish, too."

Carol looked down at her glass. "I guess that means I won't see you after graduation then?"

"Well, maybe we will. I hope so. But . . . who knows?" I ran my finger around the rim of my empty glass, then waved it at the waiter. "Scotch!" I shouted.

Carol stretched back in her chair and yawned. Her full breasts swelled beneath her thin blouse.

"Well, I guess I'm off to bed. Betsy and Sybille are probably already asleep. Do you have your key?"

"Sure. I've got it here somewhere. I'll be up in a bit."

"Don't stay up too late, Jay. We have a big day tomorrow."

"I'll be right up," I smiled. "I just want to have my nightcap."

"I'll leave the light on. And Jay . . . don't drink too much."

"Who me?" I winked. "Never!"

Sitting alone in the cool air, I watched the cars and motorbikes pass by on the Boulevard de la République. Couples strolled beneath the street lamps arm in arm. The moon was half full.

It should be good camping on the beach with Carol, I thought. *God do I like her. And tonight, here in Marseille, we'll finally be alone.*

"Voila, Madame," the waiter said as he replaced my empty glass with a full one.

I played with the ice cubes.

It's good to be going to Corsica, but it's not good to be going home.

I threw back the drink and waved at the waiter again.

"L'addition, s'il vous plaît."

He brought the check and I pulled several large colored bank notes from my wallet. I thought about the tip and flipped a 20 centime piece onto the porcelain saucer.

'Madame.' Fuck you! 'Madame.'

I caught myself on the back of the chair as I got up. The Scotch sloshed in my head. I concentrated on steering my course through the sea of empty tables without knocking over the chairs or tripping on the terrace's blue-slate flagstones. The waiter smiled as I stumbled by.

"I should have hit him," I mumbled.

Inside the lobby, I dragged my feet past the concierge's desk to search for the elevator. The gold double doors finally appeared from behind a copse of potted palms. I leaned heavily against the button and watched the little white light slowly jump its way across the overhead panel from 7 to R. As it passed 4, it blurred, then split into two fuzzy white dots. I blinked, and at 2, the lights snapped back together again. The bell clanged. I shook my head. When the doors opened, I stumbled forward into the car and squinted at the numbers on my room key. *4 ... 40 ... 407.*

I closed the gate and pushed the 4 button. The car jerked to a start, wobbled up the shaft, and jerked to a stop. I pushed open the gate and stepped out onto the thick red paisley carpet. I looked left then right.

"Now what? Where the hell is it?"

I turned left down the brightly lit hallway and followed the wallpaper past the staircase to the end of the corridor.

407. I jabbed at the lock. Once, twice. Finally, I got the key in, and the door opened. Carol had left a small lamp on. It glowed in the distance between our two beds. I pushed myself towards it and sat down heavily on the end of my bed. Her breathing was soft and gentle as she slept. As I watched her blanket rise and fall, I tugged at my shirt and pulled off my desert boot.

My eyes snapped open to the bright morning light. I stared up at the ceiling from on top of the bedspread where I lay. Next to me was my pillow. And I was still wearing my clothes from last night. My head pounded terribly. There was a ringing in my ears; a queasy feeling twisted my stomach. I squinted as the sunshine flooded through the open window.

From across the room came a gentle swish . . . swish . . . sound. Again, the soft sound—swish, swish. I pulled myself up against the headboard and stared through the shafts of morning light. Carol's silhouette sat tall and relaxed on a low bench in front of the dresser mirror. As she drew the small brush through her long chestnut hair, the gentle sound of *swish*, *swish* came again. I watched as the sun's rays turned the cascading waves of auburn transparent. Carol turned and smiled when she heard me stir. She was already dressed.

"Well good morning. I waited up for you. Where were you?"

"Oh, I had another Scotch, I guess."

"How do you feel, sleepy head?"

"OK," I lied. "What time is it?"

"It's almost nine. Hurry up. We have to get down to the harbor to buy our tickets. If you don't step on it, you're going to miss breakfast."

My stomach turned at the thought of food.

She picked up her rucksack and walked to the door.

"Hurry up now."

"OK. OK. I'll be right down. Can you order me a café crème and croissant?" I asked through lips that felt like parchment.

When she slammed the door, my head shook. As I got

up, I tripped over the crepe sole of my Chukka boot lying on the floor next to the bed. Pushing myself to the bathroom, I stepped over the doorsill and leaned against the washbasin in front of the mirror. My eyes were like red spider webs. I found the aspirin bottle and struggled with the childproof cap. Two tablets rolled onto my sweaty palm, and I choked them down. I blinked to study my stubble of beard and tangled blond hair.

As my shaking hand reached for the razor, a vicious attack of nausea struck. An explosion of sickness erupted from my stomach. My legs buckled. I gagged, staggered to the toilet. I heaved up the aspirin, the Scotch, the steak and blood into the porcelain bowl. Spittle dripped from my lips, down my chin, into the putrid mess.

Too weak to stand, I sank to my knees and gasped for breath. The bathroom lurched. I held myself, curled under the sink, fighting off the waves of dry heaves that bombarded me. My temples throbbed as though pierced by rusty railroad spikes. Rivulets of sweat ran down my nose and splashed on to the white tile floor. I reached up, yanked down a towel from the rack and mopped the puke from my face. The pungent smell of disinfectant, mixed with the stink of stale Gauloises and excrement, was overwhelming. I shuddered, gasped and vomited again into the bidet. My head hung like a heavy weight.

"The one chance I get," I mumbled. "The one chance I've been hoping for all year long, the one time I'm alone with her, the one chance to sleep with Carol—what do I do? I fuck it up! Why? Why do I always fuck things up?"

Slowly, I pulled myself up off the tiled floor to the sink. My trembling hand fought to unscrew the cap from the Visine. Each drop felt like an icepick stabbing at my bloodshot eyes. I turned from the mirror and stumbled away from the acrid stench into the bedroom to try and pack my things.

By the time we bought our boat tickets and made a tour of the old town, it was late afternoon. The four of us carried our packs down through the cobblestoned streets to the old port where the *Cora* was docked. Sybille, Carol and Betsy stopped to buy food for dinner while I picked out two large bottles of vin ordinaire.

We carried the provisions in our string bags to one of the rocky beaches surrounding the harbor. Betsy found a protected spit of sand, and we spread out our meal on Carol's towel. We sat together in a small circle Indian style and feasted on pâté, sardines, salami, fresh bread and cheap wine. Sybille's transistor radio crackled out the BBC's top hits by The Beatles, Roy Orbison and The Beach Boys. The night's soft wind mixed the strong scent of garlic from the outdoor market with the brackish smell of seaweed from water's edge into an evening potion. Tired freighters steamed across the distant horizon.

Not far away, a gang of six young French punks was splashing each other in the surf. They each took turns pushing one another down under the breaking waves. Two of them wrestled one of the smaller boys on to the beach, filled his pants with wet sand, and laughed.

A short boy in a black T-shirt and dirty cutoff jeans noticed the girls sitting by the rocks. He grabbed his crotch and waved, then pulled the ringleader, the biggest one, by the shoulder, spun him around and pointed. They strolled over to Sybille and hovered over her.

The small one snickered, "Hey, Jocko, looky here. Nice little bird, eh?"

The leader's dark olive skin glistened in the evening sun. A dagger pierced the red heart tattooed on his chiseled chest.

"You got cigarette?" he growled at Sybille.

He looked 18, about six feet tall. His French accent from the south was heavy and slurred, his teeth stained. Sybille hid behind her blonde hair.

"Got cigarette?" he repeated.

A baby-faced boy with an old leather jacket squatted down nearby on one of the large flat rocks. He started flipping pebbles onto the sand. With each toss, he increased his range, until he finally reached Betsy. One or two of the stones fell onto her blue raincoat. I got up.

"Leave her alone!" I shouted. "Why are you bothering us?"

"Why you bothering us?" the boy mimicked with a high whine.

"What do we have here? A wise guy?" the leader said sarcastically.

I gave him a nervous look. "Get out of here," I said.

The gang looked at me and laughed.

"Get out here," they mocked.

The gang tightened its circle about our small group.

"What are you . . . Anglais?" the leader asked. He turned back to Betsy and Sybille. "Fräuleins, sprechen sie Deutsche? How 'bout a piece of chocolate?"

Betsy hid her candy bar. They all laughed again.

"I want some chocolate," the leader yelled.

I flinched. My muscles tightened.

"Get the hell out of here!" I shouted. "Get the hell out of here!"

He paid no attention. The others were squatting about like pigeons. They looked uninterested, but I sensed they could fly at a moment's notice. One bumped his buddy so he barely missed stepping on Sybille. The leader picked a large rock out of the sand and held it in his grimy hand over Carol's head. He smiled at his friends, then turned to me and laughed.

"Look at this, wise guy. How do you like this?"

He threw the stone up in the air above Carol's head and just barely caught it with his large fingertips. Carol cowered. She looked up at him. He shook the rock menacingly. This time, he tossed it higher and caught it again just above Carol's head. The boy with the long red hair nudged Betsy with his stubby fingers.

"Come on. Just a little piece of chocolate. One piece."

"Do it again and I'll hit," I snarled at the boy.

"You won't touch him," the leader sneered. "You know, big boy, I killed a man once."

He looked away, then suddenly turned and ran at me.

He grabbed me by my shirt and viciously flung me down onto the sand. With his knee on my chest and one hand holding my shoulder, he quickly pulled a knife from his jeans pocket and held it against my throat.

"You wanna be cut, hot stuff?

"Stop!" Carol screamed. "Please. Let him up. We'll go. Come on girls. Let's get our things. We'll go."

The leader turned and smiled at Carol. As the girls scampered about gathering up their rucksacks, sleeping bags and food, the leader slowly got up and put his knife away. He stood up over me, looking down at me, and taunted, "You've got two minutes to get the hell off our beach."

"Jay, come on," Carol urged. "Let's go. We don't want to miss the ship."

I stood up and wiped the sand from my pants. I picked up my bag and we began to walk towards the *Cora*. Suddenly I turned. The leader was still watching us.

"Hey!" I shouted. "We'll remember you . . . you Frenchmen! You and your country!"

I shook my fist at him. He gave me the finger, laughed, then turned back to his pals. I looked at Carol.

"Why did they have to fuck up such a nice night? It always gets fucked up. I should have been stronger. I should have fought them."

"Let it go, Jay. Six against one. I don't think the numbers were in your favor." Carol squeezed my hand. "Don't worry about it. You were fine."

We walked along together in silence towards the dock to wait on line for the ten o'clock boarding.

That night, the evening's crossing was rough—furniture breaking away, people being seasick, and glassware shattering. But the *Cora* kept pushing on across the black, raging sea. The rain lashed at the ship, and the wind howled. To fight off my seasickness, I left the girls, and I went outside by the ship's front rail. As I watched the angry whitecaps crash over the ship's bow, the sea spray splashed sobering waves of cold water across my face. To keep from vomiting, I breathed in deeply the swirling sea wind combined with the strong scent from the ammonia capsules that I took from my first aid kit. With each whiff, my nausea weakened. And the ship continued pounding its way through the dark night.

Hours later, the storm began to weaken. The whitecaps gradually subsided, and the night began to turn to day. By the time the *Cora* sailed into the old port of Bastia, the rocky sea had changed to a turquoise lake, sparkling in the morning sun. Deckhands went about their chores, sweeping up the breakage, and tying the ship to the pier.

The three of us left Sybille with her German relatives at the bottom of the gangplank, and walked up the hill to the main square. We took a table outside at a small restaurant and ordered a breakfast of café au lait and croissants.

As the girls talked amongst themselves, I watched a stooped old woman across the road methodically sweep the empty square. She took her twig broom up one side of the paving stones, then down along the stone wall of the church, and then back again across the baked yellow dirt. She pushed her pile of rubble until it rested in a heap at the center of the square next to the lazy, moss-covered fountain. When Betsy and Carol finished their coffee, they went inside to wash up and pay the bill.

At the table next to ours, a French family of four that I recognized from the *Cora* sat with their morning meal. The father had just left his little girl at the curb to be sick. Her mother sat slumped in her chair and leaned heavily on her husband's shoulder, her hand to her mouth. From her widened eyes and pale face, I could see that the voyage had not been kind to them. The little girl returned to their table; the mother stood up and walked unsteadily to the road. She turned and looked back at her husband, then back at the street, uncertain of her own seasickness. She hesitated, then finally returned to the table. Her husband squeezed her hand.

The small stone church stood cradled in the morning shadows at the far corner of the square. It seemed to call to me.

I got up and walked past the pockmarked fountain with its spitting gargoyles through the dust to the rustic chapel. The heavy wooden door swung open with a groan on its thick rusted hinges. I stepped over the sanctuary's stone sill, worn thin by the centuries of faithful parishioners, into the dark dank empty chill. At the tiny tin alms box by the door, I dropped a centime through the narrow slot. Ahead, through the darkness, sapphires glimmered from the cross at the end of the nave. I walked through the thick musty air, listening to the echo of my footsteps ricocheting off the vaulted ceiling. Before me, the marbled Christ hung from his nails; his loincloth covered by multi-colored light floating down from the three stained glass windows above. With his head tilted, he stared into my eyes and filled my heart with his sadness.

Luminescent waves of gold candlelight glistened from a rickety stand of dark battered wood in the side altar. There I took a crooked candle from the small box, lit it from one of the many that burned, and pressed its base into the sand. Beneath the warmth from the rows of small flames, I sank down onto the cold stone floor and prayed.

"God, pleases protect my mother. Free her from her drinking; her problems with money. Give her happiness and health. Please, remove the difficulties in her life. Give her new hope. Let her become the woman she was—pretty, filled with life. Give her strength." I missed her, and felt her pain. "Please, God, please—help her."

Outside, the brilliant sun beat down on the courtyard's flagstones. Slowly crossing the square again through the morning's heat, I made my way back to the café to find the girls arguing.

"But, Carol, he said 'Deux cents'," Betsy whined. "You know, two hundred. Get it? Two francs. Two hundred."

"Yes, I know. I gave him two francs and you left two francs on the table," Carol said.

"I thought he meant for each one of us," Betsy insisted.

"OK. Go back and ask him for them . . . or don't. They're your two francs." Carol shrugged her shoulders.

"Come on, girls, get your things." I looked at the map. "The beach is this way."

We walked past the Governor's palace, down the cobblestone road, to the old fort. Looking down from the bluff, we could see the surf and the beach below.

"Here it is!"

I pushed back the brambles, walked past the twisted sign that warned of 'Chien Méchant' and followed the steep dirt trail down through the blue wildflowers. From the road above, Betsy stood skinny and tall squinting down through her thick glasses at the path.

"It's certainly not paradise," she complained.

"Don't you want to go down?" I asked.

"Well, what about the dog? I expected . . pa. I thought it would be something nicer."

"Come on, Betsy. Give it a try," Carol urged. "We can always go back."

At the bottom of the hill, a rotted rowboat half covered in sand guarded the entrance to a long stretch of warm, white beach. Exhausted, we spread out our sleeping bags and collapsed into sleep.

When I woke, Carol and Betsy were already beginning to make lunch.

"Come on Carol, let's search for a place to spend the night. Betsy, we'll be back in ten minutes."

We rolled up our pants and walked hand in hand through the billowing surf. Soft, heavy seaweed caught up in the froth of the incoming tide wound
its slippery tentacles around our legs.

"You know," I said, smiling, "you've helped me so much this year. Last fall, I was so unhappy—really miserable. I remember the first time I heard the word *misanthrope* at college. I thought, 'Misanthrope, that's me.' Growing up, I always *had* enough, but I never, ever thought I *was* enough. I never felt like I fit in. But, because of you, that's all changed now. You've made me happy again, Carol. You really have."

"I think it's you that's changed, Jay," she said. "You've

changed a lot since First semester. You were pretty quiet back then. You never smiled."

"Me? Come on. What about you? You never said anything. You barely looked up from your books."

"I know. I'm shy. But, you know that by now. I guess you're kind of like me. You hardly ever spoke at the beginning of the year." She squeezed my hand. "I'm glad you came out of your shell and let me get to know you."

I saw the warmth in her dark chestnut eyes.

"You know? I was thinking. There are some words, when you put them together, they mean the opposite." I kicked at the surf. "If you take 'all' and 'one,' for example, and put them together, you get 'alone.' Same thing with 'a' and 'part'— 'apart.' Most of my life I've felt that way. Never 'all one' or 'a part,' but 'alone' and 'apart.' Reality . . . life, I guess . . . usually feels foreign to me."

I picked up a flat stone and skimmed it over the waves.

"I'm sorry you're not going back to Vanderhill with me," Carol said softly.

"Me too. I'll miss you." I skipped another stone across the water. Five jumps this time. I turned and looked at her. "I'll miss you a lot."

Ahead, two children played by the shore. They looked like brother and sister. The boy was about seven with dark skin and a crew cut; the girl was younger, about five, with a short blue dress and a small straw bonnet. They were both barefoot. I pointed at their dogs, a small black puppy and a spotted bitch.

"Chiens méchants?" I smiled. "They don't look very mean to me."

At the end of the beach, nestled against a rocky cliff, was an old fishing boat circled by decaying rope and covered with netting and sand. Winches, pulleys and large wooden bobbins were scattered about its hull. Above, up on the hilltop, a crumbling cement blockhouse stood wrapped in rusted strands of barbed wire. Old pieces of a German tank spilled down the sandy embankment.

"Look, Carol. You see that dune? We can use it as a windbreak. The sand's hard, so it's perfect for cooking. After lunch, we can lug all our stuff down here."

"OK. But I'm hungry, Jay. Let's go back. And you're getting too much sun anyway."

We walked back up the beach to find Betsy and have our lunch. After washing down the last of our sandwiches with the cheap red wine, we gathered our belongings and carried them down to the wreck. The girls used stones and some tiles they found piled up on the beach to build a small stove. I went off to search the shore for driftwood.

As I looked up from my pile of branches and twigs, a strong, dark-skinned man came walking towards me covered in the pungent stink of fish. Baggy tan pants hung beneath a torn white T-shirt. His muscles bulged as he pushed a wheelbarrow through the sand. I guessed he was coming in search of the stack of tiles lying 50 meters from where our sleeping bags were spread. I offered a weak, "Bonjour," hoping to overcome any accusation of theft of his tiles or of trespassing.

He stopped and tipped his straw sombrero. "Bonjour," he said with a thick Corsican accent.

"I'm sorry." I pointed to the stack of tiles. "We didn't think they belonged to anybody."

"Oh, no problem," he said in a friendly tone.

His broad, brown nose and sunburned cheeks contrasted markedly with his crooked white teeth and bright blue eyes. His smile dampened into a taut frown as he glanced at our campsite. He gave his dark moustache a tug.

"You going to spend the night here?" he asked skeptically.

"If it's OK. One night, maybe two, if the weather's good," I said tentatively. "We're on Spring Holiday and trying to save some money."

"I don't know. It's a little early in the season for camping outdoors. It rained last night. You don't have any protection. Not even tents. You can ask the Propriétaire if you can stay in the old cabin over there."

Across the beach, where the dune slanted down from the windbreak, stood a small wooden shanty.

"Where is he?" I asked timidly. "The Propriétaire?" I was not sure what we were getting into.

"Over there. In the field. The *big* one."

"Him?" I asked pointing.

"No. He's L'Italian. The Propriétaire is the *big* man." He made a great big gesture, suggesting someone with an enormous belly. "I've got the keys over there on the hook. Come on. I'm sure it will be fine."

I looked at the girls and shrugged. We gathered up our things and followed him as he wheeled the tiles back to the little cabin. Beside the shack, a woman was hanging wet clothes on the branches of a tree. She was thin and tanned like the man. She turned, then smiled. "Bonjour," she said with a heavy accent. The young boy and girl from the beach now played by her feet with their small black puppy and spotted bitch.

"Leave your stuff here," the man told us. "I'm working on the cabin now. Putting in a tile floor. See? I call you when I'm done."

We dropped our things by the door and walked down to the water's edge. I found a large pile of dried seaweed to sit on, and opened my torn Hemingway. The girls skipped pebbles over the waves and watched the man go about his work. An hour later, as the sun was starting to fall behind the jagged mountains, the sea's wind began to build. With a shiver, I creased the page of *The Sun Also Rises* and went to check on how much progress the fellow had made with the floor.

When I stepped over the doorsill, he stood up, put his hands on his hips and stretched his back.

"Ah. Enough for today." He studied me. "Me and the family are going to have . . .. What's your name?"

"Jay. Jay Walker."

"We're going to have snack, Jay. You all welcome to join us if you want."

"We'd love to," Betsy and Carol chimed in from outside

the doorframe.

Chilled in their light garments from the sea's air, they followed me into the dimly lit room. The walls were made from boards, planks and old doors that had washed up onto the beach. High up on the wall across from the entrance was a small window that let in the afternoon light. A collection of lost articles from the sea hung from nails and pegs—an old inner tube, two straw hats decorated with bits of ribbon, pails, shovels and a tattered lifejacket. They spoke of the beach's past. Bits of broken mirrors were tacked to the walls to make the shack look bigger. For light, an old lantern hung overhead in the center of the room.

At the smaller of the two tables, the family spread out their red-checkered oilcloth. The woman took her sharp knife and sliced the long baguette. She gobbed a mixture of vegetables, onions and chicken between the two halves, then cut it in quarters. The girls unwrapped our sparse provisions. I sat on the bench between them and jabbed at a can of sardines with my knife.

The little boy and girl gathered about their parents' table straddling the bench while playing with their dogs. From behind her mother's full skirt, the little girl peeked out curiously to study us. The boy petted the bitch and shifted his dark eyes from one of us to the other. His father got up and carried half of his sandwich over to our table.

"Here, have some," he said with a smile. "You don't seem have much to eat. Help yourselves."

Betsy and Carol dug into the mess that reeked of garlic and chives. Each chose a small bit of heavily oiled chicken. The man waved his finger back and forth at Betsy with a grin. "Attention! C'est la tête, ça," he said, pointing to his head. Betsy quickly dropped the morsel onto the table and made a repulsed grimace. The family laughed until a large shadow crossed the floor.

A tall, dark figure stood in the doorframe blocking what little daylight there was before entering the room. He addressed the family with a heavy Sicilian accent and took a seat across from the small boy on the bench. Instead of taking off the tall red hat that matched his sunburnt face, he simply crossed his heavy arms on top of his bulbous stomach and stared at us with his dark brown eyes. A long, frayed rope strained to hold up his stained white trousers while his large gut tried to push free from beneath the stripes of his tight blue and white pullover. Certainly, this was "Le Propriétaire."

He carefully inspected the family's fare, then helped himself to the chicken and poured some of the red wine into a large tin cup. He emptied his drink with one swallow, wiped his mouth with his sleeve, then let rip a burp that shook the cabin. Betsy jumped. The children laughed. He raised an eyebrow and looked at us suspiciously.

"You from England?"

"No. America," Betsy giggled nervously.

"Must have cost a lot of money. 5,000 francs?" he questioned.

"More," Carol said with a grin. "That's why we're so poor now. We're broke."

"Had Germans here once. Spent two months at my place. Never got a centime." He rubbed his thumb and finger together to make sure we understood he was talking about money. "Remember English couple last year?" he asked the other man in a critical voice. "Camped here in a tent. Fifteen days."

"We were only thinking of spending a night or two . . . maybe three," I offered, "if that's OK."

"Too early in the season to sleep outdoors," he said. "You'll see in the morning. There's dew on the hay just to here." He pointed to his knee. "You say how long you plan to stay?"

"Well, we want to visit Île Rousse and Calvi in a day or two," I told him. "But we don't know about the trains or buses."

"There's only one bus," the other man said. "It leaves at six, maybe seven."

"OK. You can stay here till then," the big man grumbled. "Find out about the bus tomorrow, and leave when you wish."

"Perfect!" Carol said. "Thank you so much."

"Be sure to leave the keys with my son, Antoine here, or L'Italian."

Once the affair was settled, the Propriétaire returned to playing with his grandchildren who squealed as they ran around him calling him Pepé. When the meal was finished, the family rose and wished us a pleasant stay. On their way out, they shook all our hands and showed me how to close the makeshift shutters and lock the door. I watched them walk away up the beach, then suddenly remembered.

"Oh, Monsieur!" I called after the Propriétaire. "How much?"

He waved his hand goodbye above his head without turning. "Gratuit!" he shouted, climbing the hill. "It's free!"

The girls looked at one another incredulously. "Free?" they said in unison, and danced about in a happy circle.

At twilight, Carol and I left Betsy in the cabin as she got ready for bed, and climbed to the summit of the stony cliff nearby to see the last rays of daylight. When we reached the bluff high above the beach, the sharp sea wind slapped at our faces, and the sweet scent of lemon grass rose to greet us from the cove below. The ragged mountaintops were reflected far out into the murky green of the Mediterranean. We sat side-by-side, gazing out over the expanse of blue until the sun began to sink behind the tall, sloping peaks.

"Come on," I said. "It's getting cold. Let's go down."

Back on the rocky beach, I turned to take one last look west before entering the cabin.

"Carol! Look! Come here! Look!"

High above the rocky mountain ridge in the sapphire sky, the edges of every white cloud were now painted brightly in flamingo pink. It was as though someone had thrown a switch.

I turned to Carol and smiled. "Perhaps there is a God after all."

We huddled together amongst the jagged crags, oblivious to the sea's cold spray, and watched as the colors gradually faded away.

When the clouds finally melted in to a purple dome, Carol said, "I'm sleepy. It's time for bed."

Inside the shanty, she took off her shoes and jacket and put them on the chair. I locked the door.

"Turn around, Jay."

I heard her slip out of her blouse, skirt and panties, and get into her sleeping bag.

I hung my red suede coat on an old hook, folded my jeans for a pillow, then turned down the flame from the lantern and climbed into my bag. I looked over and saw that she was still awake.

"I love being with you, Carol," I said.

From outside the cabin came the muffled sound of the waves crashing again and again against the rocky coast.

"Jay . . .," Carol whispered. "Come here,"

"What?"

"Come here."

My heart was racing as I unzipped my bag and joined Carol in hers. Her body was soft and warm, and her moist hair still carried the salted scent of the evening. In the lantern light, I watched the damp of the sea's mist sparkle on her dark eyelashes. We held each other gently.

"This is wonderful," Carol said as she rolled towards me.

"I know," I replied. "I've been waiting for this for so long."

I bowed my head, buried my face in the nape of her neck and inhaled her cleanliness. When I put my cheek on her breast, she caressed my wet hair and drew me to her nipples. My hand found her soft stomach and then her pubic mound. She spread her legs, and let me arouse her. Her back arched slowly and rhythmically to my touch. I kissed one hip, then the other. She let me embrace her between her legs, then drew me back up to her chest, then her shoulders, then her neck. I moved my body on top of hers as I kissed her lips. She opened her legs for me and raised her knees. We moved with the sound of the waves, tentatively, tenderly. Gradually, our pace quickened. She clasped her hands behind my neck to pull herself up to me; opened herself fully to me and pulled me harder into her, again and again. When we finished, we lay quietly beside one another. She stroked my face.

"Good night," she said softly, her voice trailing off into a wistful whisper.

The warmth of happiness coursed through me. I rested my head between her soft breasts and felt sleep coming to the cadence of her heartbeat.

Tu-tump . . . tu-tump . . . tu-tump . . ..

Chug-chug . . . chug-chug . . . chug-chug . . ..

The sound of the wheels and a loud blast from the *Rapide*'s shrill whistle woke me from my dream as the locomotive entered Dijon. Still thinking of Carol, I squinted through the soil on the windowpane at summer's sunlight. Below, in the dusty street, mothers rode motor scooters beside the trestle with babies strapped to their backs. One young woman looked up and waved. I opened the window and waved back.

On the other side of the murky Saône, large, white industrial quarries lined the riverbank. The workers paused from their large cut blocks to study the train as it lumbered by. Some put down their heavy jackhammers and shook their caps at the passengers. Others merely wiped their brows, stared, then went back to their trade. In the town's center, most of the buildings were old and shuttered, connected by lines of wash. Sleepy cats sunned themselves across windowsills and fought for space with the flowerpots.

On the northern outskirts were pastures filled with livestock. In one meadow, a small boy sat in the shade and watched an old woman gather white blossoms from twisted apricot branches in her frayed, straw bag. From beneath his tree, the boy pitched stones at the crows perched on the stone wall that enclosed the field. Further out into the countryside were acres of farmland striped by rows of freshly turned earth. At the edge of a small pond, a herd of tired horses grazed on the lush green grass. Cows huddled together for warmth in the afternoon's chill. Through the shadows of dusk, the last swallows returned to their nests. Now only the highest branches glimmered in the darkening groves.

The train raced across the Seine and left the green country hills behind in the twilight. Ahead in the distance, surrounded by a picket fence of sooty smokestacks, the Gare de Lyon bathed in the glow of La Ville de Lumière.

With an explosion of steam, the locomotive lurched to a stop at the track's terminus. I grabbed my suitcase and satchel from the overhead rack and went to the window. It was easy to spot Marie-Claire with her broad face covered by a smile and her mop of blonde hair. Phillip, her thin husband, was dressed as always as a Scotsman—tweed jacket, cords, argyle socks and pipe. They came pushing their way up the station platform, squeezed between the crowd of soft drink vendors, high-priced fruit stands and newspaper boys hawking Le Figaro.

"Jay! Jay!" Marie-Claire waved. "Bienvenue!"

We hugged and kissed at the bottom of the train steps and Phillip gathered up my luggage.

"Welcome to the big city, Chéri," Marie-Claire laughed. "We have quite a night planned for you! How are Aunt Helen and Uncle Maurice?"

"Oh, they're fine. They told me to be sure to tell you that they all say 'hello.'"

"We'll still be partying tomorrow morning when we take you to the airport!" Phillip said as he gave me a squeeze. "Come on. Let's get the car."

We zigzagged through the narrow streets of Paris, down the Boulevard Montparnasse past the student cafés—Le Sélect, Le Dôme and La Rotonde. I dragged my camera with me through the Citroën's sunroof, and filmed the Champs Élysée and Place de La Bastille as we drove by. Barely did I have time to drop my things inside their apartment door before Marie-Claire whisked me back out to the car for our trip to dinner. At Les Halles, Phillip found a spot right in front of the bright red awning of his favorite restaurant, La Tour de Montlhéry.

"It's the best little bistro in Paris," he said. "I hope you're hungry. The chef's a friend of mine."

Over hearty steaks and glasses of red wine, Marie-Claire and Phillip quizzed me about their relatives. They joked about their country cousins and the stuffy closed society of Lyon and the Mollière clan.

"Did you have fun with Aunt Helen and Uncle Maurice while you were there?" Marie-Claire asked.

"Incredible. I enjoyed living with your family so much. Every moment of it. They treated me just like their son. And we had such a great going away party last night at their country home. There were over sixty students from the University. The girls brought the food and the guys brought the wine, Scotch and cognac. I've never seen so much booze. Just after midnight, a young Swedish girl with long blonde hair took the old horse out of the stable and rode it into the ballroom completely naked!"

"Maurice must have had a fit," Phillip chuckled.

"Not at all. He cheered her on like Lady Godiva until she fell off onto the parquet dance floor. After the music finally stopped, well past midnight, we played tennis on the overgrown court with the sagging net 'til the sun came up."

"Did he take you on a tour of the Roman burial mounds?" Phillip asked. "He loves them."

"Of course. After breakfast. While Jerôme exercised the tired old horse over the jumps, your uncle took Debby . . . you know, Debby, the girl with the harelip, and James and me out into the countryside."

Marie-Claire poured more wine. "How is that crazy English friend of yours anyway?"

"James? He took a flight to Egypt yesterday. He says he has a heart condition and only six months to live. So, he flew to Cairo to buy a camel. He wants to ride it back to London before he dies. He's only nineteen. I think if anything's going to kill him, it'll be the booze, not his heart. I can just see him clip-clopping down Fleet Street, Lawrence of Arabia outfit on and all, holding a fifth of Scotch in one hand and a saber in the other. When we left the château for Lyon after the party, we drank and sang all the way home. What a great time we had! I tell you, I'll always remember your family."

I did not know if it was the long train ride to Paris, the glasses of wine, or the conversations in French, but suddenly I felt exhausted and overcome with sadness. It was difficult now for me to follow my hosts' fast-clipped Parisian sentences.

"What's the matter?" Phillip asked.

I looked up from my glass. "I don't know. Something's wrong. Last week in Lyon, I was overwhelmed with sorrow. I spent my last days walking along the banks of the Rhône sobbing. I don't know what it is—if it's leaving Lyon, leaving France, or something else? I don't know what it is."

"You'll be fine, Jay," Phillip said pouring me more wine. "Let's sing tonight! Come on, bottoms up. We'll go up to Montmartre for a nightcap." Phillip paid the bill. "Don't worry, you'll be fine."

Marie-Claire gave me a hug and a kiss, and Phillip grabbed me by the shoulder.

"Come on. Let's go, my friend," he said.

Twenty minutes later, Philip squeezed the car into a small space in front of a white picket fence that encircled a small nightclub. Strains from an accordion inside the cabaret spilled out onto the street. Above the heavy oak door, a brown rabbit jumped nimbly over a small sign that read "Le Lapin Agile."

Down the dark, narrow hallway, we pushed through the red velvet curtain into a small noisy room filled with people eating, drinking and smoking. Past the crowd at the small bar, Phillip found a pair of narrow benches at a table in the back. He waved over the short pudgy waiter.

"Three cherry brandies," he said with a smile.

Across the room, multicolored spotlights marked a lanky troubadour sitting on a barstool. He sang a plaintive song about a seaman's lost love while strumming his twelve-string guitar. When the tray came, I tossed my snifter back and ordered another round.

We sang, drank, clapped and stomped our feet as the

music grew louder and louder. For the last performance, a sultry torch singer, dressed in a tight black satin gown, sang of the tawdry lives of sailors in the port of Amsterdam. As she finished her ballad, she bowed her head and let her dark eyes be covered by her long auburn hair. The white circle from the bright spotlight overhead followed the handkerchief that she dropped to the floor, slowly narrowing to a pinpoint, then flashing out. An explosion of hoots and cheers filled the darkened room.

We spilled out the side door onto the quiet, cobblestoned street with a group of newfound friends. Still singing loudly, we wove our way past the rusty bollards arm in arm back to the car.

"Marie-Claire," Phillip said as he pulled up to their apartment. "I have a surprise for Jay. We'll be back in a bit. Is that all right?"

"Well, all right. It's his last night in France. But don't be bad boys." She winked. "OK?"

"Thank you, Cherié."

Phillip gave his wife a kiss, then spun the Citroën around and followed its yellow headlights to L'Étoile.

"How long has it been since you've been with a woman, Jay?" he asked.

"Well, this spring, on Corsica. Why?"

"No, no. You told me she was an American. That doesn't count. And she's gone back to the States, anyway, right? So, you've never had a French woman. Well, before you leave France, you have to be with 'une française.'"

He took the first street to the left off L'Étoile and drove into the Bois de Boulogne to where several trucks were parked. Along the curb, four or five nervous-looking men were pacing up and down, puffing their Gitanes. Others stood back in the bushes looking over their shoulders, taking care of last-minute necessities. Phillip parked the car where most of the action was taking place.

"Here, take this. It's 500 francs. Get the one in the shiny white DS. The one with the red hair."

"The white DS?"

"Yes. She's the best! Look for the leopard skin uphol-stery." He shook my hand. "It's 1:00 now. I'll be back at 2:00. And Jay . . . have fun!"

I put the money in my pocket and stepped out onto the curb. Large sleek sedans rolled slowly by with their interior dome lights on and their headlights flashing. A woman in a long black Citroën with blonde pigtails pulled up in front of me. She rolled down the window, looked out indifferently from be-hind the steering wheel and smiled. I stared back at her timidly with my hands in my pockets. She pouted, took her breasts away from the window and drove further along where she was stopped by an eager customer. The cold night air began to cut through both my turtleneck and the cognac. I felt uneasy, not sure I wanted to be here. My excitement was mixed with both fear and apprehension.

What if I can't perform? What if I don't know what to do?

I looked up the road for Phillip's car. As I turned back, a white DS pulled up with a couple inside. When the man got out, I bent over and looked in. The dim blue dome light lit up the leopard skin upholstery and the woman's fiery red hair. I opened the door and sank into the soft foam rubber passenger seat that was already tilted back. I slammed the door, and the car rocked forward down the avenue while a tape played the soft music of Aznavour.

She looked at me with her bedroom eyes and said in English, "German?"

"No. American."

"You look German. Or maybe French."

"It's the goatee." I tried to sound older. "I'm from New York," I stammered.

"Voiture?" she asked curtly.

"What?"

"Here, or the hotel?"

"How much is the hotel?"

"Mille francs."

"Voiture," I said as I lay back in the seat.

"Service complet ou la pipe?"

"C'est combien, le service complet?"

"Sept cent cinquante service complete, cinq cent la pipe."

"La pipe, alors."

We drove several blocks and parked under a street lamp.

"Trop de lumière, n'est-çe pas?" I asked squinting up through the windshield at the bright light.

"It's the best spot," she said. "The *flics* never bother us in the well-lit areas."

While she counted my money, I undid my belt and slid out of my pants. I tried to make myself comfortable as she started to work for her 500 francs. I held her white shoulders and inhaled her heavy, cheap perfume. Gently, she cupped my cock and sucked, twirling her tongue around its tip. With her every stroke, my body became more rigid. I dug my feet into the carpeted floor mat.

Wait! Wait! I told myself.

But I could not wait any longer. I threw my back against the seat and exploded.

She gagged, then slowly lifted her head. Finished, she looked around wearily to make sure the police were not there. Brushing back her long red hair, she reached for a Kleenex and wiped her lips. As we drove back to the corner where I got in, I studied her pale complexion.

"Why don't we talk for a while?" I asked.

"Look. I've got my ten regulars waiting for me on my circuit. I shouldn't have even picked you up. I've got to hustle. I've barely made 2,000 tonight."

"Why do you do it?" I asked.

"They all ask me that. For 10,000 francs a night, it's worth it. Besides, now I speak six languages." She smiled and opened the door. "I'm sorry, but I don't have time for chit-chat. Bonsoir."

I stepped out onto the boulevard and turned back to her

car. "Bonne chance," I said.

"Toi aussi," she replied with a slight smile.

As I watched her drive off to her next anxious customer, Phillip blew his horn. He leaned out the window. "Come on. Jump in. How was it?"

"I'm not sure. She was nice. But I've never paid for sex before. It seems strange to me."

Phillip left the park and negotiated L'Étoile. He followed the Champs past the tall, regal buildings and the Eiffel Tower back to his narrow street to get me ready for my dolorous early morning departure.

As I fell asleep, my thoughts turned to Carol. I missed her.

The clanging of my alarm clock woke me at six with a hangover. I pulled on the clothes I wore from the night before, and struggled to close my bags and get my passport and ticket in order. The empty Sunday boulevards of Paris were still wet from the morning street cleaners as the three of us drove through daybreak to Orly. After check in, Phillip ordered a bottle of champagne. We sat and joked. By 8:30, the bottle was empty.

When my Air France flight was announced, that strange feeling of melancholy possessed me again. *What was it? What was I feeling? The hangover . . . leaving France . . . was it something else? I didn't know.*

"I guess I have to go," I said sadly.

I hugged them both, perhaps a little too long, then let them go. I turned and headed for the gate.

"Don't forget!" Phillip shouted after me. "We'll see you in the States in May. I have that business deal."

I turned and waved again.

Marie-Claire blew me a kiss.

I walked slowly up the boarding ramp and found my window seat. When the wheels pulled up off the runway, I felt my connection with France and all that it stood for severed. My next stop was the US.

I ordered a Scotch and chatted briefly with my French

neighbor. I twisted on the overhead air, flicked my light off and immediately fell asleep.

"Please stow your tray table in front of you." The voice, though soft, jolted me awake. "Return your seatback to its full upright position and make sure your seatbelt is buckled."

As the plane made its slow descent, I sat up, blinking, trying to make sense of my surroundings. Looking out the small window, I watched the small houses of Queens crowd the white beaches of Long Island below.

I walked off the plane into the crisp June sun. My mind was perfectly clear. I understood everything, and everything made sense. I was entirely in the moment, and well rested from the flight. Once again, America was clear and fresh for me. My thoughts were keenly organized, as my life was now. Everything made sense.

Kennedy International Arrivals was jammed with tourists fumbling with bags, passports and crying children. I waited in line as the tedious customs officials rummaged through countless pieces of luggage overflowing with vacation shopping. One agent stopped an African family to interrogate the confused foreigners about their pieces of fruit.

As I listened to all of the people around me, I suddenly realized that my ear had become incredibly acute to the English language. I was keenly aware of the many grammatical errors being made by this large crowd of American travelers.

While jockeying for their positions in line, fathers were yelling to wives, brothers were screaming to sisters. All were oblivious to the grammatical errors that they were making.

To me, their mistakes sounded like fingernails screeching across a blackboard. They exploded in my ears. Isolated from the American language for so long, I was now extremely cognizant of the proper structure for every sentence. I pushed forward to the sleepy customs agent dozing in his rumpled uniform. He looked up at me with tired eyes.

"Where's you's passport? You been here before?" His every sentence was incorrect and unclear. I did not know what to say. "I's talkin' you mistah? What's a matta for you?"

What's the object? Where's the predicate? I wondered. *What was he saying?*

He stared at me over his large ledger. It was obvious he thought I did not speak English. I started to move forward.

"Whoa. Hold ona minute. You's be patient. I's talkin' about your passport."

I fumbled inside my blazer and handed him my passport.

"Damn me. You's American? Look!" he said still thinking I did not understand a word. "Look! Your bags . . .? Your bags . . .?"

He stopped, straightened his khaki jacket, then he began again, speaking very slowly this time, using only short sentences and putting heavy emphasis on each syllable.

"Yourrrrr baaagggsssss," he said, poking his finger into my chest, then pointing beyond the glass wall. "Your bags over there. Oooverrr therrrrre. Got it?" He stamped my passport and pushed me towards the baggage claim. "Unnnderrrrstannnd?"

I nodded and put my passport back in my breast pocket.

"Goooooood."

"Thank you," I stammered.

"You's welk."

When I reached the other side of the glass block wall, I went looking for my luggage and my family. I was not sure if I was eager or apprehensive to see my father.

Descending the escalator, I saw him standing at the rear of a large crowd that was pushing against a long red velvet cord. It was easy to see that he had gained back the eighty pounds he had lost at the Duke clinic two years ago. Despite the warm weather, he wore his tan camel's-hair coat from Dunhill fully buttoned over his girth. His heavy-framed tortoiseshell sunglasses sat firmly on the bridge of his large nose; his thinning black hair was slicked back as usual with Wildroot cream oil.

I was surprised how haggard he looked. Ignoring his

outstretched hand, I hugged him; then went from cheek to cheek three times, kissing him in the French tradition. He blushed and pulled back.

"Hello, Jackson," he said. "What's wrong with your hair?"

"It's a razor cut. It's French."

"Well, we'll have to get that fixed. I'll get the car and meet you outside of Departures. Your brother's waiting for you over there. Oh . . . welcome home, Jackson. It's good to see you again."

I watched him walk away, then got my bags and carried them to the exit where Harry was sitting on a brown marble bench. When we waved to each other, I wondered why he was not more enthusiastic. After all, he had not seen me for more than a year.

"Well, hi!" I said and gave him a big hug. "How've you been?"

My brother looked up at me with sad eyes. He had grown while I was away, but he was still thin.

"Hey, what's wrong?" I asked.

"Didn't you get the telegram," he said with tears in his eyes.

"Telegram? What telegram?"

"We thought you got the telegram . . . Mother's dead."

I stared at Harry in disbelief. "Mother? Dead? That can't be right. She's only fifty-three."

"She killed herself last week." He choked back his grief. "In Florida. She shot herself."

I sat slumped over on the marble bench next to my brother, holding my head—crushed by my sadness.

I knew she was an alcoholic—but suicide? Was this it? Was this why I had been so miserable last week in Lyon pacing the banks of the Rhône in tears? Had I somehow known then?

I thought back to Locust Street, where she had run behind me with my first two-wheeler, pushing me all the way down the block until I did not fall; how she had hung my

118

stuffed deer's head on the front door at Christmas, covered its nose with red sparkles like Rudolph's; the scary Halloween costumes that she wore with her fake mole and missing teeth, out-scaring the scariest of trick-or-treaters who came to our house. This was the woman who gave me my life.

Tears came. Uncontrollable sobs. My body shook.

How could she have done this? How could this have happened? Why didn't she wait for me?

Harry put his arm weakly around my shoulders as I sat stunned, staring into space.

On the ride to my father's, I sat numb, in the back seat, staring out the window, saying nothing.

What am I doing here? Is this really real? I wondered.

"There's a telegram for you from France on the hall table," my father said as we pulled up the long driveway to his new, large one-story house.

Lyon

My dear little Jay,

You have just left this moment . . . we watched you one last time from the platform, and something very cruel squeezed our hearts, because we knew your mother was dead.

On the 26th, when the unhappy telegram was telephoned to us, we decided not to talk to you about it because of how sad you were already feeling. We called Air France to find out if there was a seat available for Saturday, and since there were none, we decided to tell you nothing. You could not have endured the awful news, and you would not have been able to make the long voyage under these conditions.

It was devastating to see you leave knowing that upon returning to the U.S., you would not find your mother waiting for you. Surely, you will feel horribly alone. We wanted to do everything for you, but how can you console a son for the death of his mother? And when you arrive in New York, I will be thinking so much of you, my dear little Jay.

You know you had a large place in our home during the past year and you really were our son.

We wait impatiently to hear from you. What happened to your mother? Was it an automobile accident? Some illness? You never said she was sick.

Your return to America will now be an awful nightmare, as you will regret not having been able to return faster to see your mother again.

You had been so happy with your time spent here in France, and now you will be thrown into the deepest hurt. Several weeks ago you told me you loved your mother, got along well with her. You worried about her. Now you will find nothing there upon your return. Poor dear Jay! How I would like to be next to you to try and bring you a small amount of comfort.

Be courageous, my little Jay.

I embrace you most tenderly from the bottom of a mother's heart.

Madame Mollière

Empty, I stuffed the telegram into my jeans, ran upstairs and locked my bedroom door. I felt terribly alone. I ignored the knocks on the door. I knew it was my father, and I did not want to let him in.

"Jay. Jay!" He pounded. "Open the door!"

Finally, I went to the door and opened it. He sat down awkwardly next to me on the bed. I held myself and slowly rocked back and forth as I tried to choke back my tears. I couldn't understand. How could this have happened?

Without ever touching me, or knowing what to do or what to say, my father tried in his own uncomfortable way to comfort me with his halting words.

Chapter 5

I woke up hung over. The ice bucket with its empty wine bottle was next to the bed, and Bonnie lay sleeping by my side. I could hear Joseph, my teenage houseboy, in the kitchen fixing breakfast. As I lay in the bright Ivorian sunlight that streamed in through the window, I felt the early morning's breeze blow through the room across my chest.

I rolled over and looked at Bonnie asleep on the pillow next to mine. She was young and beautiful, tall and thin, with an almost boyish build. Her hair was fiery red; her soft skin, the color of alabaster. She smelled fresh and clean. I moved closer to her, and her half-asleep eyes opened slowly. They were dark green, hidden beneath reddish-gold lashes.

"Good morning," I said, my nose almost touching hers.

"How are you?"

"Fine." She smiled, and stretched out her long legs and arms touching my naked body.

I lay back and stared into her

electric eyes. *Fantastic!* I thought. How wonderful it was for me to finally have had her last night—something I had longed for for the last six months. Now I was fearful of losing her. I did not want anything to ever go wrong.

I slid my arm behind her. As she arched her back, her small brown nipples came out from beneath the clean white sheet. I pulled her closer and inhaled her delicate perfume from the night before. I kissed her face, her neck and pushed my hips closer to hers. She wrapped her arms around me, and we held each other. As we clasped our hands, Bonnie's long hair drifted across my face. For a moment, I could hear our heartbeats mixing with the cries of the birds nesting in the bushes out back. She was warm and delicate. I put my pillow under her hips and climbed on top of her wonderful body. She entwined her legs around mine.

"You had too much to drink last night," she giggled, and bit my ear lightly.

My mouth went to her almond nipples; my hand found the tuft of red hair between her pale legs. I heard her purr a low moan. Gently, we joined together and began our early morning lovemaking. Slowly, I moved myself in and out as she bent her knees and raised her legs to deepen my penetration. With each thrust, I became more and more awake. As our rhythm grew faster, she held tightly to my back. I used my strength and speed to satisfy her. Above, the mosquito netting circling our naked bodies began to shake.

"I'm going to come," I whispered.

"Wait! No! Wait for me," she panted. "Wait." She raised her pelvis to me, again, harder this time, then harder again. Then suddenly, like an explosion, we both came together. Fulfilled and happy, we fell back on to the pillows and looked at each other with half-opened eyes.

Bonnie began to stir again. Slowly, she rolled herself over and put her feet on the tile floor. She turned to me and said softly, "What a wonderful way to start the day."

I watched her as she slipped into her panties.

"Don't go," I pleaded.

She hooked her bra behind her and pulled her dress on over her head. As she bent over to kiss me good-bye, I ran my hand through her hair.

"I have a four o'clock class this afternoon," she said, still smiling. "I'll see you afterwards, at dinner. Hurry up! You'll be late for your first class. Put some clothes on."

Bonnie went down the hall into the living room.

"Bonjour, Joseph. Ça va?" I heard her say.

I sat up and watched from the window as the students in their khaki uniforms went on their way to their morning classes. Bonnie waved as she rode by on her mobylette. I lay back against the headboard and thought of the months I had spent trying to win her affection. When the alarm clock rang at eight, I pushed the mosquito netting aside, and got out of bed. I stretched, then took the muslin netting and rolled it into a ball and tied it in a knot above the bed.

"Joseph!" I shouted. "Café. My head is splitting. My mouth tastes like wood. Gueule de bois." This was a phrase I had used much too often during this my second and last year of Peace Corps teaching. Hangovers were coming more and more frequently.

We had spent last night dancing with friends at a club called The Bar Climatisé in Bouaké, the country's largest city after Abidjan. The BC's uninspired name came from it being the only air-conditioned bar in town.

"Why the hell did I drink so much?" I scratched my aching head. "Don't I know when to stop?"

I walked slowly down the hall to the bathroom and took two aspirin along with my Aralen pill for malaria. Then I wrapped a towel around my waist and went barefoot into the living room.

"What a fucking mess!"

I sat at the table amongst the wreckage from last night's after-party. Joseph shuffled in with his best effort at French toast. *Pain perdu*, he called it—lost bread—and that's exactly what it looked like.

"Joseph, we've got to get this place cleaned up by five

o'clock. I've invited the missionaries up for lemonade. Don't forget. You have to put all the liquor bottles away. I'll be home at 12 for lunch and a siesta. Do you have enough money for the market?"

Joseph nodded as he shuffled back into the kitchen in his tattered khaki shorts and worn leather sandals.

"And, Joseph, be sure to keep Bonnie's money separate from mine. You know how pissed she gets if we screw it up."

I picked up the *Time* magazine to see how things were going back in the States after the Martin Luther King assassination. I grimaced with my hangover as I choked down the coffee.

First Kennedy, now this. What's going on in America? I thought. *Abbie Hoffman was right—Steal This Book!*

After taking a muddy shower with the water from the cistern, I dressed and gathered up my notebooks. Crossing the dusty road that ran in front of the line of teachers' homes, I wondered how I would get through my morning English courses. Perhaps the French-speaking Ivoirian students would be kind to me today.

"Good morning!" I shouted as I walked into the first classroom.

"Good morning," the 40 little black faces shouted back at me. My brain rattled.

There were five rows of desks, eight deep. All the students were dressed in their uniforms of tan khaki shirts and shorts, and those who could afford shoes wore them. The older students, those who were supposed to be 12, sat in the back. Most of these boys had small beards and were probably 16 or 18. With no birth certificates, it was impossible to know. They were here to stay out of the army.

There were only four girls—three black, one mulatto. They sat huddled together in the back right hand corner. Since birth, they had been told that they were simply stupid livestock, meant only to serve as channels for birth. All wore blue dresses, and wrapped black, waxed thread tightly around small, twirled, clumps of hair. Each looked as though she had a dozen six-inch antennas protruding from her head.

Since the school's English texts had yet to arrive from Abidjan, I was still using the small number of books I had brought with me from Peace Corps training. Today I was going to teach them Frost's *Stopping By Woods on a Snowy Evening.*

I thought, *What the hell do they know about Robert Frost? The only American they've ever heard of is Mohamed Ali. For that matter, what do they know about snow?*

But I was hungover, and they certainly knew something about woods. So, rather than grapple with the wisdom of my lecture, I plunged in for the next four classes.

When the twelve o'clock bell finally rang, I limped home to rest my weary head. Joseph had a light lunch waiting for me on the table in the living room. I ate half the sandwich, savored the dark local beer, then headed for the nap I had been thinking about since morning.

I lay on the bed with the alarm clock on my stomach and watched it move up and down with my breathing. Beads of sweat filled my bellybutton from the stifling heat. The hot African sun was pounding down hard on the metal roof above.

It seemed like only minutes before the alarm was clanging. I struggled to my feet, threw some water on my face, and went off for my afternoon classes.

At five o'clock, I left my classroom and walked back across the hard dirt soccer field to my house. Passing the cistern truck, first I noticed that my banana tree needed a hosing, and then, coming up the road from town, I saw the large, brown cloud of dust. Reverend Ryan and his daughter, Alice, were arriving in their blue Peugeot from their compound down the hill. Joseph stood on the terrace slowly sweeping the remnants of last night's party into the yard.

During my first year in Béoumi, the year before Bonnie came, the missionaries had nursed me back to health from a strep throat infection. As a result, I began to read the Bible and, amazingly enough, stopped drinking. The Bible reading lasted until I finished the book. Sobriety took a nosedive after six months when I went to a Peace Corps party and decided to have a J&B instead of a coke.

"Hello!" I waved as their car stopped in front of my porch. "It's good to see you both again. Here, let me help you with those packages."

Alice climbed out from behind the steering wheel juggling gift boxes and a bowl of fruit. She was a big, redheaded woman, 46 and single. She seemed to be happy working with her father at the mission for the past 20 years. Alice wore one of her large handmade dresses and her usual simple straw hat to protect her fair freckled skin from the strong sun.

"Be careful, Jay," she said. "It's ice cream cake. You're so thin. We have to fatten you up. You don't get that very often in Béoumi! And I know how much you like sweets."

She gave me a bear hug that lasted a bit too long. I stepped back, somewhat embarrassed.

"Let me look at you," she said. "Oh, Jay, you look so old and tired behind that beard."

Reverend Ryan stood straight as a post in his starched white shirt and black trousers. There was always a sparkle in his eye. His thinning white hair was neatly combed back on each side of his head. Still spry after many years of missionary work, he certainly did not look 84. He greeted me with his usual iron handshake and warm smile.

"Good seeing you again, Jay," he said while taking a chair on the patio.

"Alice, sit down," I said. "Please, sit down."

"What's all this mess?" Alice asked as she settled her big frame into one of the armchairs.

"Oh, I had Michel and Rémy over last night for chess and cocktails. I think we drank more than we played. Joseph!" I called. "Bring the lemonade. I'm so stiff from all the volleyball and dancing, I can hardly move, not to mention my head . . . let me slice this cake up and put the rest in the refrigerator before it melts."

As I left for the kitchen, Alice called after me, "Jay, have

you got it working again? And come over here when you're finished. I'll give you a good back rub."

I returned carrying three plates of ice cream cake, put
them on the table, and then sank down on one of the armchairs across from Alice. She got up and walked behind my
seat.

"Here, let me loosen those big shoulders."

"How have you been, Jay?" Reverend Ryan asked.
"We've missed you at our prayer meetings. The children like
you so much. You used to come every Sunday . . . that's until
you started drinking again."

"I think it was that party in Katyola that got me going," I
said to Reverend Ryan somewhat embarrassed. "I guess I just
wanted to fit in with all the other volunteers again."

Alice dug her fingers into my back. I winced.

"And I've been busy. Ever since school started, there's
been one Peace
Corps party after another. Last weekend I was in Bouaké; before that, Yamous-
soukro. And you remember I had that bout with the malaria
last month."

Alice continued to work the muscles free in my shoulders. Her hands were strong, like her father's, from years
spent showing the Ivoirians how to plow, plant and dig. Her
large shadow shielded me from the afternoon sun.

"Here comes Bonnie," I said. "Have you met Bonnie
Sloan? She's the new Peace Corps volunteer." I wiggled out
of Alice's grasp, stood up and waved.
"She's teaching sixiéme this year. She's from California. Sac-
ramento."

As Bonnie came up the front steps, Alice stared at her
short yellow sundress. I took Bonnie by the waist and kissed
her on the cheek. Alice sat down heavily in her armchair and
ate her ice cream cake.

"Bonnie, these are the Ryans I told you about. Alice lit-
erally saved my life last summer. I came down with strep while
the Peace Corps doctor was off somewhere in Kenya chasing

female volunteers up and down Kilimanjaro."

"That's true, Bonnie," Reverend Ryan said. "But don't forget, Jay, you're the one who pulled me out of that whirlpool in the Bandama just three weeks later." He stood and shook Bonnie's hand. "I would have gone under and never come up if Jay hadn't swum out to save me, Bonnie . . . Jay and the good Lord, that is."

Alice's freckled face had a frown on it as she shook Bonnie's hand.

"So you're from California, Bonnie. Are you a Christian?" Alice asked.

"I'm Episcopalian," Bonnie answered.

"No. No. I mean—are you a Christian?"

Bonnie looked puzzled.

"Oh, never mind, Bonnie," Alice said. "It's not important." And she took another large forkful of ice cream cake.

Reverend Ryan finished his lemonade. "Alice, I think it's time for us to be going. We have our six o'clock prayer service. Jay, it was good seeing you again," he said. "Don't be such a stranger at church. And bring Bonnie too. The Lord be with you, Jay. And you too, Bonnie."

We shook hands and I walked them to their old 404 Peugeot. We waved good-bye as they drove down the dusty dirt road back to town.

"That was some hammer lock she had on you," Bonnie teased. "I didn't think she was ever going to let you go."

"When she was nursing me back to health last year, I think she may have gotten a crush on me. But she really did save my life. My butt felt like a pincushion by the time she finished with all of those penicillin shots. Come on, let's have a Scotch. We have to go over our vacation plans for our trip to Jacqueville."

Bonnie watched me pour her drink.

"Whoa, that's enough for me."

I smiled, dropped an ice cube in the glass and handed it to her. I stretched out in the chair next to her with mine.

"Did I tell you I finally found a teaching job in Rhode

Island for next year?"

"No," she said hesitantly.

"It's a private school—St. James. It's near my father's summer house. What's the matter, Bonnie? Don't look so upset."

"I'm just sorry you won't be here with me next year," she said bowing her head.

"Bonnie, I told you that I was only going to spend one more year here. And you know I have to do something next year to keep out of the Army 'til I hit twenty-six. I don't want to fly off to the war in Vietnam after just spending two years in the Peace Corps. I had to find some kind of teaching job or be gobbled up by the draft. But, you already know this. We've talked about it before."

"Yes, I know, but . . . "

"Hey, ho, you guys!" Michel shouted from down the dusty road. "Where's our apéritif?"

We looked up from our Scotches and squinted through the bright sunlight. Wearing a much too tight blue T-shirt and short white shorts, Michel sauntered slowly down the hard-packed dirt road past the line of whitewashed professors' homes. He was short and heavy with a small beard that looked like a chinstrap. His nickname was "Le Gros," as he loved his wife's French cooking too much. And he was also known by his students as the school's most short-tempered French teacher.

Rémy followed along behind carrying my baseball bat over his shoulder. He was just the opposite of Michel—tall, thin, relaxed and athletic. He had a handsome face except for the gap between his two front teeth. He was the amiable Math teacher.

Michel came up the steps onto the patio pounding my baseball into my mitt.

"Well, old man," he said, "That was quite a show you put on last night. I don't think Annick has danced that much since we were married. Joseph . . . eh, Joseph," Michel called. "A Scotch, s'il te plaît. Hey, Jay, look here. Don't you think I've lost some weight?" He embraced his girth and shook his belly. "What do you think?"

I smiled as I scanned his portly frame. "Hardly. By the way . . . Rémy . . . Rémy, whoever won that chess match last night? I can't remember. You or me?"

"Who knows?" Rémy said twirling his finger in his Scotch. "It doesn't matter. I'm still way ahead."

"Why don't you guys join us for dinner?" I offered. "I think Joseph has finally mastered American roast beef."

"Sorry," Michel said. "Annick's cooking dinner, and I'm afraid she'd kill me if I stayed."

"Rémy? How 'bout you? You don't have a wife to boss you around."

"No, I've still got my Math tests to correct. Obviously I never got to them last night. It's tonight or never."

"I know what you mean. I barely got through my classes this morning with my gueule de bois. OK, but you guys are missing a good American meal."

"A good American meal?" Rémy laughed.

"A good American meal?" Michel kidded. "There's no such thing as a good American meal!"

They polished off their drinks and shook hands good-bye.

"Take care of Bonnie," Michel said.

"Ciao!" Rémy said.

And they walked back down the dusty road to their houses.

After dinner, Bonnie and I rode our mobylettes down the hill into town. Along the way, the black silhouettes of young girls swinging freely from the limbs of short scrub trees crisscrossed the road. Their light paneas blew in the evening breeze, leaving some half-naked. When they saw the white people coming, they became excited, shrieked and held on to one another as we passed below. At the river, a small herd of cattle clattered across the wooden bridge guided by three tall, thin men in bright saffron turbans and loose-fitting tangerine robes. They used long withered sticks to prod their cattle beneath the teak trees. These were the Tuareg, the warriors from the North. Their hard, dark bodies glistened in the twilight.

In town, small orange campfires were beginning to burn in front of the mud huts. The flames filled the night air with the thick smell of smoke and cooking meat. Mothers squatted in their fenced yards washing their babies in large porcelain bowls, while the men hung kerosene lamps in trees to light their small wooden stores. We puttered past the gendarmes' station and turned left at the prison into Bonnie's courtyard.

"Why don't you come in?" she asked holding my arm.

I looked at her. Her emerald eyes were electric in the sunset.

"You know why." I smiled. "I'd never make it home." I pressed Bonnie against the porch column and felt her breasts rub against me from beneath her thin white blouse.

"I got no sleep at all last night," I whispered. "And we have to be up early tomorrow. Thank God we're finally on vacation! The white beaches of Jacqueville await. And, besides, I haven't done a fucking thing all week long."

"I don't know about the fucking part." Bonnie laughed.

I squeezed her strong body and kissed her hard.

"Good night," I said, and got on my mobylette.

"Drive carefully, Jay."

With a quick kick, I sputtered the mobylette to a start.

"You know me." I winked. "I always do."

I waved good-bye as I drove out between the gateposts. But instead of going straight back to Le Collège, I went down the side street past the brick houses. I wanted to see the brave workers coming back from their hard day's labor.

The men were coming home now, trudging wearily along the side of the sandy road swinging the machetes they used today to clear their fields. Some of the women carried firewood on their naked shoulders. Others balanced black metal pots or bundles of plantain roots on their heads. Unaware of their swaying bare breasts, they almost danced as they shuffled along in the dirt with their rhythmic motion. Two children lagged behind playing with a small dog on a rope leash.

"Ça va?" the little boy shouted as I motored by. Then he ran behind his mother's skirt to hide from the white man.

I wanted to see the older men. I admired their strength and courage. And at last they came. Covered with open sores, and withered from malaria, dysentery and leprosy, they limped along with their pain and makeshift crutches. Last were the lepers. They let their dirty bandages trail out behind them like streamers in the wind and ignored their open sores. When the elders grew tired, they simply crouched by the roadside like nesting hens and waited for their strength to return. One blind man used a stick to find his way through the twilight. He could not see the white sickle high above the savanna that shined brightly over Béoumi. These were truly the courageous workers. I hoped I had their grit.

I turned the mobylette around and headed back up the hill to school. I thought about my nightcap—Rémy Martin or Johnny Walker Red? I was happy, but I needed a drink.

Once home, I sat on the terrace with my Scotch and watched the moon dance between the clouds.

What am I doing here? I wondered. *And how will it go at St. James when I get back?*

I thought of my younger brother, Harry, back in the States. I had not wanted to leave him behind to fend for himself. But I'd had to free myself once again from my family—the family I did not have—the one that did not exist. I could not stay any longer with my father or the memories of my mother. That night as the 747 had raced down the lonely runway for Africa, the sensation of breaking free from the family that I could no longer tolerate coursed through my body. This time, the wheels lifting off the tarmac at JFK were unlike those at Orly two years earlier—the ones that had carried me back to the States from France and to my mother's death. This was escape, and it was fantastic! The enormous feeling of relief— the feeling of leaving everything far behind—had surged through my body.

"Climb! Climb!" I had shouted as I watched the house lights on Long Island's south shore disappear beneath the night's clouds. This was the opportunity I had wanted—this was the answer—to escape again from my family. "Fly! Fly!"

I looked at my rocks glass. Rivulets of sweat ran down its sides from the African heat. In this quiet evening, high above the school buildings, the silver moon hung pasted in the purple sky.

"Life . . . fuck it!"

I gulped down the rest of my Scotch, threw the ice cubes in the bushes and went to bed.

In the morning, I rushed to meet Bonnie at the Gare de Taxi in town. We had to go to Bouaké to catch the train south to Abidjan, the capital, on the coast.

"Hold on to your hat," I said to Bonnie as I threw our bags on top of the old station wagon. "This is the same driver that went off the road last week. See his cuts? It's amazing Rémy and Michel are still alive. Come on. Hop in. We don't want to miss the train. Here, want some? I brought some wine for the trip." I took a swig and passed the bottle to Bonnie.

"No thanks, it's a little early."

"OK. Suit yourself."

I leaned back and put my arm around her. We left town heading east at a
fast clip, bouncing along the jarring washboard road to Bouaké. Ahead, another brush taxi was coming at us full throttle through a large cloud of red dust.

"Hurry!" the chauffeur yelled. "Lean forward and press your hands against the windshield."

All of us in the front seat pushed hard against the windshield to keep the glass from being shattered by the flying road stones. As soon as the other taxi sped by us heading for Béoumi, our driver shouted "Merci" with a toothless grin. With one hand on the wheel, he turned his head to address the people in the back of the car. "Six cents cinquante CFA, s'il vous plaît." He passed his hat amongst the passengers collecting his fare while doing the best he could to keep the speeding taxi from sliding off the sloping dirt road. At last, arriving at the Bouaké train station, we worked our way out of the crowded cab.

"I never thought we'd make it," Bonnie sighed as she brushed the red road dust from her blouse and slacks. "These pants were black before we left … now they're red."

I noticed again how pretty she was standing tall in the sunlight. I pushed back her straw hat and kissed her, then took her by the hand.

"Come on. We still have four more hours on the train. Can you help me with the bags?"

Women in gaily colored scarves lined the track with babies strapped to their backs. Some had faces and chests heavily marked with tribal scars. Others wore strands of colored thread that dangled from their stretched earlobes as makeshift earrings. They walked beside the train's open windows offering up dubious meats and frothy drinks to the travelers. Clouds of black flies followed their tin trays as each passed by the cabin windows.

"Stay away from that stuff," I cautioned Bonnie. "It's probably laced with guinea worm. Sure you don't want any wine?"

"No, not yet. Here, have half a sandwich."

"No, I'm fine. You go ahead." I took another swallow of the vin ordinaire.

As the train pulled away from the platform, the happy crowd of brown bodies shouted, "Abidjai-oh, abidjai-oh!" to bid us a safe journey. They lifted their hands to wave good-bye and shield the bright yellow sun from their already burnt faces.

Four hours later, Bonnie woke me from my slumber.

"Hi, sleepy head," she said. "I guess the wine knocked you out."

I rubbed my eyes and looked out the window. A light rain was falling on Abidjan.

"Boy, was I beat." I stretched. The train jerked to a stop alongside the red dirt platform. "Let's go. We have to meet Joyce and DJ at the hotel."

We grabbed our stuff and pushed through the throng of scruffy porters. Vendors wore American Goodwill T-shirts and tattered baseball caps that were intended not for them but for the poor in the Côte d'Ivoire. They hawked their cheap sunglasses and flashlight batteries among the large crowd of travelers waiting for their taxis. One cab was going to our hotel, so we climbed on to the last two dusty seats and settled back for our trip through the capital.

The taxi zigzagged in and out of the heavy traffic down the beautiful palm-lined boulevards and raced past the turquoise lagoons up the high bluff to our hotel overlooking the Atlantic. I paid the driver, picked up our suitcases and stared up at the two large sparkling towers that were the Hôtel Ivoire.

Bonnie and I walked through the lofty lobby listening to the click-clack of our shoes on the spotless marble floor. The air conditioning was a decadent luxury that we appreciated on our way to the reception counter. There, we found the dapper concierge. Speaking Parisian French, he quickly checked us in and, with a snap of his fingers, summoned a bellhop to help us with our luggage. The young Ivorian took us to our large room that overlooked the tidal pools and the ocean beaches.

"Look, Bonnie. Down there. See?" I pointed from the balcony at the swimming pool fourteen floors below. "There's DJ and Joyce on the terrace."

"Who's DJ?"

"Didn't I tell you about him? He's the guy who teaches gardening up north."

"What's he like?"

"DJ? He's a good guy. He's just down a lot. He signed up for a third year .... I don't think he wants to go home."

"What do you mean, 'down a lot'?"

"Well . . . he's full of melancholy. For example, when I first got here last year, the school wasn't finished. So, I stayed with him for a month or so up in Ferkessédougou. It was pretty depressing. When he wasn't out teaching gardening, he was usually holed up in his house with a bottle of bourbon reading *The Naked and The Dead* and listening to Leonard Cohen.

Sometimes I'd hear him sobbing on the other side of his bedroom door."

"Oh …. That's too bad. What about Joyce?"

"I know her from college. She's a nurse. They're just friends. They're not together. Come on. Hurry up! Get your suit on. Let's go for a swim."

We found DJ and Joyce sitting in chaise lounges under one of the fifty-foot teak trees not too far from the bar with their drinks. Joyce was taller than Bonnie, about 5' 5", with shoulder-length dirty blonde hair—pretty by Peace Corps standards. DJ was over six feet—thin, with curly blond hair. They looked like brother and sister. DJ slouched in his chair wearing sunglasses. He always seemed to be slouched in a chair somewhere wearing sunglasses—night or day. The glasses made it impossible to see his weary eyes.

"Hi, you two!" I shouted. "Ready for our trip?"

"Ready for our trip?" DJ said from behind his shades. "I've been busting my balls up country for almost three years building gardens. You're damn right I'm ready for our trip. How've you been, Fat Wallet? Still got that beard, eh? It's a Hemingway thing, right?"

"I'm good. Hey, Joyce. How's Katyola?" I asked. "How's the nursing going?"

"Well, they still won't use those damn water filters," she said, fixing her bikini. "To them, they're just status symbols. They won't even take them out of the boxes unless they're having company over. I don't know how they'll ever get rid of their guinea worm?"

"Garçon," I called. "Vodka tonic. A double. Bonnie?"

"Make mine a martini. Let's celebrate! Finally we're on vacation."

"Don't take too long," DJ said as he got up. "I made reservations at the *Queen Mary* down at the port. It's got the best food in town, and a harbor view with outdoor dancing. I got a table out on the fantail. We'll have a blast tonight. Hey, Jay. Do you smoke? I haven't just been growing tomatoes, you know."

"I can't figure you guys out, DJ. What's wrong with just Scotch? You put on your spooky music, *Nights In White Satin*, or something else, light your candles and incense and then risk getting busted just to get stoned. I'll stick to the booze. It's so easy. You just walk into a liquor store and say 'Give me a bottle of J&B.' What could be simpler?"

"OK. Suit yourself. All the more for me then." DJ smiled. "How's the teaching going?"

"Not bad. I've been trying to teach the kids to sing *Hoist Up The John-B Sail*. They're going to sing it at graduation. They like it better than *Stopping By Woods On A Snowy Evening*. They don't even know what snow is. I hope they'll be ready by graduation. We only have four more weeks."

"Hey, it's getting late," Joyce said. "We better get going. We'll see you two at eight. And don't be late."

As they walked away, I turned to Bonnie. "That DJ's a pisser. He's always stoned, or drunk, or both. I'm amazed he's made it through his three year stint."

"Speak for yourself, there, 'Fat Wallet.' You might want to think about slowing down on the hard stuff yourself. Sometimes you overdo it, Jay."

"Oh, yeah? Look who's talking." I pointed to her martini. "Hey, you look great in that suit. Come on. Let's go for a swim."

At 8:30, our taxi pulled up in front of the *Queen Mary*. We walked up the gangplank and found Joyce and DJ at a table in the back of the ship overlooking the docks. DJ had obviously arrived somewhat stoned and was now somewhat drunk. Joyce looked great in her white halter-top, short pink skirt and long brown legs.

"Hello, again. Sorry we're late. We kind of had a tough time getting out of the room after our swim," Bonnie said with a wink.

"What's for dinner?" I tossed opened the menu. "I'm starved!"

"Try the Scotch," DJ slurred. "It's delicious."

A young woman with dark skin and jet-black hair

leaned over our table. "Have you decided yet?" she asked. "If not, I recommend the Peking duck." Her eyes were a blend of a deep green and dark brown. Her ancestry mixed. She was a gorgeous Eurasian.

"Sure, let's do it," I said.

So, we all ordered duck—except for DJ, who passed on the food.

"A bird can't fly on one wing," he said to the waitress. He rattled the ice in his glass in her direction. "I'll have another. Hey, did you guys hear? James Brown is coming over for a concert. You wanna go?"

He used his knife and fork as drumsticks on the tablecloth to tap out the beat.

"I feel gooooood!" he wailed. "Bahda, bahda, bah. What d'ya say? It should be a blast!" He knocked over his Scotch glass. "Whoopsie."

"Sure. Why not?" I said. "Here, I'll get that." I used my napkin to mop up his mess.

Joyce looked at DJ and then at me. It was clear my friend would soon end up under the table. Bonnie put down her fork and placed her napkin on the table.

"Jay, why don't I take DJ back to the hotel?" she said. "I don't feel so well after the train ride. I think it might be the malaria again."

"I'm fine," DJ mumbled looking up from his lap. "A bird has to have a tail to . . .."

"Oh no," Joyce said. "That's not fair, Bonnie. I'll go."

"No. Really . . . I'm not feeling very well."

"You sure, Bonnie?" I asked. "We just got here."

"Yes. I think it's the malaria. Please stay. Enjoy yourselves."

"OK," I said. "Let's get him home. Come on, D.J. Up we go."

After we loaded DJ's limp body into the back seat of a cab, I kissed Bonnie good night.

"I won't be late," I told her. "I promise."

"Don't be silly. I'll be all right. Have fun."

Joyce and I watched the car pull away, and then walked back up the gangplank to our dinners and the music. As Procol Harum lamented over the sixteen vestal virgins, we danced amongst the couples on the crowded fantail and watched the running lights of cruise ships as they passed by. Joyce circled her arms around my neck and pulled me to her. I felt the perspiration on her cheek and smelled the vodka on her breath. As the band switched gears to the Stones, she pushed herself away from me.

"I can't get no… sss … sss … satisfaction," she howled, wagging her index finger above her head at the blackened sky as she strutted across the deck.

She put one hand on her hip, pouted, and mimicked Jagger pushing an imaginary top hat over her eyes. When I took her by the waist and pulled her to me, her heady perfume swirled about me in the steamy night's air. From overheard, the lantern light reflected in her dark blue eyes each time she tilted back her head and laughed.

"Hey, I know a place not too far from here where we can go skinny dipping." She giggled. "The night fisherman won't mind. And we can use the torchlight from their boats to see. What'd ya say? You game?"

"Game? Are you kidding! Sure I'm game. Let's go!" I drained my cognac and paid the bill.

Joyce took me by my hand and led me down the gangplank past the road to a narrow strip of beach. Further along, on the other side of the palmettos, a small half-moon of shore circled the inky lagoon. Not far out on the water were men with torches spear fishing from their dugout canoes. We piled our clothes on the soft, white sand, slipped quietly into the warm sea and swam together from the shore.

I watched her as she dove below the surface, then chased after her beneath the waves. The torches burning from the bows of the small pirogues above illuminated her glistening form. Shimmering flames caused by the freighter oil that covered her long, lean body leapt from her naked silhouette out into the underwater darkness. Shining sparks stretched out behind her like a comet's tail through a bright galaxy of blue phosphorescent light. Down through the dark, clear water, I followed the iridescent trail of silver bubbles. They swirled, and swirled . . . then, dying behind her, dissolved into the ocean's blackness.

I fought through the clouds of pearls that followed her, and pulled her from this maelstrom of tiny, whirling balls. We exploded up to the water's surface, filled with laughter and gasping for air. Her blonde hair was wetted back away from her face; her lapis eyes flashed in the yellow glow of torchlight. We swam together in the night until the dugouts began to gradually return to the shore.

"It's getting late," Joyce said. "We better get back."

I swam after her, back to the beach, and as she ran up onto the shore through the moonlight, I lunged for her ankle and pulled her down onto the sand.

"Hey! Jay! Let me go. Jay!" She tried to push me away. "You're drunk. Stop it!"

I climbed on top of her and tried to force her legs apart. She began to kick and slap. I used my force to hold her wrists.

"What's the matter? Hold still," I said. "You liked it in Katyola, didn't you? Remember last September? Stop kicking me, damn it!"

"Jay, stop it. You're hurting me. Stop it!" she yelled. "You've got Bonnie now."

Joyce freed one hand and hit me hard in the face, then jumped up and ran to her clothes and on towards the road. I sat alone on the sand.

Why do I do this? I wondered. *The evening had been so good, and I had to ruin it.*

I searched for my shirt, then finally found my shoes scattered about in the bushes. My belt had disappeared. I struggled with my pants, falling backwards onto the soft sand each time I tried to put them on.

Out in the harbor, the *Queen Mary* glowed brightly.

"Time for another drink."

I walked off towards the bar.

The next morning, Bonnie, Joyce, DJ and I left the hotel after a quiet breakfast to board the bus that would take us to our seaside resort. The day was sunny, but none of our four-some was feeling well. While DJ and Bonnie put their things on the roof, I walked to Joyce and put my hand on her arm. She stiffened and pulled away quickly.

"Look. Joyce. I'm sorry for what happened last night," I said. "I had a little too much to drink, all right?"

She turned, got on the bus and took a seat in the back by the window. I climbed on board behind Bonnie and used her shoulder as a pillow as we waited for our trip to begin.

An hour later, we pulled into Jacqueville, once an old slave-trading port on the coast that was now a holiday resort. Bonnie and I carried our bags to our small, grass-roofed hut. Beside the door was a rusted English cannon covered with rotting leg shackles. A hammock that stretched between two palm trees framed the blue Atlantic. Joyce and DJ went further down the beach to their cabin, a larger one, with an amber sun-face painted across the front wall. This had been a totem for the tribe who lived there years ago.

After unpacking, we all met at the outdoor café for drinks. The four of us sat in the shade while the delicate branches rustled and swayed with the breeze above. From on high, the warm spring sun flashed down between the long green palms and splashed across the flagstone terrace. Out over the ocean, pelicans soared, circled, and then plunged like stones into the sea to catch their prey.

"Not bad for a gardener, eh?" DJ said sipping his beer. "I've thought about coming here all year long. It's about time my spade and hoe work paid off."

A loud clash of shrieks and laughter came from down the beach. With a rush, ten or twelve slender, naked black bodies darted out from one of the old slave houses and spilled cheerfully onto the sand. Some of the native children ran back and forth between the bilious surf and the safety of the shore like excited puppies. Others played with shells that they used for shovels to make their sandcastles and forts. As they thrashed about yelling and screaming above the pounding waves, their mothers came onto the beach, bare-topped, wearing their withered breasts like medals from past wars both won and lost.

"Just think," Joyce said. "Only one out of ten of them will make it to eighteen."

"That's a happy thought," I said. I finished my Scotch. "Hey, DJ, let's get our trunks and go for a swim before dinner. We can take our drinks down to the beach. Come on! Grab your mug. Let's go!"

We changed quickly, and carried a fresh round of drinks down to the ocean's edge. Hugh waves were rolling high and hard onto the beach, fifteen, sometimes twenty feet tall. DJ threw the Frisbee at me.

"Come on Fat Wallet, let's go!"

He jumped into the surf and swam out past the breakers. I put my glass by my towel and dove into the frothy after him. But the water caught me by surprise. As it swelled, the power of the wave sucked me high up into its crest, and then dashed me down hard into the shallow water skinning my nose on the sandy bottom. I came up smiling and bloody, and waved to the girls. They were sitting together talking, not watching our antics.

We finished our swim, toweled off and went up to the cottages to change. Joyce and Bonnie were waiting for us on the verandah when we got back to the restaurant. We ordered our wine and seafood dinner, then watched the orange sun mix its colors on the ocean's surface. Gradually, the shiny golden caps left the summits of the emerald rollers. Seagulls rode the lulls and swells that were now covered by shredded purple blankets. We ate in silence, staring out at nature's wonderment.

When dinner was finished, Bonnie said to me, "Come, Jay. I want to walk the beach. Let's go down to the jetty."

"OK. Joyce, DJ, behave yourselves," I kidded.

We walked quietly beneath the massive curved trunks of the palm trees that leaned out from the shore towards the sea. Ahead, a group of old men sat cross-legged in their colorful robes. They were speaking slowly in Djoula, telling stories of the past. One man, perhaps the chief, with ebony skin and a white beard, used a well-polished cane to illustrate his tale by drawing pictures in the soft sand. We nodded as we passed by, and soon reached the rocks of the jetty. The wind was blowing harder now. When Bonnie turned, I saw the tears in her eyes.

"Jay, Joyce told me what you did last night. Why?"

I looked down at the sand. "I don't know . . .. It just . . . it just sort of happened. I had too much to drink, Bonnie. I'm sorry. I really am."

"I'm not staying with you tonight, Jay." She turned and walked back towards our room.

I sat alone on the sand.

Why do I do this? My life's so good. And this isn't the first time I've hurt someone I care abot with sex and booze.

I felt hollow inside, awful about what I had done, breaking the trust that Bonnie had shown me.

Why do I wreck something that's so good? Something I want so badly?

The wind grew stronger. I stood up and shivered. Wandering slowly back down the yellow beach to the outdoor café, I felt the wet sand squish between my toes, and gazed with indifference at the crabs that scampered up and down the bank along the shoreline.

When I found DJ sitting on a stool under the colored lights talking to the bartender, I pulled up a seat and put my arm across his shoulders.

"Wow, what's up?" he said behind his black shades. "You look like shit. Where's Bonnie?"

"Oh. We had a fight. You know? I always fuck things up."

"Yeah, me too. Don't worry about it. Have a drink. I'll buy."

The bartender poured two Scotches and slid a dish of peanuts our way.

"So, what are you going to do when you go home?" DJ asked.

"Me? When I go home, I'm finishing up teaching my students to sing the Sloop John B. for graduation. Then, hey, just like the 5th Dimension—it's *Up, Up And Away*! That's going to be the theme song for my going away party—*Up, Up And Away*! I'm going to play it over, and over and over again. I'm going to throw the biggest damn party Béoumi's ever seen. I mean *big*, DJ! Joseph's covering all the walls with palm fronds. The house is going to look like a goddamn beachside resort by the time he's finished. He might even put sand all over the floors. It'll be the farewell party to end all farewell parties." I took a handful of peanuts. "Out front, Rémy and Michel are going to help me dig a huge trench for the furniture. We're going to have the biggest damn bonfire Béoumi's ever seen. I'm burning everything! It's gonna look like Dante's Inferno. Everything goes! Desks, chairs, tables. I'm tellin' you, DJ, the damn flames are going to reach the sky that night! I've invited the Sous-Préfet. If I keep him plied with bourbon, there won't be any trouble from his gendarmes. Tons of guests . . . tons of friends. I'm inviting everyone. You're coming, right?"

"No. Jay . . . I mean, what are you going to do when you go home? You know—back to the States?"

I stared at DJ.

"Home?"

I reached for my empty drink. I didn't want to think about going home. I looked out at the soft drops as they started to fall from the overcast sky. The rainy season was beginning. I rattled the ice cubes in my rocks glass at the bartender.

"Scotch."

Chapter 6

Saint James

Framed in in the windshield of "The Blue Bird of Happiness," my new, blue '68 Le Mans—a gift from Sally, my father's third wife—the empty school sat sparkling on an expanse of green overlooking a strip of sandy beach and the Atlantic's bilious surf.

I pulled in between the pineapple-topped stone columns and drove up the tree-lined entrance past the tennis courts. From behind the main building, lofty Gothic spires of the distant Saint James chapel poked through the tops of towering elms. Ahead, Coach Walter Thompson waited for me on the lawn in front of the dormitory where I would live for the next nine months.

"Hi, Jay!" he bellowed, waving a strong forearm in my direction. "Welcome to St. James."

Thompson stood posed on the grass like a state trooper with his belt strapped beneath his large stomach and his legs spread far apart. His eyes hid behind the dark green lenses of aviator sunglasses.

"Sorry I'm late. I missed the ferry from Jamestown."

"Never mind. Grab your gear and come on in. We've got a lot of work to do. Wait 'til you see the new offense I've come up with for this year. I call it 'Victory '68'! It's unstoppable!"

Coach led me through the patio to the living room where football diagrams covered a large coffee table and most of the floor.

"So you played on the undefeated Dunbarton team, eh?" He slapped me on the back. "Undefeated teams don't come along that often."

"We had a great team. The line averaged 210 and the backfield 180. At 172, I was one of the smallest."

"Marge, can you bring us two beers?" he called.

"I still carry the football charm that we got at the sports banquet with W - 7 L - 0 cut into it."

"Look at this," Thompson said, no longer paying attention. "You see? This year I'm splitting the tackle and the guard. The defense will never be able to figure out the damn formation! Oh, Jay, this is my wife Marge."

Mrs. Thompson came into the living room carrying a tray with beer, a cheese dip and chips. Much smaller than her husband, about 5'1", she was wearing an apron and had her black hair pulled back in a bun.

"Hi, Jay. Walter's told me all about your '61 team at Dunbarton. He hopes our '68 season will be just as good. Has he shown you his new idea?" She put the tray on the table. "Now, if you boys need anything, just holler."

"Here, Jay, look at these."

He handed me a pile of plays and swigged his beer.

The new formation left a gaping hole in the front line next to the guard that led straight to the quarterback. I had to catch myself from laughing. I thought, *After the first three defeats, I'm sure he'll pull the line back together again; that's if the quarterback's still alive.*

"It's certainly different," I said.

"Now, during each game, I want you to get up in the tower and take Polaroids of the offense and the defense. We'll analyze them on the field and in the locker room at halftime. Then we'll make our corrections. Those Saint James Bulldogs should roll over every team we play. Oh, shit." He banged his bottle down. "I nearly forgot. The phone guy's upstairs waiting for you. Here's your key. You better get goin'." He gave my hand a hard squeeze. "I'll meet you at the Fieldhouse tomorrow—eight sharp! Wear your cleats and, here, bring this whistle."

I dragged my bags up the two flights of dorm stairs to my master's suite where the phone man was squatting outside my door.

"Hi, I'm sorry to keep you waiting. The coach just told me you were here." I fumbled with my key. "Come in."

When I opened the door, I found a small living room with a desk and several chairs adjoining a tiny bedroom that had a stove. There was a small bathroom and a small clothes closet. And in each of the three rooms, there were little dormer windows.

"Where do you want the phone?" he asked wiping his forehead.

"Oh, over there on the desk I guess. I'm just going to hang up my things. Are you from Castle Hill?"

"No, Middletown. Say, how come they let students have phones."

"Oh, they don't." I blushed. "I'm a teacher . . . a French teacher. I guess I look young for my age."

At dusk, I went down the hill to the tumbledown yachting town of Castle Hill for dinner. While driving, day or night, I always wore my sunglasses, the ones with the blue lenses. They turned the blue interior in the Pontiac to an even stronger blue. I felt warm and comfortable inside my "Blue Bird of Happiness." Lennon screamed out the lyrics of "Revolution" on the radio. Life was good.

At the narrow alleyway, I turned off Main Street and

parked on the short pier in front of a small dingy restaurant called the White Shark. There were only four tables in the tiny candlelit dining room. In the far corner was a little stage with a microphone. A parrot's cage hung above it next to a spotlight. Benches lined the walls, and an old potbelly stove separated a row of dirty frame windows. The tables were full, so I sat on one of the stools at the old wooden bar, ordered a Scotch and began to thumb through the St. James catalog.

"Hi, I'm Fraser Himes," the young man sitting next to me said. "I teach chemistry at St. James. You must be the new French teacher."

I looked over and saw a short, unassuming fellow with wavy, blond hair. As he lifted his beer, I could see the strength in his arms.

"Oh, hi. Jay Walker. Yes, I'll be teaching French this year. It's only for a year."

Fraser laughed a funny little laugh. "Yeah, I heard someone was coming in to take Croaky's spot for the year he's in France. His real name's Furgeson." He clinked my glass, then shook his empty bottle at the woman behind the bar. "Well, good luck!"

"Yeah, it's only 'til June. After that, I'll be too old for draft bait, and I'll go to New York to work for my dad."

"Not bad," Fraser chuckled.

"Say, how do you like it?" I asked. "I mean teaching at St. James and all?".

"It's OK. I've got a drunken Limey for a department head. Thornton keeps his whiskey bottles stashed out in the observatory behind the telescope. He leaves me pretty much alone. Aside from teaching chemistry, I also coach the wrestling team."

"I'm helping Thompson with varsity football this fall."

"Double 'good luck.' He hasn't had a winning season in six years. Each year he comes up with some new idiotic offense. I'm surprised they still give him the job."

"Wait 'til you see his plan this year," I laughed. "It's definitely unique."

"I bet. You'll get a kick out of your department—Gerald Rutherford and Richard Thiselton. Gerald and his wife fancy themselves as French bohemians. I think it's a carryover from their years in Paris. They throw these kinky parties with jazz and incense. He plays the bongos and likes to swap wives. Richard . . .. Don't let him get you alone in the dark! He's queer."

"Queer?"

"Yeah. He even speaks *French* with a lisp. Another Scotch?"

We ordered dinner and more drinks and listened to the guitar player strum sea shanties to his parrot Shipwreck. As we ate, Fraser pointed out the girls who were returning for their undergraduate classes at the two local colleges.

"Byerly's an artsy-craftsy liberal arts school for the rich and stupid. They say it's Castle Hill's answer to The Rhode Island School of Design with dollar signs. They're mostly crazy artists who love to screw. Saint Mary's of Victory is just the opposite. See? Over there by the parrot. It's a strict nursing school for Catholic girls. We call it 'SMV'—'Save My Vagina.' They're the ones sitting with their blazers tightly buttoned and knees glued together. Boy, are they stiff! And one other thing."

"What's that?"

"Be careful of the sailors. Last year, I had too much to drink one night and they got me in an alley and used me for a punching bag. I looked like a raccoon for two weeks before the swelling went away."

"Gotcha. I suck at fighting. That's why I thought it would be better to teach than to go to 'Nam."

After dinner and too many drinks, we stumbled out of the restaurant into our cars and drove up the hill to St. James. As I locked my apartment door, I remembered I had to meet the coach and the team at the Fieldhouse at eight, so I set the alarm for seven. When I lay on my bed, the ceiling began to slowly turn, then faster and faster until I put my foot on the floor.

The next morning, my head was splitting. I barely had

time to throw on some clothes, take two aspirin and get to the gym on time. From the back of the reeking locker room, I saw Coach introducing the team to Bob Springer, an alumnus who was now playing pro ball for New England. When Bob smiled, the muscles in his cheeks rippled.

"I'll never forget my days playing here at St. James," he told the boys. "It not only helped me win a scholarship to BU, but it started me on my path to the pros."

One of the seniors in the last row whispered to a friend, "He forgot to mention the team was two and six his senior year." They both chuckled. "He's lucky he survived the season to graduate!"

I struggled through practice with my hangover, Thompson's offense looked even more idiotic. After a cold shower, I dragged myself back to my room, took more aspirin and began to organize my lesson plans for the coming week. I wanted my French classes to be fun and interesting, like Gallard's had been at Dunbarton. If they weren't, I knew I would never hold the attention of my students. I planned to intersperse some of the French rock 'n' roll from the 45s I had brought back from France with the audio lessons I would give my students in the language lab. The heavy breathing of Jane Birkin's "*Je t'aime . . . Moi non plus*" pumping through their headsets would surly keep the boys from slumbering in their cubicles.

With a knock on the door, Fraser Hines poked his head in. "What's up?" he asked.

"Not much. Just working on my lesson plans. I'm trying to make them interesting for the kids."

"Hey, what ya listening to?"

"Blood, Sweat and Tears. Spinning Wheel."

"One of my favorites, Spinning Wheel. You know, Jay, it ain't easy to keep the kids interested — believe me. Some are spoiled. Others stupid, or they just don't give a damn. The rest usually give it their best shot . . . but I like it, even though the pay sucks. And the wrestling too. Most of them are pretty good kids."

"That's kind of how I was at Dunbarton. A lousy student, but I really tried hard. I used sports to make up for my grades. Say, I'm off to Sandy Point this weekend. My folks said I could use their summerhouse while they're away. Want to come? Mopsy's having one of her girlfriends up from New York. It could be fun."

"Who's Mopsy?"

"Mopsy? She's my stepsister. She's a riot. And she's going to bring her friend Kelsey. Kelsey's related to the Buckleys. You know, the *rich* Buckleys! She's a wild one. It should be a blast. What do you say?"

"Sure. What time do we leave?"

"Let's leave at eleven. We can take 'The Blue Bird of Happiness,' and just make the ferry to Jamestown."

"'The Blue Bird of Happiness?' Get real."

"It *is* the 'Blue Bird of Happiness.' Just you wait 'til you see how she flies."

On Saturday, the sixty-mile drive to Sandy Point took less than an hour. As we turned up the gravel drive of Quail Run, a large, gray-shingled house, we saw Mopsy and Kelsey playing croquette on the side lawn. My stepsister stood head down concentrating on her ball with a cigarette held tightly in the corner of her mouth and a Budweiser next to her bare feet. She wore her usual white Lacoste sport shirt and khaki culottes. Her short brown-black hair spilled over her dark brown eyes. She squeezed the croquet handle with her knobby knees.

"Hit the damn thing!" Kelsey shouted. "It's not Wimbledon for God's sake. Go ahead and hit it!"

Kelsey was about 5'9" with long, dirty-blonde hair. She wore a pink T-shirt over her braless breasts. Below her naked midriff, a red madras skirt wrapped around her narrow hips and covered little of her long legs. On the grass, between her sandals, were a Bloody Mary and a large bag of pretzels.

"That's tennis, stupid," Mopsy replied. "Wimbledon's tennis. Now, let me shoot, will you?"

When I honked the horn and waved, she swung and

missed her ball.

"Goddamnit!" She shook her mallet at me. "Where the hell have you been? You're supposed to have been here two hours ago. Did you bring the beer?"

We pushed through the garden gate.

"Mops, this is my friend, Fraser Himes." He smiled. "Hi, Kelsey. Long time, no see. We forgot the beer. I'll run into town—Schnider's, right? Do we still have the charge?"

"Sure. And pick up some steaks for dinner, and some cigarettes—Camels," Mopsy said. "But get a move on it or you'll miss cocktails."

On our way back from our errands, Fraser said, "So what kind of a girl is Kelsey anyway? She looks pretty hot to me."

"Well, I guess you could say she's hot . . . but some-times she can be a little too hot. She's a little on the nutsy side. Her family's got tons of dough, but she was caught shop-lifting in Bloomingdale's last month. I think she does it for the thrill of it. Her dad's always able to get rid of the jail time. But she can also be a hell of a lot of fun—we'll find out soon enough."

We pulled up the pebbled drive, put the stuff in the kitchen and then sat by the pool drinking and watching the girls swim laps in their bikinis.

Fraser talked about his summer of sailing and the Ber-muda races. He told of the parties in Hamilton, and how he had served as crew to bring one of the racing yachts back to Castle Hill. I teased the girls with my stories of life in the Peace Corps compared to their jobs in New York. For the past seven years, Mopsy had worked as an editor at *Time*. Kelsey lived off her family's money. She kept a part-time waitress job while she tried to get her acting and modeling careers going.

"Look, why don't we skip the steaks?" I said as I pol-ished off my Bloody Mary. "There's a band at the Tavern to-night and they've got good food. Let's go dancing instead. What do you say?"

"I'm always up for dancing," Kelsey said. "Mops? How

'bout you?"

"Sure, why not? I'll dance around the bar. My knobby knees should last at least for one night."

"Fraser? What do you say?"

"Yeah! Sure." His blue eyes sparkled. "Sure, let's do it."

"If we're going to go, we better go soon," I said. "The place gets jammed early, and they don't take reservations. Let's take two cars, Mops. That way we can always split up later if we want."

"That's my bro' Jay." Mopsy winked at Kelsey. "He's always thinking ahead, and he's always keeping his options open."

"Well," Kelsey said with a wry smile, "that works for me."

When we got to the Tavern, it was packed. We pushed our way past the bar to a table by the dance floor, and grabbed a waitress to order our dinner and some French wine. After putting our order in, she came back with our Côtes-du-Rhone and poured it all around. Mops lit another cigarette and quickly poured herself a second wine, then continued her reminiscence of Floyd, her fiancé, who had been killed last year in Vietnam.

"He really liked to come here," she said taking a long drag on her cigarette. "What a fucking loss. Poor bastard was so good looking. They said he never knew what hit him. Goddamn landmine." She took another strong drag. "I hate those Viet Cong sons of bitches!"

"Mops, you're right," Kelsey said. "I really liked Floyd. His laugh was infectious. And he had that special twinkle in his eye."

We went from dinner to dessert and then champagne, before walking outside into the cool Rhode Island evening. The brisk night air carried the mist up from the Atlantic.

"Let's go to the yacht club for a nightcap," Mopsy said. "I haven't pissed off old Scotty in weeks. Come on, Fraser, you can ride with me. Kelsey, you go with Jay."

Our two cars slowly snaked their way in tandem

through the empty streets to the small, inky harbor of the sleepy village. As we parked in front of the old weathered building, Scotty's silhouette appeared under the yellow light locking up the rickety front gate.

"Whoa! Hold on a minute, Scotty!" Mopsy yelled. "Open up. We're not done yet."

"Miss Dryson?" He squinted into the darkness. "If that's you, I'd better be gettin' my shillelagh."

"Scotty, please. Let us in. We need a drink," Mops begged. "We'll be good tonight. I promise."

"Now that's a likely story. But OK. Just one. Come in."

The four of us followed Scotty's small frame up the rickety stairs to the second-floor bar. We carried our drinks out onto the porch and sat watching the sailboats bob up and down at their moorings on the black water.

"So, Miss Dryson, what shenanigans have you been up to since I last saw you?" Scotty asked as he re-filled her Scotch.

"Nothing much. Tennis and work mostly," she said. "You know, Scotty, that new tennis pro's a real jerk. He won't let me on the courts barefoot anymore. What a pain in the ass! I've been playing barefoot ever since I was a kid." Mopsy looked sad behind her drink. "We were talking about Floyd."

"Ah, Floyd," Scotty said. "Now there was a good lad. What a pity. Only twenty-five, was he?"

Mopsy suddenly got up. "I'll see you all at home," she said as she went down the stairs. "Thanks, Scotty."

As Scotty cleaned up her drink and cigarette, he said, "You know, she's never been quite the same since Floyd died."

"You're right. The spark's gone out," I said. "Well, we better not leave her alone. Let's go. Here, let me sign our chits, Scotty. Thanks. Good night."

Kelsey, Fraser and I climbed back down the wobbly steps that led to the parking lot, and drove up the hill to Quail Run. We put the car in the garage and walked across the pebbled driveway to the rear gate. Mopsy was sitting on the cement curtain of the pool with her beer and cigarette, dangling her legs in the water and watching the steam rise into the night's sky.

"Good night, Mops," I said as I pushed open the front door.

She didn't answer. She just kept staring into the underwater lights.

I walked inside and climbed in bed thinking about my stepsister mourning Floyd's death. I closed my eyes and thought back to how I had felt getting off the plane at JFK and learning of my mother's death—that awful hollow pit in the middle of my gut that would not go away.

"Jay. Jay! Wake up."

I looked at the clock. It said 2:30.

"Let's go down to the beach." It was Kelsey wearing her T-shirt and torn jeans. "Come on, sleepyhead." She shook my shoulder. "It's a full moon. I feel like skinny dipping."

"OK. OK. Hold on a minute, will ya?"

I struggled out of bed and pulled on my pants and shirt. I found Kelsey waiting in the front seat of the Pontiac with two beers and her cigarettes.

"Let's drive up to the bluff at the golf club. It should be beautiful tonight," I said. "We can walk down to the beach from there."

As the village slept, we drove through the deserted hamlet past the old merry-go-round and the lighthouse to the bluff on East Beach. At the Club, I found the narrow path the golf carts used and pushed The Blue Bird up the hill to the edge of the cliff. Out on the ocean, the sea had turned into a bright silver tray.

"Here," said Kelsey handing me a beer. "I'll race you to the water."

She jumped out of the car, pulling off her top as she ran down the sandy slope. When she got to the shore, she slipped out of her jeans and waded out into the surf. I put my clothes on the beach next to my beer and followed her out through the gentle waves. I caught her in the breakers and pulled her to me by her waist. When I pressed her tight against me, her soft wet skin cut the sea's chill against my chest

"What a night, eh?" I asked.

Salt water ran off her face and the moon glowed in her eyes. She splashed me, then dove under a wave and ran back up onto the shore.

"Come on, slow poke," she cried. "See if you can catch me."

I chased her nude body as she ran along the beach. Her skin glistened in the full moonlight, still moist from the sea-water. Just as she started to climb the dune, I grabbed her and pulled her down. As she fell, she began to laugh. We rolled and rolled to the bottom of the hill tangled in each other's arms and legs. I kissed her hard as I ran my fingers through her wet hair.

"Hi there," Kelsey smiled. She kissed me back hard on the mouth as she stared in to my eyes.

I pushed her on to her stomach and entered her from behind. Pulling out, I put my prick between her cheeks, stroked her several times, and then put it in again. My thumb used her juices to lubricate her asshole. Kelsey rose up, offering me her hole. I placed my tip in her ass and slowly started to work my way inside. Kelsey reached behind her and spread her cheeks, then took my cock, moved it up and down in her crack. I found her shoulder beneath her golden hair, and bit down lightly. My fingers wound through her long curls. She rolled onto her milky bare back and had me again, lifting her knees high alongside my ribs, rocking with my rhythm. Our pace grew faster. She pulled herself up to me and held my shoulders tightly. When she reached her climax, she let out a shrill cry and threw her legs further apart. I plunged into her again and again until finally I burst up into her.

We collapsed in the moonlight and lay still until the cool night wind began its chill. Our lovemaking finished, we walked to the water's edge holding hands to find our clothes. We dressed and kissed, then followed the sandy path back up through the brambles to the ninth hole and The Blue Bird of

Happiness.

The next morning, as the four of us sat outside under the umbrella by the pool, Mopsy looked up from her breakfast plate. "You know what?" she said, "It's such a beautiful day, I feel like going down to the Beach Club? What do you say? Do you guys want to go?"

I looked at Kelsey and she gave me a coy nod.

"Sure, Mops. Great idea," I said. "They've got the lobster on Sundays at the buffet, don't they? Fraser, you game? We've got time, right?"

"Sure," he smiled. "Let's do it. What's wrong with lobster?"

From down the drive the familiar melody of blaring air horns rang out. Steve Summers' vintage Mercedes made its way up towards the carport. He was the Eastern rep for Drambuie, and his horns were tuned to play their corporate jingle. I walked out through the back gate to greet him. Always the proper Englishman, Steve was in his mid-seventies and usually wore a white suit and hat to match his white moustache— he looked like Colonel Sanders without the black bow tie. I found him polishing the bugs off his front license plate. It proudly read "NECTAR." He tipped his hat as I approached. I liked Steve because he never acted his age.

"Hi, Jay. I was wondering if your folks are up this weekend," he asked. "I've brought them a case of Drambuie. After last week's party, they're probably out by now."

"No, Steve, they're not. Here, let me take that. I think they're off to Block Island this weekend, or maybe Fisher's. You never know. I just hope Dad does better on the crossing this time. The last time out, he got so polluted Sally nearly killed him. We're going to the Beach Club for lunch. Do you want to come along?"

"No, you kids go ahead. I've already had my morning constitutional along the water. Half a mile out and half a mile back. Have fun! Oh, and Jay, don't forget to tell your dad about the Drambuie."

"I won't. Don't worry."

As I put the large carton in the garage, Steve drove down the driveway with his air horns blasting.

"That guy's really great," I said to Fraser. "Even a his age, he can really throw a frisbee. OK. Let's get the girls and get going."

The Beach Club was bustling with activity. There was hardly a parking spot in the crowded lot.

"Come on, girls. Fraser and I have to be at school by six. There's a General Assembly with the students, then a faculty meeting. Let's get some food and go for a swim. Mops, show them the buffet. I'll get the drinks. And get me some lobster."

The four of us sat together around one of the large wooden tables on the outdoors deck enjoying the sun and champagne. We were by far the youngest among the Pucci/Gucci crowd, and without a doubt the loudest. We finished our brunch and then our swim. The girls returned to Quail Run to straighten up the house and pack while Fraser and I threw the football on the beach.

"God, that Kelsey is really something," Fraser said. "Beautiful, but wacko. She came into my room last night and scared the hell out of me. She said she wanted to take a drive out to the bluff by the golf club for a swim. I told her 'Sorry, I don't have any wheels.'"

"What? No shit! Well guess what . . . she woke me up too," I said with a laugh. "We didn't get back from the beach 'til three. No wonder my ass is dragging. This time, maybe being second choice is better than no choice at all." I gave Fraser a push. "Come on. We better get going or we'll miss the ferry."

Once back at Saint James, after the General Assembly, Fraser showed me the way to the Faculty Lounge. He introduced me to Kaiser Yaeger, the German teacher from Brown, who was standing by himself in the corner. He was in his early twenties, tall with wavy hair and a glass eye larger than his real one.

Bill Proctor, the English teacher, shook my hand firmly at the bar. He had a good-looking boyish face, and well trimmed shiny black hair. His tweed sports coat, Oxford striped shirt, and red rep bow tie all spoke of his time at Yale where he had captained the tennis team. Being young, a spiffy dresser, and well built, Proctor was the teacher most noticed by the faculty wives—and he seemed to know it.

Arthur Hartton, the school's tall headmaster, stepped to the podium. Standing straight as a post, he rapped the lectern several times with his knuckles. Once the room was silent, he looked up over the microphone and began.

"Welcome all. I hope you've enjoyed the drinks and hors d'oeuvres. I know you're all still busy unpacking, so I don't want to take up too much of your time. Just briefly, I want to touch on some of the difficulties we'll be facing during the coming year."

He fixed his glasses and rocked back on his shiny winged-tipped cordovans.

"Civil rights, Black Power, the war protests and drugs will all be with us this year. The black students have already said that they will be boycotting chapel. We have to be tolerant with this group, but we also must be firm. As most of you know, last year, our foreign students from Latin America were buying drugs and bringing them back to school for their class-mates over Christmas break. I intend to make sure that this does not repeat itself. And finally, most of the senior boys are keenly aware of those women in town. We will be vigilant in making sure that there are no more afternoon rendezvouses with this kind of trade."

Hartton's face was stern as he looked over the faculty.

"You have each received in your mailboxes this year's school curriculum and the upcoming sports season schedule. If any of you have any questions concerning either, please see me tomorrow in my office. Are there any questions? Good."

He chuckled.

"This will probably be the last bit of relaxation you'll have at school 'til the middle of June, so enjoy yourselves."

The two French teachers, Gerald Rutherford and Rich-ard Thiselton, walked over to say hello and welcome me

aboard. Gerald was wearing a paisley ascot and using a cigarette holder to smoke his Gitanes.

"Hello, ol' boy. Soyez le bienvenu. Hear you'll be helping us fill Roger's slot while he's in Paris. Let me introduce you
to my bride, Renée."

Rutherford's wife sat on the couch wearing a low-cut
red dress with matching beret and lipstick. She seemed as eager to display what was in her dress as what was on her mind.

"You really must come over for dinner one night," she
said while she held my arm. "We throw these very interesting
parties. They're 'intime'." She winked. "Very 'intime'. Gerald
and I feel it helps us get to know the other members of the faculty better." She flicked her cigarette ash on the floor and
smiled up at me.

Richard Thiselton was shorter than me, about 5'5". His
dyed blond hair was immaculately oiled and slicked in place
with gel. He fingered the gold watch chain that ran through the
buttonhole of his Tattersall waistcoat as he walked over.

"Welcome to Saint James, Jay. It's Jay, right?" He held
me by the elbow as he shook my hand. "Has Gerald told you
you'll be teaching the 3s and 4s this year?" he asked through
pursed lips.

"Yes, I'm looking forward to it," I said. "I just hope there
aren't too many kids from the Paris Embassy."

"Well, I'll be teaching the 5s and 6s." He looked at me
with his piercing blue eyes. "If you ever need any help, my
door is always open. I'm in the Winthrop dorm, just above the
swimming pool. You must come over some time. I've got
some fantastic Bourgognes grand cru," he said with a tilt of his
head. "Maybe tomorrow night after dinner—that's if you're
free, I mean. And bring your bathing suit. We can go for a
swim afterwards."

He finally let go of my hand.

"Well, thank you, Richard. That's kind of . . . "

"Jay, come on." Fraser pulled me by the arm. "Let's get
out of here," he whispered. "I've got some great stuff over at
my place."

"Stuff? What do you mean by 'stuff'?"

"Never mind. Come on. You'll see."

We walked across the quadrangle to Fraser's dorm and climbed the two flights to his small bachelor's quarters. He pulled out some rolling papers from his desk drawer and spooned out some pot from a small urn on his bookshelf. With the crack of a match, he lit the tightly rolled joint and took a long drag.

"Here, try some of this."

"Fraser, I don't smoke pot. All I need is a bottle of J&B to get me where I want to go. And it's legal."

"Come on, Jay. It's OK. You'll like it. Go ahead. It's great stuff."

I fumbled with the joint, took a puff, and then another. When I started coughing, I awkwardly passed it back to Fraser. He pulled heavily, then handed it back.

Suddenly, from outside Fraser's door, came titters of laughter.

"Shit! It's the students."

Fraser quickly flushed the roach down the toilet and waved his arms about to try and get rid of the smoke. He sprayed some cologne in the air, threw open the windows, then pulled on his windbreaker.

"Come on, Jay, we've got to get out of here," he said. "Let's go down the back stairs. We'll drive into town. Once we get there, we can think of our alibi."

As we left the apartment, three or four students were standing in the corner at the end of the hall smiling. They watched as we hurried down the steps.

We drove down the hill in the Bluebird past The Breakers, the Vanderbilt's summer cottage, and parked on the wharf that led to the White Shark.

Fraser and I huddled over our drinks.

"Damn it. What shitty luck. Listen. If anything happens," Fraser said. "Here's what we'll do." He took a long pull on his scotch. "Let's say I had some acquaintances over and that one of them took out some pot and started smoking. We told them to stop, but they wouldn't, so we asked them to leave. How's that sound?"

"Sure. That should get us off the hook. Or at least I think it should," I said with a rather uncertain voice.

"OK. But we have to stick to it. Remember, no matter what, we gotta stick to it, or we're fucked. OK?"

"Sure. OK," I said trying to sound more confident.

Fraser gave me a wink.

"OK then," he said. "Bottoms up. Let's go."

The next morning, Arthur Hartton called me into his office. It was a large, dark room. There were rows and rows of musty books on heavy mahogany bookshelves, and an enormous oil portrait of the school's founder hanging above a stone fireplace. The headmaster sat at his desk in front of several stained glass windows that stretched from ceiling to floor.

"Jay, you've only just gotten to St. James, yet something serious happened yesterday. The Student Council has reported that some students smelled marijuana smoke coming from Mr. Himes' apartment last night. And, that Mr. Himes and you were seen leaving the school together shortly afterwards. Now, I've already spoken with Mr. Himes, and he has told me about his two acquaintances. I'm only going to ask you one question. Is this story true?"

I hesitated before answering. I felt the perspiration running down my back. I looked at Hartton, hoping my voice would not crack. I gripped the arms of the chair. "Well, yes. Yes, sir. Absolutely," I lied.

"Fine. Thank you for your time. You may return to your classes. And, Jay, close the door behind you, please."

Later that day, another General Assembly was called. This time, it was announced that Mr. Himes would be leaving the school due to an infraction of the Honor Code.

"What happened, Fraser?" I whispered into the phone.

"Arthur said it was my apartment, and I was responsible. Don't worry, I've already found a job working on a sailboat behind the Shark. I'll be fine."

"But, Fraser, it could have been my apartment!"

"Relax, Jay. It could have been, but it wasn't. Don't worry about it. It was my idea; it's my neck. Just keep your head down and fly under the radar. You'll be fine. I want to show you this guy's boat—38 footer. And wait 'til you see his summer 'cottage' where I'm staying. It's huge. Four security systems! I'll tell you what. If you're free next Saturday, let's get together. And I want to introduce you to some of the Byerly girls I know. We'll have a blast."

"OK, Fraser. I'll see you Saturday. Sorry about this mess."

"It's OK, Jay. Listen. Don't worry about it. It's entirely my fault."

Slowly, I hung up the phone. I was so lucky. Once again I had wiggled off the hook without getting caught.

What if it had been me? I thought. *Then what? What would my father have said?*

Chapter 7

The Wilted Stiff

W hen the doorbell rang, I put the bowl of peanuts on the coffee table and checked my watch. 4:30.

"Who is it?" I yelled walking into the hallway.

"It's me, Benny K. I got the bananas."

I opened the door and found my friend from the Downtown Athletic Club wrestling with two large bags of groceries for our beach house party. Ben Karlson was tall with bushy black eyebrows. Years of exercise had kept his 30-plus frame thin and strong.

"Come on in. Put the snacks in the kitchen, and the bananas on the bar by the blender."

"Here. Give me a hand." Ben tossed a bag at me. "Hey, Jay. Why daiquiris?"

"Thurston from the Sandbar Club told me it's the drink of choice this summer. What the hell, we might as well go top drawer. We're still three shares short and the summerhouse starts next weekend. This is our last shot to fill out the empty slots."

"There're supposed to be four or five coming. We should be able to find some suitable candidates. And if we don't get enough members, we can always charge the members that we've got more."

The doorbell rang again.

"Come in," I shouted. "It's open."

David Robidow came in carrying two bottles of rum and a sack of powdered sugar. He was short, starting to bald and twenty pounds overweight.

"Where do you want these?" he asked, huffing and puffing. "It's hotter than a witch's tit out there today." He wiped the mist from his large aviator eyeglasses.

"Witches' tits aren't hot, David. You can put them on the bar, next to the carafe. Have a daiquiri, if you want. They're delicious. I'm on my second. Ben, get some ice, will you? And turn up the air conditioner."

There was a knock at the open door. Two young women were standing in the hallway.

"Hi, my name's Arlene," the tall redhead said. "Is this where the beach house party is? I'm looking to join a group house in the Hamptons."

"Sure, come in. My name's Jay."

"Hi Jay," the thin blonde said. "I hope I'm not too early."

"Oh, Joyce! Hi. No, no. How was your winter? Have a banana daiquiri. Arlene, make yourself comfortable on the couch. Did you have any trouble finding it? This is Ben, and he's David. Excuse me, there's the door."

A short young woman with blonde hair and blue eyes was pushing at the doorbell.

"Hi." She gave a tired smile. "So this is Kips Bay? I

tromped up and down 34th Street ten times before I found it; people must have thought I was a hooker . . . I'm Debbie."

"Sorry, I should have given better directions," I said. "Come in. Make yourself at home. Do you want a daiquiri?"

The men stood at the bar talking with the women. Hors d'oeuvres were passed and more daiquiris poured. The girls were in their early to mid-twenties, and all were attractive. Ben sat near the large bay window with a photo album on his lap showing off the summerhouse.

"See? This is last summer at the beach house," he said to Debbie. "We call it the 'Wilted Stilt'. See? It sits up on these piles." Ben pointed to the large wooden posts under the house. "It's not new, to say the least, but it's right on the beach looking out at the ocean. The sun's fantastic. And it's the last house on Dune Road, so the neighbors never bother us. This is Dave. He's our chef."

"I cook a mean lobster," David said. "Friday nights we have our dinners outside on the deck."

As Arlene peeled off her sweater, Ben's eyes got larger.

"See, Arlene?" he said. "Here we are at the Air Force base playing tennis."

"Excuse me, is this the party?" a woman asked peeking in from the hall. "I'm sorry I'm late. My name's Anne Crystal."

She was wearing a loose-fitting, low-cut silk blouse with a short, black skirt and heels. Her bosom was full, and she had a teasing smile.

I turned away from the other women and focused on Anne.

"Come in. Come in," I said with a smile. "Here. Try one of these."

As Anne reached for her daiquiri, she knocked the peanut dish off the coffee table onto the floor.

"Oops. Sorry. I guess I should be wearing my glasses."

Ben, David and I watched in amazement as she went about the carpet on her hands and knees using her round-rimmed granny glasses to search for the peanuts. Her Jane

Mansfield-like cleavage was staggering to all three of us.

"Here, let me help you," I said.

"No, no," she said, looking up. "I think I've got them all. No, here's one more."

Anne stood up, brushed off her skirt and sat on the couch next to Ben.

"Here let me take those," I said, fumbling for the peanuts. "Did you have far to come?"

"No, I live on East 78th, so I just took the 2nd Avenue bus down."

"78th? That's funny. That's where Ben lives. He's between 2nd and 3rd."

"Ha! So am I. We must be neighbors. I'm right across from the synagogue on the south side."

"He's right next to it."

I filled my glass and went into the bathroom to pee and put on more cologne. I checked myself in the mirror. *Not a bad looking fellow*, I thought to myself. I smoothed my hair, smiled and went back to look for Anne in the livingroom. She was standing next to David at the bar laughing. There was a devilish twinkle in her blue eyes.

"What's so funny?" I asked.

"I was just telling David that I didn't know if your house let Jews join. He told me he's been the token Jew for the last two years. Said he'd file a discrimination suit if you guys didn't let me in. By the way, I love the pictures. What a fun house."

"Well, I've got some pull with Ben, so I'm pretty sure you're in. As a matter of fact, I can guarantee it. I mean if you want to join."

"Well, the price is right, and you guys seem like a good bunch. Sure, I'd love to join."

"Great! Here's to the summer." We clinked and drained our glasses. "If you'd like, I can give you a lift out on Friday."

"You've got a car?"

"A company car. But guess what — believe it or not, it's a metallic candy-apple red Vette with a black convertible top."

"A what?" Her eyes widened.

"Yeah. My old man still thinks he's a teenager." I laughed. "Cars are one of the few perks he gives me. Wait 'til you hear this baby purr."

Anne looked at me with a mischievous smile. "I think I've got Friday off. I can leave whenever you want."

"Let's leave early. We can have a picnic in Amaganset. There's a place right behind the old restaurant *Lunch*. They call it Asparagus Beach. The waves are great and so are the dunes. What'd say? OK?"

"Perfect! And I bet I can guess how that beach got its name. Oh, shit. Sorry. I have to go. I promised Glen Ellen I'd meet her at the gym at seven."

"I'd give you a lift, but I have to stick around and clean up the mess. See if Glen Ellen wants to join."

"See you Friday."

I watched her slender figure as she walked out the door.

"Wow, Dave! I think we just hit pay dirt," I whispered.

"Steady, Jay. I think we all have our eyes on her."

"Well . . . I really like her. Let's see what happens this weekend."

On Friday afternoon, the two of us drove out on Long Island to the Hamptons and pulled into the sandy parking lot of *Lunch* at three thirty. I grabbed the picnic basket Anne had prepared along with the cooler from the trunk. She took the blanket and towels. We followed the footpath behind the restaurant through the marsh grass up to the top of the dunes. Out over the sparkling Atlantic, the black-and-white terns skimmed along the crests of the rolling waves.

"How 'bout here?" Anne suggested.

"No, let's get a little further off the path. I think there's something better over there that's more protected. Here, give me your hand."

We walked through the dunes until we found a small hollow. Anne spread out the blanket, and I dropped the basket and the cooler next to the towels.

She stretched her arms up to the sun. "This is perfect,

Jay!"

Anne pulled off her light blue T-shirt covered with tiny white clouds and small yellow suns. It mimicked the bright azure sky overhead. She stepped out of her saffron shorts and lay down on the blanket. Her bright pink bikini showed her full bosom and dark tan. She propped her hands behind her head.

"What a gorgeous day!" she said.

"I love the view."

"Are you talking about the ocean?" Anne said with a wink as she tightened her bikini top."

"They're both great." I laughed. "How 'bout some wine?"

"Sure, I'll have white."

As we savored the crisp Chablis, off in the distance, a family walked towards us along the water's edge. The young girl in the middle held her parents' hands. All three were naked.

Anne giggled. "I knew Asparagus Beach was a nude beach. Here, try this. Hope you like turkey. It's all I had."

She moved over in front of me and gave me the Coppertone bottle.

"Can you put some of this on my back? I don't want to get burned." She leaned forward and reached back with one hand to hold up her long blonde hair.   "OK?" she asked.

I rubbed the oil onto her strong shoulders, then down her back to her narrow waist. I marveled at her brown body.

"Is that enough?"

"Sure. That's fine."

She took the last bite of her sandwich and emptied her glass.

"What d'ya say? Wanna to go for a swim? Nothing better than a dunk in the nude after lunch, don't you think?"

"I'm game. Here. Have some more wine. It's almost finished, anyway."

We raised our plastic cups and gulped our drinks.

"Cheers!" She shouted as she drained her glass. "Come on! I'll race you to the water."

Anne tossed her glass aside, kicked sand at me and took off down the dune running.

"Come on, slow poke!" she yelled. At the water's edge, she slipped out of her bikini and dove into the surf.

I ran to the breaking surf, pulled off my suit and plunged in after her. The cool, refreshing water felt wonderful. I came up sputtering, shaking my head from side to side, and staring up at the sun.

"This is heaven!" I shouted. "I've died and gone to heaven."

"No, you haven't!" she shouted back. "You're alive and well in Amagansett."

Is this really happening? I thought to myself. *Well, if it is, it's the best damn day of my life!*

We splashed each other and dove beneath the waves as they broke towards the shore. Two young men walked by naked, holding hands. They stopped to search for skipping stones and watched us frolic in the surf.

"Come on, Jay. I'll race you to the red wine."

She took off again out of the water, scooped up her suit and ran up the dune back to the blankets and towels.

"Here, get dried off." She threw me a towel. "Let me put some sunscreen on you. You'll burn your buns."

As she spread the suntan lotion across my back, I pulled the cork from the Beaujolais and poured fresh drinks.

"To nudity," I said.

"To nudity," she laughed.

I looked at her gleaming blue eyes as she rested her chin on her knees. I reached out and stroked her thigh. She looked at me and moved closer. I put my arm over her shoulder as we finished our wine. Then I kissed her, and she kissed me back. Anne stared up at my face. I blocked the sun from her eyes, caressed her cheek. She arched her back when I kissed her neck, her salty breasts, and sucked her hardened nipples. When I moved on top of her, she held me under my arms and let me enter her easily. Slowly, we started to make love under the warm summer sky. Finally, I felt the rush and came inside her.

We lay together, side by side, until the afternoon breeze picked up.

"I guess we should head off," I said. "If we get to the Wilted Stilt early, we can share the Red Room if you want to. It's just off the back deck facing the ocean. What's so supper is you can hear the waves at night."

"Sounds marvelous. Let's go."

We gathered up our belongings and headed off hand in hand for the car to start our trip back to the beach house in Westhampton.

We arrived just before six and found Henry Thurston sitting out on the front deck reading his paper. Henry was a Canadian friend of Ben's from Merrill Lynch, and the elder statesman of the house. A small man, about 5'4", with gray hair, in his mid-50s, Henry was still bitter over his divorce of 10 years ago. He often suggested that the *Times* run divorce announcements the way they do for weddings, detailing the dark clothes, shoes and handbags of both parties and giving descriptions of the hawkish attorneys in attendance.

"Market must have been slow today," I said.

"Yeah. Ben and I left about three to beat the traffic. He's on the beach jogging up to the inlet and back. Say, who's this pretty little lass?"

"Henry, I want you to meet Anne Crystal. She's new to the house this summer."

"Well, what a splendid addition. David's in the kitchen working on dinner. I put the wine in the fridge to chill."

"We'll see you in a little bit. We want to get cleaned up for cocktails."

Still covered in salt and sand, I pulled open the wooden door to the rickety old outdoor shower next to our room on the back deck. I stepped inside, and hung my towel and Speedo on a rusty nail. The water was brisk and refreshing on this beautiful sunny day and the soap felt good running across my shoulders and chest.

As I watched white wisps of clouds move across the

blue summer sky above, the shower door creaked open and Anne stepped into the stall. She joined me under the spigot, holding herself close against my body and letting the stream of soft, clear water fill her mouth and gush down her neck and breasts. I reached behind her and untied her bikini top while she squirmed out of her bottoms. Frothing with soapy bubbles, our lubricated bodies slid together. I found her mouth, her tongue, as the sun warmed our bodies. She wrapped her legs tightly around my hips as I glided up inside her. She arched her back. I pushed her against the shower wall.

"Harder, Jay. Harder."

I pulled down on her shoulders, forcing myself further up into her. With each stiff stroke, her fingernails dug deeper into my back. Finally, I erupted up into her, and she thrust back at me, pushing me against the door.

"Again, Jay. Please. Again."

"I can't Anne. You come to me."

She writhed up, then down, over and over again, hard, until suddenly, after a wave of spasms, she stiffened.

"Oh God, Jay! Oh God!"

I held her tightly until her grasp slowly loosened and her feet fell to the shower floor. She wrapped her arms about my waist and let her tongue explore my mouth, my teeth, my tongue. She grabbed my hair with both her hands, pulled my head back hard and stared into my eyes.

"Wonderful." She gave a wild laugh. "Jay, that was wonderful!"

We laughed and squeezed each other.

"We better hurry," I said. "We're going to miss dinner."

After we toweled off, I saw Ben sitting up on the bluff in the Crow's Nest with his drink watching the evening waves crash in from the sea.

"Ben," I shouted. "What's for dinner?"

"Don't know," he cried back. "I'm concentrating on the Scotch."

"We'll be right out."

We waved and went off to the Red Room.

Anne changed into a lovely flowing white sundress for dinner. I found my white ducks, pulled on a blue polo shirt and laced up my Topsiders. We walked upstairs and found David in the kitchen with a pile of two-pound lobsters.

"So, how's my Jewish partner," Anne said with a smile.

"Good, Just trying to get these lobsters done."

"Need any help?" I asked.

"Help? Hmmmm. Well, not with the lobsters, I guess." He smiled a cat-like grin and used his apron to wipe his large eyeglasses. "We're eating out on the deck tonight. If you two aren't too tired . . . maybe you can set the table for me."

"Now, David," I said with a wink, "be nice."

After the silverware and napkins were placed on the rough-hewn table out back, I mixed two Scotches and carried them out the back screen door with a slam. I found Anne curled up in a beach chair watching the sun start to set over the bay.

I pulled my chair next to hers. "A toast to summer."

"To summer."

We clinked our glasses.

"You know," she said, "all of the people I've meet so far in the house have been really nice."

"Ben tries to pick a group that works well together. Unless we're stuck for members, we usually get a pretty fun bunch for the summer. Tonight's our visit to the Windmill House, one of those stuffy group houses in town. The first weekend of the summer they have this formal black tie sit-down dinner. Kind of a 'Welcome Back to Summer' thing. We sneak in over the fence while they're eating and go skinny dipping in their pool."

"What!"

"It's sort of a tradition. We just drive over, and while the dinner guests look on in amazement, we slide down their slide bare ass naked. It's gotten to the point where they almost expect it."

"Well, if I'm going skinny dipping, I better have another Scotch. Come on."

After a sumptuous lobster dinner and much white wine, our group of housemates climbed into their cars for our trip to the Windmill House. Benny K led our caravan at 60mph down the narrow two-lane Dune Road, spending more time in the left lane than in the right.

When we got to the old shingled mansion, we parked our cars under the cover of the tall maple trees and crept across an immense, well-manicured lawn awash in bright floodlight. Beethoven's *Ode to Joy* splashed out from the dining room and filled the yard with music that celebrated this wonderful moonlit night. As the others snuck past the giant windmill towards the pool, I took Anne by the wrist.

"Wait!" I said. "Let's do a dance to Summer."

"What?"

"Yes. Let's do a dance to Summer. You get down at the far end of the yard. I'll start at the other end. When I wave, run to me, and I'll run to you."

Anne giggled and took off like a shot for the far end of the beautiful green lawn.

When I reached my position, I waited for the anthem's crescendo, then waved my hand and started to run towards her like a young Nureyev at the climax of the *Ninth Symphony*. As she ran to me, the folds of her white dress flowed out from behind her like the Winged Victory streaking across a green carpet. We ran past each other, to the opposite ends of the immense yard. We turned, and again, like matador and bull, charged towards one another. We came crashing together in the middle of the yard. I caught her by the waist and hoisted her skyward. I held her high above me, and pirouetted around and around in the lush, deep grass. Finally, out of breath, I brought her down, and we hugged and kissed each other.

"Come on," I gasped. "Let's go cool off."

Just as we reached the white fence that circled the pool, we saw Joyce wriggling out of her clothes. Her blonde hair glistened in the moonlight, as did the scar on her face from last summer's automobile accident. With each of her steps up the slide's ladder, our laughter became louder and louder.

"One . . . two . . . three!" we all cried.

Joyce flew down the slide with a large splash into the pool's warm water. Ben's large silhouette quickly followed, shaking the ladder back and forth as he climbed to its top. He lay on his stomach and came screaming down the slide into the moonlit pool head first.

"Come on, Anne. Let's go," I said.

I dropped my clothes, climbed the ladder, and went down the slide into the pool. Then came Anne, followed by David and finally Henry.

When the people inside the house heard the commotion, two diners came out onto the verandah to investigate. They smiled and waved when they saw us. The tall man took off his formal wear, ran across the driveway, and dove into the pool to join our naked band. Next, a tall brunette unzipped her lovely pink evening gown, sprinted across the grass, and jumped in holding her nose. First the pink flowers from her hair floated up from the bottom of the pool. Then she burst through the water's surface with reams of laughter.

Some diners, apparently the more conservative ones, or perhaps those new to the house, peered out from the curtained windows, shocked by such an outrageous performance. Others gathered on the side porch to satisfy their voyeuristic tendencies, trying to decide if they should join in our adolescent behavior. By midnight, the party was winding down, so we found our towels, thanked our hosts and, under the glow of moonlight, returned to our beach house.

In the morning, Anne and I both rose early to join Benny and Joyce for an early morning jog down the beach. By the time we got back, we were exhausted.

"Breakfast," Anne panted.

"Eggs," Joyce begged.

"Bloody Marys," Ben howled.

"Mimosas," I bellowed.

We hurried from David's spread in the kitchen onto the back deck, carrying our plates into the gorgeous sunlight. Ben jabbed at his runny yellow yolks with the points of his toast.

"Say, Jay," he said, his mouth half full. "Gene Fulton and Judy Campbell will be coming by for a swim and lunch later on. Why don't we pull the old furniture-firewood trick?" He raised his bushy black eyebrows with a smile.

"Do we have any left?" I asked.

"Furniture-firewood trick? What furniture-firewood trick?" Anne asked.

"The boys think it's funny when a new couple comes to visit us to casually break up some of the old furniture and feed it into the small metal fireplace," Joyce said. "Usually, the guests look completely dumbfounded. They think we're all nuts. Then we tell them it's just a joke. Usually, they still think we're all crazy."

Everyone laughed.

"Sure, let's do it! I remember the last time Bob and Maraid came by. They thought we were completely insane."

As we carried our dishes into the kitchen, we heard a car pull up the graveled driveway.

"That's Fulton now," Ben said. "Act naturally everyone."

A voice came from the bottom of the steps. "H-h-hello? Any b-b-buddy home?" Judy Campbell and Gene Fulton came around the corner onto the deck with their towels and beach chairs.

"Where in here, Gene. Come in."

They stepped between the sliding glass doors into the living room and collapsed on the couch.

"White wine?"

"S-s-sure," Gene said. "And one for J-j-judy too."

"We were just going fire up the Weber," Benny said. "It's still a little damp in here."

"Damp? It must be n-n-ninety degrees out."

"Here you go, Judy. Here, Gene." I handed them their drinks. "I'll get the wood, Ben."

Nonchalantly, I walked over to a ragged kitchen table

chair and slowly broke it into several small pieces. Judy and Gene's eyes popped. Incredulous, they watched as I put the broken chair on top of the newspaper in the Weber. Ben threw in a match and the shellac from the wood caught immediately.

"Here, let me help you," Ben said.

He went over to an old folding beach chair and broke it into smithereens. Before throwing the canvas backing and splintered wood into the fireplace, he added a small end table. Judy and Gene's mouths dropped. They could not believe what they were witnessing.

"More wine, Gene?"

"N-n-no thanks." He looked at Judy in amazement. "N-n-not right now."

Henry came in from the deck.

"Hey, fellows," he said. "I think you're going to need some pails of water. The smokestack's so hot it set the roof on fire."

Ben and I jumped to our feet and grabbed the ladder off the back deck, while Henry brought a pail of water from the kitchen. We scampered up onto the roof and used a fire brigade to douse the flames.

"I guess we overdid it a little bit this time," Benny laughed. "Usually, the roof doesn't catch on fire."

"Gene, Judy . . . you should have seen the looks on your faces," I chuckled."

"Well, we kn-n-new you were nuts, but t-t-that confirms it."

"Gene, they didn't tell me the part about burning down the house." Anne laughed. "I guess they keep that from the new house members as a precaution."

"OK. Now that that's done, let's hit the beach." I wiped the soot off my hands. "Come on, Anne. There's volleyball, Frisbee and bodysurfing waiting."

After lunch and a siesta, Ben and I threw the football on the beach until David called from the deck that we had to leave for dinner.

We drove to the Japanese Garden in town and sat

outside under the glowing lanterns. All ten of us squeezed around a long table eating sushi and drinking sake as a nearby bug zapper marked time to the oriental music.

Paul Choate, a new member to the beach house and a bear of a man, and his girlfriend, Diana Plakas, came in late. Paul, whose weight was pushing 320, was always on a diet. So instead of eating dinner, he spent his time emptying the tiny white saki cups and fiddling with the small swizzle sticks. At the end of the meal, he leaned across his line of little empty porcelain bottles.

"Hey, Jay. Bet I can beat you back to the Stilt."

As he fumbled for the keys to his BMW, Anne and I ran from the table and jumped in my car. We sped off, taking the shortcut through the parking lot by the boat basin and headed for the Inlet Bridge. I went through the "S" turn at the country club at 70, when Paul's convertible flashed out in front of me from a side street and accelerated up the ramp and over the bridge. I raced after him down the slope onto Dune Road and pulled even with his roadster before we both turned right and raced on for the beach house. He screeched into the driveway ahead of me laughing and waving. I slid to a stop just behind his rear bumper.

All four of us fell out of our cars in hysterics, holding our sides, when a police cruiser pulled in behind us with its red lights flashing. The door swung open and a tall trooper stepped out wearing hat, boots and sunglasses.

"License and registration from both of you," he said sternly.

Arlene, David and Debbie tried to stifle their laughs from the deck above as they watched the proceedings unfold. Sheepishly, Paul and I produced our documents and waited for the officer to issue us our summonses.

"We're sorry, officer," I offered as I took my ticket.

The squad car backed out of the driveway and disappeared down Dune Road.

"Well, I guess summer has officially begun," Paul said. He found an empty flowerpot by the garden and took it to the bar. "Come on everybody, let's celebrate!" Plugging the hole in the bottom of the pot with his thumb, he filled it with Boodles. "Give me oodles of Boodles," he shouted, taking a large swallow.

Sunday morning was dark and dreary, so Anne and I packed our things and left early for New York. With the top down, we listened to oldies on CBS and the rumble of the Corvette's exhaust driving down Montauk Highway. At exit 70, I turned onto the extension north towards the Long Island Expressway.

As we came over a small rise, I pointed to a vivid 50-feet tall reddish-tangerine iron sculpture.

"See that, Anne?"

"See what?"

"Over there, in the potato field. There . . .. Right there behind the fence." I pointed again. "See the big reindeer's head?"

"Oh. Wow! It's pretty."

"See how he's looking up at the sky? It's called *The Star Gazer*. When I look at it I see Calvary."

"Calvary? What's Calvary."

"That's where Christ was crucified."

"They didn't teach us that in Hebrew school," Anne said with a laugh.

"They hung Christ from a cross on Calvary and crucified him. Afterwards, he rose again. There was a second birth, a chance for redemption. That's what I've always wanted to be—a star gazer. Always looking up. Always hopeful. What do you think?"

"I like that—star gazer . . . but, maybe for you, instead of a reindeer it should be a bronco." She winked. "That's for the rebel in you, Jay."

"A rebel, huh?" I squeezed her knee. "Well, here's one rebel who really loves being with you."

"You're silly." And she leaned over and kissed me. "But star gazer . . . I like that."

Just after two, we pulled in front of Anne's apartment

building on East 78th Street. As she grabbed her duffel off the back seat, I asked, "How 'bout drinks and dinner on Wednesday?"

"You don't slow down, do you? Sure, Wednesday's fine. I'll skip the gym."

"Good. I'll meet you at the Colonial Club after work. 67th Street, just off Park. It's one of those stuffy clubs my father had me join." I laughed. "And no jeans. I'll give you a call on Tuesday. Bye"

It was early on Tuesday night when I heard the ringing. I rolled over and picked up the phone.

"Hello?"

"Jay?"

"Yeah."

"You been sleepin'?"

"Yeah. Who's this? Is that you, Ben?"

"Yeah. How come you're sleepin'? It's not even nine yet."

"Yeah, I know. I'm beat. I had a shitty day at the office. Tuesday's always a shitty day."

"You want me to call you tomorrow?"

"No, that's OK. What's up?"

"You goin' out to the house this weekend."

"Yeah."

"Could you do me a favor?"

"Sure. What?"

"We need some firewood, and my car's in the shop. Could you stop and pick some up on your way out to the house?"

"Geez. I'd like to help you out, Ben, but I'm taking Anne out with me this weekend. With all our stuff, I won't have any extra room in the Vette. There'll be no place to put it."

"OK. I'll call David. Say . . . what's this with you and Anne? How's that goin'?"

"I don't know. Things seem to be goin' pretty good. I really like her, and when we're together, we have a good time . . . so, so far, so good."

"So, you like her?"

"Yeah. We have fun together. I'm seeing her tomorrow night at the Colonial Club."

"So, it's serious?"

"I don't know. I'll just see how it goes. Say, how you gettin' out to the house?"

"I'll take the train."

"OK. See you Friday."

"OK. Nite."

"Nite."

I rolled over and went back to dreaming about Anne.

Wednesday evening, I was running late as usual. Driving up Park Avenue, I wondered, *What does she look like again?* I tried to recall her facial characteristics. I remembered she was blonde and short. *What happens if I get to the Club and can't recognize her?*

When I pushed through the heavy wooden revolving doors, Tommy, the hall porter, greeted me. "Good evening, Mr. Walker. There's a young lady waiting for you in the East Room."

I climbed the marbled steps with trepidation. At the doorway to the East Room, I hesitated, turned and went into the men's room to pee, fix my hair and straighten my tie. After a second glance in the mirror, I walked across the polished hallway. At first, the large room looked empty. Then, at the far end of the room, I saw a small figure sitting with her back to me on a crimson couch in front of the fireplace. Now I remembered how pretty she was. Anne turned and smiled at me as I entered the room.

"Hi. Sorry I'm late."

"That's OK. I was afraid you wouldn't recognize me."

"Are you kidding? I'd know you anywhere. Did you get a drink? Good. Maggie, Scotch please," I said to my favorite waitress. "So, how have you been?"

"Fine, except my job's driving me crazy. I guess it's what you get when you work for The Hartford Insurance Company."

"Insurance? You didn't tell me you were in insurance. That's what I do. I had trouble with my first stint, too. I worked for Chubb for a year. It was like that. Working for my father's no bargain either. I feel more like an employee than a son. Thanks, Maggie." I put my glass on the table next to Anne's. "I have so much trouble just trying to talk to him. He always keeps himself at a distance, a big distance."

"Well, at least at work I don't have a father to contend with. But I hate my boss and I hate my job."

"Maybe I can help you get over to the brokerage side. I've got a good friend at Henken & Jackson." I finished my drink. "Ah, that tastes great! Maggie, another, please. Let's take our drinks upstairs. We can get something to eat. Oh Maggie, one for Anne, too, please."

As we exited the elevator on the third floor, I showed her the oil paintings of the Club's most prestigious members; three US senators and a president were included. Before going into the dining room, I took Anne into the library.

"Late one night I was in here studying for an insurance exam when the door opened and a congressman came in with his girlfriend. I was off in the corner behind a tall fern, and they never saw me. They started going at it right here on the table in front of the fireplace. I don't know if he had a wife waiting in the dining room for him or not. I just watched the whole thing from my armchair."

"Sounds like an interesting club."

"I guess it can be."

When we entered the dimly lit dining room, Robert, the maître d', greeted us with his usual friendly smile. As always, he was wearing his pince-nez glasses and had his thinning hair pulled across the top of his head.

"Good evening, Mr. Walker," he said with a slight bow. "It's been a long while . . . since last night, I believe," he said with a laugh.

"Now, Robert, behave." I shook his hand with a ten-dollar bill. "Can we sit at the corner table?"

"By all means, Mr. Walker." He pocketed the ten. "Right

this way."

The dining room was decorated with heavy burgundy drapes and portraits of past Club presidents. The few tables that were taken were occupied by much older couples. They spoke quietly over bouquets of fresh-cut flowers and small candles.

Anne looked around the room at the silver-haired couples. "Boy, they sure are old."

"It's kind of fun being one of the youngest members. They're probably talking about sex," I kidded. "Robert, two Scotches, please."

As Anne looked over the menu, she said, "I'd like my family to meet you."

I put the wine list down. "OK."

"We're getting together on the 25th for my nephew's bar mitzvah in Seaside. I was hoping you'd come."

"Bar mitzvah? What's a bar mitzvah?"

She looked surprised. "You WASPs are really something. Don't you know anything? It's a coming-of-age celebration. They're very big on the south shore. It usually turns out to be more of a party for the parents than for the boy. But the boy still gets plenty of gifts."

"Sounds about the age I was when I got my motorcycle."

"Motorcycle? Motorcycle! You certainly don't look the type."

"That was before Dunbarton," I laughed and waved over Robert. "Two filet mignons, please, Robert . . . medium rare, and a bottle of the Nuits St. Georges." I handed him back the wine list and menus.

Anne sipped her Scotch, then reached over and took my hand. "Now tell me a little bit more about you."

"Me? There's not much to tell. I work for my father in insurance. That's about it."

"Come on. Any brothers or sisters? Tell me about your mother."

"I've got a brother—Harry. He's 23 and lives in Atlanta.

Harry's trying to break into theater. My mother died in '64."

"Oh, I'm sorry. How did she die?"

"My mother? Car accident." I sipped my scotch and asked, "Now tell me, what about you, Anne?"

"Nothing fancy," she said. "I grew up in a Jewish home on the south shore, went to AU, and then landed this job with the Hartford."

"Here we are. Filet mignon, medium rare." Robert slid our plates onto the white tablecloth and poured the red wine.

"My father's married to his fourth wife," I said. "By the way, he's having his birthday party at El Morocco on the 10th. Would you like to go?"

"El Morocco? What's El Morocco?"

"You JAPs are really something. Don't you know anything?" I teased. "It's a private club in the East 50s. Kind of the flip side of this one. It's done up in a blue-and-white zebra motif. There's a Kasbah in the back and a live band for dancing."

"Sounds like fun. I'd love to go."

"Another bottle of wine, Mr. Walker?" Robert asked.

"No thanks, Robert. We're done here. We'll have cognac in the library."

As I signed the dinner check, Robert whispered in my ear with a laugh,
"Mr. Walker, your signature is always so much better at lunch, and your women are always so much better at dinner."

"All right, Robert. That's enough of that now. Have a nice night."

"What's that all about?" Anne asked.

"Robert's also the maître d' at the lunch club I belong to downtown. He always has some kind of little joke for me at the end of each meal."

We walked down the marbled hall to the echo of our footsteps and pushed open the studded red doors. The dark, musty room was filled with stacks and stacks of leather-bound books. On the other side of the reading table, two tall armchairs stood framed between majestic bronze andirons. Robert brought in the cognacs, and put the snifters on the small mahogany table in front of us.

"Will that be all, Mr. Walker?"

"Yes. Thank you, Robert."

"Very well, then. Enjoy your evening, Mr. Walker." And he left us with a slight bow.

I took the poker and stirred the logs. Anne sank into one of the large armchairs and crossed her legs. In the warmth of the flames, we drank our cognac and watched the shadows of the flames dance across the Persian rug.

"It seems like I've known you a lot longer than 10 days," I said.

"Me too. Much longer. You know, in spite of all your trappings, you're really not too bad a guy."

"Thanks." I smiled. "Thanks a lot."

"Every once in a while, I see some pretty good stuff hidden underneath that veneer of yours. I guess you've been pretty lonely since your mother's death. What an awful way to die . . . a car accident."

"Give me some time, and I might show you more. Say," I said changing the subject, "I have an idea. Why don't we go to Max's Kansas City?"

"Where?"

"It's a great bar down on 17th and Park. The music's fantastic. Sometimes Janis stops by with her band. Or Lou Reed comes in. It's packed with hippies. Kind of a Peter Max happening thing. Or there's dancing at the Filmore on St. Marks with the J. Geils Band."

"Jay, I really can't . . . I can't stay out late tonight."

"OK. Regine's then? It's not far—The Regency Hotel at Park and 59th. It's a little expensive, but it's a great disco. Or Doubles in the Sherry-Netherland."

"Jay, I can't tomorrow's a work day."

"OK. How 'bout my fraternity club, Saint Barnabus' Hall, on 64th and Park. It's right nearby. Charles makes the best Planter's Punch in town. No . . . wait. I know. Let's go to Teddy's! You'd like Teddy's. It's just around the corner. Come on. Let's go to Teddy's for a nightcap. Just one. I've got Dad's car outside. Then I'll give you a lift home."

"OK, Jay. You never give up, do you? But just one. It's a 'school night'. My boss throws a fit if I come in late. She's one of those really tough dykes."

"OK. Deal. Just one." I took her by the arm.

"Jay? Just one . . . promise?" She looked at me dubiously.

"Promise!" I winked.

We went downstairs, said goodnight to Tommy and pushed outside. A bright, clear sky lit up 67th Street. The night's air was cool and fresh. Tonight, New York was at its finest.

"This way. I left the car on Park." I took her hand and we walked to the corner. "Here we go." I unlocked the passenger door.

"Shit! *This* is your father's car!"

A blue-and-silver Rolls-Royce Corniche hugged the curb. The license plate said WALKER.

"Yeah." I laughed. "He buys them used, so they're half off. He doesn't buy them at all; his company does. It drives his business partner nuts. I always park it on the street. Apparently no one ever steals a Rolls."

When we got to Teddy's, there was no place to park.

"I'll just leave it by the fire plug," I said as I opened her door.

"You can't do that."

"I do it all the time. The cops never seem to ticket Rolls."

The small bar was packed with couples in their twenties. Some were standing by the pinball machine; others crowded around the five tiny tables with their drinks. Most of the men wore blazers and the women little black dresses with pearls. Next to the door, Midnight the cat lay sleeping on the bar by the window curtain.

"Hi, Frank. Two Tidalwaves, please. Come on, Anne, let's bowl."

I dropped two quarters into the slot and sprinkled

sawdust on the alley. Anne hitched up her dress and shot the silver puck.

"Damn! A split."

"Here. It's easy. You just have to bank it. Let me show you." I bent over her from behind. "OK. Give me your hand. Ready? Go." The silver puck flashed down the sawdust-covered alleyway, and the two pins snapped up. "Bingo! A spare."

We drank our drinks and bowled until Frank came over.

"Jay, we're shutting down. It's time go."

"Ah Frank, just one more round," I begged.

"No. 1 a.m. That's it." He crossed his muscular arms across his apron. "See you tomorrow night."

"Oh, come on, just one more."

"Jay, you've had enough," Frank said.

"OK, OK. I'll see you tomorrow. Good night Frank."

I scratched Midnight between the ears and left twenty dollars on the bar for Frank. As we walked out onto the deserted street, I used Anne for balance.
There was a ticket on the windshield.

"Shit."

As she helped me into the car, I gave her a sloppy kiss.

"Now, be careful, Jay. You don't want to smack up your old man's car. You've had a lot to drink tonight."

I sat behind the wheel trying to get the key in the ignition.

"Oh, right, Little Miss Goody Two Shoes. Like you haven't? Why don't we try Swells or Mortimer's for a nightcap? I bumped into Jagger the other night as he was leaving Mortimer's with his entourage."

"No, Jay, it's time to go home."

"OK. OK."

On 78th Street, I squeezed into a spot behind Ben's Fiat.

"Come up for coffee. You'll never make it home like this."

I struggled up the three flights to her small apartment. Anne went in the kitchen while I looked for the bathroom. A loud crash brought her running.

"What in the hell was that?" she asked.

I was holding my right index finger and trying to keep the blood from dripping on the carpet.

"I had a little accident trying to take a piss. I was leaning against the wall
and fell. I think . . . I think I broke one of your pictures, not to mention pissing all
over the floor."

"Here, let me look at that . . .. I don't think it needs stitches. You'd better stay here tonight. If you want, we can go to the hospital in the morning."

She wrapped my finger and helped me slip out of my suit and tie. I was asleep as soon as my head hit the pillow.

The next morning, I was roused by the throbbing pulse in my finger. I opened my eyes and found Anne propped up on an elbow looking at me.

"Oh, my head."

"Shhhh." She put her finger on my lips. "Rabbit, rabbit, rabbit. It's the first thing you have to say on the first day of the month." She smiled. "It brings you good luck."

"What month . . .?"

"Shhhh. Just say it."

"Rabbit, rabbit, rabbit," I muttered holding my head with my good hand. "I hope it works and the Rolls is still downstairs."

"I can see it from the window. Oh, look. There's Ben."

"Hey, Benny," I shouted. "Over here. Rabbit, rabbit, rabbit."

Ben was outside on his fire escape reading the morning paper in the sun and smoking his pipe. He heard his name, looked around and was surprised to see us wrapped up in bed sheets waving at him from across the street. He waved his pipe and smiled.

"Benny, want some breakfast?"

"No thanks. Just had my wheat germ."

"Here, Jay, drink this." Anne handed me a large mug of

coffee. "You had way too much to drink last night."

"I know. I know I overdo it every once in a while. I better get going. Dad'll be pissed if I don't get the car back by nine. Can you help me with my jacket?" I finished my coffee and went to the door. "I'll call you later."

"Here's your tie."

"Thanks. Sorry 'bout the picture."

Mid-afternoon, Anne picked up her office phone.

"Hi, it's me. Busy?" I asked.

"No. Just pushing papers from one pile to another. How's the finger?"

"OK. Listen, there's a party tonight. Steve Martin's in concert up in Tarrytown. Ben and Dave are taking dates. Want to go?"

"I was supposed to meet Jen for dinner tonight. I suppose I could cancel."

"Good. I was hoping you wouldn't say, 'No.'"

"What time do we leave?"

"I can pick you up at five if that's OK? We're having dinner at the Chart House. I think you'll like it. It's right on the water. After dinner. we're driving over to the theater."

"Sure. Sounds like fun. I'll see you then."

At five o'clock, Ben, Dave and I had our cars lined up on 78th Street. Anne came out her front door in a white blouse, short black skirt, white sandals and a pink scarf wrapped at her neck. I spritzed the smell of Scotch from my breath and put the Binaca back in my pocket as she opened the car door.

"Hey, you look great! Hop in. We've got to be at the Chart House by six."

I kissed her on the cheek and then followed the others onto the FDR Drive and up the Bruckner. On the Hutch, Ben pulled alongside, rolled down his window, reached over and handed Anne a bottle of champagne.

"Bottoms up," he smiled, and then sped up ahead to Dave.

At the Chart House bar, we ordered our food and more

champagne. Dave sat with Brenda Charles. Her short red hair blew in the river breeze. And when we told our jokes, her green eyes sparkled. Kitty Germain had her arm around Ben's neck. She was laughing and drinking. Tall and thin, her long brown hair matched her legs. During dinner, we all teased Anne as the newcomer to the group.

"Let's finish up guys," Ben said. "We're going to be late."

We downed our drinks and paid for dinner, then drove in tandem to the auditorium. The show opened with a short film. Steve Martin was a waiter juggling cats with an arrow through his head. Then, when the lights came up, he stepped out on stage.

Ben nudged my arm. "Be right back. Gonna get a drink. Want anything?"

"Sure, whatever you're having."

I pulled Anne closer to me and settled back to listen to the jokes. Fifteen minutes later, Ben returned balancing two tall glasses filled with a thick, pink liquid.

"What in the hell's this?" I asked.

"It's all they had. Goddamn Swiss Mix is sponsoring the show."

"Ugh! Tastes like toothpaste."

"At least we won't have to keep running back and forth," Ben smiled. He pulled two full bottles out from underneath his sportscoat. "I swiped these from the display case while I was waiting in line."

"Watch it!" Anne said. "You're getting it all over me."

I put my glass and bottle between my feet, then mopped the pink spot from Anne's dress.

"Have some?"

"No, I've had enough . . . and Jay, why don't you slow down a little bit?"

"Don't worry about me, I'm fine."

When the show was over Ben and I stumbled over the empty bottles and followed the crowd to the exit. Outside, the rain was coming down in sheets, and people were scampering every which way through the parking lot to find their cars.

"Wait here, Anne. I'll be right back."

I threw my collar up and ran out into the rain in search of my car. Twenty minutes later, I pulled up honking for Anne.

"Come on! Make a dash for it," I yelled through the cracked window.

She splashed through the pools of water carrying her shoes and slid into the passenger seat.

"I've never seen it so bad," she said as she rang the wet from her hair.

"If it gets any deeper, the motor will conk out. I know a motel not too far from here. Why don't we go and dry out instead of heading all the way back to the City? What do you say? OK?"

"Are you OK to drive? It's pretty bad."

"I'm fine. It's just a couple of miles down the hill in town."

"Well, if you're sure, then let's stop. I'd love a hot bath."

As the wiper blades flashed back and forth, I squinted through the windshield, searching for the exit. "Here we go. Route 125A. We'll be there in ten minutes." I turned down the steep hill towards town, but at the curve at the bottom of the road, instead of turning left, the car skidded straight forward on the wet leaves and slid off the road. With a crash, the Corvette lurched to a stop under a guardrail.

"You all right?" I asked. "Wait here. I'll go see how bad it is."

I ran to the front bumper and tried pushing the car backwards up the hill in the pouring rain.

"Sit behind the wheel!" I yelled.

"What?"

"Sit behind the wheel. On the count of three, give it the gas in reverse. Ready? One . . . two. . . .." I lunged against the front bumper, and the car shot backwards onto the road. Most of the right headlight and fender remained behind in the mud. Drenched, I got in the car.

"Damn it. What a fucking mess!"

"I think we better just go home, Jay. I'm tired and wet."

"You sure you don't want to go to the motel? It's just—"

"Yes, I'm sure. I think I better drive."

"No, Anne, I'm OK. I promise."

I turned the car around and slowly followed the one headlight beam down the Taconic to New York. When we arrived at Anne's, she opened the car door.

"Thanks, Jay. I'm sorry about the car."

"Can I come up?"

"No, not tonight. You better go home."

I smiled weakly and gave her a good night kiss before pulling away.

The next morning, I dropped the car at the repair shop and boarded a crowded downtown bus for the financial district. The heat was stifling; the windows were all stuck shut. I squeezed in between an old man in an overcoat and the rear door pretending to read the *Journal*. My head pounded to the music of my neighbor's Walkman.

We crept down Second Avenue, the bus stopping and starting with jerks at every stop. The driver tried to jockey his way through the bumper-to-bumper traffic, hitting the brakes, accelerating, jostling the passengers back and forth. The smell of bus fumes finally got too strong. I had to get off. Standing on shaky legs, I pushed the yellow exit strip with one hand and covered my mouth with the other. I waited in the stairwell, praying desperately for the doors to open. Finally, at 28th Street, the bus came to a stop. I pushed open the rear doors and stepped out into the heat. I followed the overwhelming stench from a line of old trashcans to a near-by alleyway. There I sprayed the building's brick wall with vomit.

"Goddamnit! Why do I drink so much anyway?"

I used my clean handkerchief to wipe my lips, walked back to the curb and looked for a cab. My head began to spin again. I bent over and retched at the curb. The puke splattered up from the sidewalk onto my wingtips. I looked at my hand-kerchief, then used my sleeve to wipe the sweat from my brow.

"I have to stop this."

My empty stomach settled, and I hailed a taxi to take me downtown to the World Trade Center.

Midafternoon, I called Anne from my office.

"Hi. I'm sorry about last night," I said. "I guess I had a little bit too much to drink. Are you coming out to the Hamptons this weekend?"

"Sure. It's my weekend, and the weather's supposed to be perfect."

"Can I give you a lift? The car'll be out of the shop by Friday."

"Well . . . if you'll behave yourself, I don't see why not."

"Great! We can have dinner outside at Magic's."

Friday night after drinks and dinner, we left Magic's, the small, pubby restaurant in town, and headed back to the Wilted Stilt. I put the top down and drove slowly up Main Street past the Marrakech disco towards Dune Road.

"You didn't say much at dinner." I took Anne's hand. "Is everything OK? You're usually more chatty."

"Yeah. I'm OK. I just had a bear of a week at work." She smiled back at me. "I'm really beat. That's all."

At the top of Key Bridge, we saw the sparkling lights of the pleasure boats moored offshore beyond the beach clubs and the white crashing whitecaps of the Atlantic rolling in. Powerboats in the inlet passed back and forth under the bridge while overhead seagulls glided on the soft breeze back to their evening berths. The radio played the Grass Roots' *Let's Live For Today.*

"Why don't we stop at Moran's?" I suggested.

"Jay, it's late. Why don't we just head back to the house?"

"Come on, just one drink." I squeezed her thigh. "It'll just take a sec'. It's on the way, and there's a band. I have something I want to talk to you about."

I swerved the car into Moran's dusty parking lot and took a spot in front of the giant rusty anchor by the front door.

When we walked inside, there was a tall, thin blonde in

a white tank top, torn jeans and snakeskin cowboy boots choking a mike in front of her back-up band. Leaning out over the stage, she scanned the crowd with her piercing blue eyes.

"OK . . .. This one's from Carole King . . .. *Smackwater Jack*!"

She pounded a clear Plexiglas Fender against her hip and belted out the lyrics.

"*You can't talk to a man . . . with a shotgun in his hand.*"

I motioned Anne away from the music to two stools at the bar in the back.

"How 'bout a Jellybean?" I asked.

"No, thanks."

"Black Russian?"

"No, Jay." Anne stared at me with stormy eyes. "Nothing for me."

"Sure? OK." I caught the bartender's eye.

"Hi, Jay. What'll you have?" he asked.

"Three Wise Men. And, Billy, make it a double."

In a minute, he came back with my concoction and a smile.

"Here you go, Jay. Johnnie Walker, Jim Bean and Jack Daniel's. A double."

I took a sip, then looked at Anne. I began slowly.

"Anne, for the past couple of weeks there's been something rolling around in my head like a marble." I took another swallow. "Ahhh." I looked her in the eyes. "Anne, I know we haven't really known each other for all that long, but I've felt something very special about you ever since we first met. I don't know if you feel the same way, but I'd like to make our relationship more serious. I care for you. I care for you a lot. I don't think I've ever felt this way about anyone else. You make me feel whole. What I'm trying to say is, what . . . Anne, what would you say if we got engaged?"

Anne stared at me in disbelief.

"Engaged? Jay, I hardly know you. I like you a lot, sure, but I think we ought to give this more time. We've only just started to date."

"Hardly know me?" I stammered. "There's not too much more to know. What you see is what you get. Look," I said hesitating, "you're the first person I've ever asked. I feel we'd really be good together. What do you say?"

"Jay, it's getting late. I think we better go. We can talk about this back at the house."

I finished off my drink and slammed the glass on the bar. "Come on. Let's go then."

I took her roughly by the arm and threw a $20 bill on the bar.

"Thanks, Billy."

"Night, Jay."

I spun out of the parking lot in a cloud of dust and zig-zagged down Dune Road to the gravel driveway of the Wilted Stilt and pulled in. We carried our bags in silence up the creaking stairs and around to the Red Room on the back deck.

"Goddamnit, Anne," I said, pulling off my clothes. "Look. I've never asked anybody else. How can you not be sure?"

Anne said nothing. Suddenly I grabbed her and threw her onto the bed.

"What's the matter?" I shouted. "Aren't I good enough for you? What's
wrong with a WASP?"

Trembling, she looked up at me with frightened eyes.

"Jay, you're drinking too much. You're drunk."

"Don't tell me I drink too much." I shook my fist at her. "I can handle it; I know when to stop."

When I went to grab her, Anne lunged past me. She snatched the car keys from the top of the dresser, and ran out the door across the back deck to the stairs. Naked, I chased after her. I hurried down the stairs as she jumped into the car and locked the doors. She fought to get the key into the ignition.

I banged on the window. "Anne, let me in."

I seized onto the car's side mirror as she screeched backwards down the gravel driveway.

"Anne! Stop! Stop!" I clung to the mirror. "I'm sorry," I screamed.

She continued to drag me with her down to the main road.

"Anne, please don't leave me," I cried. "I need you!"

When she saw my tears, Anne stopped the car. I walked in front of the headlights to the driver's side. Anne stared in horror at the deep gashes on my knees and across my feet.

"Wait!" she said. "Jay, wait! Let me pull up. Oh God, Jay! Look at you. You're bleeding everywhere."

"There's a first aid kit in the trunk," I said.

She picked the twigs and small stones from my gashes, then soaked the cotton with peroxide and carefully cleaned the gravel and dirt from my wounds. I winced as she dabbed the iodine on my cuts. She took a small can of Lanacane from the kit and spayed the antiseptic up and down my legs. Then she used a roll of gauze to bandage my knees and feet as best she could. With each wrap, the cloth filled with more blotches of blood. I began to shiver. She took the blanket from the car and wrapped it around me.

"Jay, put your arm around me. Here, let me help you back up the stairs."

"Let's sit in the Crow's Nest for a while. I'm feeling nauseous and the night air helps."

We walked down the path towards the ocean to the steps that led to the small deck on the bluff. Carefully, I lowered myself down into one of the deck chairs. We sat side by side in the dark staring out at the crashing waves. Above, a sickle moon cut through the white wisps of clouds.

"Jay." She held my hand. "Jay, listen to me. You need help . . . but I can't help you. I don't know how to. My cousin's been going to AA for almost five years now. Jay, it's working for him. He can take you to a meeting."

I looked at her with sad, tired eyes. "Anne, I know I drink a little bit too much every once in a while. But I've been drinking all my life. I can handle it. I promise."

"Jay . . . Jay, look at me. I really care about you. I really do. But, if you don't go, then . . . then, I'm sorry, I can't see you anymore. We can't see each other anymore."

My head was starting to clear and the pain from my wounds was growing stronger.

"Anne . . . let me think about it," I said with a grimace. "Can you give me a hand. I think I have to go to bed."

As the wind's stronger gusts came chilling, I limped away from the sand dunes back to our room with my bloody arm around Anne's shoulder.

At lunchtime on Monday, I sat in the back of a gloomy church basement on John Street and listened to a striking young woman with long chestnut hair and the greenest of eyes tell of her descent into alcoholism.

"So, stay with AA! Use the twelve steps," she concluded. "Remember, if you're alone, you have no family, you're not alone any longer! Now AA is your family. And, you never have to drink again. If you're new or just coming back, get telephone numbers, and use them! Get a sponsor! Get a home group! And above all else, always, always remember, 'It's the *first* drink that gets you drunk'. Now let's close with the Serenity Prayer."

I stood in the large circle, holding hands with two strangers, trying to mouth the words with the others, "God, grant me the serenity to accept the things I cannot change . . ."

I thought of my mother.
Why couldn't she have found this place?

Chapter 8

I hesitated in front of my father's corner office, then knocked twice.

"Come in," my father called.

I walked in past the large teak elephant guarding his door with its ivory tusks, the one he brought back from Nairobi during his trip around the world last year.

"Morning, Dad. You're looking very spiffy."

He looked up and straightened his dark blue custom-made Seville Row suitcoat that was squeezing his portly frame.

"Well, I'm a very spiffy guy."

When he ran his hand through his oily hair, I thought back to when I was a child and rode on his shoulders to see the elephants and clowns above the crowds at Ringling Brothers, Barnum and Bailey circus. I remembered messing his hair and feeling the greasy Vitalis. That was before the wall between us had been built.

"Have you got a sec?"

"What is it, Jay?" Frank Walker frowned. "I'm rather busy."

He rolled his wrist and glanced at the Patek Philippe with its shiny alligator strap. The blue sleeve and white monogrammed French cuff that highlighted the dark hairs on his small hand hung heavy with a gold engraved FW link. The Walker family crest on his signet ring glistened in the morning sunlight. Behind the narrow slats of his office windows, a lazy helicopter passed across the cold winter skyline of Manhattan.

"I'm trying to be out of here by five today." He tapped the ivory elephant paperweight with his gold Cross ink pen, then rubbed his bad knee. "I've got my doctor's appointment uptown."

"It's kind of important. Can I close the door?"

I sat across from my father in one of the two plush red leather armchairs facing his antique desk. I looked past him at the collection of photographs on the mahogany credenza. Within one of the silver frames was a picture of me in my early twenties on top of the Empire State Building standing next to the observation deck's 25-cent telescope. That was the way I first felt after joining my father's firm—on top the world. The photo stood next to a bronze plaque with the company motto, "Where there's a Walker, there's a way." I was still on top of the world, on the 101st floor to be exact, but now that motto was no longer working for me.

"Dad, do you know it's been eight years now since I joined the firm?" I asked. "Do you remember last year? I spoke to you about the progress I've been making here . . . or I guess I should say not making."

My father straightened his legs the way he always did when he was put in an uncomfortable situation. Pushing his pile of paperwork aside, he looked across at me through his tortoiseshell glasses.

"Jay, are you sure you want to talk about this now?"

"Yes," I continued with a shakiness to my voice. "Yes,

I've been thinking about this for quite a while. I need to talk to you now. What I've really come to do is resign."

Frank Walker stretched the tight-fitting shirt collar from his portly neck.   "Why do you want to resign?" He fidgeted with the gold letter opener from Tiffany's.

"Like I told you last year, I still don't see any commitment to my future here. I've worked hard for the past eight years; gotten in early, left late. I don't know if you know it or not, but sometimes I come in on weekends, Saturdays, Sundays . . . sometimes I spend the night here on the couch." I looked at my father, then went on. "When I joined the firm, I studied hard for all the tests the way you asked me to. I got all the degrees and titles you wanted me to get. But it didn't make a difference. Nothing happened. I don't want to resign . . . but I feel like I'm just another employee. After eight years, I'm still getting no direction, no encouragement and no support. I'm 34 now, and I have to think about my wife and my kids. I've gotten an offer from another company paying me considerably more money."

"Which firm?" he snapped.

"French & Son over on Broad Street."

"Jackson." My father called me by the moniker I so despised. "I kid you not. I'd be very careful if I were you. I've heard some pretty bad things about them. You say they're paying you a good buck?"

"They're doubling my salary."

My father winced.

"Let's face it; it hasn't worked out for me here." I looked hard at him. "I wish it had. I really do. But, in all this time, there's never been any communication between us. I've never known why; I probably never will. But, you and I both know that I'm getting nowhere here. If I stay, I'm afraid there will be still more people brought in over me. I really don't have a choice; I can't stay any longer."

"Jay, it's your decision. If you want to resign, resign. But, I'll need two weeks' notice to fill your spot." Frank Walker looked down at his well-polished, custom-made Church shoes from England then back up at me. "Jay . . . you know, you used to call me 'Sir'."

I got up and looked at him sitting in his armchair across from me.

"I was younger. Is that all?"

"Yes, that's all."

As I reached the door, he added with a smirk, "Oh, Jay. By the way, I was going over your expense report for this month. How are your financial problems coming?"

I turned and looked at him. "Financial problems? I didn't know I had any financial problems. But, thanks for asking."

Without looking back, I walked away from my father. The envelope containing my counter-offer—higher salary, more time spent in sales, new car—still lay inside my suit jacket pocket. Had he asked me to stay, I would have said yes in an instant.

On my way back to my desk, I passed the President's office. Through the cracked door, I saw Dave Thatcher laughing loudly on the office intercom.

At noon, when I left the World Trade Center, I knew my life had suddenly changed, never to be the same again. I found a corner pay phone and called French & Son.

"Mr. French? It's Jay Walker. I've thought about your offer, and I'd be happy to start in two weeks. Yes, I should be able to bring several clients with me . . .. I'm glad you're pleased . . .. I look forward to seeing you soon also. Good-bye."

I had been working at French & Son for three weeks when Jim French called me into his dark office after lunch on Friday.

"Jay, we're happy with the way things have gone since you joined the firm. Your work here in the short time you've been with us has been outstanding. Everyone likes you, and the accounts you bought to French & Son have made a significant contribution. But . . . I'm afraid I have some bad news for you." I slumped in my seat. "We've heard from your father's attorney. He plans to bring an action against you and us for a breach of your non-compete agreement. Apparently your father feels that if he lets you take clients from his firm, then his other employees could do the same thing."

I stared at him in disbelief. "I never thought he'd do this," I said.

"I'm afraid we'll have to give the clients back to him if you can't change his mind. Do you think you can talk to him?"

My body shook. I felt sick to my stomach. "Let me try," I said weakly. "I never thought he'd do this."

That afternoon, Anne and I packed our things and left for my stepsister's house in the Hamptons. As soon as we arrived at Mopsy's, I began composing two scripts to read to my father on Sunday asking him to withdraw his lawsuit. The first script was a plea to him on a personal basis as his son. The second was on a professional basis as a businessman.

Sunday morning, as she finished her breakfast, Anne asked, "What do you think he'll say? Do you think he'll drop the lawsuit?'

"I don't know. We'll just have to see."

"Jay, are you sure you have to read the scripts to him? Couldn't you just talk to him?"

"Anne, after all these years, you know we've never talked. He's never ever said anything to me. You know that. I don't know why, but it's always been that way. Maybe it's because of his childhood, being adopted, or having to drop out of Princeton, or maybe something else . . . I'll ever know. But, I just can't talk to him. I've tried. I really have. But I've never been able to talk to him. This is the only way I can talk to him—I have to read him my scripts. I don't know of any other way. Come on. It's almost ten. Let's pack our things and go."

We were barely able to squeeze our two suitcases into the small Nissan. Without telling me, my father had decided to downsize my Corvette to a less expensive car. My car phone had also been done away with.

As we drove along the LIE on our trip west to my father's compound on the north shore, I rehearsed the scripts that I was soon going to be reading to him. My palms were sweating as I thought of this confrontation—a confrontation I dreaded. I gripped the wheel tightly and tried to concentrate on what I was going to say to him.

"Jay, relax. Just try to relax." Anne put her hand on my lap. "It'll be OK. I'm sure he'll understand. Are you sure you want to read them to him?"

"You asked me that before, Anne. I told you. I have to. I can't talk to him. Don't you see? I never could."

"But why?"

"It's . . . God knows why. There's always been a block. I don't know why. I've already told you that. We've hardly ever had a real conversation. And if we ever did, he was always so damn uncomfortable. If I did speak to him, I always felt like he was either belittling my judgments, or that I was disappointing him . . . that, somehow, I was letting him down. Even in the family photographs, when you look at them, and look at my father, he always looks uncomfortable. Usually he's looking away from the camera—he never looks at the camera."

Anne turned to me and asked, "Why do you think he's that way?"

"I've spent a good deal of my life trying to find the answer. I've gone back to my childhood—all the way back to when I was a small child. I've wondered, 'What did I do to make him so displeased with me?'"

"Do you know the answer?" Anne asked.

"No. And I don't think I'll ever know. One day, I was walking with Thatcher and him. We were going to an insurance luncheon at the Hilton. I was walking down the sidewalk about ten feet ahead of them. I heard my father say to Thatcher, 'See how well his blazer fits him? How good he looks?' I felt so proud. But he could never say anything like that to me directly—I think maybe somehow it hurt him too much. I don't know."

Suddenly we came upon the small, wooden sign that marked the entrance to the secluded Sheep's Path Lane. We turned into what looked like a tunnel, and followed the narrow lane down the hill. Branches of tired elms overhung the shaded street like a canopy. On either side of the road were ivied brick walls that protected the large sequestered estates that hid behind the tall latticework gates. The bumpy dirt road passed by the obligatory black metal nameplates marking each driveway with their crisp white letters: Pell, Auchincloss, Mellon, Prescott. We came to two plaques separated by a round, red Holmes Protection sign—one said Walker, the other Pogue. The beach club was straight ahead.

We turned to the right, and the long split-rail fence took us past the Pogues', up a pebbled drive to a two-storied brick manse. Black shutters framed each of the twenty windows. Above the blue-slated roof, four large red brick chimneys broke towards the chilly turquoise sky. To one side, a thick copse of tall birch mimicked the home's black trim and peeling white paint. At the end of the long stretch of manicured lawn, we reached the opening in the sculpted boxwood hedge and parked the small Nissan on the cobblestones next to my father's Rolls. The Winged Victory gleamed from its blue and gray hood, and the license plate, FW 21— twenty-one for his favorite restaurant—glistened from the trunk.

Ahead stood two imposing red doors marked with large brass knockers held in the teeth of matching lions' heads.

We stepped out onto the pebbled drive and walked through the immaculate stepped English garden that trickled down to the front of my father's main house.

At the end of the lawn, in the smaller gardener's cottage, Florence, my father's fourth wife, was sitting at an easel in an upstairs window painting. She had been living alone in the cottage ever since her son Billy died from a drug overdose last month.

When she heard our car doors slam, Florence opened the window and waved.

"Hello, darlings!" She gave a wide, toothy smile. "I didn't realize you were coming today. How nice!" she called through clenched jaws. "I'll be right down."

Florence soon stepped out into the north shore sun, tall and thin as always with little makeup, to give us hugs. Her hair was gathered behind her narrow face in a bun to show off the diamonds that sparkled from her ears. She carried herself very straight—shoulders back, chin up. Florence did not look her sixty years.

"Well, how are you? It's been ages! Just ages!" She took both Anne and me by the arms and led us through the garden to the main house. "Come in . . . Come in before you freeze to death!" She pushed open one of the heavy front doors. "Just let me put my things away and wash this paint off my hands. I'll be right back. I think your father is in the den."

The interior was immaculate, spacious and sterile. Matching circular stairways that led to the upstairs bedrooms bordered the curved entrance hall. Its checkerboard black-and-white marbled floor, glistening from repeated polishings, spilled on to a large French Aubusson rug in the living room.

Carrying her smock in one hand and her brushes in the other, Florence disappeared through the swinging door into the kitchen.

"Nelly, fix drinks. We have company!"

The living room was decorated with three large sofas covered in floral chintz and over-stuffed pillows. They surrounded the marble fireplace where four large logs crackled. Bouquets of fresh flowers were arranged delicately on each of the antique mahogany tables. And nestled amongst the oriental vases were silver-framed photographs of ancient relatives and drooling dogs. Oils by Lautrec, Utrillo, Pissarro and others adorned all four walls. I gazed at the portrait of my step-mother, the one done by Dalí years ago. There, in the foreground, a young beautiful blonde Florence smiled out at the room. Over her shoulder were drooping watches and chests of drawers. Almost hidden in the surrealist desert landscape, a small bishop figure dressed in a red priest's habit sat on a white horse with a lance. Here was Dalí's joke. He had painted Florence's second husband, who was Jewish, as a minute equestrian Catholic priest. Next to the painting, French doors led to a large, awninged terrace. Their glass panes framed the outdoor fountain with its gurgling bronze sculpture of

Donatello's *David* brandishing his sword in the nude.

"Here we are," Florence called. Her footsteps moved quickly across the marbled hall. "Here we are. Try this—it's tea with fresh mint! It's delicious. That should warm you up."

We sat across from her on the couch, awkwardly smiling and sipping our drinks. Then I asked, "Is Dad free?"

"Oh, I'm sure he is, Jay. He's probably reading the *Times* or watching the golf; trying to rest up for his knee operation on Thursday. Go tell him hello."

I put down my glass, stood up and straightened my slacks. I gave Anne a quick kiss. She looked at me nervously. Slowly, I walked from the living room back into the entrance hall and then down the hallway past the winding staircase.

The television was playing softly in the den. I stopped at the end of the corridor and went into the small bathroom with its marble basin and monogrammed hand towels. Even here, a tableau by Degas hung above the toilet. I looked at my nervous face in the mirror, combed my hair and fixed my collar. When I reached the den door, I found it ajar. I hesitated, then pushed it open.

The room was dark, decorated in rich reds with velvet and silk-striped crimson wallpaper. Across from the double doors that led to the terrace, embers glowed in the deep fireplace. A half-finished Bloody Mary sweated under the shade of an Oriental lamp. Scattered about on the Persian rug was the Sunday *Times*. The *Social Register* and *Who's Who* lay open on the mahogany coffee table.

Hunting scenes matted in red with ornate gold frames hung about the large, red leather armchair where my father sat. His heavy girth settled him deep in his seat. A shaft of winter sunlight pierced the curtained window and reflected from his oily hair. His bad leg rested elevated on a small red leather ottoman in front of him.

I took a deep breath. "Dad?" I tried to smile. "Dad? Hello, Dad."

Frank Walker looked up from the membership book of the Brook Club.

"Hello, Jay," he said sternly. "I didn't know you were coming out today."

"I've come to talk to you about the lawsuit."

My father stiffened. He never liked it when someone confronted him unexpectedly with an awkward subject from which he could not escape.

"Why don't we let the lawyers work that out?"

"Dad," I blurted out, "I want to ask you to withdraw your lawsuit."

He clenched and unclenched his small hands. The black hairs bristled about his signet ring and alligator watchband.

I sat down across from him in one of the armchairs and took out the two scripts from my sports coat pocket. Without looking up, I began reading the first document that begged him not to continue the lawsuit based on the bond of family.

"Dad, I don't know why we can't get along, I never have," I stammered. *"As your son, I've tried as best as I know how to strengthen the ties between us over the years. I'll never understand why this has been so difficult and why I've failed. Maybe it's because you're so tough. You seem not to want to let me in."*

Without looking up, I could see my father purse his lips from the corner of my eye.

"I've always wondered, 'Is it me? Have I done something wrong?' I know sometimes it may have seemed I took the things you have given me for granted. Perhaps I did not show it, but I was always grateful for and did appreciate the things you gave me. I know sometimes I drank too much too. And God knows, I'm lousy with money. Perhaps you could say that I'm the dissolute son. But, is this what has kept us apart? I'd always hoped to create a bond between you and me, one that unfortunately has never existed. It's taken a long time for me to finally realize that this dream of mine may never come true."

When a scowl crossed his face, I squeezed the script tighter and forged on.

"I'm sorry that things are in such a mess now. And I'm sorry we still can't talk to one another like father and son. If I haven't lived up to the expectations of what you wanted me to be, I'm sorry for that too. But please, don't embarrass me at my new firm—please don't sue me."

I put the first script on the coffee table and opened the second that spoke of my years of commitment at Walker & Co.—hoping that perhaps my words of supplication might somehow soften my father's resolve.

"I'm also sorry that things did not work out at Walker & Co. I had hoped for many years that they would. I joined your firm eight years ago wanting to contribute, to be a strong player on the team, and hoping that one day perhaps I would be allowed to run your firm, and then pass it on to my children." My voice was strained. I went on. *"During the eight years I spent at Walker & Co., I feel that I worked as hard or harder than any of your other employees. Do you know that in eight years, I have only missed three days of work, and that often I would come into the office on weekends? Whatever job I was asked to do, I did. In spite of that, never was I ever given any guidance or a chance to become part of the management team. Although I worked hard at Walker & Co., got in early, left late, I know there were others, even those new to the firm, who were paid more than—"*

"I paid you a good salary!" he said with an air of truculent superiority.

"I earned that salary!" I shot back.

My father winced.

I paused a moment to compose myself, then began again.

"I know there were others, even those new to the firm, who were paid more than me. And during my eight years at your firm, you brought someone in over me—not once, but twice. Unfortunately, then it became clear to me that there was little I could do that would result in any kind of significant recognition for me at your company. Once I finally came to this conclusion, I was left with no other choice but to look

elsewhere for a new opportunity. I had to get on with my life. That is why I left—to try and build my own life and career, certainly not to hurt you. I'm sure you don't know how hard it was for me to leave. It's not what I wanted to do. I wanted to work with you, earn your admiration and eventually be given Walker & Co. to run on my own. And then, in turn, to have my children run the company, and then their children. It's sad. Now nothing will be passed down between us, and there will be no more Walkers at Walker & Co."

I saw my father staring at me with his marmoreal glare. I read on.

"Remember before I left your company? Your only comment then was that I had to give you two weeks' notice so that my slot could be filled. For those two weeks, I worked just as hard as ever. After I left and joined French & Son, several of my clients called me and said that they wanted to continue to do business with me. These are clients that I developed over the years and brought on board myself. I grew these accounts without anyone's help and provided all the services that they required. And yet, while at Walker & Co., never was I given any credit, acknowledgment or compensation for them. In fact, my impression was that these few accounts were more of a burden than a value to your firm—that they were really of no significance."

I looked up and saw the irritation building on my father's face. His small hands squeezed the arms of his red leather chair.

"It was they who asked to come to French & Son. It was not me who asked them. So, now I ask you, please let them follow me. Allow me to start my career at French & Son without a lawsuit between father and son. I will honor my noncompete agreement with you. But these accounts, I honestly feel do not violate that covenant. They are mine. They belong to me. Let me get on with my career without a fight between us. Please … just give me a chance at my new company. Take back your lawsuit."

I put the second script on top of the first and looked

across the den at my father's indifferent visage.

"Perhaps you're wondering what effect I hope might come from these two scripts? Well, aside from the obvious, I also hope that perhaps one day this estrangement between you and me might somehow diminish." I stood up, and, through tear-filled eyes, asked in a soft voice, "I often wonder . . . Do you love me? Did you ever love me?"

He shifted his weight uncomfortably and stared at me. There was no expression on his face. He said nothing.

A wave of sadness crashed down upon my body. I tried to stand tall.

"I don't know if this has helped in any way to bringing us closer together," I said weakly. "But I wanted to say these things to you. I hope you know that I . . . I . . ." I choked back my tears, "that I love you—that I've always loved you."

As I turned and walked to the door, he did not say goodbye. He said nothing.

Florence was carrying fresh drinks into the living room. I looked at her, then turned to leave.

"Jay, wait!" Anne called. "Florence, I'm sorry, we have to go now. Wait, Jay."

"Why darlings, what's wrong? Do stay for lunch, won't you? Nelly has made salmon canapés with fresh caviar. They're delicious."

Anne put her cup down. "No, we really must go. You probably don't know this, Florence, but Frank's suing Jay for taking clients to French & Son."

"What?" She looked stunned. "No! That can't be right. He'd never do a thing like that."

"Anne, we have to go," I said. "Let's go."

As I pulled open the heavy front door, the sun spilled in across the marble tiles. Walking hand in hand, we followed the flagstones through the clumps of snow out to the parking area and got in the car.

"How'd it go?" Anne asked,

"Not well," I said wiping my eyes. "But at least I had my

say. I'll always be thankful for that. I did my best, Anne."

She put her hand on my thigh as we drove along the Long Island Expressway in silence back to Manhattan. I felt relieved. It was finally done. At last I had spoken to my father as a son and as a man. And at last, I had finally expressed my feelings to him. By the time we reached the Holland Tunnel, the intimidation of his power was already starting to ease.

"You know, Anne, my father has always portrayed himself as a powerful man; he always carries himself with an air of superiority. I had to get away from that—from his power and his superiority. He has always had a sense of privilege and self-interest about himself. I had to go somewhere to get away from that . . . somewhere where he couldn't reach me. I had to escape . . . escape from him. First, I tried France, then Africa in an effort to be free of him." I shook my head. "Of course, I should have known that no matter how far away I went, I could never escape him completely—that he would always be there in the back of my mind." I turned and looked at Anne. "But what makes things easier for me now is that I think I've finally discovered that underneath it all, my father will always have a need in him . . . a need for confirmation . . . confirmation of his own importance . . . his own self-worth. He will always be looking for this from those around him—the ones he feels are above him in his social circle. I'm so glad I'm not like that."

Anne smiled. "I am too," she said with tear-filled eyes.

"You know, ever since I was a young boy, I desperately yearned for his love. It's sad that I never knew this was something he was incapable of giving. For years, as I grew up, I endured his subtle criticisms while I tried to please him. But now, finally I've realized that this will probably never be possible. So, I'm going to stop trying. It's just not worth it. From now on, let's start focusing on us and our wellbeing. Agreed?"

"Agreed," she said with a smile.

That night, as I lay next to her, the day's events ran through my head. For some reason, I felt empty and alone. Switching off the light, I rolled over and put my head on her soft stomach, drawing her closer to comfort me. At first Anne flinched and stiffened, but then she rolled towards me. As she ran her fingers through my hair, I reached under her legs, using my strength to raise her pubic mound to me. I pushed the top bed sheet back and buried my head between her legs. Gently, I put my tongue in her, moving it from side to side, and then up and down. She writhed slowly. I sealed my mouth to her, caressed her with my lips, nose and tongue. My shoulders forced her to the headboard, further separating her legs. I climbed to her stomach, her breasts, her throat. I kissed her hard on the lips and rubbed her nipples. I entered her, withdrew, and entered her again.

She took my mouth with her lips, pushed her tongue deep inside while my hips continued to move strongly up and down. Locking her ankles behind mine, Anne grabbed at my shoulders with her long fingernails. She lifted her pelvis higher and harder to meet my thrusts, moaning with each stroke until I came. Our bodies were sealed to each other until finally she came, then came again.

I felt comforted and warm lying there in the dark with my head on her breast, listening to the faint rapid beat of her heart. How lucky I was to be with Anne tonight. It had been months since we had last made love—anger in our marriage had been brewing. As I waited for sleep to come, I first listened to her soft breathing, and then said a simple prayer.

"God bless my mother. God bless Sally. Thank you for my wife and thank you for my children. Amen." And then, before falling asleep, I added, "God bless my father."

Thursday morning, I sat working at my office desk when the phone rang.

"Jay, I've got some bad news." It was Dave Thatcher, President of Walker & Co. "There was a problem today with your father's knee operation," he said in his usual stern voice. "The X-rays never showed the blood clots in his lower leg. Once the doctors made their incision, the clots raced to coat Frank's lungs. He suffocated on the operating table. It should have been a simple operation. I was supposed to have met him at '21' for lunch after the operation. But they didn't know about the clots. There were five doctors there standing around the operating table, but they couldn't save him."

The telephone rocked in my limp hand. Then my grip changed. I squeezed the receiver until my fingers turned white. Then finally my anger melted into vindication and relief. At last he was gone.

"Jay? Are you there?"

"Yes," I said.

"Florence is at New York Hospital," I heard Thatcher say. "Can you go up there right away?"

"What? Where? New York Hospital? Oh, sure. Let me call Anne. We'll go up right away."

I hung up the phone slowly, waited, then punched in Anne's office number.

"Anne Walker."

"Hi. There's been an accident. Dad never made it through the operation today. He's dead."

"Dead? How can that be? Jay . . . you sound funny. Are you all right?"

"Yes. I'm fine. I'm fine and relieved. Florence wants us to join her at New York Hospital. There's no rush. She was never on our side. I'll meet you at the subway—Wall and Broadway. OK?"

"OK. I'll meet you there."

"Anne, don't rush. Take your time. There's no need to rush. He's dead."

"Jay, are you sure you're OK?"

"Yes, I'm fine . . .. You know what?"

"No? What?"

"Now that he's dead, what did he have? Nothing, really—some clothes, some books—just . . . just things. That's all he had—nothing but things. Certainly not family. And you know what?"

"What, Jay?"

"He died alone . . .. It's sad. It's really sad. And, in the end, he had no friends."

"Be good to yourself, Jay. Now that it's over, try to be

good to yourself . . .. I'll see you in twenty minutes."

We found Florence sitting slumped in the corner of the stark Visitors' Lounge. She raised her head when we entered the room and walked quickly to me. I held her small, frail body loosely while she sobbed. Her shoulders shook as she buried her face in my chest. Then she turned, reached in her bag and handed me a large manila envelope.

"Jay, I have your father's obituary from the Social Register. And I brought this portrait photograph of him from Bachrach. Can you quickly run them over to the *Times* for me? That's what I did for Billy last month. Your father would want them to be in the paper tomorrow."

I looked at Anne. "Do you mind if I run this over to the *Times*? I can meet you at home later on."

"No. It's OK. Go ahead. I'll see you at home."

"Oh Jay, there's one other thing. Here." Florence put my father's signet ring in my hand. "He wanted you to have it."

I looked at the Walker family crest with the griffin's head and neck holding in its mouth a bloody hand. Waving on the banner beneath the Welsh shield was the motto *omne solum forti patria*. I thought back to my years of Latin at Dunbarton. It was from the Roman poet Ovid—*every land a homeland for the courageous man*.

"It's all he left you," she stammered. "He's leaving all of his Walker stock to your brother. Harry now owns forty-nine percent of the company."

"Really?" I looked back down at the ring. "How kind of him." I looked at Florence again. "I guess I've found my homeland now."

"Homeland? What do you mean?" Florence asked.

"Never mind."

"Oh . . ., and, Jay. Thatcher called," Florence said. "He's going to have his lawyers at the funeral home—Frank Campbell's. He wants you to sign some legal documents."

"Seems like a fitting place to be signing legal documents," I said with contempt.

"You know, Jay, Cambell's is the Tiffany of funeral

homes in New York. And, afterwards, I'm having a horse and carriage take the coffin to Saint James."

I turned and took the elevator to the lobby.

Outside, the low January sun was setting on York Avenue. Standing alone, I watched the cars pass by through the gray slush and smiled—inviolable. I eschewed the long line of waiting yellow taxis at the cabstand, and started my long, slow walk across town to Times Square.

Why rush? I thought. *He's dead . . .. At last . . . he's dead. And finally, at last, I'm free!*

On my way west, I thought of my father who would soon lie amongst the Walkers in their regal sepulcher. *For him, no matter what it was, it was never enough, or never good enough to satisfy his demands—rich wives, expensive cars, large homes. If it was the best, he wanted it . . .. I don't even know why he wanted it—it seemed like the getting was far more important to him than the having . . . . Maybe this was his struggle . . . to climb back up the rungs to the elite—to put himself above others . . .. Perhaps this was some kind of solace for his adolescence.* I wondered. *Did any of this make him happy? I don't know . . .. No, I don't believe it ever did.*

As I walked slowly through the snow towards the *Times*, I noticed piles of the season's discarded Christmas trees. They lay sleeping on the New York City curbsides covered in tired tinsel blankets and the pungent stench of canine perfume waiting for the garbage men to come and take them away.

For me, on this day, finally I was no longer waiting . . . no longer waiting for that feeling of relief to come. At last, I was totally engulfed by freedom — invincible.

Chapter 9

I put my demitasse down on the dinner table's white table-cloth and looked out through the restaurant's frosted window. Across the cold East River, the glow of lower Manhattan shivered.

It's been years since we've lived our marriage as a couple. We're completely separate now, I thought. *I get up before dawn, go to AA, then go to work. When I get home—at seven if I'm lucky—our conversations are nonexistent. I have so little*

interest in the few things she says . . .. Her life's not important to me any longer. We stopped kissing…touching…caring long ago. Our marriage has stopped. Friends think everything is fine. We never mention our problems—not even to each other. It's like a slow death—painful, inevitable—tearing us apart.

I finally broke the silence and said, "Anne, I don't understand it. We're each making over $100,000, and we're always broke. I can hardly sleep at night because of all the bills."

She looked up at me from her uneaten meal. "Wouldn't it be great if you just stopped spending money? Maybe wipe out some of that credit card debt instead—what is it now? $50,000? $60,000? Higher? That might help; don't you think? Did you have to buy those skis?"

"I need them for racing."

"Christ, Jay. 'I need, I need.' That's all I hear from you. What about us? What about your family?"

"Look. Racing frees me," I shot back. "Like the booze used to. It rids me of my demons."

"You mean it rids you of our money. You're not Bill Gates, for Christ's sake! Won't you ever get it, Jay?" she said in her usual sarcastic, biting way. "First you have to *earn* the money . . . *then* you spend it. And there's this novel concept called 'saving.' Ever heard of it?"

"I'm trying, alright? I wasn't born with an instruction manual about money shoved in my diaper. And, God knows, my father never gave me any advice—any advice about any-thing. If I get the OTB account, we'll be OK."

"Nothing but the best for Jay Walker," she snapped. "I guess it always has to be that way, right? But, you know what? You'll always be in debt, Jay. You'll always be broke!" Anne glared at me. "You criticized you father for his love of things. But what about you? It seems to me that you're just like him—well, aren't you?"

"Of course I like the clubs and the cars. Who wouldn't? But I'm not like my father. I don't need them to validate my success the way he did. He craved those things for status and prestige. I can take them or leave them. They're not important to me. But since I can have them, I take them."

"You always do whatever you want to do. And you never play by the rules. You never have . . . I don't know, Jay . . .. Why don't we just get the check and go?"

I glanced at Anne's tired face, then called to the waiter, "Check."

We left Fulton's Landing and walked through the snow to the car. Closing my door, I said, "I'm surprised you had so much to drink tonight. You usually stick to vodka and grape-fruit juice."

She looked at me with tired eyes. "I feel like shit. I thought the wine and cognac might help. I'm sure I'm losing the ITT account. That's the last thing I need. And, as usual, you didn't have much to say."

I turned the Corvette around and headed for the snow-covered road leading to the Brooklyn Bridge.

"I'm worried about my accounts too, Anne. My commissions are barely covering my draw. My book's $550,000. They said they want me to raise it to a million if I want to keep my job. I said to Friesen I'd love to have a million-dollar book. At twenty percent, instead of making a hundred and ten, I'd be pulling down two hundred. It's kind of a no brainer, isn't it? Thank God for my expense account. I've been hitting that up for two thousand every month, and they've never ever questioned me on it. And it's tax free. You know, Anne, I haven't slept well in months. Jason's always up at 3:30 bawling with his nightmares. Does he ever sleep? I can't really blame him, though . . . battling his goddam learning disabilities all day long. And Nicholas never goes to bed before 10:00 . . .. I think I'm getting the flu."

"You might feel better if you didn't stay up so late working on your goddamn computer," she yelled. "And it would help if you didn't leave the goddam lights on every morning when you leave for AA."

"Listen, Anne. If the kids had some rules, they'd know where they stand. You let them do whatever they want. No wonder they're always awake. At least with me, they know if certain things aren't done, they'll be punished. Why don't you try to be firm with them? You always give in? You're firm with me all the time."

"Don't feed me that crap. I'm doing just fine with the children," she shot back.

When I swung up onto the icy ramp leading to

Manhattan, there was a line of red taillights that stretched all the way to the top of the Brooklyn Bridge.

"You know, Anne, if you'd spend a little money and turn up the heat,
the kids would sleep better. Jason wouldn't get up so early, not to mention how tired I am of sleeping in my sweats. It's so breezy in the bedroom, you'd think all the windows were open."

"Look, I'll turn the heat up when you get out of debt. You run up the bills, I turn down the heat! Got it? Ask French for that raise you've been whining about for so long. Shit! Where do all these cars come from? We're going to be late for the babysitter."

"Why didn't we talk about this at dinner? You just sat there looking miserable."

"Jay, we haven't had a real conversation since Nicholas was born. And I've been thinking a lot about work."

"I was thinking about when we took that horse and carriage ride through Central Park after we left our wedding reception. It seems like only yesterday ...." "That was six years ago, Jay," she said with a bitter bite. "Damn it! We're stuck on this fucking bridge."

Anne reached over and slammed the horn.

"Relax. That won't do any good—can't you see there're a hundred cars ahead of us."

"It's better than just sitting here."

"Anne, why don't you come back to marriage counseling with me, instead of us constantly yelling at each other all the time? Maybe we could learn to talk to one another again. Why can't we communicate? Is it so hard? Other married couples do. Let's try to be a team again. Would it kill you to try and be more flexible?"

"For Christ's sake, Jay, don't give me that communication crap again. That shrink of yours is worthless," she shouted. "Be a team? Are you kidding me? All you think about is your job and yourself. How about calling my office once in a while just to ask me how things are going, or if I'm still alive?

Have you ever tried to see things from my point of view? You're so goddamn self-centered! Everything has to revolve around you! And you're always so damn angry."

"Me angry? That's bullshit! You're the one who's always walking around pissed off all the time. I've been busting my ass for the past six years trying to earn a living for you and the kids. You're the one who's always so goddamn confrontational. Why can't you at least try to make the marriage work? Give a little bit? Would that kill you?"

Anne suddenly shoved the car door open and stepped out into the snow. She started walking back down the bridge to Brooklyn between the lines of cars. I watched her in the rearview mirror until she disappeared into the swirling storm, then slammed her door shut and reached for the phone.

"Beth Hunter 'ere. 'ello?"

"Still haven't lost that English accent, have you?"

"Why should I? I'm a Brit, after all. How've you been, Jay?"

"Not bad. I was wondering if you're free for a drink tonight?"

"Don't give a girl much warning, do you? Well . . . OK. You just got lucky."

"Good! I'll be there in 20 minutes."

The snowy streets of the West Village were empty when I pulled into a spot on Waverly Place just after 10:00. I rang the intercom in Beth's lobby.

"Hi. It's me. I'm downstairs in the Vette."

"Be there in a sec," she said in her smoky voice.

I walked back to the car and sat watching the blades move the snow back and forth off the windshield. I only wished I could clear away the mess of my marriage as easily as they cleared the ice from the glass.

The lobby door pulled open, and Beth ran down the path slipping and sliding in her cowboy boots. A pink paisley scarf was wrapped around her neck and knotted at her throat. She wore her denim shirt unbuttoned and tied just above her pleated mini skirt. When she brushed the snow off her

Yankees cap, I saw she had cut her hair short again. The chocolate color matched her dark bedroom eyes.

"Hey! That wasn't very nice, was it?" She gave me her familiar warm, wet kiss. "Next time, give a girl some warning when you ring her up."

"I tried to call you earlier," I lied.

"Rubbish," she smiled. "I've been home all day."

In the dim light, I could see the small scar on her upper lip, the one I always liked to nibble on. I kissed her back, then drove off to our favorite restaurant, *211*, on West Broadway. When I pulled up to the curb in front of the stairs that led to the front stoop, I could see Cal at his usual spot just inside the red door.

"Bon soir, bon soir, Messieurs Dames," he said with a smile. He turned smartly towards the rear of the restaurant and led us to our high-backed booth. "Toujours Perrier, Monsieur Walker?" Cal asked.

"Oui, toujours."

"And for mademoiselle?"

"Double Scotch," Beth giggled putting, her hand on my lap.

When she turned towards me, her face was bright and gay. "So, how are things with you, Old Boy?"

"I'd rather not discuss it. My wife's still driving me mad."

"All bollixed up, eh?"

"Yeah. If it weren't for the kids, I'd probably leave."

"Rubbish. You're never going to leave her, now are you? And the kids? I've forgotten . . . how old are they?"

"Pardon, monsieur-dame." Cal put our drinks on the table in front of us.

"Nicholas just turned three, and Jason will be five in March. They're both great. They're all I've got really."

"You raising them Jewish?"

"No, Unitarian, or whatever they want to be. How 'bout you? How're things?"

"Not bad. Since I saw you last, I had my cat fixed and I'm starting to get checks again from my ex in London."

"Good old Nigel. So he's finally found his fountain pen, eh? Say . . . why don't we finish up here? I feel like dancing. There's that new club, *Private Eyes*, just around the corner on Hudson. It's supposed to be pretty hot. You game?"

"Dancing! Sure, let's go."

Beth polished off her Scotch, and we walked through the snowflakes back to the car.

When we pulled up to the curb on Laight Street, there was a long line of people waiting to get into the disco. I took Beth's hand, and we followed the line around the corner to the club's front door on Hudson. I led Beth up the ramp to the front of the line and shook the bouncer's hand with a $20 bill.

"Hi. My name's Jay Walker. I have reservations for tonight."

He laughed pocketing the twenty. "Yeah, and I'm Elvis Presley. Get in line bud like everyone else."

"You know, I fired someone like you just this morning." I smirked as I turned to leave.

"Yeah, well, I'm not on your payroll, jerk." He pushed me off the ramp down into the snow. "And don't come back, punk!" he yelled.

"Bugger off, you bum!" Beth shouted. "Here, Jay, let me help you. Are you OK?"

"Yeah."

I brushed off my sportscoat, and we got back in the car.

"Never mind. Let's drive over to the river," I said.

Beth lay her head down on my lap and opened my zipper. She found my cock and gently stroked it. Her warm tongue slowly licked it. She cupped its head lightly with her lips. My erection grew harder and larger. I lay my hand gently on the back of her head, lacing my fingers through her soft, brown hair, while she bobbed up and down—sometimes slowly, sometimes quickly. She sucked hard on my dick, then pulled up and all the way off, like pulling a lollypop out of her mouth, with a smack. She circled the rim of its hard head with the tip of her tongue, then plunged down, taking all of the shaft deep in her throat.

"Beth! Beth! I've got to pull over before we hit something."

I swung the car into a dark spot in front of one of the concrete construction walls next to the Hudson River, put the top down and turned up the heater. As the snow gently fell on us, Beth slipped off her panties and hitched up her skirt. She climbed over the gearshift, straddling my soft brown leather seat, and sat on my lap facing me with her knees bent. I pushed the seat back, and she unbuckled my belt. I reached up, spread open her blouse and pulled her to me. I entered her easily, as she worked her pelvis like a corkscrew, moving faster and faster.

"Do you like it," she whispered.

"Yes. Of course. Oh God, yes!" I muttered.

She pushed me deeper and deeper into her. I bit her lip. Her kisses tasted of Scotch. She dug her fingernails into my neck, pulling me to her breasts. Then suddenly I exploded up into her. She reared back and forth, again and again with each of her orgasms until she was finally finished. Slowly, she climbed back to her seat and dressed. We sat for a while in silence letting the snow fall on us as we watched the ships slide along the dark river.

"I have to go," I said at last.

I put the top back up, turned the car on to the West Side Highway and headed back to Beth's apartment.

"Want to come up to the flat for a bit?"

"No thanks. I really have to go."

Beth waved goodbye from the lighted doorway.

"Don't forget to call me," she yelled. "Cheerio!"

She turned and walked into the lobby, swinging her hips.

As I drove down West Street thinking of Beth, a large lighted billboard glowed through the snowflakes. Atop an old, deserted bank building, Johnny Walker stood in a trim, red hunting jacket with one of his shiny black riding boots on the front bumper of a Bentley. He was holding his walking stick under one arm and smiling down at a young blonde wearing a long white dress, holding a rocks glass full of Scotch. *"When you know enough to know the best,"* the sign said.

God, I'd like a drink. Apart from wet dreams . . . I haven't had sex at home in months.

I put the car in the garage and walked through the lobby to the elevators. Upstairs, the boys were sleeping. Anne had left a light on in the bedroom. I undressed and climbed in bed next to her wearing my T-shirt and sweatpants. Tonight, before falling asleep, rather than masturbating, I prayed.

"Dear God, please help me."

Chapter 10

It was just after 7pm. I stood alone in the phone booth on the concourse of the World Trade Center, one hand holding the receiver and the other ready to press down on the disconnect lever. My heart racing and beads of perspiration forming on my brow, I finally dropped the quarter into the coin slot and dialed Walker & Co. With each ring, I became more and more anxious to hang up. Three rings. Still no answer. I waited for the seventh ring, the eighth, then put the phone back in its cradle.

"No one's there tonight," I said with relief.

I had broken into my father's office many times before to steal information that I used to try and take clients and prospects away from Walker & Co. But this night, tonight, would be different.

I could no longer use the tenants'

entrance to Tower One as I had been stripped of my building pass when I resigned from Walker & Co.   But, "Where there's a Walker, there's a way."

I had found another way to reach my father's office on the 101st floor.

I walked slowly across the hard, shiny, marble floor towards the young, white-suited concierge. He stood tall and thin behind a dark wooden podium, engulfed by large, multi-colored arrangements of exotic flowers. As guests arrived, he greeted them with, "Welcome to Windows on the World. Please form a line to your right."

A large group of tourists had already gathered in front of me for their ride to the restaurant on the 107th floor.

I've got my cover again tonight, I thought somewhat relieved. *No one will see me in this crowd.*

"Windows on the World?" the concierge asked with a smile.

"Yes," I stammered.

"Right this way." He waved his gold-braided cuffs in the direction of one of the two enormous elevators.

I made sure to enter the elevator first, ahead of the group of mostly Germans and Japanese. By stepping far ahead into the back of the car, I would enter the restaurant last hidden by the large crowd of passengers.

The elevator started with a lurch and began to rattle as it clicked off the floors in increments of ten. At the 70th floor, people began to giggle awkwardly. Some opened and closed their mouths to ease the pressure on their ears. Finally, the elevator came to a sudden stop at 107 and the doors opened with a gush of wind.

"Good evening, ladies and gentlemen. Welcome to Windows on the World," the hostess said above the noise of the crowd. "Coat check is straight ahead and the restrooms are to your right. Please stop at the reception desk on your left and confirm your reservations."

As the bewildered visitors stumbled about trying to understand the instructions, I stepped out to the left behind the

crowd, making certain not to make eye contact with the hostess. Rather than confirm a reservation, I continued down the
hall as I had done so many times before. The dimly lit corridor
led past rock sculptures. Between the small *Wine Cellar* restaurant and the Dining Room, I had discovered a small door
that led into the kitchen.

 I walked slowly through the soft yellow light halfway
down the hallway, where I stopped and waited, pretending to
admire a large indigo crystal. I needed to wait for a screen
from the hostess so she would not see me slipping into the
kitchen. Finally, a large man came walking towards me. As he
passed, I quickly turned left and, with a nervous shove,
pushed open the kitchen door. A waiter carrying a full tray of
soup staggered backwards. With a crash, two bowls of vichy-
ssoises covered the floor. I kept moving forward with my eyes
fixed straight ahead on the Fire Exit. I forced the metal door
open and fell inside.

 So far, so good, I thought, *except for the soup.*

 I took the stairs to 106 where the banquets were held,
and then continued down to 105, 104, 103 and 102. I knew
that each of these doors was locked from the outside. Rivulets
of sweat trickled down my back, and the strength in my legs
began to fade. At the 101st floor, access to the hallway was allowed. So I slowly pushed open the stairwell door and peered
out. I looked left, then right. No one was in the deserted hallway, so I stepped out onto the plush carpet. Just as the door
locked shut behind me, the elevator bell rang. I heard the
doors slide open and men speaking.

 "Damn it," I whispered.

 I moved quickly down the hall to the men's room, sat inside one of the stalls and waited nervously. As I locked the
stall door, the men's room door swung open. It sounded like
there were three people—probably washing up after an early
dinner. They were all speaking in some Asian language. I took
the handkerchief from my suit's breast pocket and wiped the
perspiration from my forehead. It seemed like hours before
they finally finished their evening ritual and left. Cautiously, I

exited the stall, went to the men's room door, and checked the hallway. Again, all was quiet. I walked past a corridor of offices to Walker & Co.'s large front mahogany door. I stared at the brass letters that spelled out my name.

"Take the firm away from me, will you?" I sneered. "Let's see if I don't get you bastards!"

I fumbled in my trousers' pocket for the old front door key and forced myself forward to the lock. I tried the key . . . again . . . then again, but the lock would not open.

"Shit! They must have finally changed it."

The elevator bell rang loudly behind me. I retreated quickly around the corner back to the men's room. Again, I waited in the stall, but no one came in. After ten minutes, I checked the empty hallway.

"I'll get in the back door," I chuckled. "They never use it."

Down the hall, away from the elevators, I knelt down by the back door knob and took out my plastic tools. Frustration grew as I tried to work the lock open. I grumbled each time the plastic hook slipped off the curved bolt.

"Stubborn bastard. Open up!"

Suddenly I heard someone coming from the elevators. I froze. I was trapped in this dead end corridor. The footsteps kept coming.

"What do I do?" I wondered in a panic. *"Walk forward . . . just stay here?"*

As the footsteps got louder, I started to mumble, "Oh, God. No! Please, God. No!"

My heart was pounding like a drum.

Just as the footsteps were almost upon me, a middle-aged Asian man came weaving into the hallway's intersection. I held my breath. He looked down, fumbling for his key, and turned away from me. He zigzagged down to the other end of the corridor and poked at the lock until his door finally opened. He staggered through the doorway into his office.

Feverishly, I returned to my job, desperately jabbing at the lock. Over and over, the plastic hook caught the metal bolt.

But each time it slipped off before opening the lock.

"Goddamnit. He'll probably be coming back any minute."

Then, *click*.

I breathed a sigh of relief.

"Finally."

I put my tools away and gently pulled open the door. As usual, the office was dark. I put my small flashlight in my mouth and used my hands to feel along the wall. As I moved past the fax machine, my elbow hit a vase of flowers. It teeter-tottered back and forth, then rolled off the table and landed with a thud on the rich tan carpeting in the middle of my father's red and blue monogram. I stared at the firm's logo woven into the rug—the large blue W for Walker. I smiled and replaced the Chinese jar intact.

"Thank God the Old Man always bought the best—'the best money can buy,' as he would say. How in the hell would I have cleaned up the pieces?"

At the end of the wall, I knelt down on all fours, turned off my flashlight and cautiously peered around the corner.

Nothing but the bright lights of Manhattan far below the dark empty office.

I took the lamp off my old desk and plugged it into the outlet by the copy machine. Now, in the soft light, I began to prepare myself for tonight's special meeting. I carefully spread out my handkerchief on the office floor. Tonight, Thatcher's turn had come. I was going to seek revenge on the man who had taken my father's firm from me.

"That fucker Thatcher's probably pulling the ol' man's Rolls into the corporate parking spot downstairs right now."

I heard the ring of the elevator bell outside the office's main door.

"That must be the bastard now. Eight o'clock. Just like clockwork. He always checks the payroll on Thursday nights. Well, he'll regret he made the trip this Thursday. Sweet revenge."

I covered my trembling hands with the tight-fitting

rubber gloves, and hurried to assemble the parts that I had left on the handkerchief. I screwed the silencer onto the chrome barrel and then attached the barrel to the pistol's stock. The chamber was ready. I only had to squeeze the trigger.

Before the front door opened, I turned out the light, stepped back, and steadied my shaking arm against the corner of the file room door. From where I was hiding, I could see a flashlight sweep across the reception area and shine into the main office space. I tightened my grip on the gun's handle and steadied my arm against the wall. The figure walked slowly into the larger room and cast the light from one side of the office to the other. As I started to squeeze back on the trigger, a glint of light reflected off a badge on the person's hat.

"Shit! The fucking Port Authority Police," I whispered. "They must suspect something. I bet Thatcher called them in."

The officer slowly made a final pass with his flashlight over the main room, then turned and headed for the exit. He had not noticed the misplaced lamp that remained on top of the copy machine.

They must have caught on, I thought. *That's probably why the lock was changed. Well, Thatcher, you've bought yourself some extra time. But, sooner or later, you have to show up. And when you do, asshole, I'll be waiting.*

I went about my usual task of reviewing the new business files that I found in the various desks and in the metal drawers in the file room. After making copies of the information that was useful to me, I replaced the lamp and left the office by the front door to take the elevator to the empty lobby.

The following afternoon, when I returned to French & Co. from an uptown appointment with a new prospect, I found a message on my desk. Jim French wanted to see me at 2:00 in his office. I checked my watch. It was 1:45. Fifteen minutes later, I walked down the hall and said hello to Maggie.

"I got a message the boss wants to see me."

"Yes," she said with a smile. "He's expecting you. You can go right in."

I pushed open the door and found Jim French sitting in

his darkly lit office. Ken Liebfeld, Paul Farmer and Bernie Katz, the outside counsel for French & Son, were standing behind him.

"Have a seat, Jay," Jim French said.

I sat in one of the three leather armchairs in front of his desk. Jim French's face was drawn and serious. He looked from Ken to Paul to Bernie, and then back to me.

"Let me get right to the point, Jay." He straightened his tie and swallowed. "I've been told that you're breaking into your father's old office. Is that true?"

I stared at him in amazement. *How did he know?* I dropped my eyes, and said weakly, "No. No, it's not."

"Jay. Look at me. I'll ask you once again. Have you been breaking into your father's office?"

I looked up at Jim French. Now there were tears in my eyes.

"Yes . . . yes, Jim, it's true." I felt sick to my stomach and began to shake. "I'm so sorry. I really am. I was just trying to bring new accounts over to your firm. I hope you'll forgive me."

"Jay, as you can imagine, this is a very serious matter. Will you wait outside, please?"

It seemed like hours before I was called back in.

"Jay, first of all, I want you to know that I like you—and, if I could, I would even keep you at the firm," Jim French said. "But my counsel has told me that you have to resign. There really is no other option. I'll need your resignation on my desk in the next thirty minutes, and then you have to leave the building. No one here will say why you left the firm or that you were asked to leave. Do you understand?"

"Yes, Jim," I said feebly. "Again, I want to apologize for my behavior, and any trouble it has brought you."

"Goodbye, Jay," Jim French said without shaking my hand.

I went back to my office, humiliated that I had been so stupid as to get caught. I wrote out my resignation letter in long hand, sealed it in an envelope and gave it to Maggie on my way out of the office. Outside, I found a pay phone on the corner of Wall and Broad.

"Anne? Anne, listen. Somehow, Thatcher found out I was breaking into Walker & Co. I'm sure he told Jim French. I just had a meeting with French and his lawyer. They forced me to resign. I don't know what I'm going to do."

"Oh Jay, I'm so sorry. But don't worry. We'll think of something at home tonight. Are you OK? You don't sound very good."

"Yeah, I'm OK."

"Why don't you go home now and get some rest? I'll see you at six."

When Anne came home, I was lying on our bed, still wearing my suit and shoes. I rocked back and forth holding myself making low, groaning sounds.

"Jay? Jay, it's me. Are you OK?" Anne shook my shoulder. "Jay! Jay!"

I held myself in a tight ball staring at the pillow.

Chapter 11

Golden Acres

Anne took my hand and led me from the Nissan. Jason and Nicholas followed behind, pushing and shoving. It seemed to me that my small family was walking in slow motion through the burning sun. Two hundred feet ahead was the Admissions Building, a modern one-story structure. It looked cold and threatening on this blistering hot 4th of July.

"Wait!" I pulled back. "I want to think."

I sat down numb on a small concrete bench trying to decide.

Should I go in? Do I want to commit myself again . . . a second time in a mental hospital?

A middle-aged woman dressed in street clothes walked out the doors. She stopped in front of me.

"Can I help?" she asked.

I looked at her kind face.

"No. No, I think I'm OK. I'm just trying to figure out . . . .. I'm not sure I need help. I don't know if I want to go inside."

"It's a fine place. One of the best," she said. "They'll certainly help you here. Well…whatever you decide, good luck." She smiled and continued on to her car.

I looked at Anne. "Let's go see," I said wearily.

Inside the first set of metal doors was a small white buzzer set to the side of the two locked wooden doors. Anne rang and the inner doors clicked open. As we walked through the empty lobby, the air conditioning gave a pleasant chill from the strong Connecticut summer heat outside. Ahead, behind a large circular reception desk, stood a neatly dressed Asian man. He greeted us with the wave of a red folder.

"Hello, Mr. Walker. Welcome to Golden Acres. We've been expecting you. My name's Charles Woo. Doctor Charles Woo. Please come in."

He shook Anne's hand, then mine, with a firm hand-shake.

"This must be Jason. And you, young man, must be Nicholas."

Nicholas hid his face in Anne's yellow skirt.

"Please follow me." And he took me by the elbow.

He led us to a small private office just off the rotunda where there was a long table surrounded by six chairs.

"Can the boys wait outside?" I asked.

"Certainly. We're not busy today. It's the holiday," he said. "One of the nurses will keep an eye on them. Have fun boys. You can go play." Dr. Woo closed the office door and turned to me. "Now, just a few formalities. Do you mind if I ask you several questions?"

I shook my head. "No. Go ahead."

"Well, first, why do you look so troubled? What's the matter?"

"I'm still not sure I really belong here."

I saw the concern on Anne's face. "You have to do this, Jay. You… "

Dr. Woo interrupted. "Well, then why did you go to Harrington Hospital?"

"Why don't you tell him, Anne?" I said.
"When Jay was fired… "

"I had a good job. A really good job," I said.

"OK, Jay. That's fine. Now let's let Anne finish," Dr. Woo said.

"Well, I found Jay that afternoon at home lying on our bed. He told me that he wanted to leave this life… his life. That he had no desire to live. Several days later, Dr. Zagorski, his psychologist, called. He told me not to leave Jay alone. That he could be a danger to himself. I told Dr. Zagorski I couldn't watch him all the time. That I work. That's when he recommended that Jay go to Harrington. Four days later, they released him. Jay talks a very good game, and he talked his way out of the hospital." She looked at me anxiously. "Then, leaving the hospital, when we drove back to Manhattan, he became frightened. He thought I said we were going to drive out to visit his step-mother in Southampton, not drive back to the apartment in New York. He became very angry. The closer we got to New York, the more angry and frightened he became. After we got home, it was like before. He couldn't function. He'd spend each day in bed paralyzed by fear. I tried . . . I didn't want the children to see."

I butted in.

"Harrington was an awful place. Every floor was locked. Patients were spilling out into the narrow hallways. At night there was yelling and screaming. It lasted all night long. They strapped one old woman into her wheelchair. She'd sit there tied up with duct tape constantly banging her head on the desk that was attached to her wheelchair. They had me spending my days making moccasins and belts. I swore I wouldn't spend the 4th of July in that dingy hole."

Dr. Woo looked up from his clipboard. "How bad has the depression been, Jay?"

"I was getting so close to reaching my goals. My family,

my profession, my debts, my faith. Everything I wanted in life was coming together."

"Then you were fired?" Dr. Woo asked.

"I lost everything. Once my job was taken away from me, I felt hopeless. I'd lost everything I'd worked so hard for. I'd become one of the golden boys at one of the largest brokerage firms in the world. Then, I lost it all. And I had no idea how I could ever get it back. I felt too tired and too old to start all over again. I didn't have the strength to start again. I saw myself eating out of trashcans."

I stared out the window, then turned back to Dr. Woo.

"Every morning, I'd struggle to get out of bed and get dressed in my suit and tie. But I had no place to go. No place except AA. And every time I went to AA, I would listen to the subway's rumble beneath the meeting room floor. My mind would drift to jumping on the tracks. To save money, I gave up my garage space by our apartment and moved the car to a cheaper place on a rooftop garage near the river. Each time I parked the car, I had to walk ten blocks to get home. I began to study the height of the garage's roof. Jumping from the roof or on to the subway tracks, these all seemed like solutions to my problem. They seemed perfectly acceptable. I didn't care anymore. And I couldn't get these thoughts to stop." I wondered, 'How am I going to care for my sons?' Then I remembered the life insurance. I had $440,000 of life insurance for the boys."

Anne reached across the table and took my hand. I held her hand tightly—I was desperate for help from anyone. I looked at her, then Dr. Woo.

"One morning while my family slept, I sneaked out into the hallway in my pajamas. I was going to take the elevator to the 36th floor and jump. I'd already studied the roof from the children's playground on the esplanade. It was high enough, 36 floors. But when the elevator came, I couldn't do it. I turned around and went back into the apartment and slipped back into bed."

"How do you feel now, Jay?" Dr. Woo asked.

"Even today, as Anne was driving up here, I was thinking 'Wouldn't it be nice, so nice… just open the car door and slowly roll out onto the macadam of the thruway at 60 or 70 miles an hour? Finally, the pain would stop.' I have trouble remembering what year it is, what day it is. I can't think clearly. I feel totally lost. Totally abandoned. I feel completely empty inside."

"At home, I'd catch Jay looking up at the rooftops." Anne started to shake as she spoke. "Today, when we stopped at Burger King for lunch, he was walking slowly behind us. I saw his reflection in the windows studying the traffic going by in the street."

"Anne, do you think Jay should be here?"

Anne looked at me with fearful eyes. "Yes . . . yes, I do. He'd be safer here."

Dr. Woo looked at me.

"Jay, we can help you here."

"I just want to be happy like other people, that's all. I want to feel good about myself again. Why is that so hard? Right now, nothing matters. I don't care about anything anymore. If I do stay here, I have to be in an unlocked building. Not like at Harrington. I felt like an animal there."

"I think that's alright," Dr. Woo smiled. "But you have to promise not to try to run away."

"I promise," I lied. The thought of escape was already in my head.

"Well good." The doctor smiled. "Jay, do you have everything you need?" "I think so. I've packed my best clothes. Anne told me Golden Acres is for the rich and famous. She said it's more my kind of place - completely different from Harrington." I laughed and shook my head. "I never thought I'd be picking out a posh loony bin."

"Alright then. Good. Now, all you have to do is read these and sign them for me." He handed me a pen and stack of papers.

I picked up the pen without looking at the documents. As I signed by the red Xs, the pen shook while I gave away my rights to Golden Acres.

"Fine." He took the papers back and put them in his briefcase. "Alright then. This way, please."

Outside in the upper parking lot two strong orderlies took my bags from the Nissan and put them in the Golden Acres van. They drove me down the hill to the Main House while Anne and the boys followed behind.

The van jerked to a stop in front of a majestic old building with a sprawling front terrace. On one side of the main door was a large window that showed a comfortable living room inside. On the other were two windows that spanned what looked like a large dining room. The van door slid open and I stepped out into the glaring sun. Walking up the flagstone steps, I spotted three surveillance cameras hidden discreetly amongst the ornate molding on the blue-gray slate roof. One of them marked our progress as we walked to the front door.

Two middle-aged nurses dressed in street clothes rather than uniforms were waiting to take us upstairs to my second floor room. With each step on the worn staircase my fear grew. I looked for locks on the windows and doors as we walked down the narrow corridor. There were none. The older nurse, the one with the nametag Becky, shoved my door open. I pulled back into the hall.

"What's wrong?" she asked.

"I thought it would be more modern. Larger. With sliding glass doors. A swimming pool. I thought this was for the rich and famous."

The other nurse, Jenny, tried to stifle a short low cackling laugh. She stood behind me, encouraging me to enter the room.

"I thought I'd be on the ground floor with sliding glass doors by a swimming pool."

My eyes darted from one wall of the small room to the other. There was barely room to turn around. A worn white bedspread covered the sagging single bed. The armchair in the corner was losing its stuffing. A tired chest of drawers with peeling varnish leaned against the far wall. Faded striped wallpaper encased this tiny box. Only the view from the small window had any redeeming grace. It looked out onto the large rolling front lawn that stretched like a green carpet from the front door down to the visitors' parking lot and the main front gate. It was an awful room. I felt trapped.

"It's just temporary Jay." Jenny nudged me forward. "We just want to keep you near the nurses' station for a while. We're just down the hall if you need anything. We have to keep an eye on you for a while at the beginning. You understand. We don't want you running away just after you've joined us." She laughed her cackling laugh. "After a week or two, we'll move you to another, bigger room."

"A week or two?" I looked at Anne with pleading eyes. "A week or two?"

"We just want to get to know you, that's all, Jay." Becky looked at Anne and the boys and smiled. "Jay, it's time for your family to leave now. "

Shaken and frightened, I turned to my sons, drew them to me and hugged them both tightly.

"I'll miss you two guys."

"But Dad, aren't you coming home with us to watch the fireworks?"

"No Jason, not this year. You have to take care of Mommy now. You're the big brother, right?" Slowly, I let them go. I wiped away a tear and turned to Anne and gave her a loveless kiss.

The door closed, and I stood alone in the room.

How did this happen to me? Is she really trying to help me? Or does she just want to get me out of the apartment?

From the larger window I saw the white doctors' office building across the path below. Just under my window, the professional staff was using a side door of the Main House to come in to lunch. I turned, stared at my bag, then slowly began to unpack my things. I could not find my razor, nail file or drinking glass. My sneakers were missing their shoelaces and my belts had been removed. The orderlies had even taken the

Listerine.

I'm in recovery. Don't they know I'm in recovery? I'm not going to drink my fucking Listerine for God's sake. I'm in recovery and I'm in a fucking lunatic asylum.

On this sunny Fourth of July afternoon, as I lay on the bed, tears rolled down the sides of my cheeks.

The dinner bell woke me at six. I stared at my tired face in the mirror, then joined the men and women downstairs waiting in line with plates. The long buffet table had an enormous selection of fine meats and vegetables. The opulence of the food was staggering.

"Is it like this every night?" I asked the fellow in front of me.

"They try to get us to eat. Most of us had stopped before coming here."   He turned away and filled his plate with roast beef, mashed potatoes and asparagus.

I took some of the turkey and carrots and went to a long table in the middle of the room where a woman with hair dyed pitch black sat at the head in a bright red floral dress. She was middle-aged, heavy set and wore thick pink pancake makeup. Her dark red lipstick was painted from one side of her face to the other stopping at her ears. She said nothing, but attacked the first of her five turkey drumsticks like a typewriter carriage. She snatched the second leg before the first bone hit her plate. Then, on to the third and fourth without ever looking up.

A tall, fat man with oily skin sat across from me. His girth stretched the buttons on his plaid vest and brown tweed jacket. Both his hair and his beard were parted down the center. On his plate was nothing but peas. He divided the green pile down the center, making sure that each side was of equal size. Then, carefully with his dinner knife, he took one pea at a time on the flat of his blade, slowly balancing the pea before the tip of his tongue. Then, like a Gila monster, he snapped each pea into the back of his mouth and swallowed it with a gulp.

I only ate half my meal, and then went back to the buffet table to search out dessert and coffee. Ten warm pies and three cakes waited next to large tubs of vanilla and chocolate ice cream. There were even red, white and blue Independence Day cupcakes and cookies.

At this rate, I thought, *I should put back the 30 pounds I've lost by week's end.*

As I ate my cake and ice cream in silence with my head down, I thought of the family and the job that were lost, and the distant New York City life that now excluded me.

How will I ever get it back? How will I ever find a job?

The ice cream and coffee had no appeal, so I left my seat and walked outside to the backyard.

As I stepped away from the bright lights of the Main House into the dark night, I looked above at the starry expanse of the heavens. The night air was cool and refreshing on my skin. My sense of claustrophobia began to subside.

Five women, all dressed in T-shirts and jeans, sat gathered together at a small wooden picnic table smoking and talking. It looked like most of them were in their early twenties, all thin, with heavy eye makeup.

"Hello," I offered.

One smiled, the dirty blonde with sad eyes who was sucking her thumb. But the others were more interested in their conversation. I crossed the small back lawn to the brick garden wall and watched as fireflies zigzagged amongst the black ivy with their blinking lights.

One of the girls laughed loudly. I turned and looked.

"Higgins says I should be out of here in two to three days," said the tall girl as she pulled on her nose ring.

Another pushed her purple hair back, took a hard drag on her Lucky and blew smoke rings at the moon. Spiky thorns from purple bougainvilleas circled both of her pale, thin arms. A third tattoo of a diamonded yellow cobra circled her neck.

"I'm in for as long as my insurance lasts," she said with a smile. "They call it the 28-day cure. Funny how that works - after 28 days, when the insurance runs out, you're cured."

The small blonde wiped tears from her eyes with a Kleenex.

"Bobby and I are gettin' married when I get out. I just know we are. Just as soon as he buys a car. I've always wanted to marry a guy with a car. I'm sure he'll come back."

What am I doing here? I thought. *How did my life get so screwed up? This isn't what I planned.*

I found my way to the pay phone booths in the hall next to the large living room and called my sponsor.

"Ian? Hi, it's me. They've got me locked up again, Ian. I can't take this much longer. I feel trapped. I've got to get back to my family."

"Listen, Jay, it'll only be for a short while. I'm sure they'll help you."

"I'm scared to death. I don't know what's happening to me. I'm so frightened I'm having trouble just talking. I can't stand being here all alone. I don't feel like I'm alive. The grounds are lovely and the food's great, but I don't give a shit. None of it makes any sense. I have to get out. Can't you help me?"

"Jay, use the Serenity Prayer. Remember when we worked the Steps? Think of what you can change and what you can't."

"Everything in my life feels fake, Ian. It's like something out of Kafka. None of this makes any sense. The isolation. I'm cut off from everything."

"Jay, you can do this, I know you can. Don't give up. Try to accept it. You just got there. Give it a chance. Try to let them help you. You know you can…"

"It feels like jail, Ian. The loneliness is killing me. I have to get out. They're giving me so much medication my hands are shaking. I can hardly hold the phone. I can't even speak I'm so fucked up. The words won't come out. I still can't shower, shave or get dressed. I don't even want to. I forget to eat. I try to tell myself that everything's going to be OK. But I know it's not. I'm scared, Ian. And I feel so lost. Completely lost."

"Jay, give it a try for a couple of days. I'm sure it'll get . . .."

"I don't know if I can last that long, Ian. Everything feels like it's closing in on me. I'm trapped in here with a bunch of lunatics. I'm afraid to go to bed, and I'm afraid to get up. I'm starting to feel like I'm one of them. How do I get back to being normal?"

"Jay, it's almost 10. Why don't you turn in? Read a couple pages of the Big Book."

"I'm … I'm trying to read *The Seven Story Mountain*. But, I can't even get past page five."

"Then say some prayers tonight. And tomorrow talk to your doctor."

"I'll try, Ian. I'll try."

"'Bye, Jay. Good luck."

I brushed aside the tears with a shaking hand, then walked slowly back to my tiny room.

10:30 was "Meds," so I lined up with the rest of the second floor patients. At the counter I was given my small paper cup with my Lithium and a cup of water.

"Make sure you swallow the pills," the nurse barked. She stared at my lips with her fox's eyes. "Don't try and hide them under your tongue. That's it. Drink them all down. Now let me see. Open up. Let me see."

I returned to my room, dropped my clothes on the floor and finally fell asleep at one-thirty without washing or brushing my teeth.

The dream began in a small apartment. I noticed the light on my answering machine flashing and hit the button.

"Hi. This message is for Jay Walker. This is Francis calling from Integrated Behavioral Health," the answering machine said. "I'm calling about the forms we sent you. We still have not gotten them back yet. If we don't receive them back in the next two weeks along with your doctors' reports, we'll have no other choice but to stop your disability payments. If you have any questions, please call me at 1-800-417-1000. Thank you and have a good day."

"They don't want me to be successful. They don't want me to have a family. They don't want me to be happy. They

don't want me to live."

I woke up with a scream, soaked in sweat. Panic, bewilderment and fright all coursed through my body.

"I won't let them take this from me. I won't." My heart pounded. "Why am I here? I've to get back to New York. I have no schedule here, no structure, no job. There's nothing for me to do here." I looked around in the dark. "What am I doing in this strange place, frightened and alone? I've to get out of here. Nurse," I cried. "I can't stay here. Nurse!"

My door flew open and two night nurses ran into my room.

"Nurse. I have nothing to do." I stared at them, my eyes wide, my body shaking.

"Jay, what do you mean? 'Nothing to do?'" The small nurse put her arm around me.

I pushed her away.

"I don't have anything to do," I yelled. "Can't you see? I can't stay here. I have to go home. It feels like all the walls are closing in on me."

She held me again. "Jay, everything will be alright. Everything's going to be fine. You have your daily activities."

"You'll make new friends," the older nurse said. "You can always read or exercise in the gym. There's the swimming pool. And you have your group therapy."

"I need control. I don't have any control here. I have to try to start my career over again. I don't have time to stay here. I have to get back to work. I have to find a job. Don't you understand?"

"Jay. Try to relax. Just relax. There'll be time for all that later. First you have to get well again. Lie back. Lie down here. Here, this will help you." I felt a jab in my thigh as she pushed the needle's plunger down. "Now try to get some sleep, Jay."

I lay back in bed frightened and confused.

"It will be alright, Jay. It really will. If you need anything, just call us. We're right around the corner."

One of the nurses switched the light off. The other drew the door closed. And the black engulfed me again.

What am I doing here? How did things ever get this bad? I wondered.   Slowly, I drifted off.

I spent the next afternoon pacing back and forth across the blue-slated terrace in front of the Main House; back and forth, over and over, again and again. I went from the yellow hammock at one end of the terrace to the small green hedge at the other. Back and forth. Each time I reached the hedge, there were the three forbidden small slate steps. They led to the driveway that was off limits. Each time I reached them, I stopped and pushed my shoe tip an inch over the edge of the top step. Then I looked quickly over my shoulder and smiled at the hidden rooftop camera that stared down at me, constantly tracking my course back and forth.

"You see? I've crossed the line again," I said to it. "You see?"

I walked slowly back again to the yellow hammock, then turned and went back to the steps. Like a caged tiger, I prowled the terrace like this for the next four hours. But I still could not free myself from the tension that held me.

I kept thinking, "How can I get out of this place?"

I looked down from the terrace at the sprawling front lawn that spread out across Golden Acres. I studied the circular drive.

"If I sneak off the patio into the bushes, go behind the houses, and then down the road to the main street, then I'd be free. But there's too much open space. They'd see me on the cameras. I have to go at night."

After lunch, walking back up to my room, I studied the corridor that led from my small bedroom past the bathroom to the far end of the hallway. I looked around carefully before going past my room down to the T at the end of the hall. To the left was the nurses' station, but to the right, the hall continued past the reading lounge where the staff did the weighing and blood pressure tests. At the end of the corridor was a staircase that I had never noticed before.

This must lead to the side door on the first floor, I thought.

I had to be careful. If I were caught, they would surely send me to the locked Acute Care Unit at the top of the hill, and I'd never be able to get out of there. The next morning, the house was quiet. All of the patients were at their planned activities. In the bubble mirror that peeked around from atop the doorframe, I saw the nurses' station. Two nurses sat at their desks absorbed in their administrative tasks. Cautiously, I moved down the hallway past the reading lounge.

"Excuse me!"

A tall man coming up the steps nearly knocked me down.

"Oh, hi. I was just getting another magazine."

I backtracked into the lounge and started to fumble through *Sports Illustrated* and watched the man continue on down the hall to the nurses' station. Once he was gone, I left the lounge and continued down the staircase. At the bottom of the steps, I found myself at the back of the Main House's kitchen. The door was held locked with a large chain and padlock. Freedom was just on the other side.

"Shit. I'll have to find another way."

Back in my room, I lay down on my bed to nap and fell right to sleep.

I am on an island, a small island, across from a small lagoon, in a small town in the south of Australia were the sun was shining. There is a main ferry house with a pier stretching out into the lagoon were people are gathered. Everyone here is so innocent and friendly. The women for the most part have short-cropped hair. One woman that I met has reddish hair with lovely blue eyes. The women are so friendly. They play games. They don't hurt anyone. They are remarkably open. There are also some animals like iguanas or armadillos. They are very strange games that the people play. Everyone is friendly. They don't bother you. They are open and warm and loving. People just go about their ways. They don't bother you. They just do things that make them happy, and they don't bother anyone. They are very open. They are not concerned or embarrassed about themselves. There are some who were naked. I thought they might be Aborigines. Most are thin. But the people are just together. They go about their ways to-gether, doing things together, not judging—friendly—loving. I try to fit in, but I am amazed, I am amazed about this place. It is like no other place in the world that I have ever seen. There is no judgment. There is no embarrassment. I try to explain this to the woman I met. But she does not seem concerned with it. She is more concerned with me than with herself—with living a good life, with being nice, with being understanding. Then she went away. I lost her. I came upon a group playing some sort of game that I do not understand. They want to in-clude me in the game, but I tell them that I do not know the game. I go up a hill to a group of simple houses with open thatched roofs so that the sun can come in. There are boards and platforms. Some of the women wear iron body attach-ments that suggest sexual things. One of the women that I saw is incredibly muscular, incredibly strong from living a life outdoors—a pure life, eating healthy food. She does not notice her muscularity, she just accepts it, takes it for granted. She is not proud of it—it is just who she is.

There is an ocean liner, a huge ocean liner, out in the middle of the ocean. There are people on the ocean liner. It is pitch black and cold. The ocean liner is crashing through the waves—going through the black night. On the ship, we are go-ing through a storm. The rain is lashing at the ocean liner. The wind is howling. The sea is rough and raging. White caps are all about the ship. The bow is crashing down through the large waves. It is a medical ship that is pounding through the huge waves in the dark of night. There are children in positions to medically help their fathers live; or they have the option to not help their fathers survive. Their fathers' lives are dependent upon the medical choice the children make to either help the fathers survive or not. The fathers are very ill, and, for a father to survive, a child has to either participate in a medical fash-ion. If the child decides not to participate, the father will die. All of the fathers are dying. They can only be saved by their chil-dren who either volunteer or do not volunteer to help their fathers survive.

On the medical ship there are wards after wards, filled with fathers in beds. They are all dying, and it is up to the children — it is only the children who can help the fathers survive. The children must determine — decide — whether or not they want to help the fathers survive. Each child can volunteer to provide the life source so that the father can live. Some fathers have their sons sitting at their bedsides providing the transfusion that will let them live. There are other fathers who are in beds with an empty chair by their bedside who are dying. The empty seats are where the sons are letting their fathers die. Only the sons can prevent their fathers from dying. My father is not here.

I say to one of the boys who is going to help his father survive, "It must be difficult to have this power—to be in this position—to be willing to help your father survive." I begin to sob. "I don't know if I could do it. It must be hard."

There came a sharp knock on my door. I sat up and rubbed my eyes.

"It's open," I said.

A thin man in his forties walked in leaning heavily on two brown, worn, wooden canes.

"Hi. Tom Forster. Just moved in down the hall. Came by to say hello. I'll be your neighbor for a while. They're moving me up to the ACU in a day or two. I can't use my wheelchair down here."

"Jay Walker."

I looked at Tom's delicate frame and broad face. His receding hairline was underlined by thick eyebrows and a dark mustache. Long black sideburns dropped below his cheekbones. He held himself on his two canes.

"I hear you're pretty new here," Tom said.

"Yeah. I came in on the 4th. I was at Harrington in Queens for four days before coming here. God, what an awful place that was. I couldn't stand it. People screaming in the halls. But, it kept me from killing myself, I guess. They had me in a locked ward." We looked at one another. "I don't know about you, Tom, but for me, life still doesn't make much sense. They think I'm bipolar. You know . . . manic-depressive. Most of the time I go sky high, but once in a while I go very low. I like it when I'm up high, speeding around. But it's not good for my bank account. I piss away a ton of dough. I call it 'being in the penthouse'. But it's a hell of a lot better than being in the basement. The doctors are trying to keep me between the lobby and the third floor with my meds. This time I really crashed. It was like being at the bottom of a deep, dark well. No one could help me get out." I gazed out the window. "Pretty quiet around here with the holiday. What are you in for, Tom?"

"Same thing. Clinical depression. I got this virus when I was 17, and they didn't think I'd ever be able to walk again. As you can see, I've learned to get around pretty well with my sticks. But recently, I've been getting up every morning and crying my eyes out. I don't know what's wrong. Finally, my wife and I decided that maybe some professional help would be a good idea."

"Sometimes I wish I could cry more often," I said. "It's just recently I've been able to cry. Things suck so much, there's nothing much else to do. Most of the time I don't seem able to feel my feelings, or feel anything actually. All of my feelings seem locked away in a freezer somewhere."

"Well, to me, you look like one of the more normal ones around this place," Tom chuckled. "I don't know if that helps any. I saw a woman sitting outside talking to one of the trees a couple of minutes ago. Her lipstick went from ear to ear. Then there's this guy out back. They say he's a genius. He's been sitting out there ever since he got here three months ago writing his treatise. He showed me the journal he's been writing in. It's all gibberish. Nothing but gibberish. He only writes on the first page. He writes down the page. But then, when he gets to the bottom, he goes back up to the top and starts all over again. He never turns the page. He just starts over again at the top, writing one sentence on top of the other. The page is covered completely in blue scrawl. And he just keeps writing. They say he's been at it ever since he got here three months ago. Someone should tell him to turn the page." Tom scratched his head. "This is really some place, eh?" He smiled. "Anyway, I've got to get ready for dinner. Nice to meet you."

As Tom hobbled out of the room, I thought, *Good thing you don't know how fucked up I really am. I've got to get out of this place.*

Friday afternoon was my walk. I went downstairs to meet Sara, my nurse. She was shorter than me, about 5' 2", soft spoken, with a round, warm face. Her brownish-gray hair was pulled back in to a bun and held in place with a long wooden chopstick. Sara was more friendly and understanding than most of the staff. She seemed to truly care about me. It was only with her that I could leave the terrace. Stepping down onto the oval roadway with her was like opening a prison door.

"You know, Sara, my breakdown came at just about the same time of year as my mother's suicide. I only realized that yesterday. She killed herself in late June. And years ago, my grandmother tried to do the same thing in the summer."

I could see the sunlight sparkling in her tears.

"Do you suppose there's a connection, Sara?"

"Perhaps," she said. "But don't forget, Jay. When you had your breakdown, you didn't have any alcohol to hide behind. Unlike your mother, you were facing life sober. You didn't have a crutch."

"But I'd been doing fine without the booze until my breakdown. Now I feel like I've totally changed. I'm not the same person any more. Before, even sober, I had no fear. I'd run the 6:30 am AA meetings, be in the office by 7:15 getting ready to make my cold calls; exercising every day - jogging or skiing depending on the time of year. That's all gone now. Now I have no interest in anything anymore. I always said that I never understood people killing themselves. I thought, 'Even if a door slams shut on your life, if you're patient and wait long enough, another door's bound to open.' And when I'd meet people who said they thought life was tough, I didn't know what they meant. To me, life never seemed like a struggle. But now I've become one of them. I've totally changed. Life doesn't seem so easy anymore."

"You're probably just starting to find out who you really are," Sara said. "For the first time, you're looking at some of the painful parts of your life."

"Like what? I've been able to handle it all right up 'til now."

"Look at your marriage, Jay. Didn't you say things have been rocky for a long time? That really only your children give you something to care about? And what about your parents— your mother and your father? Have you accepted your mother's suicide, or not being able to ever communicate with your father? And what about your resentments, and your feelings of deprivation and entitlement?"

"I know I stuff my feelings. I know that that's because I don't want to feel them. But Sara, right now, I don't have a clue what I'm going to do with my life. My thoughts are so jumbled up. And I always feel so tired. I used to know exactly what I wanted—where I was going, and how I would get there."

"You just have to give it time, Jay. You've been through a lot. And you've been through a lot sober. Eventually your hopelessness and confusion will end. You'll see. They'll be replaced with a new meaning for your life. Try to be patient with Dr. Burns in your one to one sessions, and also in Group. Don't forget it takes two or three weeks for your medication to start working. Until then, try to accept the things that have happened to you. Look at what you have to be grateful for. Be patient, Jay."

"I'm trying, Sara. But what do I do in the meantime? I don't think I'm getting anything from Dr. Burns. And I'm still paralyzed by the fear and the loneliness."

"Patience, Jay. I know it's hard. You know, in AA they say that it's like peeling an onion. It takes time to peel away the old layers. And often times, what you find below hurts.

Change takes time, Jay. And it's painful. Let us try to help you here."

"You know, Sara, before I was so optimistic."

"Jay, what about hobbies?"

"Hobbies?"

"Yes, don't you have any hobbies you still care about?"

"Well, photography was one of my passions. I'm pretty good at it. I take pictures wherever I go. Jason and Nicholas are my favorite subjects. My apartment is covered with their photos. Maybe my wife can bring me my Nikon. She's coming up next week."

"I'm afraid you can't do that. You see, it's important to the patients at Golden Acres that their anonymity be protected. Taking pictures might interfere with that. We've been taking care of the rich and famous for over sixty years."

Up from the bottom of the hill came what looked like a long-haired leaping gnome. The short old man was skipping up the oval towards us, first hopping onto the lawn and then back off it again onto the tarmac. His thick white eyebrows matched his wild bushy hair that bounced up and down with each leap.

"Who's that, Sara?"

"That's Jeffery. He's been with us a long time."

As he skipped along, he twirled one hand above his head, pulling his white shirttails further out of his baggy trousers. Suddenly he stopped his prancing and bent over a small yellow dandelion. Without picking it up, he touched his nose to its delicate petals to smell the flower's fragrance. He stood up, put his hands on his hips, stretched his back, then pushed his long ragged hair out of his eyes. He stared at the teal sky above, before looking down at the dandelion again. He smiled the broadest of toothless smiles and spoke to it.

"I'm not nuts, you know. I'm not nuts at all. 'Take your medications! Take your medications!' That's all they tell me. I take my meds. But, I'm not nuts."

He continued his skipping, going right by us, up the drive, hopping on and off the lawn waving his white Golden

Acres wristband above his head.

The six o'clock bell rang for dinner.

"Jay, I think it's time to go back," Sara said.

"Thanks for taking me around the oval tonight, Sara." I looked at her kind face.

"I enjoy talking with you, Jay. Maybe we can do it again next Friday."

"Sure," I lied. I knew I would be gone by then.

On Thursday afternoon, I stood by my window, looking for Anne to arrive. Just after three, the white Nissan pulled into the parking lot at the bottom of the hill. Anne got out and began her walk up the oval drive to the Main House. I met her on the terrace, took her hands and kissed her lightly on the cheek.

"I'm happy you came. How was the traffic?"

"Not bad, actually. It looks as though you're starting to gain back some weight. Why don't we sit down? It's a lovely day."

"I haven't noticed . . .. How are the boys?"

"They're fine, actually. They miss you. Maybe next time I can bring them with me."

"Anne, I want to leave here. I want to leave here soon. I hate being cooped up in this place. They're always watching me." I pointed to one of the cameras on the roof. "The only time I can leave the terrace is when I have an escort or there's some group activity—swimming, or the gym, or something. I don't have any interest in their group activities."

"Dr. Burns said you should try to get involved. Actually, you've always liked to exercise. That's all you did in New York."

"I've tried. But I can't. Don't you understand? I don't give a damn anymore. I don't give a damn about anything anymore. And I'm always exhausted. All I want to do is to be left alone. To be left alone and to sleep. I have no enthusiasm for anything. I don't care anymore."

"Actually, Jay, you were a great salesman. Don't be silly. You'll be able to do it again. You just need some rest. Do you need any more clothes from home?"

"Anne, can't you see that I've changed completely? I'm a different person now? Everything has fallen apart. I've lost everything. I'm not only frightened about the future, but about the present and the past as well. I don't know if I'll ever be able to get back on my feet again. I've completely lost control of my life."

"Well, you certainly had control when you were stealing from Walker & Co.," she said sharply. "If you weren't copying files from your father's office, you'd never have been fired. And you wouldn't be here now. I told you not do it, actually— that's kid shit!"

"Kid shit? What!" I stared at her in disbelief. "You never told me not to do it. Don't you remember? It amused you. You thought it was funny."

"Stop it, Jay."

"How can you *not* remember? We'd meet at Windows on the World when I was done copying policies to celebrate. Sometimes, you'd even have your parents meet us. Don't tell me you can't remember that?"

"Well, it wasn't a very good idea. Look where it got you."

"I was only trying to make money for you and for our family. It was all for us."

"Actually, it was a pretty stupid thing to do. Why can't you play by the rules like everyone else?"

"Stupid. You didn't think it was so stupid at the time. If it was so stupid, why didn't you tell me to stop?"

"Jay, keep your voice down," Anne snapped.

"Keep my voice down. For God's sake, Anne, can't you give me a break just for once? I need your help now more than ever, not your criticism. Look what I've given you. I've introduced you to my friends, taken you to my clubs, gotten you a job at an Ivy League firm. I taught you my lifestyle. Now you know how to navigate your way about New York society. Can't you try to give just a little bit?"

She glared at me.

"Look, Jay, it was a long drive up here. Jason kept me up all night last night. My job's killing me. And since we let the maid go, I've been doing all the housework myself. I didn't come here to fight. If we're going to argue, I'm going to leave."

"Fine, leave if you want. I don't care. I'll be OK without your help."

"This is the thanks I get? If you can't see that I'm trying to help you, I don't think there's any sense in me coming back again."

"Everything has to be such a big deal with you. Why can't you open up a little bit, show some . . . "

Anne jumped to her feet.

"I've had it with you!"

She stormed down the terrace steps to the oval drive that led to the park-
ing lot. I walked to the edge of the terrace and watched her walk away until she was nearly at the bottom of the roadway.

"Anne," I shouted. "Please don't go. Anne… I'm sorry. I'm sorry for what I said."

She stopped and looked back at me.

"Anne, please come back," I shouted. "I'm sorry. Please come back. Don't leave."

She hesitated, then slowly turned and walked back up the oval and stood in front of me.

"Jay, remember . . . I'm only trying to help you. I know it's difficult for you to see that now. But you still have a family in New York that cares about you. We want you to get well. I care about you, Jay."

"And I care about you too, Anne. And the boys. I'm sorry. Sometimes I just get so angry."

"I'm not sure when I can come back next time. It's hard for me with work and the kids. I'll try and call you next week and let you know."

"Anne, I'm trying. I really am. But I want to be a part of the world again. Not cut off. Be careful on the way home. Drive safe." I looked down at her through my tears. "I wish I could go with you."

With downcast eyes, she said in a soft voice, "The doctor said that once the medication is working, you should be able to come home in several weeks. Good-bye, Jay."

"Good-bye. Thank you for coming."

I watched her walk to the parking lot and drive away in the small Nissan.

I wonder if she's given up on me?

Being four years sober, I seldom thought about drinking. But tonight, after dinner, I decided to go to the AA meeting in the large building across from my second story room.

The meeting was dull and boring and poorly attended. There were only three people at the table—and only because they were required to be there. They knew and little about the 12 Step Program. But they knew a lot about drinking.

I pushed my chair back from the table and walked over to the window. I looked across the path up at my room. My window was not far from the ground below—maybe 25 feet.

Chapter 12

T hat night, after dinner and meds, I lay under my bedcovers staring at the window.

If I take the screen off, I can drop down . . . and I'll be free. I have to be careful; the damn nurses check beds every 15 minutes. I'll go tonight—go out the window. I have to get out of here. I have to . . ..

After the nurses' 4:45 bed check, I went to the window and removed the screen. The night was still dark and no one was on the path below. I went back to my bed and looked at the window. Then back to the window. I sat on the windowsill and looked out. Nothing but silence. I stood up and backed away. Perspiration now covered my brow. I measured my body for a second time against the window frame. Yes, I could fit through the opening.

I tried to force my body out the window, but fear held me back. I tried again.
Just go!
But my body recoiled from the open window

frame.

Then suddenly, as if I were in a dream, I went past my bed and out the window. I felt my fingers clawing the outdoor siding of the Main House as I fell to the ground. I crashed hard on a large metal drainage grate I had not seen hidden in the shrubbery, and listened to the shatter of my heel bone. A bolt of white-hot pain coursed up my leg and through my body. I vomited into the bushes.

Slowly, I pulled myself up as best I could. Through the early morning darkness, I limped to the wrought-iron handrail on the path and up the stone stairs. I lurched across the wet grass. With each step, the pain in my foot grew worse. On the other side of the Doctors' Office Building, I went down the hill into the darkness towards the employees' parking lot. The two stone columns at the gate led me to Golden Acres Road and then to the woods on the other side.

With the awful pain in my heel, I could no longer walk. So I crawled through the underbrush over the leaves and through the brambles until I found a small pond in the middle of a clearing. The July sun began to break through the pines and splash across the water. Music from the chirping sparrows carried on the breeze, and above me, a swallow, soaring on its white-spotted wings, bounced across the pink morning sky. There I collapsed exhausted against a fallen tree.

The screech from the rooftop bullhorns on the medical buildings jarred
me from my slumber. Police cars raced up the oval drive, lights flashing, sirens howling.

I smiled.

Good ol' Alice. She must have checked. I guess she saw the window open and called Dr. Burns; he'll be pissed. Called the cops. From the sound, I guess they miss me.

I laughed.

Now what? No money. No foot. How in the hell am I going to get back to New York? There's no chance. So much for seeing the kids.

A bushy-tailed squirrel dug in the ground beside the

258

pond. It plucked an acorn from the earth, took it to the water's edge, and washed it. It put the acorn in its mouth, then jumped up onto the tree trunk where I lay.

"Why can't I be free like you?" I asked the squirrel. "Live in the woods, eat off the land . . . like Thoreau at Walden. Why not? No rules. No jails."

The squirrel cocked its head and stared at me with its beady brown eyes. It took the acorn from its mouth, held it out in its paws, and offered it to me. Then it put it back in its mouth and scampered away.

Across the swamp, a truck rumbled down a bumpy dirt road. I ducked behind the log until it passed. It had come from the small house up the hill at the end of the road. I watched through the trees as an old, gray-haired woman wearing an apron walked from the mailbox back up the driveway with her morning mail. The slam of her front door echoed through the woods. Alone, I listened to the wind as it bent the pines.

Now what? Just lie here? What's the point? I've got no food, no money. It's like everything else—another one of my dumb ideas. Great. Just fucking great!

The morning air was chilled. I shivered, cupped my hands and blew on them. I ran my fingers through my hair.

What's the use? I'll never get away. I might as well give up.

I crawled over the twigs and leaves and hoisted myself up the embankment next to the road to look for help. Across the street, some of the hospital staff were pulling into their parking spots for the morning shift. A young nurse got out of her blue Ford and locked the door.

"Hello!" I shouted. "Can you help me?"

The woman squinted into the sun. She shielded her eyes until she spotted me lying by the pavement.

"What's wrong?" she called.

"I'm hurt."

"OK. Just wait there!" she shouted back. "We'll be right there. I'll get some help."

Minutes later, one of the gray Golden Acres vans came

down the street with its red lights flashing and stopped in front of me. Two young orderlies jumped down from the cab dressed in white medical garb.

"You OK? We've been looking for you since the alarms went off," the shorter one said.

"Jesus! What did you do to yourself?" the other man asked.

"I don't know." I looked down embarrassed. "I guess I hurt my foot."

"Come on, Mel. Pick him up. Let's get him in the van and take him back up the hill."

They grabbed me by the arms, helped me stand, and slowly put me on the bench in the back of the truck. They brought me back to my room in the Main House where Dr. Burns was waiting. The portly old man was staring out my open window at the ground below with a scowl. He turned, annoyed. Adjusting the white lab coat that matched his thinning hair and neatly trimmed mustache, he waddled around to the side of the bed and peered at me through his gold half-rimmed glasses.

"You were only trying to escape, Jay? Right?"

I dropped my eyes. "Yes," I muttered.

"What?" he snapped.

"Yes, that's all. I was only trying to escape. I had to get away. I couldn't stand it here anymore."

He wiped his oily forehead and frowned.

"Let's see," he said. "Get up on the bed." He took hold of my ankle and shook my foot back and forth. "Doesn't hurt?" he asked, surprised.

I shook my head. He still looked perturbed.

"Probably not broken then, but we'd better have it checked anyway. Dr. Walsh in Danbury, he's an orthopedic. The orderlies will drive you down." He walked to the door. "We'll start the ECT as soon as you get back."

I called after him, "ECT?"

The old man turned and smiled. "You know, Jay . . . shock treatments."

At noon, two orderlies in white uniforms put me in the back of one of the Golden Acres vans for our tip to the Danbury Hospital. It wasn't long before we reached the turnpike, and the urban landscape of Connecticut now sped past my window. I sat quietly on the back seat with my leg up, and listened to Mel and Bobby talking up front about some of the young female patients.

"Nothing worse than nutty druggies," Mel said.

"Yeah." Bobby smiled. "But for a night, what the hell? It might be fun, right?"

"What if they squeal?"

"Who's going to believe 'em?"

Can I get the rear door open? I wondered. *All I have to do is slide it open and roll out onto the pavement and be done with it.*

I pulled my leg towards the door, leaned against the van window and tugged at the handle anxiously.

Shit. Bobby has to open it.

When we pulled in to Danbury Hospital, two orderlies in white gowns were waiting for me at the Emergency Entrance with a wheelchair. They pushed me past the sliding glass doors down the hall to Admissions.

"You've got to fill out the forms and then wait to be examined," the nurse said from behind the counter. She handed me a clipboard.

I looked up. "I don't have my insurance card."

"That's OK. Do the best you can."

Ten minutes later, as I struggled to finish the forms, a tall man in his forties, wearing a lab coat and glasses, walked up to me.

"Hi. I'm Dr. Walsh." He shook my hand. "How does it feel?"

"Not bad, as long as I don't try to walk on it."

"They tell me you had a little accident up at Golden Acres."

I flushed with embarrassment. "Yeah. I tried to leave via a second-story window. Pretty stupid, huh?"

"We're going to have to take a few snapshots. Wheel yourself in here. It'll only take a minute. Let me have your papers."

After the x-rays were taken, I waited in my wheelchair by the common area where the doctors worked, my foot elevated and wrapped in a new Ace bandage. Across the room, a young nurse was clipping up films on the lighted wall panel. As she worked, her platinum ponytail swayed back and forth beneath her starched white cap with its shiny hospital pin. I watched her white stockings. Each time she reached up on her toes to hang a negative, their seams stretched over her firm calves to the hem of her trim white uniform. After arranging the four x-rays, she came down off her tiptoes, stepped back from the board and studied the pictures.

"Oh my God!" she gasped.

Her face turned ashen. She held her stomach and covered her mouth as though she were going to be sick.

"Are those mine?" I asked.

She turned suddenly and looked at me, then quickly snatched the pictures down.

"I better put you in here," she said anxiously. "Let me put you in the casting room." She pushed me rapidly away from the x-ray viewing area. "The doctor will be right with you," she said nervously. "Just wait here."

I glanced about the room at the sinks and counters all covered in plaster dust and at the rolls of white gauze stacked on the shelves. In one corner, tiny electrical rotary saws used to remove old casts hung on the wall.

Can I use them on my wrists? I wondered. *What if I screw it up? I'll have to explain the scars for the rest of my life.* I was confused. *How do you slash the second one after slashing the first, anyway?*

The door swung open and Dr. Walsh came in carrying the films.

"You should have used the stairs," he said waving his glasses at the x-rays. "You've done one hell of a job on your calcaneus."

262

"Calcaneus?"

"Your heel bone."

"Is it bad?"

"Bad?" The doctor gave a wry smile. "Worst I've ever seen."

I swallowed hard. "Shit. Usually, I get away with these things. Somehow I manage to wiggle off the hook. But, every once in a while, I get caught. I guess this is one of those times. It's what I call my lightbulb philosophy."

"Your what?"

"Most of the time in my life when something goes wrong, I look at it like dropping a lightbulb. Usually when my lightbulb drops, it doesn't break. It just bounces and doesn't break. So I get off the hook without any consequences. But, every once in a while, like today, when the bulb drops, it shatters, and I can't put it back together again. That's when I can't change the outcome when something bad happens. I can't turn it around and make it good again. All there is is shattered glass. So basically, every once in a while, I'm screwed."

He laughed. "Well, Jay, I'm sorry to tell you . . . not only has your bulb shattered, but so has your calcaneus. Your heel bone will never be the same. You'll probably always have some kind of pain for the rest of your life. If you want, once it heals, we can break it again and then fuse it. But for now, there's nothing much to do but keep it wrapped and elevated." The doctor shrugged his shoulders. "Sorry, it's the best I can do. You'll have to use the wheelchair until it mends. After that, if it's still bad, let us know and we'll break and fuse it. It might need a pin. Of course, you'll lose your flexibility."

"I'll have to live with it, I guess." I smiled. "I can always walk on my hands, or maybe on one foot for the rest of my life—that shouldn't be so bad."

The doctor laughed and walked away, waving my file in the air.

Just after two, the gray van pulled in between the two stone columns at
Golden Acres. Bobby did not stop at the Main House, but

drove further up the hill to the Acute Care Unit—my punishment for trying to escape.

I was to be moved to the locked facility, the ACU, a
clean one-story building, much more modern than the tall,
three-storied Victorian Main House at the bottom of the hill.
The biggest difference was that I would no longer be allowed
outside. I was being locked up.

Mel helped me down from the van into the wheelchair.
The hot July sun splashed up from the driveway. I began to
sweat. They pushed me past the outside doors and rang the
bell. The lock buzzed open, and we passed through the thick
glass doors into the air-conditioned sanctuary of the reception
area. Nurses smiled as I rolled up to the admissions counter.
None wore the standard hospital garb. The ACU was a private
medical facility—very private.

A tall nurse with long red hair and strong arms came
around the counter and smiled at me. Her eyes were green,
her high cheekbones freckled. Her nametag said Marybeth.

"Welcome to the Acute Care Unit, Jay. We have your
room all ready for you."

She pushed me away from the exit, down a quiet hallway past a line of private bedrooms. It looked as though every
room was empty. At the end of the corridor, we turned right
and she rolled me through the open door into a large, modern,
air-conditioned room. The furniture, carpeting, bedspreads—
everything smelled new. The large double bed was covered
with a light brown comforter that matched the drapes that
hung at either end of a large picture window. And the drapes
matched the rug that matched the wallpaper.

I smiled. "Well, it's not the Main House, is it?"

She swept back the sheer white curtain for a panoramic
view of the sprawling green grass carpet that rolled down the
hill to the Main House.

"Unfortunately, the food's not as good. We don't get
everything they get down there. You'll probably want to clean
up before dinner. It looks like you've had a rough day. My
name's Marybeth. If you need anything, just push the buzzer

over there."

"Thanks. I'm fine," I mumbled.

Once she closed the door, the loneliness came crashing back again. I missed my children desperately; I even missed my wife. New York seemed a million miles away.

I wheeled myself over to the dresser and searched the drawers. Everything suitable for self-harm had been removed—no light cords, glasses, string, knives or plastic bags. I pushed past the bed into the polished bathroom, picked up the comb and tugged at the brambles in my hair. I sniffed at the pink bar of perfumed soap, then washed the dirt off my hands and face. I watched myself in the mirror as I brushed my teeth—black circles under my eyes, gaunt face from not eating, scraggly beard that I had no energy to shave.

"Man do you look beat," I said to the face that stared back at me. I spat the toothpaste in the sink.

"Jay, may I come in?" a firm, deep voice at the door said. "It's Dr. Burns."

I rolled myself into the bedroom. "Sure. I'm just cleaning up."

"How are you feeling, Jay?"

"Fine," I lied. "I'm trying to get used to the wheelchair. It's kind of hard to move around with my leg sticking out."

He walked to the window and looked out at the grounds.

"Jay, I've scheduled you for a series of ECT treatments. You don't have to take them if you don't want to . . . but I would, if I were you. They'll help your depression and bring back some of your energy. It's up to you, Jay, but I feel it's the right thing to do."

"Shock treatments?" I looked at him cautiously.

"Electroconvulsive therapy . . . shock treatments. Call them what you will. But don't worry, Jay. They're safe. Trust me." He shifted his weight from one foot to the other. "We've been using them since the '70s with great success. The only side effect might be a temporary loss of short-term memory, but you'll get that back quickly. If they work, your family should be allowed to visit with you again very soon. I'm sure the ECT will make you feel better. What do you say? It's your choice."

I hesitated. "I don't know."

Dr. Burns looked annoyed as he walked to the door. He turned with a scowl on his face.

"There's an opening for you today at four. Believe me, Jay, they don't
hurt. It's not like *One Flew Over the Cuckoo's Nest*. I'm only trying to help
you, Jay. This is your last chance. And, for God's sake, shave that damn beard."

He slammed the door.

"Then give me a fucking razor," I grumbled. "My choice, my choice. Like hell it's my choice. One way or the other, they'll fry my brain whether I like it or not." My body shivered. "What the hell am I going to do?"

Later that afternoon, there was a gentle knock at the door.

"Hello? Jay? Hi. It's me, Gini," a soft voice said, "your nurse."

The young nurse was busty with chestnut hair that matched her dark brown eyes. About five feet tall, she stood erect and had a pleasant smile.

"I brought you a safety razor, and it's time for your shot."

"What shot?"

"You have to have it before the ECT," Gini said holding the needle. "It helps control the seizure."

"Seizure? But I'm not even sure I want the ECT" I looked at her anxiously. "Can you give me a little more time?"

"Jay, Dr. Burns says it's the only thing that will help you get better quickly. You have to have the shot in the next fifteen minutes. You're scheduled for 4:00. It's your choice." She turned on her small heels and walked to the door. "If you want the shot, press the red button above the headboard. Remember, Jay. Fifteen minutes, or it's too late."

I stared at the digital clock. 3:29.

"Fifteen minutes. Goddamnit! Goddamnit! Shock treatments. Do I want to have shock treatments?"

Confused and afraid, I looked at the clock. 3:37.

Do I care? Do I?

I looked at the clock again. The numbers flipped. 3:44.

I want to get better. I want to get out of here. But shock treatments?

Even though I still was not sure if I wanted the ECT, my hand reached up behind the pillows and pushed the button.

What the hell? What difference does it make anyway?

After the shot, Gini wheeled me through the rotunda and down a long hallway to the lab.

"They'll be with you in a minute," she said, patting me on the shoulder. "Good luck, Jay. That was a sensible thing that you did. And believe me, the treatments are very efficient."

She smiled, turned and left me in front of a sign that said "ECT." The door opened, and two orderlies wheeled out a thin, young woman strapped to a gurney. The girl was wrapped in a large white sheet and her brown hair was matted against her wet forehead. She was unconscious. They left her in the corridor and pushed me into the small room, brightly washed in white light.

I squinted as I left the dark corridor. Together they lifted me out of the wheelchair up onto a long table covered with a white sheet. One attendant wrapped me in the sheet and then loosely buckled two thick leather belts around my chest and then two more around my legs. The other fixed an electrical halo to my head. I glanced around the room, frightened by the shiny instrument panels and overhead electrical machines that crowded down on top of me. Dr. Burns leaned over my face.

"Jay, we're ready to start the ECT treatment," he said staring into my eyes. "This is Dr. Sander, and this is the anesthesiologist, Dr. Cohen. They'll be helping with today's ECT. Remember, Jay, you'll feel no pain."

Dr. Sander dabbed swabs with petroleum jelly on my scalp and temples and then attached blue and red electrodes.

The orderlies cinched the leather belts tighter around my body while Dr. Cohen held a plastic mask with elastic straps above my face.

"Jay, I want you to count backwards from ten," he said. "As you do, I'm going to place the mask over your nose and mouth. I want you to inhale deeply. Deeply. Do you understand?"

I nodded yes—frightened, scared.

"Start now."

"Ten . . . nine . . . "

He lowered the mask onto my face and held his hand firmly on top of it.

The heavy smell of ether made me gag. I tried to take deep breaths but the white sheet squeezed me tightly. I felt like a caterpillar trapped inside its cocoon. I tried to squirm free, but the belts kept me tied to the table. I gagged again. Dr. Cohen pushed down on the mask with both hands. I felt the plastic cup cut the bridge of my nose.

"Eight . . . seven . . . "

I tried to shake my head. I struggled to get free, to get out of the straps, but I could not move. My eyes darted nervously from the bright light above my head to the doctors in their white coats. I strained against the straps. They still would not budge.

"Six . . . God, please help me."

Terrified, I tried to find Dr. Burns. I looked left, right, above. I could only see Sanders turning the knobs on the console next to my head.

"Five . . . four . . . "

My heart pounded. Sweat trickled down the sides of my face from underneath the metal halo.

"Three . . . "

Dr. Cohen's hands felt lighter now. I turned back to the bright light. No longer did I feel that I was suffocating, but rather drifting up through the ceiling, off to some world outside the room.

"Jay? Jay? Can you hear me?"

I felt someone shaking my shoulder.

"Jay, are you all right? It's Gini, your nurse. How are you? How do you feel?"

My eyes fluttered open, and the fuzzy glare of the ceiling light slowly pulled into focus. As I ran my fingers through my hair, I felt a sticky gel.

"What's this gooey stuff? And what's the bandage on my foot?"

"You've just come from your first ECT session, Jay. You've been asleep for two hours."

As she straightened the pillow behind my head, I could smell her lilac perfume.

"I guess you don't remember. Dr. Burns told you you'd lose your short-term memory for a while. You only have seven more sessions. The goo's from the electrodes, and the bandage is for your heel."

"What's wrong with my heel?"

"Don't you remember? You fractured it when you jumped out the window."

"Jumped out the window? What window? What do you mean?"

"You jumped out your window down at the Main House."

"I did?" I thought hard. "Now I remember. I tried to get away." I looked across the room. "And there's my trusty wheelchair."

"That's right," Gini said smiling. "Now why don't you see if you can get ready for dinner by yourself? You'll have to wash those blond locks of yours and get rid of that goo. If you need any help, just push the button."

I struggled to get from the bed to the wheelchair and then into the bathroom to clean up for dinner. As I wheeled myself past my desk, my eyes focused on the pile of coins. I stopped and counted them; seventy-eight cents.

"Seventy-eight cents. That's it? That's all I have? Is that all my life's worth? And $83,000 of debt. How will I ever get out of this mess this time?"

After cleaning the gel from my hair and scrubbing my face with soap, I wheeled myself down the hall past the rotunda into the dining room. Some people had already served themselves and were sitting with their dinner trays at the five tables for four. As I moved to the back of the cafeteria line, I saw Tom Forster from the Main House sitting in his wheelchair with three other patients.

"Hi, Tom. We match."

"Hey, Jay, we meet again. What are you doing up here, and what happened to your leg?"

"I guess I'm not as well-balanced as you thought. I tried to leave the Main House last night via the second floor."

"Oh sure. What'd you do, jump out a window or something?"

"You're right. I jumped out my window."

Tom's eyes widened. "But Jay, you seemed fine down at the Main House."

"I had to get out, Tom. I couldn't take being cooped up there anymore."

Tom put his tray on his lap and wheeled his chair away. "I hope to be leaving tomorrow, but not by any window," I heard him mutter.

Others were still waiting in line in front of the cafeteria window to pick up their food. I tried to squeeze into the line to get a tray, but my wheelchair would not fit between the tables and the wall.

"Hi, my name's Lou," a voice said from behind me. "Let me get that for you." Lou was wearing a bright red Che Guevara t-shirt and khaki slacks. He was over six feet. "Go find a place for dinner."

I maneuvered my way around the tables to an empty spot looking out on to the deck. Soon Lou came pushing his way through the crowded room carrying two plastic trays above the heads of the patients who sat packed around the tables.

"Here you go. Mashed potatoes and roast beef. They say the food up here's not as good as you'd get if you were still down at Main House, but it's not bad. I heard you had ECT today. How'd it go?"

"I'm still alive. It scared the hell out of me at first. But after a while, like with most things now, I really didn't give a damn. So I just went ahead and did it." I rubbed my temples and looked up at Jim. "Once I let them give me the shot, there wasn't much room left for changing my mind. What I really don't like is how after it's done, they wheel you out wrapped up in a sheet comatose for all the world to see."

"You know," Lou said, shaking his head, "if it were me, I wouldn't let them do it. My shrink's suggested it several times for my depression, but I've always given it thumbs down."

"Burns is pretty high on it," I said. "I'm not looking forward to the next one. But it's true what they say; I didn't feel any pain. Hard to believe, huh? They want me to have another six or seven sessions. They say after that I'll be sane." I smiled at Jim. "That means I'll be able to go home."

"Well, I hope it works. See you later." Lou gathered up his tray and walked to the door.

A woman in her forties sat down across from me and poked at her food. Sad, sleepy eyes looked out over her pale Scandinavian cheeks. Their color matched the soft robin's egg turtleneck that covered her full breasts.

"Hi, my name's Jay. What brings you to Chez ACU?"

"I'm Janet. I'm from Darien," she said without looking up. She fiddled with her gold earring as she inspected the broccoli with her fork. "I had everything I wanted," she began. "You know—money, a husband, children, two homes, horses. I just wanted the bottle more." She pushed the mashed potatoes to the side of her plate. "It pulled me down slowly at first, then finally into the darkest depression I'd ever known. I felt like I was in the burn unit of my soul."

I stared across the table at her beauty and her sorrow. Her blue eyes glanced up at me. She smiled and brushed back a strand of blonde hair from her lovely face. White gauze bandaged both her wrists.

"One minute I was doing triathlons and showing horses;

the next I was gobbling pills and guzzling booze. I couldn't stop. So, I tried suicide—twice." She lowered her eyes, twisted her water glass, then took a sip. "Before I slit my wrists, I pricked my finger. I wanted my nail polish to match the blood when they found me." Slowly, she raised her eyes and looked at me over the rim of her glass. She smiled a coy smile and leaned towards me. She offered me her hand, and I took it.

"Before I got sober, at the end," I said to her, "all I could think about was the next drink. But when I crashed, when I came here, I had gotten sober. Funny how that worked. I guess I didn't have the booze to protect me from the pain any more. I'd lost my armor; the armor booze gave me. So I was trapped. I couldn't drink and I couldn't not drink. It's a shitty place to be. I had no place to run to for comfort. For the first time in my life, I had to feel my feelings. That was the hard part, the hardest part." I shook my head. "I'm not very good at it. I don't let myself feel."

"I have to go," she said. She pushed her chair out, got up and walked away, her plate still full.

Before going back to my room, I asked one of the male nurses whose name was Hal if I could have a plastic bag to put over my bandaged foot before I showered.

"Sure, man, no problem. But, hey, I'm going to have to stay with you when you shower and get the bag back when you're done. Is that cool with you? Security purposes, you know. We don't want to find you with a sack over your head."

After I showered, I gave the bag back to the Hal, then settled into my modern new surroundings. Through the thick double glass, I looked out at the stars before falling asleep between the clean, fresh sheets.

Friday was a sparkling bright day. This meant 'Deck Time' at the ACU.

After lunch, just before 2:00 PM, a large group of patients huddled together in the Activities Room, jostling for position in front of a large sliding glass door. On the other side was a 15 by 20-foot outdoor deck that was screened in by a 12-foot-high wire fence with lights. Deck Time was nirvana for the smokers. They pushed and shoved back and forth like race-horses in the starting gate waiting for the bell.

At exactly 2:00 PM, the orderly turned the lock. With a gush, the first crowd of smokers rushed forward snatching folding chairs and benches. Most congregated in the shade of their favorite umbrella table designated for the smoking crowd. I watched from a corner of the deck in my wheelchair while they babbled about various tidbits of obscure trivia. As they talked, their pile of butts grew larger and larger until their communal ashtray overflowed onto the table. Aside from their storytelling, bumming cigarettes and lights from one another was a large part of the social interaction.

There were others suffering from more acute depression who moped about, occasionally throwing in their two cents about whatever topic was being discussed. Some just stood by themselves, rocking back and forth with their arms folded across their chests and their heads down in the beautiful sunlight.

One smoker was Jack, a tall, thin bipolar patient. He lived in town and had an affluent family background. Jack always insisted on being the director of the group's topics of conversation. Today, his animation was more manic than usual. Holding court, Jack raced on and on about a multitude of different topics. He was particularly proud of his knowledge of past military and political events, as well as his green Lacoste polo shirt and saffron sharkskin slacks. He emphasized endless details in his diatribe while rapidly tapping out a rhythm with his brown crocodile loafers.

As I sat alone under a distant umbrella, I watched with amusement as he led the group's conversation with incredible rapid-fire details about the Kennedy assassination in Dallas.

"You see, there's no way there could have been an accomplice," Jack pontificated. "Oswald, he was a crack shot, and the Book Depository gave him the perfect view. It wasn't that far away." He repeated this mantra over and over again whenever anyone would offer an opposing view.

"No! No!" he would shout. "There's no way there could

have been an accomplice." Each time he would jump up, then sit down again, then jump back up.

Mary was another one of the smokers on the deck. She was in her mid-forties, married and overweight. As she chain-smoked her cigarettes, she mumbled to no one in particular about her family and how unfair life had been to her. Usually she would stay apart from the others, but today she mingled with the smokers.

"What about Jackie?" she sniffled in her frumpy, rumpled checkered dress. "Poor Jackie. What a shock. Seeing her husband's head blown into a million pieces."

Next to her stood Charles, a portly young man. He too was manic and fancied himself as the group's stand-up comic. "Well, you know Mary, there's always Crazy Glue. Or maybe she could have just swept up the pieces and put them in her pink pillbox hat."

I smiled as Charles mixed his brilliant mind with his sardonic sense of humor on whatever topic of conversation was at hand. He presented himself as a successful but somewhat obnoxious real estate executive at his father's prestigious New York firm. As Charles continued on, his antics bordered on the malicious. He used his boarding school background to belittle those about him with lesser education. Finally, when the group's conversation did not suit him, he moved his pudgy frame to a distant table on the deck and sulked like a spoiled child.

Phil, the most pompous orderly at the ACU, was the one in charge of Deck Time. He leaned against the glass doors in a crisp white shirt and trousers with white socks and white shoes. No matter how hot it was, he always stayed in the sun, getting his ebony tan to an even darker shade. His job as supervisor was to clock the length of Deck Time— twenty minutes sharp. As usual, he watched the patients with disdain, tapping his billy club in the palm of his hand. Finally, he strutted about the deck like a movie star, shouting, "Times up! Period's closed. Period's closed."

"No. No, it's not! We still have three minutes," Hank

yelled. He was one of the newer manic patients and still wore his blue pajamas. "There's still time for one more cigarette. It's only been seventeen minutes."

Phil straightened his white, starched shirt. This was the chance he had been waiting for. He swung his billy club and struck Hank brutally across the back of his neck. He grabbed him by his pajamas and wrestled him to the ground. They rolled across the wooden planks, knocking over aluminum chairs, their arms and legs flailing. Two aides quickly ran out onto the deck from inside. One pulled Phil off of Hank and pushed him against the brick wall. The other helped Hank to a chair and dabbed at the blood that ran from his nose with a handkerchief.

Phil smoothed his oily hair and his white uniform. He stood in front of the patients with his legs spread apart, clutching the billy club tightly across his thighs.

"See! Now you know! Now you know who's in charge here," he gloated. "When I say it's twenty minutes … it's twenty minutes. Understand? Let's go! Everybody inside. Smokes out."

Phil used his billy club to push the herd roughly past the sliding glass door back inside the dark ACU.

"Hurry up. Let's go!" he shouted.

That bastard, I thought. *He's the one who should be locked up.*

Saturday was rainy and overcast, so group activities were planned indoors in the main room. Nine chairs and tables were assembled in a circle for patients taking drawing class. I sat in my wheelchair with my easel on my lap and watched as the others painted their pictures.

One woman, who was in her teens and had attempted suicide three times, only used a black marker. Her name was Hope. She began slowly and meticulously. But as she worked, she crossed over the lines of her drawing and drew faster and faster until her entire canvas was covered in black. When she finished, she put each of her paintings next to her other black canvasses.

Nancy, a thin young woman with a harelip, sat next to a man who was painting a rose. She was obsessed with my silver wheelchair and rigid leg. As she did her paintings, she would vary one only slightly from the next. She called each of them "Man in the Iron Chair." Sometimes my chair would be blue or sometimes red, but I was always a stick figure with my leg raised straight out in front.

As she drew, Nancy constantly surveyed the room to see where the staff was. When no one was watching, she put her painting down, got up quietly and slipped out of the room. Minutes later, she returned. Bits of her last meal stained her black turtleneck and the smell of vomit filled the room. Around the corner came one of the orderlies carrying a wastepaper basket.

"God damn it, Nancy. Next time when you purge, use the toilet. Now go to your room and clean this out!"

I enjoyed this art therapy. Each time, without meaning to, I would draw the same thing, a pink heart in a silver cage. When I saw my "Caged Hearts" hanging on the cafeteria wall next to the other patients' paintings, I was proud. Each of my drawings was slightly different, but they all looked like lonely valentines trapped behind the crooked bars of circus wagons.

I wondered. *Did my father have a caged heart, too?*

Monday morning, I thumbed through *Psychology Today* in Dr. Burns' plush waiting room, and I thought about our private sessions.

What a waste of time. I still don't know if I'm even really depressed. And what if I am? What good has Burns been? He should have retired years ago.

I watched the receptionist. Her starched lace blouse had its Victorian collar buttoned high up to the top of her neck. She wore her brown hair pulled back into a tight bun that held a number two pencil. It looked like a yellow thermometer that was taking the temperature of her head. Her right breast prominently displayed her bronze name tag—Priscilla. Note pad, phone, keyboard—all were aligned with precision on her mahogany desk.

When the doctor's door opened, she quickly straightened her black-framed eyeglasses. A mother and father exited with their daughter. The young girl was dressed all in black with a blue streak running through her black hair. A leash went from her waist to her mother's wrist.

"Jay, you can go in now," Priscilla said.

All of Dr. Burns' files were stacked in neat rows. Everything—books, family pictures, pens—was in its place. On the walls, various diplomas were mixed in with oil paintings of English fox hunting scenes. Dr. Burns sat comfortably behind a large mahogany desk in his white lab coat. His gold tooled leather desktop had recently been oiled.

"Good morning, Jay. Sit down. How are you?"

"I was able to shave and dress myself this morning. And my appetite seems to be coming back."

"Good. Good." He spun his armchair around to find my file on the credenza behind him. "You look better when you shave, and that should make you feel better, too," I heard him say as I stared at his back. "The nurses tell me you still don't like 'Group' very much."

"I don't mind it. I just feel that I'm not really getting much out of it."

He turned around, holding a thick file with my name on it. "Well, stick with it, Jay. It should help you. How's the heel?"

"I think it's getting better. The swelling's down, and the purple's almost gone."

"Are you taking your medication?"

"It's hard not to. The nurses watch me like hawks."

"Sleeping OK?"

"Fine, unless I'm jumping out windows."

"That wasn't a smart thing to do, now was it? Dr. Wash said that you'll be walking with a limp for the rest of your life, you know." He penciled a few notes, then looked at his watch. "Well, we have to stop now. But, stick with it, Jay. Seems like you're getting better."

On Saturday morning, while I lay in bed reading *L'Étranger*, there was a knock at the door.

"Who is it? I'm finished with the ECT."

"Jay, it's me, Gini. Your boys and your wife are here." She smiled. "You can go home now."

"Go home? I wasn't told I was leaving today. Are you sure? Gini, I'm not sure I'm ready to leave yet. I don't know if I'm really well enough to go home. No. Gini, I don't want to!"

"Jay, it's supposed to be a surprise. Dr. Burns says it's been four weeks now, and that you're much better. Besides, your insurance runs out today. The orderlies will help you with your crutches."

"But, Gini, I'm not sure I want to leave. I'm not sure I'm ready yet. What if I have another breakdown? Then I'll have to go through the ECT all over again. I don't want to do that. I feel safe here . . . .." I backed away. "You are my family now."

"Jay, you'll do fine. Believe me. You'll do fine. Here's your family."

"Hi, Daddy!" Jason called from the hall.

"Daddy! Daddy!" Nicholas yelled as he ran to me and hugged me.

"Hi, Nicholas. Hi, Jason. Boy did I miss you two guys!" I ruffled their blond hair and looked at their clean smiling faces. "You've both grown so much. Look at how big you are!"

"Daddy, how'd you hurt your leg?" Jason asked.

I looked at Anne. She shook her head.

"It's a long story, Jason. I'll tell you later." I turned to Anne. "I'm not sure I'm ready to go home yet."

Nat took my hand. He looked up at me with tears in his eyes.

"Daddy, it's OK now. You'll do fine. I know you will. Please come home."

Chapter 13

P aralyzed by fear, I hid beneath the secure warmth of my bed covers and listened to the *clickety-clack*, *clickety-clack* of Anne's NordicTrack. I was terrified of getting up and facing the day. Those goddamn birds . . . chirping, chirping, chirping. They're always chirping. Why are they so damn happy all the time?

Slowly, I pulled myself up and went into my sons' bedroom to help Jason and Nicholas get ready for school.

Despite my best efforts, when Anne came in to check on my progress, she saw Nicholas wearing a turtleneck—she did not like it.

"I'll do it!" she snapped. She tore it off and replaced it with a blue collared shirt. "Can't you do anything right?"

At the breakfast table, she re-set the place settings that I had put out and changed the cereal boxes. She stared at me to make sure I knew how inept I was even at this simple task.

After Jason and Nicholas finished their cornflakes, Anne bundled them off to their buses, slamming the front door without a kiss good-bye.

I sat alone in the dark apartment by the living room window looking down at the people below rushing through the courtyard on their way to work. They looked like ants, owned by their jobs with no free will.

I left my half-eaten bowl of cereal in the kitchen sink and walked to the bathroom to take my medications. On the shelf next to the toothpaste was my box of straight-edged razor blades. I hesitated for a moment, thinking about my wrists and the relief I could get. All I had to do was fill the bathtub with warm water and let my life slip away.

I shook myself and quickly took the container of anti-depressants and slid the medicine cabinet door shut. A haggard face covered by melancholy and a two-day beard stared at me from the mirror. I felt sick to my stomach, frightened by this gaunt visage that had once been strong and confident. I swallowed my pills and went back into the bedroom to sleep some more.

At 11:00, I woke. I hated being awake. It meant that I had to face the day—and life. I would have to find something to do to fill the hours until it was time to sleep again.

I picked up the *Times* classifieds and looked for a job that I did not want. Today there were no insurance ads, and I felt relieved. I had no strength. I simply did not care anymore.

At 1:00, I remembered to fix myself some lunch. I was able to get the can of tuna open, but burnt the toast. I sat in the safety of my bedroom in front of the computer eating without tasting my lunch and scanning the web for insurance jobs I didn't want.

The phone rang, jarring me from my thoughts.

"Hello? Jay Walker," I said in my most confident,

insurance salesman's voice.

"Hi Jay. Anything new?" Henry asked.

"Oh. Hi, Henry. No, nothing yet. It's slow this time of year, you know." My voice was betraying my fear. "Henry . . . you're one of my oldest friends. So, let me be honest with you—I'm scared. I keep trying to figure out how I got here? How did I end up like this?"

"Jay, don't give up. Many friends of mine have hit rock bottom at one time or another, me included, and somehow we've all bounced back. You'll see. You'll bounce back too. Just give it time."

"I'll keep trying, but it seems hopeless."

"Just keep hanging in there. You'll find something soon. I'll give you a buzz next week."

"Thanks, Henry. Thanks for calling."

At 2:00, I left the protection of the apartment to drive uptown and see my psychologist. As usual, I arrived late.

Dr. Zagorski opened the door. He was a thin man in his forties, bald with a black beard. Since he said so little during our sessions, I called him the Stone Buddha.

"Jay, you're late again. I've told you before. You're supposed to be here at 2:15. It's 2:30. What was it this time?"

"Sorry. I'm still afraid to go outside, and keeping track of time is beyond me . . . and I couldn't find a parking space. New York sucks!"

"Why don't you take the subway?"

"I told you last time, I don't know what I'll do if I get near the tracks. Before I went to Golden Acres, the shiny silver rails and the rumble of the trains attracted me. Now they scare me away." I frowned. "I guess you don't remember, do you?"

Zagorski glared at me as he settled in to his leather armchair. "So tell me, Jay, what's on your mind today?"

"I spend most of my time thinking about the years I spent building my career . . . how I got to the top. Before, I was able to get up every morning at 5:00 and run the 6:30 AA meeting at the All Saints Church. I'd be in the office by 7:30 and attack my morning's sales prospects. I worked so hard . . .

so hard, for so long. When I got fired, the prestige and the fast action were ripped away from me. Not to mention my $125,000 salary. Now, when I think about work, it makes no sense to me. My life makes no sense. When I think of having to begin all over again, building a new book of business, I'm overwhelmed. I don't see how I can ever do it again."

Sobs suddenly grabbed me from deep inside, stealing my speech and racking my body. Waves of tears flowed down my face. I tried to speak, but no words would leave my mouth.

"Here. Take this." He handed me a Kleenex.

Finally, I was able to catch my breath and compose myself. I looked at him through tearful eyes.

"How can I start all over again. I can't—it's too hard. I can just barely organize the job clippings and computer print outs on my desk. I can't even keep my phone messages straight. I can't do anything right. Maybe my mother was right. Why not just do what she did? What difference does living or dying really make anyway?"

Zagorski leaned forward in his chair. "Jay, remember what I told you. Suicide is the most selfish act of all. You're not thinking about that again, are you?"

"No. Shit. I just hate re-hashing the same stuff with you week after week. Am I getting anywhere?"

"Jay, you still have a big problem getting in touch with your feelings—it's what we call alexithymia. You barely seem able to show any feelings at all . . .. Well, we have to stop," he said in his soft voice. "I'm afraid time's up."

When I stood up to leave, a bolt of white-hot pain shot up my leg from my broken heel bone. As I limped to the door, I heard Zagorski say, "And, Jay . . . next week, be on time. And don't forget to leave your check on the table by the door this time."

I drove back down the FDR Drive to Battery Park City to pick up Jason and Nicholas at their bus stop. They alone gave me the courage to be outdoors.

While I waited by the curb, engulfed in the usual crowd of chatting mothers, I looked about nervously to see if any of my ex-colleagues from work might be walking by after a late business lunch. I was terrified that one of them might see me unbathed and sloppily dressed. They all knew I had been fired.

The boys' buses came around the corner at the same time and all the mothers pushed forward waving at their children. I could see both Jason and Nicholas sitting by their windows looking for me. The happiness that they brought me was all that I knew now; Nicholas with his athletic ability, and Jason, my special boy, trying his damnedest to overcome and deal with his learning disabilities. I hoped they did not sense how afraid I was of the day, or of the future and of life. I needed their unconditional love desperately now. They were all I had, and I did not want to frighten them away.

Jason bounded down the bus steps with his backpack swinging. It made me think back to the time when I jumped down my school bus steps to meet Buttons on the corner. Jason jarred me from my daydream as he caught and squeezed me tightly. Nicholas grabbed my leg.

"So how was school?" I asked them as I ruffled their hair.

"Mrs. Miller is still cranky, Dad," Jason complained.

"Did finger painting today, Dad." Nicholas held up his hands to show me his small multi-colored fingers. "Mrs. Small wants me to bring a smock next week."

"OK. We can make one out of an old sheet." I smiled. "Come on. Let's go upstairs and tackle your homework."

Once their schoolwork was finished, I sat my sons down at the computer to play their games.

"Guys, I'm gonna take a short nap," I said with a yawn.

I set their 'Share Clock', then retreated to the safety of my bedroom. Once under the bedcovers, I was instantly asleep.

I stood next to my father's hospital bed. A small drop of blood came from his ear and slowly rolled down the side of his face. Another drop of blood fell from his other ear. It ran down his neck onto the collar of his pajamas. He no longer looked big and powerful. Instead, he lay there emaciated and scared. Just above his lower eyelids, his scarlet blood slowly swelled up and rolled from his frightened eyes down on to his cheeks. He wanted to say something to me, but instead of speech, there came only a gurgle. His throat was filled with his warm red blood. As he tried to speak, blood spilled from his nose and mouth and ran down onto the bed sheets. He lay there, small and frightened in the pool of blood. As his crimson life-blood spilled from the bed to the floor, I went to the closet and got two large buckets. I put one bucket on either side of his bed and watched them fill with his blood. The blood kept com-ing.

"Why didn't you ring the alarm bell?" Dr. Burns was standing in the doorway.

My father looked helplessly at Dr. Burns, then at me.

The front door slammed, and my eyes snapped open. Anne was home, carrying groceries from the market for dinner no doubt. I was sure that her mood was still full of anger, and that she would not join the three of us at the dinner table.

I only ate a small portion of my meal, then carried my half-full plate and utensils into the kitchen to clean them and put them in the dishwasher.

Rather than let me help, she grabbed them from me with a curt, "Let me do it. You always use too much soap." She tossed the food in the garbage then washed the plate. "I don't know why I have to cook the food if you're not going to eat it."

"I'm really not hungry . . . Anne, can't you see? All I'm trying to do is help."

"Well, if you want to help, pay attention to the things I ask you to do," she said with a clenched jaw. "Did you pick up the dry-cleaning today, like I asked?"

"I'm sorry. I forgot."

"Typical," she muttered. "It's always the same. For Christ's sake, Jay, it's been a year now. When are you going to snap out of this depression bullshit?"

"It hasn't been a year. This is April, not July."

"Whatever."

I retreated to the safety of the bedroom—wounded and dejected. For the next two hours I browsed the web. At last it was 9:00, and I could climb back into bed to wait for the next day.

Anne woke me at 11:00.

"Jay, wake up. I'm too tired to read the boys any more books. You have to get up."

I dragged myself from the bed to the boys' room, sat on the floor, and read them my favorite story, *The Little Prince*. Jason fell asleep as soon as I began, but Nicholas lay on his stomach wide awake and begged for more at the end of each chapter. Finally, my exhaustion caused me to lose my temper.

"That's it, Nicholas. It's time to go to bed now."

I was always tired and desperately needed the safety and solace of my queen-sized bed. Only there did I feel safe.

"Daddy, please . . . only one more story," Nicholas whined.

"Nicholas, it's midnight. I'm going to bed."

I slammed the book shut and returned to the security of my bedroom.

Anne heard Nicholas' sobs.

"Don't you hear him crying?"

She ripped off the bed sheets with a vengeance, and stormed into the boys' bedroom to read Nicholas more books. I was glad to have the warm bed all to myself.

At dinner on Thursday, Anne announced that Tina had called her at the office.

"Tina's girlfriend's backed out of their trip to Cancun," she said. "Tina asked me if I want to take her place. It's a last-minute thing; I'd have to leave tomorrow. The boys are off from school this week. Do you think you can handle them on your own? I really need to get away."

This is her first solo vacation since our wedding, I thought. *So is the marriage finally over? Has she given up on me? No! She'd never leave me. She could never cope with the two kids by herself.*

"Sure, why not?" I smiled. "I'm sure the rest will do you good. The boys will take good care of me, and I'll take good care of them. And you'll be home before we know you've been gone."

"Are you sure you can handle them?"

"Yes, we'll be fine."

The day after Anne left, shortly after midnight, Jason woke up crying. I dragged myself from my bed and went into the boys' bedroom and sat next to my son.

"What's the matter, Pal?"

"I'm scared. I want Mommy."

"She'll be back soon, Jason. There's nothing to be afraid of. Nicholas is right here and I'm right next door."

"I'm frightened. I've got nightmares with these big monsters. They've got these yellow horns for eyes."

I looked at my son sitting upright, frightened and confused on his small bunkbed. He was holding his rabbit puppet, its plaid skirt worn from years of cuddling. His lower lip was trembling.

"Can I watch TV, Dad? Can I watch *The Muppets*?"

"Sure, get your blanket and your pillow. I'll take the cushions off the couch."

I took his small hand and led him down the hall into the living room and put *The Muppets* into the VCR.

Jason had trouble positioning himself on the couch cushions. I helped him straighten out his twisted bedding and get settled in with the pillows.

"Don't be afraid, Jason. Everything's OK. Give me a hug."

He hugged me loosely, while I held him tightly. I thought how good it was to hold my son and feel his coarse hair against my cheek. Unlike his brother's soft blonde hair, Jason's was rough and dirty brown, like Anne's. Once he fell asleep, I left him on the couch and returned to my empty bed.

Hours later, Jason was pulling on my bed covers.

"Daddy, where's Mommy?"

"Hi, Jason. What time is it?" I looked at the digital clock.

286

5:06. I could see the drizzle falling against the bedroom windows.

"Can I come in bed?"

"Sure, Pal. Hop in."

As he climbed into bed, I watched his little potbelly. I remembered when I was ten and how my classmates called me 'Fatso.' How unalike my two sons were: Nicholas coordinated, lean and gifted, and Jason so sensitive and plagued by his learning disabilities. I loved them both desperately, but in different ways, proud of Nicholas and proud of Jason, too, but more protective of my older son. Jason, much more than Nicholas, needed my help and love.

Before long, Nicholas came in rubbing his eyes and carrying his one-armed teddy bear. He was naked, and even at five, I could see the muscles in his strong, tiny legs. Unlike his older brother, Nicholas always seemed to wake with an erection.

"Morning, Daddy."

"Hi. How'd you sleep?"

"Good."

"OK. Let's have our breakfast and then we'll all get dressed and maybe go out."

"Dad, can we watch TV?" Jason asked. He liked to escape into a world of fantasy.

"Not until you have your breakfast and get dressed. I also bought a new computer game for you to try. While Mom's away, I don't want you boys watching too much TV. You guys watch TV all the time when Mom's around."

"OK. Dad, can you help me put on my shoes and socks?"

"Sure, Jason. You've almost got that down. I'm proud of you. Come on, let's get dressed. Then I'll fix you guys some pancakes."

After breakfast, I sat with the boys on the living room rug playing games and listening to music. I thought how odd it was for me to be caring for my two sons like this. My father had raised me in such a different way.

By noon the rain had stopped, and I took the boys across the street to the World Financial Center for lunch. We sat together at a small table by the window in Au Bon Pain. Across the street was the World Trade Center.

I thought back to the years I had spent working there for my father on the 101st floor. I had wanted to take over the firm and then give it to my children. That would never be now. And it was not too long ago that, instead of going to Au Bon Pain for milk and peanut butter and jelly sandwiches, I would take my boys next door to Foxhounds for Shirley Temples while I drank cognac. How lucky I was to have been able to break the chain of alcoholism in my family.

"You know, I really like being with you two guys," I said, rubbing their heads. "You're very important to me, and I always have fun when we're together. Jason, you're doing great with getting dressed. I know it's hard for you. And Nicholas, you're doing great with your homework."

"Homework's easy, Dad," Nicholas bragged, "even in my gifted class."

"When you help me, it's easy to get dressed, Daddy." Jason looked up at me with his big blue eyes. "But it's still hard for me to tie my shoes."

"One day, it'll be a cinch, Jason. We just have to practice more. Don't worry. And if I lose my temper with you, Jason, I'm sorry. I'll try to be more patient."

"That's OK, Dad." Jason patted me on the shoulder. "I understand."

"Come on, you two. Let's finish up and go home and play on the computer."

Outside the restaurant, I held their hands as we crossed South Street; then let them go and watched them race each other into the apartment building entrance past the doorman to the elevators.

For dinner, the vote was unanimous—pizza. We ate together in front of the TV watching a tape of *The Wizard of Oz*. By the time Dorothy returned to Kansas, it was 10:00, and the boys' eyelids were starting to droop. I took them into their bedroom and read them a story from the Children's Bible until they both fell asleep.

The rest of the week passed in much the same way. The children knew that my rules were not to be bent—there were no exceptions or extra minutes to watch TV. They would have to wait until their mother returned before they could start their whining again to get their way.

Sunday evening, when I got home with the boys after church and the movies, Anne was unpacking her suitcase in the bedroom.

"Hi, Honey, welcome home," I said. "How was the trip?"

"Hi, Mommy, what did you get us?" Jason asked.

She hugged her children and handed them each a small brightly wrapped package.

"Now go play in the living room," she said. "I have to talk to Daddy."

She sat in the corner of the bedroom in the small wicker chair. Her face was half lit by the bedside lamp, and tears glistened in her eyes.

"Jay, I have to talk to you." She wiped the tears away. "Jay, I've tried to be a good wife, but I can't go on like this anymore. There's no more love. That's all there is to it. It's all gone."

This can't be happening, I thought. I slumped down heavily on the bed and stared at Anne blankly. I felt nothing.

"Anne, why don't we try the marriage counseling again? I still don't know why you stopped going in the first place. Or we can call Reverend Forester. I've spoken with him in the past, and he's always been helpful. He's had his own problems, and he's the one who got us to Dr. Zagorski for the marriage counseling. Have you thought about the children? It's important that we stay together for them."

"The boys will be fine, actually. I think it's better than having them see us
fighting all the time, and living in a home with no love."

She pushed back her hair and looked away.

"Anne, has our life been so bad compared to what most

other people have? What about our trips? We've been to Paris, cruised the Caribbean, weeks in Florida, skiing in Vermont. All I wanted was a nice home, a loving family and a good job. You know, when I gave you your Valentine's Day cards and roses this year, you didn't even say 'Thank you.' Did you know how hurt I was?"

"Jay, let's face it. Our marriage stopped working years ago. We haven't had sex in months, forget good sex. I'd hoped you'd change, but you'll never change. We'll never communicate. And there's too much to forgive—the drinking, the money . . .."

"Anne, whatever happened to 'For better or for worse, 'til death do us part'? I've always said 'I love you.' It's been years since you've ever said it back. Why have you decided that it should end now of all times? Now when I need you. How can you leave me now? We can make things better again—I'm sure of it. I think I'm starting to get stronger . . .."

"I'm sorry, Jay. I'm really sorry. I know this isn't a good time for you for this to happen, but I can't wait any longer. I've been thinking about this for months. Look, Jay, I have to get on with my life. I'm really sorry, but it's finished. I don't love you anymore. The marriage is over!"

"Are you seeing someone else?"

Anne stared at the floor, then raised her head.

"I met Tim at work a while ago. We're just friends, but he wants to see me more often. He's getting a divorce. He's fun. He makes me laugh."

"You mean Tim McLeay from AA? You don't mean him, do you? He's been listening to me pour my heart out about my job and my marriage at every AA meeting. It would have been nice if he'd told me he was dating my wife. I gave him my résumé last week. What a fucking bastard!"

"We're not dating. We're just seeing each other every once in a while. He heard you sharing about our marriage at one of your AA meetings. So, he called me and asked me out."

"I can't believe it. I've planned all my life to have a

family that would hold together. What about all that I've given you, shown you, taught you? Is this the thanks I get? And what about the kids? I don't want the same mess for my kids that I went through."

"Jay, it's too late. Try to be reasonable."

"I am being reasonable. I have been reasonable."

I ran my fingers through my hair and shook my head. I looked up. I could see in her face that it was over—the marriage had ended. "When do you want to tell the children?" I said weakly.

"We can tell them after church on Sunday at the playground, if you want."

I lay against the mountain of pillows stacked against the brass headboard and held my head in my hands. I gazed at the pictures on the wall—Anne helping me run the marathon, me standing next to her father before he died, the photo of Anne and me on the Staten Island Ferry. I turned and looked at my wife. Tears were falling on her blouse.

"So what do you want to do?" I asked unsympathetically. "When do you want me out?"

"You don't have to leave right away. Next month is fine. I'm away on business the week of the 13th. The children can stay with my mother. Why don't you leave then?"

I got up and looked at my wife. I felt tired and drained.

"I'll be out next month."

I walked into the living room to see my children. They were all I had now. I sat on the sofa between my two sons and stared at the cartoons, numb, stunned by the fact that Anne and I had finally gotten to this point. Everything that I had planned for my life was now gone. Somehow, I would have to find a way to start over again, all over again, from scratch.

How did the love die? I wondered. *I didn't want to have my mother's or my father's life for either my family or for me. No divorce! No alcoholism! No suicide! How did it all get so far off track? It wasn't supposed to happen this way. I'd planned to have a good life, a good job, a good marriage. Sure, the marriage hasn't been good for a long while. That's true. But*

*there were good times, and the two kids. Jason came along. Nicholas was not far behind. Did she still love me then? Our lives had their usual ups and downs, like most marriages, but I always thought our lives were still good, better than most . . ..
Now it's over. It's all over. It's time to go.*

"Daddy! Daddy!" Nicholas called. "Mommy says it's time to go. It's time to go to bed. Will you read us a story? Pleassssssse . . .."

Chapter 14

The banging of the construction work from the street below blew in through the open window and roused me from my dream. Still tired, I lay in bed waiting for the clock radio to sound before falling back to sleep.

In an office filled with many rooms, I stood between Dave Thatcher and my father. The three of us were arguing over my paycheck. I was trying to pull the check away from them, and they were pulling back. Finally, the check tore in

half and I fell backwards onto the plush carpet designed with my father's initials.

"What am I doing here? Do I still work for Walker & Co.?" I screamed.

I ran away from them as fast as I could, headed for the exit. As I passed Anne, I saw she was wearing a floral gown that was tightly cinched under her bosom. Instead of pulling the dress up to cover her large breasts, she nonchalantly let them squeeze out over the top. She smiled at me, and waved slowly as I ran by. Everywhere I ran was a dead end. There were no exits.

Finally, I came to a small door that led to my tiny studio apartment. Inside was a large, fat lady with a big bust who was the wife of a florist. She was trying to make the apartment better looking with bouquets of flowers. I sensed that she was also looking for sex, but she did not come right out and say so. Instead she gave me subtle hints as she showed me how to make my studio apartment more attractive using large plants. When we left the apartment, it was night outside, and we met three Englishmen going to a pub. They were walking into town, but they were not sure where the pub was. So the fat lady, who was a local, went with them to show them the way.

My eyes flashed open. Just like every morning, I was disoriented and panicked by the day. A knot grew in my stomach. And a fearful reluctance kept me from putting my feet on the parquet floor. I felt sick and confused.

"How early do I have to get up for the job interview?" I wondered. *"Did I set the alarm correctly? I have to be in Short Hills by 11:00, and then be back in New York in time to take the boys to karate."*

I put my head back on the pillow to get away from the day and sleep some more.

I stood inside the wrought-iron door at a zoo, watching the hunchback limp away with his ring of keys. The animals were slowly perishing. As one large alligator began to rot, it changed into a large, bull-chested creature with the head of a bearded man. While it lay dying, another alligator approached it for the kill. It stuck its snout in the bull-creature's bellybutton, and started to eat it from the inside out. Then it put its snout down the monster's throat. The centaur-like beast looked helplessly at me while the alligator continued to devour it from within. Slowly, it dragged itself closer and closer to the iron fence with the alligator still halfway down its throat. At last, it found a sharp spike on top of the fence. It hoisted itself up and plunged the back of its neck down onto the spike, spearing the alligator inside its throat.

The soft music from the meditation tape began to play from the radio, stirred me from my dream. The dread of facing another day, particularly today with my interview, was frightening. I felt completely isolated in my tiny hovel.

The digital clocks on the VCRs and radio alarm clocks screamed at me "Get up!" 8:17, 8:17, 8:17, 8:16. I had spent the last twelve months trying to coordinate all four of them — 8:19, 8:19, 8:19, 8:18. I pulled the pillow over my head to block out the sunlight.

"I have to get up."

I forced myself to throw the bedcovers aside and put my feet on the cold wooden floor. My dizziness was cut by the pain from my left heel, reminding me of my episode at Golden Acres. Sickness swelled in my stomach. I hobbled to the window to look for Nicholas waiting for his school bus with Anne. I loved watching him in the morning standing with his classmates on the corner below. The clock on the desk shouted 8:38. His bus was just pulling away.

"Damn it! Damn it!" I pounded my fist on the desk. "Why didn't I get up earlier?"

Loneliness engulfed me.

I pushed myself into the bathroom and slowly began my daily routine, a ritual I clung to like rungs on a ladder to pull myself up out of my black hole and into the day.

I started with my dose of Zoloft, 200 milligrams. Then, reluctantly, I reached up and took the Atra razor and lime-scented shaving cream down from the top shelf of the medicine cabinet. I waited impatiently for the water in the basin to become lukewarm. Now I could shave—first the sideburns, then the cheeks, next up underneath the nose and finally down the neck. I watched the grim face in the mirror as I slowly washed the razor. I hesitated, then put it back in the cabinet.

Next, the dental floss—always green, always mint-flavored. Then the electric toothbrush with the double-colored toothpaste, blue and white, from its sink-top dispenser. Finally, the non-alcoholic mouthwash. Only recently had I been able to break away from the gold mouthwash of Listerine to the newer, gaudy blue kind. I did not like its sweet taste, and would rectify my folly once the bottle was finished.

I froze.

"What do I do next?"

My eyes darted about the bathroom.

"Ah, that's it." I became calm again. "The shower."

The warm water helped drain some of the tension from my body as the ritual of my shower began. High up on the shower caddie was the shampoo—Vidal Sassoon. Nothing but the best for Jay Walker. For the past fifteen years, I had always had my hair cut by Olya at Sassoon despite my debts. For $110, she made me look good.

I took a small dab of face scrub from the pale green Clinique tube as I shampooed. Jason called this my "hard sand." The way it woke up my face made me feel better. Next was the conditioner. Again, Vidal Sassoon. And the light blue body scrub. Always Clinique. The only variable was the shower gel. Sometimes I chose Paco Rabanne or Calvin Klein, other times Polo or Perry Ellis. I studied the plastic containers on the glass shelf. Perry Ellis! I lathered my body and smelled the deep, rich, musky fragrance. How sad it was that this creative young designer was no longer alive.

What a waste. He was so young. So talented.

After the shower, I listened to the weather on 1010 WINS to plan what I should wear while I dried my ears. Two Q-tips, damn it! Not one, as Anne had always insisted, but two, damnit, one for each ear. She'd chastised me for years for this extravagance.

Why do you think they put cotton on both ends? she'd *nag. Don't you get it? You're only supposed to use one Q-tip for your two ears. Fuck her!*

I fortified my receding hairline with Rogaine before spraying my body with Right Guard deodorant and Hermès cologne. I smiled at the mixture of fragrances, and the remembrance of my father always saying that the small maid's room in the back of his spacious Sutton Place apartment where I had lived for a year smelled like a French brothel.

Today, I had the strength to make the day bed. I straightened the covers and replaced the throw pillows in their usual order. The big ones—blue, then white, then green—in the back. Medium size—brown, then multi-colored—in the middle. Then the small ones—red next to black and purple next to burgundy.

I stared into the closet.

"Which suit? The one I wore for the last interview? That would be the easiest."

Usually I wore the one from Paul Stuart and added maroon suspenders, charcoal gray socks and my still-new black Gucci loafers. My brown shoes were on the front of the shoe rack. The black ones behind.

Each suit hung with a complementing tie wrapped around its wooden hanger. All of the hangers were wooden. They had to be.

Never did I have to bother deciding which shirt went with which suit. There were only white ones, but very good white ones. Each tailor-made with my monogram in a silver diamond shape on the chest. The "W" was in the middle to split the first and second initials. And there were tailor-made holes in the collars for my gold collar pin.

Underwear, in the drawer just above the sock drawer, was simple. Like the shirts—white only.

The socks were over the calf from Paul Stuart. The ones in the drawer closest to the river were blue, the color of the Hudson. The gray socks were in the middle, and the black ones on the side by the dark closet.

I went through the motions of dressing slowly. The dark gray suit with the subtle white chalk-mark stripes. A white handkerchief and a soft red Hermès tie. Then the collar pin, cufflinks, tie clip—finally my father's signet ring and Patek Philippe watch — the only two things he had left me in his will.

My uniform complete!

Finished! Finally finished. I took a deep breath. Now I

was in what Dr. Zagorski called my "Full Metal Jacket." I started to feel some of the confidence I had lost with my breakdown slowly coming back into my body.

I looked around my small studio apartment. The many photographs I had taken of Jason and Nicholas, now hanging among the dying plants, brought a weak smile to my face. They showed the boys feeding the ducks in Southampton, or hiding behind the palm trees in the Winter Garden. On the desk, a stack of unpaid bills lay next to the pile of newspaper clippings of job offerings that had gone unanswered.

I squinted in the hall mirror. Still tired? Still worried? On the contrary. I looked pretty good. I was relieved. I looked like one of the many who headed off to work in New York City every day. I straightened my tie and brushed back my hair. I took my worn Gurkha attaché case off the hall chair for appearance rather than need. It was part of the image, and it amused me. Out of work for over two years, but no one ever asked me why I was carrying a briefcase. I locked the door and stooped to pick up the *Times* and the *Wall Street Journal* off the hall carpet. I scanned the headlines on the way to the elevator to seem informed for the interview banter.

On interview days, I was not afraid that I would not get a job offer, but rather that I would. Then I would be forced to decide whether or not I could leave the safety of my apartment and try to function in the workplace like a normal person in the outside world. I would have to decide if I really wanted to work again. And, if so, was this the job that I wanted? Most of all, was it a job that I could do?

I hurried to the garage for the station wagon and stopped quickly across the street at Au Bon Pain to pick up my coffee and croissant. I glanced at the New Jersey map on the seat next to me, then checked the clock on the dash. I was usually late to most of my appointments. Today, for once, I wanted to try and be on time for my interview.

I winced as I turned in front of the World Trade Center. I still could not bring myself to enter the Towers, fearful of the humiliation should I bump into one of my old colleagues. I had come to hate these buildings. Gazing at them from my apartment window, I always wished they were gone.

Luckily, the traffic on West Street was light. Before I knew it, I was through the Holland Tunnel and headed west on Route 78. The September day was clear and sunny, and I felt better than usual in my business suit with my Burberry raincoat stretched out on the backseat. I had been on many trips to New Jersey before, either visiting clients or chasing prospects when I was working. So, I felt comfortable behind the wheel with the power of the car beneath my foot.

As I sipped the coffee and ate my croissant, I listened to the weather and traffic on the radio—sunny and bright, no delays. The knot in my stomach was starting to unravel, and I was content to follow the cars in front of me at 65 while I let my thoughts run to my boys. *Do they know how much I love them?* I wondered. *Jason, beautiful, and Nicholas, precocious.* I marveled at their inquisitive minds. The chirping of the radar detector signaled the cop ahead hiding in the bushes and brought me back from my daydreams. I picked up the car phone.

"Hi! You've reached 212-707-5080. We are away from our phone right now. At the beep, please leave a message for Nicholas, Jason or Anne."

"Hi guys, it's me. I'm off to New Jersey this morning for a meeting today. If I'm late getting back for karate, you know where the Hide-A-Key is — in the stairwell on the first landing. If I'm not home by the time you guys arrive, just wait in my apartment. I love you. Bye."

I put the phone back in the cradle and turned right onto Route 24. At the Short Hills Mall exit, I saw the modern three-story building where Bellinger/Carver was located. I took one of the visitors' spots in the half-full parking lot. My watch said 11:00.

I checked the board in the lobby and took the elevator to the third floor. My suit jacket felt tight, and a rivulet of perspiration trickled down my back. I tugged at my collar, swallowed hard, then pushed through the shiny glass door that opened onto a modern, well-lit office.

The receptionist smiled. She wore heavy blue eye makeup and two large scarves that matched the color of her bright blonde hair and ruby lips. A bevy of multi-colored beaded necklaces covered her flat chest. Dangling from a rhinestone lanyard about her neck were her rhinestone eye-glasses. The nameplate on her desk said "Shirley."

"Hi, I'm Jay Walker. I have an appointment with Lou Si-lener and Arthur Woodlof. I hope I'm not running too late."

"Have a seat, Mr. Walker," she said chewing her gum. "I'll let them know you're here. Here's an application to fill out."

I took the clipboard and nervously flipped through the pages.

Why do they always ask me to do this when they already have the exact same information from my résumé?

I pulled my gold Cross pen from my suit coat pocket, filled in the three pages, gave the clipboard back to Shirley, and then looked around the plush office. Fish swam lazily in a large tank to the rhythm of the Muzak. Tall, green ferns bookended the large mosaic on the wall.

"This sure beats New York City, Shirley. I was beginning to forget what grass looked like."

She laughed and popped her gum.

"Oh, my name's not Shirley. I'm a temp. I'm Myrtle."

"Well, Myrtle, I tell you, getting a parking spot in under twenty minutes was a real treat."

I scanned some of the insurance periodicals that were on the table and saw in *Business Insurance* that French & Son. was doing well, climbing to number six nationwide. The headlines also mentioned their layoffs. They were getting stronger by cutting staff. No one was watching me, so I quickly slipped the magazine into my attaché case.

I had just begun to thumb through the pages of *Agent and Broker* when a voice said, "Jay? Hi, I'm Lou Silener. Come in. I want you to meet our President, Arthur Woodlof."

Lou was a tall, thin man in his fifties with a gray flattop and strong handshake. He was not wearing his suit coat, and when he smiled, he showed a chipped front tooth. I followed him through two glass doors and down the corridor to a large corner office.

"Arthur, here's Jay Walker. Jay, this is Arthur Woodlof."

Appearing to be in his mid-sixties, Woodlof wore a navy blue chalk-striped suit. His hair was white, and he had piercing pale blue eyes. He sat bolt upright in his armchair.

"Welcome, Jay. Sit down," he said looking preoccupied. "Make yourself comfortable."

He stacked some papers on his mahogany desk and then joined us around a large glass-top table.

"Lou showed me your résumé," he said with a smile. "It's impressive."

He took off his gold reading glasses and focused his eyes on me.

"So tell us a little bit about yourself."

"Well, first, there was boarding school in Connecticut. Then college and the Peace Corps. I call it my 'Ernest Hemingway' phase—studying in France and working in Africa for two years. When I got home, I used my French to teach in Newport. A year later, when I was too old for the draft, I left teaching and came to New York to work for my father's firm."

"Jay, I was wondering, why did you ever leave Walker & Company?" Woodlof asked.

"It was one of those father/son things. I worked hard, but it was never really good enough. So, finally I pushed off. Not long afterwards, I tripled my salary at French & Son."

"I guess what Lou and I are wondering is . . . what happened at French & Son? And why have you been in the job market for so long?"

"Good question." I tried to muster a smile. "As my new firm began to grow stronger, management kept raising their sales goals. At the end, they only wanted Babe Ruth players, and I wasn't able to hit 500. They wanted $1,000,000 in commissions. I was at $650,000. So, they let me go along with thirteen or fourteen other sales guys. Then they fired all our back-office staff. It saved them a lot of money, and they got to keep our accounts and commissions. Since then, I've been trying to find a job similar to my old one, but most brokerage firms are downsizing now. The job market's been tight for the last several years."

Woodlof looked at Lou and then back at me.

"So tell me, Jay, if you were to come on board at Bellinger/Carver, do you think you still have the contacts to bring in the business? And how much and how quickly do you think you can bring it in? In other words, to put it bluntly, Jay, how much are you good for?"

"Well, sales is a two-way street." I squirmed in my seat. "I think a lot of my success will depend on the firm I join. That's why I haven't accepted any offers up to this point," I lied.

"You don't have a non-compete with your old firm, do you?" asked Lou. "You can go after your old accounts, right?"

"We need $100,000 in commissions the first year," Woodlof added. "Can you do that?"

"Oh, sure. And when French let me go, they said they didn't care who I went after."

"Well then, I don't think it should be too difficult for you to bring in a good chunk your first year," Lou said. "We're not as big as French, but we have all the resources you'll need."

Woodlof looked at me hard. "Jay, I'll tell you what. We recently hired someone from another large firm. Here's the deal we made with him. We offered him all of our resources and we agreed to give him fifty percent of all the commissions he brought in. He took the offer on the spot. How does that sound to you? There's no salary or benefits, you understand. It's straight commission."

I tried to hide my disappointment.

"I certainly appreciate your offer, Mr. Woodlof. If it's all right with you, I'd like to think it over for a day or two. Most of the firms I've been talking to have been offering me a base plus commissions," I lied again. "Some also provide an allowance for my car, garage and car phone."

"But, Jay, you know you're an unknown quantity here,

and you've been out of a job for a long time," Woodlof said. "Quite frankly, I don't see much of that old eye of the tiger. You have to have that if you're going to be in sales, you know." He stood up. "Well, think it over, Jay, and get back to Lou."

"We could always change the deal once you start to put some business on the books." Lou smiled.

"You have a fine firm here, Mr. Woodlof. I certainly appreciate the opportunity to have had this discussion. I'll get back to you by Wednesday."

"Fine," Woodlof said. "Thanks for coming out, Jay."

He gave me a hard handshake.

Outside in the parking lot, I opened the car door and threw my attaché case on the passenger seat.

"Fifty percent of all I bring in, but no salary! Are they nuts? I'll have to start from scratch again." I slumped behind the steering wheel and held my head. "I can't do it. Fifty percent of zero? What will I live on? I don't even know if I can bring in any business."

I punched the steering wheel.

"'I don't see that old eye of the tiger. You have to have that if you're going to be in sales, you know.' Of course I know that, you asshole. I've been in sales for ten years. Why the fuck do I keep doing this? Do I want a job, or not?" I shook my head. "What's the use? Fuck it!"

I pulled out past the Mall and headed back to Battery Park City. This time the speedometer stayed between 80 and 90 as I thought about the meeting.

God. How much longer can I keep doing this? There's absolutely no excitement any more. I'm fucking burnt out. I'm too tired to keep doing this.

On the ramp to the Holland Tunnel, the traffic was bumper to bumper.

Damn it! Can't New York ever get it right?

I grabbed the Jersey map and slammed the car phone with it.

"Move!" I shouted.

A blue Paramount Plumbing van nudged its way in front of me. Their logo of the finger turning off the faucet crossed my windshield.

I worked my ass off for that account. Wining and dining Jack Rubin, kissing his consultant's ass. Smokey Ridge Farms, Fur Coat Factory, Gold's Optical. I winced. *Alfonso, Complete Drugs—they're all gone now. I worked so damn hard for every one. And no one ever helped me. I did it all myself.* I slammed the steering wheel. *They're all gone now. I've lost them all.*

While staring ahead at the line of cars, I thought of all the clients and prospects I had worked on over the years. All the goddamn cold calls I had made. Hundreds, thousands of goddamn cold calls. The weekends spent in the office.

I was good. Really good. What a waste. I busted my ass for so many
years bringing in those accounts. Now what do I have to show for it? Nothing. Why did I ever break into my father's office? Why?

Half an hour later, after fighting through the tunnel traffic, I turned into the garage. I pulled my attaché case off the passenger seat and walked down South Avenue towards my studio. I watched the cracks in the sidewalk as the thought of all that I had lost kept growing and growing in my mind.

Passing the Financial Winery, I stopped at the window. Allen was behind the counter, arranging the tiny cordial bottles. When I pushed the door open, the bell rang, and Allen looked up with a smile. He was a big man with white hair, thick glasses and ruddy cheeks. His sparkling blue eyes matched his shirt that was open at the neck. He wore baggy, brown pants and Nike sneakers.

"Jay Walker, I haven't seen you in here for years! How have you been? I thought you'd stopped drinking."

"I have," I said with a weak smile.

"Maybe you should start again." Allen chuckled. "My business has been off ever since you stopped." He arranged some papers on the counter, then peered at me over his half lenses. "Say, Jay, you don't look like your old self. What's up? You've dropped some weight. How have you been?"

"I'm OK," I said nervously. "Hanging in there. You haven't changed a bit. So what's new?"

"Not much." He looked back down at his papers. "Jay, I'm sorry I never got around to giving you the insurance."

"That's OK." I surveyed the store. "I need some Scotch for a friend. Is it still in the back?"

"Just where it's always been."

I walked past the racks of French wines and cognacs to where Allen kept the large wooden crates of Scotch. There were quarts and fifths. I pulled out a fifth of twelve-year-old Chivas Regal.

"Your old favorite, eh?" He winked.

After I paid, I said feebly, "Have a great day, Allen."

"You too, Jay. Take care of yourself, and don't be a stranger."

I stopped at my mailbox and pulled out a large stack of bills, then took the elevator to my tiny apartment. Inside the dark room, I lifted the Chivas from its silver bag and put it on the glass-top table in front of my bed. I started to open the golden bottle, then stopped and put it down again. I walked to the phone and punched in number four on the auto-dial for my therapist.

"This is Dr. Zagorski—"

"Hello, Dr. Zagorski."

"—I can't come to the phone right now," his message crackled. "If you'll leave your name, phone number and a—"

I banged down the phone and sat weakly on the edge of the bed.

Slowly I reached out, picked up the bottle and twisted the top. A loud
crack from the black cap shattered the silence. The husky smell of Scotch drifted through the room. Behind the highball glasses in the kitchen cabinet, I found a large rocks glass, put in two ice cubes and a twist of lemon, then poured the amber liquid from the bottle.

A soft smile crossed my lips while I listened to the familiar sounds of the ice splintering and the *glug, glug, glug* of the nectar gushing from the bottle. I well-remembered that strong, musky aroma. My taste buds began to water. Lifting the glass to my lips, I hesitated, then held the glass out, pondering the Scotch as I swirled it over the ice and inhaled its strong fragrance.

I stopped, and put the glass down, then reached inside my pants pocket. I pulled out my anniversary coin from AA and placed it on the table next to the bottle. I looked at the Roman numeral VI.

"Six years! Six years of sobriety. Fuck it. I've lost everything else. Why not my sobriety, too?"

I took a large gulp, let the warm ambrosia wash about my mouth, then swallowed. As the heaven slid down my throat, I felt the burning I had not felt for so many years, and the sensation of the Scotch radiating through my body. How quickly my palate remembered that raw taste.

"Ahhh."

Thoughts of my mother's drunken phone calls to me at Dunbarton, the icy relationship with my father at the office across the street, the awful final years of my marriage—they all came back to me.

All I ever wanted was a happy family. I swore my life would never end up like my mother's. I thought I'd escaped that fate. How did it happen? Why am I so powerless? I held up the empty rocks glass. *Is this the answer?*

I took another glass of Scotch with me to my desk and pulled a sheet of my father's embossed stationery from the faded beige Cartier box. At the top of the page, the maroon family crest rose triumphantly on the rich, heavy paper. The head of the knight holding its sword spoke of the strength and courage of the Walker family.

I began to write.

Love is the tenderness that holds life together

It overcomes the bitterness of the day's disappointments

Provides the sweetness that leads to happiness

With it, we return to youth's innocence

And know again the beauty of life's gentleness

We become whole through the softness of love

Without love, the pain and suffering of our existence grow

And steal the freedom that we have to become strong

Then there is only despair

I dropped the Cross pen on the floor, and emptied the glass. That warm feeling of numbness that I remembered so well was gradually coming back, bringing with it relief from the painful memories of the past and the present. I stared wearily at the photographs of Jason and Nicholas that covered my walls, then drained the last of the Chivas from the bottle into my glass, and swallowed it down.

I walked unsteadily out into the hallway and pushed open the stairwell door next to the elevator, stopped, then climbed the stairs to the 36th floor. I forced open the rusty safety door and stepped out onto the roof's black tarmac. A cool breeze from the Hudson blew gently against my face. On the other side of the river the New Jersey shoreline shimmered.

I often wondered after my mother's death why anyone would kill themselves when they never knew what might be just behind the next door or just around the next corner. I always thought if life got bad, no matter how bad, it would change at some point. Eventually a door would open, and things would get good again. But now, for me, there were no more corners. There were no more doors.

I walked past the air conditioning vents to the roof's gutter.

Now, at last, the pain will stop. The loneliness will finally end.

I found a place to put my father's signet ring and watch that Florence had given me after his death. I wanted to leave these for my children. As I stood up, I caught my balance. I stared down between the tips of my loafers at the small playground thirty-six floors below. Most of my afternoons and weekends were spent sitting there on the bench watching my boys.

Last Saturday, when I sat next to the sandbox watching Jason and Nicholas play, I'd looked up to study my building's roof. Where would I land? Now, far below me, the red autumn leaves fell from the elm trees. They swirled along the esplanade, squeezed under the railing and floated away on the Hudson's choppy waves.

I edged forward. Through the tears, I looked at the bright azure sky above and the sunlight sparkling like diamonds between the Hudson's white caps below.

Is this what I'll do? What my mother did? Take my life, too? "The most selfish act," Dr. Zagorski always said.

Suddenly there was an awakening. The bonfires of my anger and resentments no longer burned, and the feeling that I had been wronged was gone. Instead, I saw that there was hope. And I saw all the good things and years that I had had and still had ahead of me. I saw that my sons would never leave me.

"No," I said softly. "No, I won't do this. I can't do this. I'll forgive myself . . . I'll forgive my mother . . . and my father too . . .."

"Daddy! Daddy!"

I turned from the roof's edge and looked through the tears in my eyes. Jason and Nicholas were standing in front of the rooftop door staring at me. My two little boys.

"Daddy?" Nicholas ran over and took my hand.

"What are you guys doing up here?" I asked. "How'd you get here?"

"You told us, Daddy. You left us your phone message. We know you're always late," Nicholas said with his hands on his small hips, "so we came over like you said."

"I know. I know. I'm sorry. I'm going to change that."

"I got the Hide-A-Key," Jason said, proudly waving the key. "I'm the tallest. And, I saw you going up the stairs."

"Saw me going up the stairs?"

"We had to get the Hide-A-Key in the stairwell, Dad," Nicholas said. "Then we saw you going up the stairs."

"That was one long climb," Jason panted. "One-hundred-and-forty-three steps. I counted 'em all."

Nicholas looked up me. "What are you doing up here, Dad? Are you crying?"

I knelt down between my children, pulled them to me and hugged them tightly.

"No, it's just the wind. I wanted to see how far I could see. I was over there this morning looking for a job." I pointed at New Jersey. "I wanted to see if I could see where I had gone."

"Come on, Dad." Jason shivered. "I'm getting cold."

"OK. Let's go downstairs. We're going to have to hustle if we want to be on time for karate. You know I'm always late."

"Dad, when we get back, can I play on the computer?" Jason asked. "Nicholas always goes first."

"Sure. We'll set the 'Share Clock'," I said. "We have to be fair. And you have to help me clean up the mess in my apartment, too. I've never been able to do it by myself. There're papers everywhere." I looked down at my unsuspecting sons and smiled. "I really love you two. You know that don't you?" I kissed them both and tousled their hair. "I'll always love you."

I turned and walked to the door.

"Hey, Dad," Nicholas said, "You dropped your ring and your watch."

I looked in Nicholas's small hand.

"I don't need them anymore, Nicholas." I smiled. "Why don't you keep the watch? Here, Jason, this ring is for you. Don't lose it. It was your grandfather's."

"I won't Dad. I promise."

You're my family now. You're my new family. They

belong to you."

"Are you sure, Dad?" Nicholas asked.

"Sure I'm sure. I don't need them anymore."

"Thanks, Dad," Nicholas said, buckling the alligator strap around his wrist.

I watched them as they raced down the stairs together. For the first time in many months, I heard the laughter of my children and knew that they loved me. Now I knew that I had the happiness and love that I had been searching for for so long. And that it would never, ever leave me.

How could I have forgotten? I thought. *I'll always have you two. Today . . . tomorrow . . ..*

Chapter 15

Tomorrow

D*ear Lou,*

I enjoyed meeting with Mr. Woodlof and you yesterday to discuss our mutual interests. I believe that your firm does offer the opportunities that—

The phone rang, jarring me from my computer.

Wonder who this is? Must be the boys calling to wish me a happy birthday.

"Jay Walker," I said in my best business voice.

"Jay? Is that you? Jay . . . Hi. This is an old friend. I don't know if you can guess who it is."

"Well . . .," I said, confused, to the feminine voice. "Well, yes, you're probably right. I'm sorry, but I really don't recognize your voice."

"I don't blame you," the voice laughed. "It's been years since we last met. Do you remember the old Waterville train station and the Fall Festivities at Dunbarton? Do you remember your blind date?"

"Barbara? Barbara Lockland? Is that you?"

"Yes! Yes, it's me. Hi! You'll never believe it, but yesterday morning I was going through the phone book looking for my friend Susan Wade. I just got back from Paris and I wanted to tell her 'Hello.' I was looking for Susan's number when I saw your name. It was the only Jay Walker in the book. 'It can't be the same Jay Walker,' I thought. But then when I called yesterday and listened to the message on your answering machine, I knew it had to be you. How have you been?"

"God, I'm great . . .. I mean, I'm OK. What about you? Barbara, how have you been? God, it's been so many years."

"What? I can't hear you. What's that noise?"

"Oh, it's the Beatles, 'Here Comes the Sun.' It's my new favorite song. Wait . . . I'll turn it down. There. Well, how have you been?"

"I guess you can imagine; a lot has happened. Married and widowed for one. I'm Barbara Du Val now. How 'bout you?"

"Married and getting divorced. I'm still Jay Walker. Where are you?"

"Darien, but from time to time I get down to New York to visit friends. And I go to design shows. That's why I was calling Susan. There's an interior design presentation in the City for the next three weeks that I want to see. They're having a champagne reception on Thursday, and I thought maybe I might come down and see the show. If you're free, maybe we could meet."

"I'd love to . . . but, I have to tell you—I'm not drinking anymore."

"Not drinking anymore. Wow! That's something."

"I hope you don't mind. It'll have to be a ginger ale reception for me. Is that OK?"

"Sure. We have a lot of catching up to do. You'll have

plenty of time to fill me in. Can you meet me at the Kips Bay Boys' Club on East 30th? It's 330 East 30th . . . at 11:30. It's this Thursday. Is that OK?"

"Thursday? Sure, I don't have the kids 'til 3:30, and I'm not working."

"Kids? How many kids?"

"Just two. Jason and Nicholas. You'd love them."

"OK then. It's a date. I hope you recognize me."

"I'm sure you haven't changed at all."

"Well, maybe a wrinkle or two. If you want, we can go to JoJo's for lunch afterwards."

"HoJo's?"

"No. It's JoJo's"

"Oh. OK. That's fine by me. I'll see you Thursday."

"It should be fun. I'm looking forward to it."

I hung up the phone and smiled.

"After all these years—Barbara!"

Thursday morning, I got out of the cab in front of the Boys' Club and climbed through fall's bright sunshine up the old brownstone's front stoop. For a moment, I stood at the door trying to picture Barbara again. I straightened my tie, then pushed the buzzer.

"Come in," a middle-aged woman said as she opened the door. "Are you here for the reception?"

"Yes, I'm looking for a friend."

"Well, you go right up there. It's the first room on your right."

As I mounted the stairs, I wondered if Barbara would be here already. Would I recognize her? A mixture of loud conversations came from a small room in the front of the townhouse. In the alcove next to the bar stood a group of women talking. One, whose back was turned towards me, wore a powder blue turtleneck and gray flannel slacks. A crocodile belt circled her slim waist, and crocodile loafers adorned her small feet. Standing tall and slender, she let her long auburn hair fall over her delicate shoulders.

"Ginger ale," I told the barman. Cautiously, I took my

drink to the window where the women were standing.

"Don't you just love how the chaise lounge is done?" the woman in a tight gray suit was saying. "He's such a great designer. What do you think? Do you like it, Barbara?"

"I'm not sure about the chintz," the other woman said with a laugh.

I recognized the lilting laughter in her soft voice at once. "Barbara?" I said.

The woman turned, somewhat startled. Then I saw the sparkle in her green-brown eyes, her full lips and long, thick brown hair. It felt like I had left her only yesterday at the Festivities dance—that embarrassing incident I still so well remembered.

"Jay!" Barbara tossed back her head with an excited laugh. "After all these years."

I offered her my hand, but she hugged me instead. I felt the warmth of her cheek on mine and inhaled the soft fragrance of her perfume.

"It's been so long. Let me look at you." She stepped back and smiled, flashing her dark green eyes. "Just as dapper as ever. You look smashing, Jay. So, tell me now . . . how are you?"

"Fine," I stammered. I looked her up and down. "Barbara, you haven't changed a bit since . . . ." I blushed. "You look beautiful! It's been such a long time, hasn't it?"

"Too long! Much too long! So much has happened since then. Oh Jay, I want you to meet my friend, Susan Wade. Susan, you remember Jay from Festivities a hundred years ago at Dunbarton, don't you? And, Jay, this is Mercedes Austin."

"Remember?" Susan peeked over her half-frame reading glasses. Their bright blue frames matched her eyes. "Of course I remember. Jay's roommate was the one who fixed me up with Phil Cartwright. Quite a weekend for a sixteen-year-old."

"You look great, Sue." She was heavier than she had been at Dunbarton.

"Hello, Jay." Mercedes held out her hand, adorned with immaculate rose red nails and a large diamond ring. "Barbara was saying she hoped you'd come. Are you interested in interior design?" she asked with a sly grin.

"Oh, no. Not really. For me, interior design is a table and a chair. You'd know that if you saw my apartment." All the women laughed. "I came to meet Barbara for lunch."

"That sounds like a good idea. Are you hungry?" Barbara asked.

"Sure. I'm ready whenever you are."

"I've seen enough. Let's go. I left my car across from JoJo's. We'll take a cab up, and then I can drop you off after lunch. Is that OK?"

"Sounds fine to me. What kind of a place is JoJo's?"

"What kind of a place is JoJo's?" Mercedes' strong, guttural laugh shook the long red hair that covered her pale, freckled shoulders. "You've never heard of JoJo's? It's only the hottest spot in New York!"

"I'm afraid I've been out of circulation for a while," I said with embarrassment.

Mercedes smiled at me with sparkling brown eyes. "Well, this will get you back in circulation in a hurry. Have the lobster with truffles."

"Would you two like to join us?" Barbara asked.

My heart sank. I wanted to be alone with her.

"Us? No thanks," Sue said. "Mercedes and I have some shopping to do. Hermès and Versace await."

Mercedes grinned. "After what you told me, Barbara, I'm sure you two kids have a lot of catching up to do."

"OK then. But be sure to call me, you two." Barbara waved good-bye to the group. "Come on, Jay. I'll get my coat."

"Susan," I said, "it was nice seeing you again after so many years. Mercedes, I enjoyed meeting you."

I flagged down a cab on Second Avenue and climbed into the back seat next to Barbara. As she rolled down the window, the breeze filled the car with her light perfume.

"64th and Lex," she said. She squeezed my arm. "Jay, I can't believe you're here. Let me look at you. You really haven't changed at all."

"It's you who looks great! I'm so glad you called. God, you know, even after all these years, I feel like it was just yesterday we were together."

"Yes, just like yesterday," she said with a smile. "I don't know why I waited so long to call you."

Several minutes later, Barbara told the driver, "It's on the right, over there . . . the dark red building. We'll get out here."

While I fumbled in my jacket for my billfold, Barbara handed the cabby a ten.

The restaurant's name, *JoJo*, was written across the rusty red townhouse wall in black script. Yellow flames flickered inside large carriage lanterns on either side of the front door. Going down the stone steps into the vestibule, we left the bright sunshine behind for the darkness of this small French bistro.

"Hello, Maurice. Business is good I hope," Barbara said slipping out of her mink.

"Fine thank you, Mrs. Du Val. It's so good to see you again."

The maître d' gave me the coat check.

"Your table in the back?"

"Yes. That's fine. Thank you, Maurice."

We followed the maître d' through the main dining room to a smaller room in the back with four tables.

We sat side by side on a banquette that was covered in dark red velvet.

Barbara turned to me and said, "Jay, it's really been too long, hasn't it?"

"Like Daisy and Jay," I said, "but they only had to wait five years. For us, it's been over twenty."

"Daisy? What do you mean Daisy? And, Jay . . . you mean you? Is Jay you?" Barbara looked puzzled.

"No, no. You know. Gatsby . . . Jay Gatsby and Daisy Buchanan. You know Fitzgerald's book, right? The one with West Egg. Only we're not in West Egg."

"Oh ... no . . . I don't read novels very much. I don't have any time . . .. I'm so busy with my interior decorating business. And I'm really not a big fan of fiction."

"Drinks, Mrs. Du Val?" the waiter asked.

"Oh, yes please, Philippe. I'll have a blonde Dubonnet. Jay, how 'bout you?

"Tonic and lime for me, please."

"And one tonic and lime, Philippe."

"Right away, Mrs. Du Val." The waiter left for the small oak-wood bar just off the entrance hall.

"So, Barbara, let's go back. Tell me what you've been up to for all these years?"

"Well, I've been getting by." Her eyes sparkled like her diamond earrings. "First there was design school, Paulsons; then I went to work for Mr. Mat. I created my own line. One night in Boston, I was at a design gala, and met this young man. He was a successful French artist. Philippe Du Val was his name. And I fell in love. We moved to Saint Paul de Vence in the south of France and had a wonderful son, Bernard. Later, I found out that I wasn't the only one that Philippe was in love with."

"I know that feeling."

Barbara smiled.

"So, we separated. When I left Philippe, Bernard and I moved back to the States ... Connecticut. When Bernard was four, his father was surfing off the coast of Gibraltar and had an accident. He broke his back. Eighteen months later, he died." She hesitated. "That was hard for both Bernard and for me. But now ... guess what. Bernard's a Fourth Former at Dunbarton. Can you believe it?"

"Dunbarton." I chuckled. "Well, that's great!"

"Yes, but . . . well, he's not doing very well. He's in the bottom half of his class academically."

"The bottom *half* of his class? When I was there, I was

the bottom of my class."

"Come on, Jay. Not you."

"Barbara, it took my roommate almost three years to convince me that the fifth quintile was not a good place to be. In fact, I didn't even know what a quintile was for three years. No matter how hard I studied, my grades were always awful. Because I did so poorly at Dunbarton, for many years, I was dumb. I had zero self-esteem and no less self-confidence."

"I can't believe it."

"What made it worse was that every Sunday night I had to call my father and give him a report on my dismal grades. He always said, 'Jackson,' he called me Jackson — I hated the name Jackson. 'Jackson,' he'd say, 'I just don't understand it. When I was at Dunbarton the good grades just came rolling in.' But several years ago, at one of my Dunbarton reunions, I found out from my friend Judy Daniels—she's the school Archivist—that when my father was at Dunbarton in the late twenties, he had worse grades than I did. She found a letter in my father's file from the school's Headmaster to the Dean at Princeton saying that for my father to receive his diploma from Dunbarton, he would have to do well at Princeton. Then, guess what? There was another letter. It was from the Dean at Princeton. He told the Headmaster that my father should not be granted a diploma. My father had been expelled from Princeton in his sophomore year due to two years of poor academic performance. I couldn't believe it. Dad had always told me that he had to leave Princeton in 1930 because his family lost all their money in the Depression, not because he flunked out."

"What! Jay, that's true?"

"It is. All of it. Not only did he never graduate from Princeton, he never graduated from Dunbarton. For all those years, he'd been lying to me about how good his grades were and why he left Princeton. And he never told me that he only went to Dunbarton for three years—not for four like me ."

"I can't believe it."

"I made me think of a book I once read called *The Duke*

of Deception. It was Geoffrey Wolff's memories of his father, an incorrigible liar."

"Wow, that's really something."

"While I was down in the archives looking at his file, I came across several short stories he wrote for the school's literary magazine. One was about a confederate soldier with one leg. Another about a street sweeper on Wall Street. I found it odd how sad they were. He lived with his parents on Park Avenue with butlers, maids and Rolls Royces."

The waiter put a blonde Dubonnet in front of Barbara and gave me my tonic and lime.

"Something else, Mrs. Du Val?"

"No. Not right now, Philippe. We're fine. Thank you," she said with a smile, and then turned towards me. "Tell me, Jay. How have things changed for you since Dunbarton?"

"I guess. First of all, I feel different about my father now that I have discovered more about who he really was. The other day I was listening to the radio and heard this song. It's called *No More.* When I listened to the lyrics, I realized it was about a father and a son. They never had a relationship, but in the end they were finally able to have one. At the end of the song, there's a connection that grows between them. It's a hard song for me to listen to, but still, I think, for me, that's finally happened between my father and me. I've been able to recognize that my father did the best he could do."

"Jay, that's wonderful — wonderful for the both of you. It's so good that you've been able to find forgiveness … and also gratitude."

"Yes, I think it is too. It's a huge burden off my shoulders. For so many years, he was living inside my head without paying any rent. The line in the song that stood out for me was '*No more curses you can't undo, left by fathers you never knew.*'"

"Wow."

"There's another thing. After all these years, I found out that I'm not stupid. My wife convinced me take an IQ test. I ended up in the 98th percentile. It wasn't my intelligence that was holding me back; it was my family. With all the chaos in my family life, I wasn't able to concentrate on my studies, no matter how hard I tried. The only thing I *could* do at Dunbarton was athletics. I'd take my frustrations out on the teams I played against. Sometimes, when I got too aggressive on the football field, the coaches had to pull me out for a play or two to let me cool down."

"So things are different for you now?"

"Not exactly. Even today, I still keep some anger bottled up. That's why I ski so fast and pound the pedals on my bike so hard—it helps me get rid of my anger. When I'm out there, on my skis or on my bike, I love making those big, fast, sweeping turns ... going fast down the hills. It gives me such a tremendous feeling of freedom ... such a feeling of power. It helps me get rid of my demons."

"It sounds to me like you've changed, Jay."

"I guess I have. But not as much as I'd like . . . but I do feel better about myself now. I have more self-esteem and my confidence has grown."

"I can see that," Barbara said with a smile.

Maurice arrived. "Excuse me, Mrs. Du Val. The lobster?"

"Oh, yes please, Maurice. For both of us. Oh, Jay, is lobster all right for you?"

"Sounds wonderful."

With a small bow, Maurice turned on his heel and disappeared.

"You know, Jay, you could have asked me." She took my hand. "I certainly never thought you were dumb."

"It's good to hear you say that. With my grades, I didn't get much of that from my family or any of the faculty."

"That's too bad."

"It sure didn't help . . .." I looked into her beautiful eyes. "Tell me more about you, Barbara."

"More? There's not too much more to tell. Here I am, a wealthy widow living in Connecticut, working in my design company with a wonderful son. That's about it. But, Jay, what's this not drinking all about?" She pushed her drink to the side, away from me, slightly embarrassed. "It must be hard."

"That's OK" I said with a laugh. "I can be around the stuff. I just can't drink it anymore. I've probably spilled more booze than most people drink in three lifetimes."

"It's alcoholism … right?"

"Yes. You know, I've always thought of it like the lepers I saw when I was in Africa. I'd watch them coming home from the fields in the evenings. They'd stop and squat down in the dirt on the side of the road holding their filthy rags with their fingerless hands. They'd try to scrub the maggots from their oozing wounds. But they never felt any pain…. Of course, slowly, they would die."

"Is that what alcoholism was like for you, Jay?"

"Yes. More or less. In the beginning, I used alcohol to numb my feelings and kill my pain. It worked for a while…it filled the empty hole I had inside. But not only did I not feel any pain, I didn't feel much of anything else either. In the beginning, alcohol was my best friend. And then it became the most important thing in my life. I couldn't see the damage it was doing. Not only to me, but also to all those around me—to my family and to my friends. In the end, just like with the lepers, it began to slowly kill me…until my soul was nearly dead."

I looked up at Barbara; her eyes, brimming with tears, were fixed on mine. "How did you stop?"

"I'm one of the lucky ones. One day, I finally saw how much hurt I was doing to both myself and to others. In AA, they call it a spiritual awakening. So, with the help of AA, I was able to stop. Unlike most alcoholics, despite my drinking, I hadn't lost any of my material things over the years. It's only now, six years into sobriety, that I've lost what most alcoholics lose from their drinking—my wife, my job, and my home . . . but, oddly enough, I'm happy now."

The lobsters arrived on their Limoges plates swimming in truffles.

"Another drink, Mrs. Du Val?" the waiter asked.

Barbara looked at me. "Why not? We're celebrating . . .

aren't we, Jay?"

"Yes … yes we are," I said with a smile.

"Yes please, Philippe, another round." Then Barbara turned and looked at me again. "So, Jay, it must have been hard to stop."

"No. After all those years of drinking, once I stopped, it felt like I was finally home…like a huge burden had been lifted off my shoulders. And, thankfully, I haven't lost my two children. Now, for them, I'm trying to be the father I never had. What's strange is that AA says that liquor is only a symptom. There's much more going on than just the booze."

"Jay … You said 'The father you never had.' What did you mean by that?"

I looked at her looking at me—after all these years, there she was sitting next to me.

"Jay? Jay! Did you not get along with your father?"

"What? My father? Oh, no. No. Unfortunately, I never did. It's one of the reasons I have so much trouble making friends with men. For me, trusting men is difficult."

"Why didn't you two get along?"

"It's hard to say. Once, while I was in France, I wrote home and asked him to send me some magazines that I had left in one of the closets at his house. I found out that while he was looking for my papers, he came across letters I had received from Deborah Wilcox, an old girlfriend, while I was at Dunbarton. Almost every letter spoke about the alienation that I felt towards him. I think this made any chance I might have had to have a good relationship with him much more difficult."

"Whoops. That wasn't good," Barbara said with a smile.

"No, that definitely wasn't good. Then last year, Sally, his third wife, told me that my grandmother's second husband adopted my father when he was two. She said my father never knew his real father . . . that Walker wasn't his real name. It was Smith. Perhaps, since he didn't have his father, he didn't know how to be one to me. My therapist thinks that he was envious of me, but I can't figure that out. Me? Why would he be envious of me? Materially, he had so much more . . .. Maybe he saw something in me that he wanted. Or maybe he saw his rebellious first wife—my mother. I don't think I'll ever know."

Philippe arrived and put fresh drinks on the table.

"I'm sure he also saw a great deal of my mother in me—and I'm sure while I was growing up, I upset him with some of the things that I did. I'm sure he saw that I was not like him...that the material things that were so important to him were not important to me. I was much more like my mother—carefree, adventurous, daring . . . somewhat crazy. I'm sure he saw that."

"Your mother was like that too?"

"Yes. I think it was because of her that, all my life, I've always fought against authority. If someone says, 'You can't do this' or 'You can't have that,' I'm defiant. I fight fiercely to *do it* or to *get it.* You know what our family motto is? 'Where there's a Walker, there's a way.' It's something I use all the time. Me being a rebel must have irritated him terribly. He worked so hard to ultimately win back all the material *things* that his family lost in the Crash of '29. And he was an only child—he had to do it all by himself."

"It must have been hard for him growing up … right? Did he talk about it?"

"Only about a few things . . . but he would tell me about them over and over again."

"Like what?"

"He told me how he'd have to sell his blood as a young man in New York to pay his rent. Or, when he was forming an insurance agency with two business partners, how he was drafted for the Korean War, and had to leave the firm. He'd tell me how he went off to basic training but was excused be-cause of an old Dunbarton football knee injury. And that when he returned to the company, his business partners would not take him back."

"He told you that?"

"Yes. He had to start all over again from scratch."

"Wow. Coming from such an affluent family, that must have been hard."

"I'm sure it was. He'd tell me how he had to walk the docks in Brooklyn to sell insurance to the stevedores to get his own business going. I knew all of these stories by heart."

"Do you think he was making these points to remind you how well off you were in comparison to him . . . the opportunities you were given as you were growing up? Maybe, unlike him, that you lacked for very little?"

"I don't know . . . you're probably right . . .."

As Philippe cleared away our plates, he asked, "Some dessert, Mrs. Du Val?"

"Jay, would you like to try the flan? It's very good."

"Fine."

"And a demitasse?"

"Sure."

"Two demitasses and two flans," Philippe said. He nodded and headed for the kitchen.

"So, Jay, did he help you as you were growing up? Did he give you advice and encouragement along the way?"

"No, not really. Unfortunately, he didn't or couldn't. He gave me some *things* along the way, and I took advantage of the *things* that he gave me—the fruits of his labors, so to speak. I was proud to have gone to Dunbarton. I enjoyed being a member of the private clubs in New York, and I loved working for a firm where my name was on the front door. These *things* were there for the taking, so I took them . . .. Do you think I was wrong?"

After a pause, she said, "I'm not sure. Did you appreciate the *things* your father gave you? Were you grateful for them?"

"Yes. I think I did appreciate them and that I was grateful. I do now."

"So, if that's true . . . I'm sure it is true . . . I don't see any problem in doing what you did."

I saw she meant what she said.

"You really didn't have much of a choice, did you?" she asked.

"No, I don't think so. And there's one thing . . . there's one thing that I'm truly happy about."

"One thing? What's that?"

"Before he died, I was able to tell him that I loved him. I feel so lucky that I was able to do that."

"I'm glad you did."

"Voilà! Two demitasses and two vanilla flans. Will there be anything else, Mrs. Du Val?" Philippe asked.

"No, Philippe. We're fine thank you." Barbara took a sip of her coffee, then looked at me. "What ever happened to Walker & Co.?"

"Before he died, my father gave the business to Dave Thatcher, his business associate. Two years later, Thatcher sold it and retired to Florida. There's no more Walker & Co. anymore . . . ."

"I remember you told me how you'd hoped to run the company yourself one day . . . . I'm so sorry that never happened. But what about all those other dreams of yours . . .?"

"Dreams? What dreams?"

"Jay! Don't you remember? At Dunbarton . . . . Your dreams . . . the ones you told me about at Dunbarton."

"Oh, now I remember. Those dreams." I laughed. "I guess I was a little naïve back then."

She reached out and took my hand. "How's it going now?"

"A little rough—soon to be divorced and no job. Anne left me just after I lost my job. It's funny. Just before we separated, she said to me that she saved my life. She had me go away for a while when I got depressed. But for me, I saw it the other way 'round. For me, it felt like she walked out on me just when I needed her most . . . but I've been getting by. I do some reading and writing. I'm trying to finish my novel. And I go on job interviews whenever I can . . . I'm getting by. And I have my boys, thank God. I hope to take them skiing this winter. My wife, or ex-wife, or whatever she is—we used to ski at Stratton all the time."

"Stratton? I have a house in Dorset. Bernard and I ski

Stratton almost every weekend in the winter." She looked at me with a smile. "What do you think? Maybe Bernard, Jason and Nicholas can do some skiing together this winter."

"I think that would be great! My kids are just starting, but they're both quick learners . . .. They kind of ski like me — out of control and fast."

"Well, then cheers. Here's to winter and to skiing!"

After we finished our demitasses and flans, Barbara got the bill.

"Let me pay for that," I said. "Or we can split it."

"No way." She smiled. "You can get the next one." She added the tip and put the bill on her house account.

Maurice was waiting by the coat check.

"Au revoir, Madame Du Val," Maurice said as he helped her on with her coat.

"Au revoir, Maurice." Barbara discreetly shook his hand with a twenty-dollar bill.

He turned to me with a slight bow. "À bientôt, Monsieur."

At the garage across the street, the attendant pulled up a robin's egg blue BMW.

"Hop in," Barbara said. "Let's put the top down and drive through the park."

"Barbara, I'd love to, but I really have to get back to Battery Park City. I have to pick up the kids at 3:30. I'm trying not to be late for my family anymore. It's a novel concept for me — being on time. But I'm getting better at it."

She laughed. "OK. We'll do it next time. Put your seat belt on and hang on."

We drove down the FDR in silence, each with our own thoughts, the wind ruffling our hair. When we got to my building, I climbed out.

"Barbara, thanks so much . . .. Thanks so very much. It was great seeing you again! I mean really great! I hope we can do it again."

"Jay! Of course we will. What do you think? I'm not going to let you just disappear again. So, you have to call me . .

.. You have to call me tomorrow! You hear?" Barbara handed me her card. "I want you to come and see my house in Connecticut. Guess what? it's got a white picket fence all the way 'round. Remember those dreams of yours, Jay Walker! Now promise me you'll call. You have to call me tomorrow! Tomorrow! You understand?"

I smiled.

"I promise," I said, and bent over and kissed her on the cheek.

"Who knows?" she said with a wink. "Maybe we can pick up where we left off. What do you think?"

"Maybe." I smiled. "You never know."

She smiled back and gave a quick wave. As she pulled away from the curb, she said, "And hang on to that dream of yours—to have a happy family."

I stood watching her as she disappeared down South Avenue in the afternoon sun. Her blue license plate read **STARGAZER.**

Epilogue

Piazza della Signoria

Piazza della Signoria

I sat at a small round table in front of my demitasse wearing my new Burberry. It was just after ten, and the rain had stopped. She too wore her raincoat that matched mine. I looked up from the front page of the *Herald Tribune*.

"Did you see this thing about Trump?" I asked her. "He says he wants to build a wall."

"Uh-huh," she said again.

"He says he's going to have the Mexicans pay for it."

"Uh-huh," she said again.

Absorbed in the paper's crossword puzzle, she paid no attention to the lemon zest that waited on the rim of her saucer. Instead, she peered intently through the lenses of her tortoiseshell sunglasses trying desperately to decipher the secrets of today's enigma. Slowly, she went about eliminating one of the alphabet's 26 letters, and then another until, finally, the answer to the newspaper's clue revealed itself to

her and she inked in the empty boxes.

"Jay?" she asked. "What's a nine-letter word for cheer-
ful that starts with
e–b?"

"You should know that one. We argue about its pronun-
ciation all the time. It's *eb*ullient."

"Oh, yes. That's it." She filled in 9-Across. "You mean
eb*ulli*ent."

I smiled and looked at her. She was still beautiful—her
lips perfectly red like her fingernails, her hair pulled back and
immaculately colored brown, blonde and silver.

"You're still making those little grunting sounds, you
know. You've been doing it for the past six months now. How
come?" she asked. "You never did it before."

"That's what you do when you get old. And I'm getting
old. But, hey, I'm trying to stay alive," I said with a smile. "And,
hey, at my age, you know, it takes a lot of work."

"Are you looking forward to getting home to Connecticut?"

I smiled. "Not really. I still have to paint that damn white
picket fence again."

Pigeons cooed and splashed in the puddles about the
piazza as they searched for remnants of early morning break-
fasts. In the corner of the square, across from the statues in
the Loggia, the *David* stared out from his perch with his piercing eyes, majestic and unabashed by his nakedness as the
Japanese tourists strolled by with their Nikons. It was cool for
April with the wind blowing in from the Arno. I pulled the collar
of my trench coat higher around me.

We had no plans for today. We were just going to walk
about, possibly stroll over to the Ponte Vecchio to visit the jew-
elers and the goldsmiths. And I had to stop by the pushcart
merchant and buy the small statue of the David. Afterwards
we would lunch at one of Hemingway's old haunts . . . or perhaps simply make love in our hotel room.

I tried to steady my hand as I sipped the dark concoction from its tiny white porcelain cup. The biting brew kicked

my mind into a clearer awareness. In the dark lenses of my wife's glasses, I studied my reflection—a few more wrinkles, some gray hair.

I smiled as I reminisced. I had done well at the firm over the past several years. One of its best producers. And this year, I had won our trip to Florence. I was pleased.

As my thoughts turned to my family, I was pleased that finally I had made peace with my father, and that despite her troubled life, I knew I loved my mother.

And I was pleased that I loved this woman who sat across from me. And I was pleased that I loved my two sons. And that now, finally . . . I had my family.

I gazed across the Piazza della Signoria and, feeling *eb*ullient, began to softly sing,

"There's nothing you can do that can't be done . . .
Nothing you can sing that can't be sung . . ."

~

Made in the USA
Middletown, DE
29 June 2021